Virtual Lotus

Virtual Lotus

Modern Fiction of Southeast Asia

Edited by
Teri Shaffer Yamada

Ann Arbor
THE UNIVERSITY OF MICHIGAN PRESS

49884985

10-22-02

Copyright © by the University of Michigan 2002
All rights reserved
Published in the United States of America by
The University of Michigan Press
Manufactured in the United States of America
⊛ Printed on acid-free paper

2005   2004   2003   2002   4   3   2   1

A CIP catalog record for this book is available from the British Library.

Library of Congress Cataloging-in-Publication Data

Virtual lotus : modern fiction of Southeast Asia / edited by Teri
   Shaffer Yamada.
      p.   cm.
   Includes bibliographical references.
   ISBN 0-472-06789-3 (Paper : alk. paper)
   ISBN 0-472-09789-X (alk. paper)
      1. Southeast Asian fiction—20th century.   I. Yamada, Teri
   Shaffer.
   PL3508.8   .V57   2001
   895—dc21   2001006441

Contents

Singapore

Thailand

The Philippines

Vietnam

Acknowledgments

During the past seven years, the magnanimity and creativity of over fifty people—authors, translators, and consultants—brought this project to fruition. I dedicate this anthology to them with my deepest gratitude. And to all the talented writers who could not be included in this first compact edition, I express my sincere regrets.

I also wish to acknowledge those who skillfully negotiated the labyrinth of politics, copyright, and authors' permissions for Southeast Asia, particularly U Saw Tun at the University of Illinois, Urbana; John Marston at the Colègio de Mexico; Bac Hoai Tran, Susan Kepner, and Nguyen Nguyet Cam at the University of California, Berkeley; Tomoko Okada at the Tokyo University of Foreign Studies; and Nina McPherson for "The Story of an Actress" by Duong Thu Huong. A number of writers and scholars facilitated valuable contacts in the region: K. S. Maniam, Shirley Geok-lin Lim, Frank Stewart, Marivi Soliven Blanco, and Paulino Lim Jr., to mention just a few. I would also like to thank Indonesia scholar John H. McGlynn of The Lontar Foundation for his comments on the manuscript and for his assistance in obtaining authors' permissions in Indonesia.

Finally I would like to mention California State University, Long Beach, which provided release time for this project during 1996. In particular I am indebted to the research librarians Vicky Munda and Dian Olsen for their patience and proficiency. I am also deeply grateful to Frank Fata, Associate Dean of the College of Liberal Arts, in his capacity as mentor over the years, and to my associates in the Department of Comparative World Literature and Classics, especially Roland Bush and Karl Squitier. My colleague Ray Lacoste has been exceptionally gracious, devoting precious time to making editorial comments on the manuscript. Ultimately, the success of this project is also due to the spirit and creativity of my dear friend Christi Lacoste and to the forbearance of my son, Yuzo. Suggestions for short stories to be included in a future edition are warmly accepted by the editor.

and east of India, is a region of rich geological diversity and cultural complexity with a population of approximately 519 million. It was known in some classical Indic texts as the Goldenland (Suvarnabhumi), signifying perhaps its early entrepreneurial promise as a region of important trade routes. Travelers, merchants, and peripatetic mendicants, spreading the great traditions of Buddhism, Hinduism, and Confucianism from India and China, were the first to influence the region's cultures. Themes and characters from the two Hindu epics, the *Ramayana* and the *Mahabharata,* are still interwoven within some contemporary fiction, as are traditional Buddhist and Islamic elements.

Islam was introduced by Muslim traders during the thirteenth century and later became an important cultural force that is still prominent in Indonesia and Malaysia today. Europe's turn came in the early sixteenth century. European languages (Dutch, Portuguese, Spanish, French, English) and Christianity contributed to the region's linguistic complexity. This process—Westernization, or modernization—unleashed by the European encounter accelerated during the nineteenth century due to economic and technological changes wrought by Europe's industrialization and modern imperialism. In the late nineteenth century, European literary styles, such as romanticism, naturalism, and realism, along with new systems of public education and print technology transformed the region's traditional literatures as writers explored and popularized the new genres of the novel and the short story. In the twentieth century, as Southeast Asians experienced wars and decolonization, America continued to exert its influence beyond the Philippines into Indochina as the pace of modernization increased.

Like other geographical designations and boundaries imposed on the "Orient" during the Age of Imperialism, the name "Southeast Asia" both describes and invents reality. It was first used during World War II to define Lord Louis Mountbatten's area of command; subsequently, it gained popularity during the Second Indochina War. Today, Southeast Asia consists of ten nations: Kampuchea (Cambodia), Indonesia, Laos, Malaysia, Myanmar (Burma), Negara Brunei Darussalam (Brunei), Singapore, Thailand, the Philippines, and Vietnam. Slightly over half of the region is on the Asian mainland, with its deltas, coastal mountain ridges, river valleys, and interior mountain chains; twenty-four thousand islands, known as the archipelagos of Indonesia and the Philippines, comprise the rest.

Because of the complex cultural diversity found in Southeast Asia, a pan–Southeast Asian identity does not exist, irrespective of the emphasis on regional similarities promoted by the Association of Southeast Asian Nations (ASEAN). What links the writers in this anthology is the complex experience of modernization during the twentieth century. This experience is not uniform; it varies among countries and regions. It encompasses different colonial experiences and different histories of nationalism and decolonization. While differences should not be ignored, neither should similarities. One shared pattern across the region is the debate about "literature for the sake of society" or "literature for the sake of art." Every country in Southeast Asia has experienced this debate, albeit at different times in modern history. The intensity of this argument—its threat to political power—sometimes has garnered a severe response in the form of censorship or other governmental policies about politically and socially correct literature. Southeast Asian short-story writers, who so often publish in newspapers and magazines, are often most directly influenced by censorship policies.

Another experience shared by writers throughout the region is the politicization of language. Vernacular language and literature became the medium for national identity construction in opposition to the "imposed" colonial language. During the colonial period for each country there were typically two sets of writers: those who wrote in the colonial language and those who wrote in a changing vernacular. (Undoubtedly some writers wrote in both.) This pattern shifted toward a valorization of the vernacular language in many nations fighting for their independence. Nevertheless, some writers today still continue to prefer the colonial language as their literary medium of expression, particularly in Singapore (where English is the national language), Malaysia, and the Philippines. A similar politicization of language has an impact on writers in other nations with Commonwealth or Francophone legacies, such as India and Algeria.

The modern short-story genre, in any language, exemplifies a relatively recent Western form of fiction. Its adoption by Southeast Asian writers indicates their participation in something new, something different from the "traditional." Since the 1960s, every country in Southeast Asia has had writers creating modern short stories. In this post-independence period, associated with an increasingly unmitigated process of modernization, subjects popularized by writers across the region include changing gender roles, religion, alienation, and political corruption. Some shared literary styles include culturally nuanced variations of critical and socialist realism, romanticism, and existentialism.

One trend in stories from Laos, Cambodia, and Vietnam reflects the lingering impact of the two Indochinese wars, while an older generation of writers may continue to reminisce about the impact of Japanese aggression during World War II. Contemporary short-story writers in Southeast Asia continue to create either experimental or socially engaged literatures and sometimes stories that combine both qualities, while broad sectors of the reading public demand titillating romance novels, thrillers, or comics for light entertainment.

To do justice to the literary creativity found in each Southeast Asian country would require the production of a multivolume series of encyclopedic length. In contrast, this compact anthology represents an initial step toward establishing Southeast Asia's modern fiction within the disciplines of contemporary world literature and cultural studies. The short introductions preceding each unit and story provide some cultural context. More literary history will be provided in a subsequent volume on the history and significance of the modern short-story genre in Southeast Asia. Although each story reflects the unique expression of an individual author's experience, I hope the Southeast Asian short stories in this anthology will be read with E. Ulrich Kratz's comments in mind, "as part of a universal tradition which binds together most modern literatures."

Burma

The modern Burmese short story developed from Western contact, which began in 1612 when the British East India Company sent agents to Burma to open trade. For the next two hundred years the Burmese resisted the efforts of British, Dutch, and Portuguese traders to establish trading posts on the Bay of Bengal. Power of self-rule was lost during the Anglo-Burmese War in 1824–26 and two subsequent wars. By 1886, the British East India Company had expanded throughout Burma and the area had been annexed to India. Burma became a separate British colony in 1937 and won its independence in 1948.

Up to the end of the nineteenth century, Burmese literature consisted predominantly of religious texts in verse. In 1886 English was adopted as the official language, which stifled new literary experimentation in Burmese. In the twentieth century, a venue for short stories, gradually written in more succinct Burmese, was provided by newspapers, whose readers enjoyed romance and adventure fiction. During the 1920s short-story characters acquired greater psychological depth as the genre became more popular.

From 1930 to 1942 literature came to reflect a growing national consciousness, partly in response to a worsening economy. In December 1937 a group of students established the Nagani (Red Dragon) Literary Society to publish their own political writings sympathetic to Marxism. Issues regarding identity, social welfare, and political independence became important in short fiction.

Burma became a key battleground in World War II with the Japanese invasion in December 1941. Literary activity largely ceased during the war period due to Japanese censorship. As soon as paper became available after the war, magazines and journals flourished, and different literary journals became associated with specific political groups. After World War II, the importance of reestablishing Burmese as the language of education was recognized, along with the need to rebuild the educational system. To this end the first literary prizes for Burmese fiction were established by the Burmese Translation Society in 1948, the year Burma became independent from Great Britain. As civil war broke out in the early 1950s, social conditions worsened, causing writers to take up controversial subjects. Over the next few decades, the novel and short-story genres became literary symbols of a changing society. A nationalist trend in literature continued through the 1950s. Writers were concerned with the problem of identity and the effect of change on traditional life. The scope of short stories widened to include the lives of people in various classes, and character development became more subtle and realistic.

This relatively unrestricted era of literary expression and cooperation ended in 1962. The Revolutionary Council established the Press Scrutiny Board and organized the first National Literary Conference as a forum to discuss the new government's proposal that "literary workers" should support its objective of building a new socialist society. This objective would become a focal point of contention in the late 1960s and early 1970s.

By the early 1970s, many privately owned literary magazines had been denied publication licenses since they frequently published short stories expressing opinions unacceptable to the government. The government also maintained control over publishers' licenses and the paper supply for publications. After the prodemocracy turmoil of 1988, a military junta, the State Law and Order Restoration Council (SLORC), overthrew the civilian government; changed the country's name to Myanmar in 1989; and established a new state-controlled literary organization, the Myanmar Writers' and Journalists' Association, solidifying the trend toward strict state control of writers.

Government censorship has affected writers. Some practice self-censorship out of political necessity or stop writing, while others resort to allusion and irony to conceal a political subtext. Nevertheless, the short story remains the most popular and important literary genre in Burma today. Themes continue to include the problem of identity and the question of change in the traditional lifestyle. New issues include the impact of modern values on the traditional extended family, value conflicts between village and urban life, and the tension between an educated avant garde and uneducated folk perceived to be dwelling in the past.

In 1997, the SLORC changed its name to the State Peace and Development Council (SPDC), but it has not altered its policy on censorship. The following short stories represent several examples of contemporary Burmese literature. Please note that the order for authors' names in Asian languages is typically family name first, unless there has been some outside influence on the author's culture—Spanish influence in the Philippines and Islamic influence in Malaysia, Brunei, and Indonesia—or the author has adopted a Western name or pen name.

Ne Win Myint

"Thadun"

Ne Win Myint, whose real name is Khin Maung Win, was born in 1952 in Minbu District, Upper Burma, in the oil town of Yenan-gyaung. He began his writing career in the 1970s and has been a prolific short-story writer. He won the National Literary Award for Short Stories in 1992.

Amateur plays have long been an important source of public entertainment in Southeast Asia. The play in "Thadun" is for a religious festival signifying the importance of institutionalized Buddhism in Burma. It is based upon a sequence of events occurring when the sheltered Prince Siddhartha finally escapes his pleasure-filled palace grounds only to encounter an old man, a sick man, a dead man, and a mendicant. Siddhartha's subsequent selfless actions, based upon his understanding of the impermanence of ego and self, form a stark contrast to those of the character Thadun and his friends. In fact, this story may be an allegory of political corruption in contemporary Burma. Thadun and his friends represent the egocentric and incompetent generals of the SLORC, and poor "Riches Corner" represents Burma.

Ne Win Myint frames the story with an obvious disclaimer locating the event not in the present but the past. This signals to the reader that the story actually critiques the present. Vietnamese and other writers across Southeast Asia must also be cautious or very clever in their literary representations to evade jail and the censor's power. Such writers include Indonesian writers Seno Gumira Ajidarma ("The Mysterious Shooter Trilogy") and Yudhistira ANM Massardi ("Interview with Ravana").

This is a story about a small incident that happened during the days of the village chiefs. I should set the record straight because I fear some people will think that it happened just recently. It isn't a story about

"Thadun," by Ne Win Myint, published in *Ba-zinyin-gweh and Other Short Stories* (1995). Permission to publish granted by the translator, Patrick A. McCormick, with the author's consent.

anything very out of the ordinary. It's just about five people who performed a small one-act play.

A monk from Fig Tree Creek invited some men to a meeting about a Hsunthein Pwe, the ceremony and festival to donate food to monks. Of course they had to go to the meeting—the monk was revered all throughout the region. Fig Tree Creek wasn't a town but little parts of a village that weren't considered neighborhoods anymore. These little parts were called "Corners." There were five in Fig Tree Creek—Hand Clap Corner, Alo Lei Corner, Riches Corner, Central Corner, and King's Road Corner, where the rich people were found a little ways away from the middle of town. Alo Lei, Hand Clap, and Riches Corners were extremely poor and the people there led a hand-to-mouth existence.

That year, as in every other, everybody wanted to attend the Hsunthein Pwe, which was usually so large that the whole village had to be involved. Three people from each corner had to attend the meeting with the monk, including three from Riches Corner. As had been the custom every year, the village headman talked about how he wanted the ceremony to be as well attended as in previous years, about how last year's drums had worked out fairly well, about how he thought that more people might come if each Corner took on a different responsibility and put on a *pwe* open to all who wanted to come, and about how the villagers would be able to see the plays only if each Corner put on its own. Everyone made promises quite easily since the festival would take place provided the weather was favorable.

But after the meeting was over, the three old men from Riches Corner went home unhappy.

"Well, how are we going to do this? He said each Corner should take part of the responsibility and contribute one short play each."

The other two couldn't answer. Each one knew about their Corner, which had to deal with the impossibility of putting on a play when they had to work hard just to eat and didn't have a population of even a hundred people. Not counting the old men and women, children and girls, there would be about ten men at most. Out of those young men which one would put on makeup and go on stage to perform in a play? Suppose they were willing to go on stage. What dance would they perform? Who would teach them?

"This only happened because the other Corners said they could do it. They agreed to it because they didn't want to be outdone. What dance will people from our Corner do? What a depressing thought . . ."

They went back home with long faces. "We still have time. We won't be doing it until the end of the monks' rainy season retreat, so we still have a little time to get ready and rehearse. But who will put on what play?"

One of them suggested, "From the few men in our Corner, how many young men do we have? How about if we gave the responsibility to Thadun and his friends?"

"What about women? Who will be an actress? The girls have a hard enough time finding clothes to wear as it is. Where will they get costumes? Let's think about this a minute."

"You're right, I don't know what we should do."

"Wait a minute, let's try asking Thadun."

The three old men couldn't think of a play for Riches Corner to put on. They didn't know what to do. Finally they got Thadun, the town drunk, to be their leader. Thadun was meddlesome but knew a little about drums and gongs and could play the small and double-headed drums. You could say he could sing, but if the oboe was playing in C-sharp, he would be screaming, not singing, five notes lower. Even so, he was "Our Thadun, the Singer" in Riches Corner.

"I think we can make it work. Let's ask him."

Thadun and his four friends looked in surprise at the three old men before them. In their entire lifetimes, the village elders had never entrusted them with this kind of responsibility. It wasn't that no one had ever relied upon them, but it wasn't like the Corner couldn't survive without them. Nor had they ever been told they had to maintain the dignity of Riches Corner. But that day when the village elders called on them, they were given a real responsibility. They were told to think about their responsibility, that it was a play the entire village would see, that it would be a Hsunthein Pwe, that every Corner had to bear a different responsibility, that they would suffer if Riches Corner's performance was bad. Put on whatever singing, one-act play or fantasy piece you like. Don't let anyone interfere, don't let anybody influence you. You can make use of anything from any home in Riches Corner. But Riches Corner has to play an important part in this Hsunthein Pwe.

"Well, Thadun, do you think you can do it?"

Thadun glanced at his four friends. They looked back at him because it was all up to him. Actually, all of them knew about their Corner. Only the name contained "Riches." They knew it was very poor. Not every house had a door; not every household owned cattle or oxen. How were they going to put on a one-act play in a Corner where people led a hand-to-mouth existence reaping paddy, gleaning through odds and ends, and picking leaves? Thadun thought it over. After a moment, he said, "We can do it. I'll do it."

The three village elders were very happy, especially to be able to finally transfer the responsibility they had to take, out of reverence for the great monk and fear of the village chief, onto someone else's shoulders.

"Can you really do it, Thadun?"

"Of course I can."

"How many people will it take?"

"Five."

"What?"

"That'll be enough, just us five."

"Thadun, can a play be put on with just five people?"

"Yes. We'll only need the five of us."

"What about women? Won't you need some to put on a play?"

"No. There won't be any women."

"What?"

None of them had ever heard of a play being put on without women, with just five men performing. So along with feeling happy, the three old men also began to feel uneasy.

One of them asked: "You know it's going to be a play for everyone in the village to see, don't you? Don't be careless. I know your skills. Are you really thinking of having just the five of you perform without any women?"

"Please don't worry. A Hsunthein Pwe is a religious occasion. I've thought about that, too. Riches Corner may be poor, but I can handle it."

"Well, fine. But what about costumes?"

"We won't need any. We'll only need an old monk's robe and a prince's costume."

"Hmmm."

"Please don't worry. Just find what I ask you to."

"That much we can do. What will the other three wear? Which play will you put on?"

"Let's not announce the name yet. Let's just say it's a one-act play. I'll announce it only when the time is near. The other three don't need any costumes."

The three old men from Riches Corner just couldn't understand. He said he'd put on a one-act play with five people. He said he didn't need any costumes. He said he didn't need any women. He said he couldn't say which play he'd put on. He said he'd keep it secret. Anyway, at the

Hsunthein Pwe, it would be fine to say that it was Thadun from Riches Corner's one-act play. That's what they agreed to in the end.

The time for the Hsunthein Pwe finally drew near. Thadun and his friends had not actually done a thing in the time that other people were busy practicing in the orchestra, beating drums, preparing food for the monks, making offerings to the spirits of the festival and of theatrical performances, and rehearsing their singing and lamenting. Here's what others were doing. Hand Clap Corner was going to put on "Theriwa Wanizza," "The Glass Ball Seller," to a prerecorded soundtrack. In the background they were going to play Shway Man U Tin Maung's tape and have people lip-synch and perform. They had a person covering aluminum cups with gold paper for the play.

Alo Lei Corner was going to perform the play "Kitha Gawdami," also to a tape. They went to the city to rent costumes. People said that the woman performing "Kitha Gawdami" was very haughty. Of course the people from the Central and King's Road could afford anything. They were doing choral dancing and a small one-act play. But Thadun and his friends remained unworried. A few days before the event, Thadun still hadn't told anyone the name of the play he was going to put on. The four men he was performing with didn't know what they were going to do. In reality, they should have been rehearsing—their play should have been well rehearsed by that point. They should have known what the orchestra was going to play in the background, who would appear on stage, and who was going to say what.

But Thadun wasn't worried. The three old men, on the other hand, were quite worried. They had rented a costume for Thadun with the little money they had and borrowed a monk's robe from a monastery, but even then Thadun hadn't done anything, so they summoned him. Some of them had started to get angry by the time he and his friends arrived.

"Thadun! Don't just sit there watching everybody else practice. You've got to put on the play in three days. You haven't done a thing yet. Are you really going to do it?"

"Of course we are. We're practicing this evening."

"Will that be enough time? And what about your people? Do you know the plot of the play?"

"It won't take long, it's just a one-act play."

"Which play is it going to be?! You should be able to tell us by now."

"It'll be one of the life-stories of the Buddha, 'Siddhartha's Vision of the Four Signs.'"

The three old men were completely flustered. "Siddhartha's Vision of the Four Signs"? Even though they had spoken ill of him, if Thadun did something, it always turned into something great.

"Keep going. The play . . ."

"What's the problem? One of us can play Prince Siddhartha with the rented costume. One can shave his head and play the Monk. One can play the Old Man, another the Sick Man, and another the Dead Man. We won't need any actresses. We won't need any other costumes. We don't really need to do that much acting. We'll perform the scene where Siddhartha has his vision in the garden. We'll have Nga Pyu play the song "Yathawdaya" on the mandolin in the background. That's all there is to it."

"Wow! Sounds good."

The three old men were quite pleased. So they continued to depend on Thadun. Look at the money others were wasting playing trinket and bauble sellers in plays like "Kitha Gawdami" and "Wunnapahta." Their Thadun was putting on "Siddhartha's Vision of the Four Signs." Riches Corner's play was going to stand out. Only Thadun had visionary thinking. It was going to be great . . . it should be instructive religiously, too . . . it wouldn't be expensive. How nice that Riches Corner was really going to be outstanding at the Hsunthein Pwe.

The three old men believed in Thadun and his play based only on what he told them. Thadun's four friends knew which play they were going to put on only then. In any case, they had to rehearse for the remaining one or two days, so they had to start that evening. The mandolin player would also have to practice, starting that evening. They were going to ask him to go over the section starting, "The Old Man, the Sick Man, the Dead Man and the Monk, when he saw the four of them, Siddhartha repented. He couldn't live in the world of humanity any longer," from the song "Yathawdaya."

The actual night of the Hsunthein Pwe included plays and choral dancing from four Corners. In the end Riches Corner did not put on "Siddhartha's Vision of the Four Signs." The village headman gave the three old men dirty looks, and they in turn bit their lips in anger. Imagine Thadun and the others talking big about "Siddhartha's Vision of the Four Signs"; let them wait for their punishment.

The three old men were angry and humiliated. Thadun was all done up in his costume and makeup. It seemed he couldn't find the other four. He felt ridiculous.

"Too bad. Thadun, you said it would all work out."

"I planned it all out carefully. I was going to play Prince Siddhartha. Kya Youn was going to play the Monk. Nga Tei was going to play the Dead Man, Sein Maung was going to play the Sick Man, and Kyaw Hla was going to play the Old Man. I planned it all out in detail. Kya Youn said he didn't want to shave his head and wear that double-layered monk's robe. He said he'd play Prince Siddhartha. Nga Tei said that if he was just going to be lying on his back on stage the whole time, he didn't need to go on at all. He just wanted to play the Prince. Kyaw Hla looks like an old man so I told him to play the Old Man, but his girlfriend told him not to and said they'd be through if he did something like that. If he wanted to act, he should play the Prince; if not, don't do anything."

"What about Sein Maung?"

"He was no good, either. He's just skin and bones so I told him to play the Sick Man, but he said playing a sick man would be degrading. He said he'd be the Prince. It was my play, so of course I play the leading role. Those other guys were being sneaky."

"I see. Where are they now?"

"They've disappeared. I don't know where they went to get drunk. I couldn't find them when I looked."

That night, what could Thadun do with just a costume, makeup, and the three old men biting their nails and glancing around nervously, when they didn't have an Old Man, a Sick Man, a Dead Man and a Monk anymore? Let people swear at him. He couldn't help it. Thadun was still waiting for his friends to play all those roles.

It's been a while since then. Even though this incident happened back in the days when we still had village chiefs, even today when something similar comes up in conversation, the villagers in Fig Tree Creek still repeat the story of Thadun and enjoy making an example out of him.

1995

Translated by Patrick A. McCormick

U Win Pe

"Clean, Clear Water"

U Win Pe, born in 1936, is a well-known artist, film director, short-story writer, and musician. He studied at Mandalay University before leaving to pursue an artistic career. He became a filmmaker but began writing short stories in the 1980s when shortages of film stock gave him extra time.

The author's famed sense of humor is clearly expressed in "Clean, Clear Water," in which a clash occurs between Western scientific reason and traditional sensibility. A parody of class, gender, filial-status privilege, and authoritarian arrogance also shapes the satirical humor of this story. The kind of cooperation manifested in the family forming the core of this story is more associated with Burma's past than with the present. The issue of a technology clash also comes up in Sila Khomchai's humorous "The Family in the Street" (Thailand) and Aminah Haji Momin's "Foolish" (Negara Brunei Darussalam).

People like Ba Gyi Kyaw are truly unique.

But before I tell you why, let me first introduce him to you. Ba Gyi Kyaw is the reigning patriarch of the Kyaw clan. In his own family there are Khin Maung Kyaw, Tun Shwe Kyaw, Tun We Kyaw, Me Than Da Kyaw, We San Da Kyaw, Kyaw U Kyaw . . . there are lots of them! Then there are his sisters and brothers and all their sons and daughters, grandkids, and great grandkids. They are all Kyaws. The parents may give their children whatever names they like as long they include "Kyaw." Sometimes they put it at the beginning, sometimes at the end. Most of them prefer it at the beginning, but it doesn't really matter. The important thing is just that it's there.

Ba Gyi Kyaw's full name is Tun Aung Kyaw, which means brilliant, successful, and famous, although he himself is really none of these

---

"Clean, Clear Water," by U Win Pe, published in *Dhana* magazine (November 1992). Permission to publish granted by the translator, Robert Vore, with the author's consent.

things. Hearing this, you may want to ask why, then, he should be called unique. To which I would simply answer that *unique* is precisely what he is; and his uniqueness is what this story is about.

Since Ba Gyi Kyaw is the eldest Kyaw, he has complete authority over the affairs of the family. He's free to get upset with or scold any of the others just as the mood strikes him, which it seems to do surprisingly often. What is his work? Well, to tell the truth, he doesn't work at all—not at a regular job, that is, on account of his considerable inheritance. Not only that, but he lives and eats in the Kyaw family house, where he considers it his privilege not to pay any expenses. The younger Kyaws never protest this arrangement. Ba Gyi Kyaw is, after all, the eldest among them, so they all chip in to provide him with whatever he needs.

There is one characteristic in particular that makes Ba Gyi Kyaw unlike anyone else. You might even say that because of it the whole family is greatly in his debt, for in this one special matter no one can match his genius; no one is as interested, as capable, or as knowledgeable as he is. And that's the truth. What I mean is that Ba Gyi Kyaw is peculiarly obsessed with the family toilets. In the large brick house and adjacent compound where the Kyaws live there are five toilets in all—three in the main house and two out back by the servants' quarters—and Ba Gyi Kyaw is forever busying himself with them. They always have to be kept clean and tidy and free of odors. The floors have to be rinsed regularly; and when it's time for them to be scrubbed, they have to be scrubbed. The water toilets have to be kept fully stocked with water, and the dry toilets must have an ample supply of toilet paper. All the necessary accouterments have to be ready at hand in sufficient quantities at all times.

Ba Gyi Kyaw himself makes frequent use of all of these toilets, choosing whichever one is most convenient at the moment. In fact, Ba Gyi Kyaw makes more use of the toilets than anyone else in the family. At the very least, he can be seen going to one or the other of them fourteen, fifteen, even sixteen times a day. And each time he uses one, he carefully inspects it. If he finds anything amiss, he immediately commands whoever happens to be around, whether it be the cook, the gardener, the driver, or even the nanny, to drop whatever they're doing and tend to the disorder. There can be no arguments, and only after the toilet is put fully right again are the hapless conscripts allowed to go back to their work.

Ba Gyi Kyaw also oversees the maintenance and repair of the toilets. If anything needs fixing, he draws up the cost estimates himself and then gets the family to put up the requisite amount of money. There can be no arguments about that either. The money ready, one or more of the younger Kyaws are sent to purchase the necessary materials, and Ba Gyi Kyaw calls in the best carpenter or mason—whichever the situation may require—to do the work. He'll tolerate no shoddiness. After each job is finished, he makes a careful, fastidious inspection; everything must be neat and precise down to the most minute detail.

Sometimes he even hurries home from out of town for fear that the toilets aren't being properly attended to. If he finds they've been neglected in any way, he becomes consumed with rage. To his way of thinking, toilets are a person's world, the most important things in life. Time and again he says that a person's health, wealth, wisdom, and mental balance depend upon toilets more than anything else. He says that people conceive their most worthy thoughts, opinions, and plans while in the toilet, even if they don't care to admit to it. He says he himself came up with his own best ideas while on the toilet. Well, *that,* at least, may well be true, but what exactly he came up with no one knows or dares ask.

Even the ancient scientist Archimedes, says Ba Gyi Kyaw, developed his famous theory on the density of solid objects while in the toilet. Once, when the school-going Kyaw nephews and nieces retorted that Archimedes had been in the bath and not in the toilet when he had his revelation, Ba Gyi Kyaw swelled with anger, declaring that the bathroom and the toilet were one and the same thing. When the nieces and nephews pressed their argument, and looked even to be getting the better of the situation, Ba Gyi Kyaw rose as if to strike his young antagonists, and they wisely desisted.

Ba Gyi Kyaw's practical expertise when it comes to toilets is undeniable, however. He knows all about waste treatment chemicals, from basic lime preparations to the latest dry and liquid sanitary disinfectants developed in the West. He can explain why and how urine waste must be treated differently than solid waste, he can expound on the relative merits of this or that brand of toilet paper (bought, mind you, with family funds), and he's an authority on toilet soaps. He knows all there is about everything on the subject and has become such a recognized expert that housing and building contractors regularly consult him about the toilet systems in their various projects.

Not long ago, Ba Gyi Kyaw undertook to study the role of toilets in world history. In looking at his sources on Burma, he was disappointed to find that, although there is a great deal of information about uniquely Burmese innovations in many areas of culture and the arts, regarding toilets there is precious little. He says that beginning with the Thaye and Pagan periods, during the eleventh century A.D., no direct evidence of toiletry is to be found in literature, mural art, sculpture, or anywhere else—although he admits to a slight possibility of having overlooked something.

He became particularly distraught when he read of the famous alchemist from the Pagan era, Shin An Zagana, who had once become so disgusted with an unreactive compound that he threw the offending amalgamate into the toilet, only to be amazed to see that contact with the noxious toilet waste caused the metal to undergo an immediate alchemical transformation. It was a truly strange and wonderful event. What shocked Ba Gyi Kyaw about the story, however, was not that Shin An Zagana's experiment could have been such a brilliant success, but that Pagan's toilets could have been so incredibly foul. On the other hand, Ba Gyi Kyaw expresses great esteem for the water closets of Turkey, and he will eagerly explain to anyone who cares to listen that the fame of the so-called Turkish baths derives in no small way from the fact that they include good toilet systems in addition to the popular bathing houses.

The Kyaw family is often subjected to Ba Gyi Kyaw's sermons on the matter of toilets. At such times, Ba Gyi Kyaw demands complete attention from his listeners and fumes with anger if anyone dares let their concentration wander for even a moment. Oblivious to the feelings of others, he brusquely contends that those who fail to heed his words are of the lowest class of people, with no hope of ever rising in the world—that they are, in short, complete and utter ignoramuses.

Thanks to Ba Gyi Kyaw, all the Kyaws have become sanitary experts, and the entire family enjoys well-ordered and clean toilets. It is to this missionary zeal for toilets, then, that I refer when I say that Ba Gyi Kyaw is unique. Nobody, and I mean *no*body, is as crazy about toilets as he is.

In another of his recent undertakings, Ba Gyi Kyaw started reading up on the latest developments in scientific bathrooms, including toilet architecture and methods for preventing the spread of disease. He made separate studies of toilet filth and putrefaction, the release of noxious odors, the microbiology of infectious agents, and the mechanisms by which epidemics begin and spread.

Ba Gyi Kyaw made a special point of studying plans for pathogen-free sub-toilet septic tanks. With the ideas he gathered from his research, he designed his own pure-water collecting tank and developed special formulas for the chemical purifiers to be used with the new system. When the plans and special formulas were complete, he boasted that, if his seven-tiered under-toilet tank were used together with the chemicals he devised, the water that drained into the lowermost chamber would be absolutely pure—would be, he said, perfectly free of sediments and microbes and suitable for either bathing or drinking.

The rest of the family had no choice but to indulge Ba Gyi Kyaw when he made such claims. They offered no arguments, feigned great interest, and remained silently agreeable. Ba Gyi Kyaw, however, was not satisfied with just this. A mere show of interest was not enough; he wanted open, full-hearted support. He therefore insisted that a working prototype of the new toilet be constructed right there in the family compound. At this, the rest of the family began to hedge. They all heaped praises on the new toilet, said they believed in it, liked it, and were amazed by it, but they argued that there were already a sufficient number of toilets around the house and that there was no need for another. They also pointed out that the new toilet would cost at least 150,000 *kyat*, an outrageous sum that they could in no way afford to pay.

But their protests were all to no avail. Whatever toilets they already had were of no consequence, Ba Gyi Kyaw said, because the building of this new one would be such a demonstration of enlightened thinking and advanced design technique as to border on religious experience. He also argued that building the toilet and proving its effectiveness would bring recognition and acclaim to the entire family. For all these reasons it was unthinkable to him that the project not be put forward. As for the money, well, Ba Gyi Kyaw simply insisted that the rest of the family divide the expenses among them and contribute their respective shares. Indeed, what else could they do? So incessant were his demands that, just to put an end to them, they came forth with the necessary funds.

Thus it was that in the southwest corner of the Kyaw compound a host of reputable masons and carpenters began building Ba Gyi Kyaw's giant toilet. They worked at a feverish pace almost without stopping until construction was finished, on schedule, exactly three months and seventeen days after the initial groundbreaking. Then it was the turn of the Kyaws themselves to get to work, for once the new toilet was in place it had to be tested, and that meant filling it up. So, in spite of the perfectly good bathrooms in the main house, everyone had to use Ba Gyi Kyaw's new experimental toilet. This took some time, of course, for to be fully sanitized the toilet water had to pass through all seven stages of the filtering process. And in the meanwhile, poor Ba Gyi Kyaw waited in restless anticipation, unable to either sleep or eat. Not for a moment would he consider transferring sewage from the other toilets to the new one—the experiment simply had to be run through its natural course or all would be for naught. Finally, after four months of the entire family, young and old, religiously patronizing the new toilet, every section of the great tank had come into use, and filtered water at last began to trickle into the lowermost reservoir.

On an auspicious day about another month later, when enough water had accumulated in the bottom section of the tank, Ba Gyi Kyaw scooped some of it into a glass and presented it to the rest of the family. The water was undeniably clear, but they all kept at a respectable distance all the same. No one dared pick up the glass, or even smell of its contents. They praised Ba Gyi Kyaw unanimously and heartily. "Hurrah!" they cried. "It's a success! The water is good enough to use for anything! Bathing, washing . . . anything!" What they said of the water was very probably true, but still, what *were* they to do with the stuff? There were both a deep and a shallow well in the family compound, and these provided the family with all the clean water they needed. Why should they use filtered toilet water? But then that, too, was something nobody dared ask.

News of the toilet spread throughout the neighborhood and caused a considerable amount of talk. People exclaimed how marvelous the new toilet was, how successful the experiment had been, and so on, but no one would go near the treated water. Ba Gyi Kyaw grew increasingly indignant at their ignorance and stupidity. If no one would cooperate, the experiment would be a failure no matter what anybody said. So what did he do? He decided that on a certain Sunday the entire family was to stay at home; no one was to go anywhere or do any work. And since he was the oldest in the family, they all obeyed—the day came, and everyone dutifully remained at home.

About nine o'clock in the morning, a man arrived at the house carrying with him a bag neatly filled with sophisticated scientific instruments. Ba Gyi Kyaw introduced the visitor as Mr. U Maung Maung Ba, a professor of biochemistry, and explained that he had come to test the toilet water. The professor, he said, would take a sample of water from the last filter tank of the toilet and analyze it for clarity, metal content, the presence of pathogens and particulate matter, and so on. In short, he would determine scientifically if it was really as clean and safe as it looked, and then report his findings to the entire family. This said, Ba

Gyi Kyaw scooped some of the water up into a very clean and clear glass and handed it to the professor. In front of everyone, the professor proceeded to divide the water into small portions, which he then commenced to examine, each in turn, using such extremely intricate procedures as to leave no doubt whatsoever as to the accuracy of the forthcoming results.

Some three hours later, the testing was complete and the professor announced in a bold voice that the water from the last filter tank of the great toilet was clean enough to set the standards for water purity. He confirmed that it could be used for drinking, bathing, washing—whatever one wished. Ba Gyi Kyaw was elated. He said not a word, but his face lit up with a broad, ecstatic, self-satisfied smile. Then, still smiling, he scooped up a full glass of the water and held it out to the family, entreating them to each take a small sip. Coax as he might, however, he could get no one to do as he asked. They all heaped praises on him and loudly proclaimed their amazement at the wondrous success of the experiment, but they adamantly refused to drink the water, or even to so much as taste it.

Ba Gyi Kyaw's smile vanished and his breast filled with angry, bitter spite so great that for several long moments he was at a complete loss for words. Finally, he turned to the professor and explained that, although the Kyaw family believed the results of the analysis, they were not yet prepared to act upon what they knew to be true. He therefore requested that the professor settle the matter once and for all by drinking the water himself. Ba Kyi Kyaw had no sooner finished speaking than the professor's face turned sour, then became resolutely stern as he flatly rejected Ba Gyi Kyaw's petition, claiming that he had originally agreed only to analyze the water and was therefore under no obligation to drink any of it.

In the ensuing silence, Ba Gyi Kyaw became frantic, his mind groping desperately for a next move. What, he thought, could be done? Then all at once he knew, and he made his decision. There was this thing that had to be done, an important matter that had to be resolved, and if everyone else refused to do it, he would. Slowly, he took hold of the glass of filtered toilet water, raised it, and made ready to drink. The entire family looked on in rapt attention. The professor stood unmoving, transfixed with anxious anticipation. Ba Gyi Kyaw himself began to quail, his body trembling slightly. Then, with the glass suspended in his hand, he . . .

1992
Translated by Robert Vore

Ma Sandar

"An Umbrella"

*A prolific writer, Ma Sandar, born in 1947, has published about sev-
enty short stories and twelve novels. She was awarded a literary prize in
1982 for a collection of short stories and one in 1994 for her novel*
Alwan Eikmet Pan.

*"An Umbrella" reflects a humanistic, cross-cultural perspective on
relationships, aging, and the sexual double standard. Ma Sandar is
known as a realist employing an idiosyncratic mixture of humor and
sadness in her fiction. This story reflects her penchant for social satire
and her sensitive depiction of life among the common people.*

*The gender-based double standard is an important subject for both
male and female writers. In Mary Loh's "Sex, Size and Ginseng" (Singapore) and K. S. Maniam's "The Kling-Kling Woman" (Malaysia) the
female protagonist subverts the norm. Other short stories, like Sri
Daoruang's "Sita Puts Out the Fire" (Thailand), reflect how acquies-
cence may be a safer path.*

Ko Yay Geh was dozing off, leaning against the wall. He had a short
cheroot that had gone out and was being lightly held in the corner of
his lips. Every time Ma Sein Mya saw him like this, she got a feeling of
uneasiness in her mind. Then she remembered the words her mother
often used to say: " A woman who has no husband to lean on is like a
person walking in the rain without an umbrella. There is no one to
shield her from the rain and wind."

Even though she married him out of love and by her own choice, Ma
Sein Mya was not quite satisfied with her husband, Ko Yay Geh. It is
true that he gave her all of his small salary without keeping even one
pya to himself. However, she became very irritated when she could not
hold on to it, for the money diminished gradually until there was noth-

"An Umbrella," by Ma Sandar, published in *Sandar* magazine (July 1990). Permission to
publish granted by the translator, Than Than Win, with the author's consent.

ing left. By the middle of the month, Ma Sein Mya repeated the following words twice a day: "Since we have a bunch of kids, it's not enough to depend only on your salary, Ko Yay Geh. We need to plan for some extra income."

To this, the snoozing Ko Yay Geh agreed by straining to open his eyes and saying, "Um . . . of course! You plan that. Plan. Plan." Then he tried to close his half-open eyes.

"I'm asking you to do it because I don't know how to. I'm asking you!" Ma Sein Mya curtly retorted. Ko Yay Geh's eyes became a little wider and he sighed unobtrusively.

"Okay. In that case I will have to do it."

"How are you going to plan it?"

"Oh! Do I have to do it right away?"

"All you have to do is to say it. What's so difficult. Say it. Say it now!"

"Oh! Do you think it is easy to say it? If I'm that good why am I working as a clerk? I'd be working as a director general or a managing director."

Ma Sein Mya gave Ko Yay Geh a big dirty look. She muttered. She banged things around. At that moment, bad luck fell upon the eldest and the middle sons, who happened to be messing around in front of their mother and got a good spanking from her.

Ko Yay Geh heaved a big sigh. He took the short cheroot out of his mouth. Then he put it back. He reached for the matches and lit it again. He ignored everything as if he did not see nor hear any of it. He puffed on his short cheroot until there was a lot of smoke. About ten minutes later he leaned back on the wall again. He puffed on the cheroot absentmindedly. After ten more minutes he narrowed his eyes and dozed off again.

"Whenever I talk to him it always ends like this. You don't know how fed up I am." Ma Sein Mya poured her heart out to her elder sister Daw Sein Kyi, whose husband, Ko Yu Swan, was part Chinese.

Even though he had the same habit of sitting and leaning against the wall like Ko Yay Geh in the evenings, Daw Sein Kyi's husband did not doze off. He constantly used his abacus. It seemed like he was always calculating in his small head which commodity he should sell, which commodity he should be buying at a reduced price, and which commodity he should be storing. He was someone who could contrive to increase his monthly income in accordance with the ever-rising prices of food and commodities. That is why even though there were five children in both of the families, Daw Sein Kyi's family was able to have elegant meals with the good white Nga Kyweh rice, meat and fish curries with enough oil.

Ma Sein Mya, on the other hand, was rather fed up with life. She told her sister, "We never make ends meet each month. We have to borrow, or pawn, and it's always a vicious circle."

Even if Indra, king of the gods, showed up in his headdress and said, "Ask for anything you desire," it was unlikely that she would even make a wish to reach Nirvana within a few days. It was more likely that her prayer would be: "Dear Lord, may my husband Ko Yay Geh be a good provider like my sister Daw Sein Kyi's husband." However, it did not seem that the magic emerald slab in the world of the thirty-three gods hardened to remind Indra that a good person was in trouble.[1] The king of the gods did not show up. And so, while Ko Yu Swan was diligently using his abacus, Ko Yay Geh kept snoozing.

"Ko Yay Geh is a good man." Even though her sister had never responded to Ma Sein Mya's complaints before, this time she defended Ko Yay Geh. Her daughter brought them a plate of *lahpet thouq,* pickled tea-leaf salad. "He doesn't drink, gamble, and have affairs," continued her sister while pushing the salad plate toward Ma Sein Mya. "When you become husband and wife, loyalty is more important than financial matters, Sein Mya. How can you have a happy marriage if you can't trust each other?"

Ma Sein Mya gave her sister a quick glance. She immediately noticed a gloomy pair of eyes full of hurt. "What's wrong sister? Is Ko Yu Swan . . ."

"Yes, your brother Ko Yu Swan has a mistress," said her sister curtly, turning her head away from Ma Sein Mya. "The girl is young. She's also beautiful. About the same age as your elder niece Mi Tu."

"Wow! His own daughter's age!" muttered Ma Sein Mya in shock. She thought that Ko Yu Swan was only devoted to doing business. She never thought he would be interested in seeking other pleasures.

"As for me, I'm over forty, close to fifty. I'm fat. My stomach is bulging. My waist is thick. There's no way I can compete with a young mistress in good shape, Ma Sein Mya."

"Oh God! . . . Oh God!" Looking at her sister's protruding stomach, Ma Sein Mya secretly called out to God. Even though it was not as

---

1. It is believed that Indra sits on an emerald slab that is soft like velvet. Whenever a good person is in trouble, the slab becomes hard as a reminder for Indra to assist that person.

bad as her sister's, her stomach was also protruding. Her abdomen was thick; the waist was also thick. She noticed that her stomach and waist were in a straight line. She remembered how once in a while Ko Yay Geh jokingly called her "Miss Turtle Waist" or "Miss Frog's Butt" instead of her real name "Ma Sein Mya."

Besides, it had been a long time since she wore a shapely bodice. And so, not only was her body below the waist ugly, it was certain that her body above the waist was not a pretty sight either. As for her face, even before she got married it was only mediocre. Now without powder and lipstick . . .

"Oh God! . . . Oh God! I wonder if Ko Yay Geh also would like to have a mistress if he could afford it." This unhappy thought came to Ma Sein Mya while she put a spoonful of pickled tea-leaf salad into her mouth in a delirium.

"Has it been long since you found out?"

"Uh huh. About two months, I think." Ma Sein Kyi wiped her tears. "Of course he tries to cover it up. Since he looked suspicious to me, I followed him without his knowledge. I found them right away."

"What did you do then?"

"Me?" Elder Sister Sein Kyi clenched her teeth tightly. Then as if to swallow something, she gulped laboriously and gave Ma Sein Mya a weak smile.

"I left that place quietly so that he wouldn't know."

"Oh no!"

"Think about it. What would he do if he knows that I know? He would move forward boldly since it's no use hiding from me anymore. From supporting her secretly, he'll support her openly. I have five children. I'm just sitting and eating what he earns. I have no skills . . . If we divorce, how will I get an income? Since there's no divorce yet, I think it's better to pretend that I don't know anything about it."

This time Ma Sein Mya really admired her sister. But she also felt a deep sorrow for her. It was certain that if Ko Yay Geh behaved this way her reaction would not be the same as that of her sister.

"You are angry with Ko Yay Geh for not earning enough money. He can't find a lot of money, but everything he earns goes into your hand. Shouldn't you be satisfied with that?"

"Should I be satisfied?" Ma Sein Mya asked herself and became very sad. How could she be satisfied with a head of the household who was always sitting and dozing off whenever there was free time—in a poor household like theirs.

"You know Ma Shu Kyi, don't you? Ko Yu Swan's sister."

"Yeah. I know."

Ma Sein Mya recalled that Ma Shu Kyi was fair-skinned, slender and very pretty before she was married. She got married to an officer who worked in a department that brought in a lot of extra income. Ma Sein Mya heard that they lived quite elegantly and had saved quite a bit of money.

"Her husband is very nice if he doesn't drink. But as soon as some alcohol gets into his body, he picks fights with her. He'll try to find any old reason to scold and beat her."

"Oh, really?"

"When he's sober, of course he'll say, 'Ko Ko made a mistake.' Of course he will pacify her. But this Ko Ko keeps making mistakes again and again. So poor Ma Shu Kyi is always in tears . . . She came yesterday. One cheek was swollen. Ko Yu Swan was so angry that he was even saying, 'Why don't you divorce this animal?' and so on and so forth."

"Yes, of course. Divorce him."

"But they've already got two children. Will it be easy to divorce him? And in our culture, a widow might get respect from people. As for a divorcée, even the neighbors don't respect her," said Elder Sister Sein Kyi reflectively. Her lifeless eyes looked grim and dark. The colors were dim and faded. "Nowadays I meditate at night when I'm free."

"You do?" Ma Sein Mya knew that even though her sister had a tender heart, she was not a very religious person.

"Earlier of course, I thought of all kinds of things—whether I should cut my hair, or perm it, take an aerobic dance class, or go on a diet to become slender. But whatever I do, a person over forty is over forty. I'll never be pretty again like a twenty-year-old. When I realized all this, I gave up. Now I read prayer books. Meditate. I'll only try to have peace of mind this way."

Ma Sein Mya heaved a deep sigh. She thought: "Why are there so many unpleasant marriages in this world? If there is money, there is no loyalty. When there is money and loyalty, there is no compassion. For those marriages with compassion, money is lacking. Since basic needs are not met, people become short-tempered and have fights."

"This is depressing. I'd better go home." Ma Sein Mya got up and readjusted her long Burmese skirt. She saw a reflection of a not-so-pleasant-looking body with a loose bodice, a protruding stomach, and a thick waist in the cupboard mirror.

"Hmmm. It's worse because there are no pretty new clothes to decorate this body and turn it into a bearable sight," thought Ma Sein Mya bitterly while looking at the reflection in the mirror with a frown.

"Hey, are you leaving already?"

"Yeah. I haven't prepared dinner yet."

"Here. Here. Take some snacks for the kids." *Ama* Sein Kyi gave her a packet of biscuits and twenty-five *kyat*. "It's so cloudy and dark. Did you bring an umbrella with you?"

"Yes, I did. Here it is." Ma Sein Mya reached for her big umbrella which was full of holes and patches and put it under her arm. The black color of the umbrella had faded due to its old age. You wouldn't need an umbrella this big for a little drizzle. Her sister gazed at the umbrella under Ma Sein Mya's arm for a while and gave a forced laugh.

"Ma Sein Mya, do you remember what mother used to say often?"

"What?"

"That a woman without a husband is like someone walking in the rain without an umbrella."

"If only mother were here I would like to tell her that I'm using an umbrella; but if that umbrella is a ragged one, I still get soaking wet from the raindrops that keep dripping."

This time both of them looked at each other and laughed heartily. Then *Ama* Sein Kyi quite loudly said, "The good folding umbrellas and the ones with steel handles are not reliable either. When there's strong wind and rain they turn inside out."

On the way home it rained heavily. So, Ma Sein Mya had to use her old umbrella. Since it was a locally made cloth umbrella, it did not turn inside out like the folding ones.

"It should be enough that it does not turn inside out. Tolerate the leakage. Tolerate it," said Ma Sein Mya to herself.

The rain got to her from the side. It also beat her from the front. On ·top of that, the umbrella cloth could not keep the rain from dripping on her. By the time Ma Sein Mya got home, her whole body was soaking wet. Also the biscuits in the plastic bag that *Ama* Sein Kyi gave were moist and soggy.

"*Ama* Sein Mya, were you caught in the rain?" asked Than Than Khin from next door. Her little face, full of *thanakha* powder with thick circles on her two cheeks, lit up the gloomy room like a little light-bulb. "The rain is really heavy. It never rains but pours. I'm lucky that I didn't go out today."

(Than Than Khin owned a treadle sewing machine. She was a

seamstress. However, since the blouses she made were not so shapely, there were not many customers. Every afternoon, she dressed up and went out. Even though she said she did some buying and selling, Ma Sein Mya did not know for sure what she sold and what she bought. Ma Kyawt from the front house gossiped: "How much income will she get from sewing? Will it be enough for the mother and daughter to eat? You don't know what she is up to going out in the afternoons." Sometimes young mischief makers from the neighborhood sang out from the dark some lyrics from a well-known romantic song: "Ma Than Khin. Oh, Than Khin. I'd only like to see you beautiful like a flower. I'm also concerned that like a little flower you will wither away. I'm concerned."[2] And they giggled.)

"I did take my umbrella along, but I still got wet."

"Hmmm. When the rain gets really heavy, how can you remain dry with an umbrella of this size?"

"Oh, it's also because the umbrella is ragged. It would have been better had I walked in the rain without it."

Ma Sein Mya handed the biscuit packet to her middle son with her left hand and with her right hand forcefully threw the umbrella down on the floor of the front room. She was irritated with the ragged old umbrella as well as with Than Than Khin, who was smelling sweet and looking beautiful.

"Daughter, bring me a kimono from my cupboard. I'm going to use it as a bathing garment," she yelled out sarcastically while gathering the lower end of her long Burmese skirt and squeezing out the water from it. The older son, however, not realizing that it was only a sarcastic remark, muttered with surprise, "You have a kimono? Do you?" With wide eyes he looked at the faded Chinese print garment that the middle daughter brought to her mother.

"You stupid ass," swore Ma Sein Mya in her mind at her son while changing. She picked up the wet skirt that fell near her feet and squeezed out the water. Even though she had not glanced at Than Than Khin, she could hear her whisper: "When the rain is really heavy you get wet no matter what kind of umbrella you are using, *ama*. At least this one makes you look dignified."

1990

Translation by Than Than Win

---

2. These three lines are from a famous Burmese romantic song.

Daw Ohn Khin

"An Unanswerable Question"

Daw Ohn Khin (May Thet Su), born in 1942, is now a retired school-teacher. "An Unanswerable Question" was awarded first prize in the 1995 short-story competition that is held each year by the Sar-pay Lawka Publishing House in memory of their leading writer, Mo Mo (Inya), who died in 1989.

Contemporary Burmese life is starkly depicted in "An Unanswerable Question." The author writes elliptically about the unsatisfactory economic system; the lack of employment opportunities for the young, causing them to leave the country; and the alarming inflation rate, which renders the Burmese kyat *worthless compared to other foreign currencies. In contemporary Burma's culture of growing materialism, parents exert subtle pressure on adult children to obey them, no matter what the individual cost.*

The difficulty of finding work in a poor economy and its toll on the individual are also the subject of Mey Son Sotheary's "My Sister" (Cambodia), Khai Hung's "You Must Live" (Vietnam), and Bun-thanaung Somsaiphon's "A Bar at the Edge of a Cemetery" (Laos).

Just at present things were not going well for Ko Tut. Or to put it more correctly, he was feeling pretty miserable. One reason was that his best friend and roommate, Ko Moe Gyaw, had gone back to Rangoon a few days ago. It wasn't so much the parting from a long-time companion that he minded as the fact that his friend was going back home to his own country, to where Ko Tut's own family was. His friend Ko Moe Gyaw had been abroad for more than four years, nearly five now, and his parents felt their son had been away from them far too long. They kept begging him to return, and as he'd managed to save up quite a bit

"An Unanswerable Question," by Daw Ohn Khin, published in a collection of the year's twelve best stories in July 1996. Permission to publish granted by the translator, Anna Allott, with the author's consent.

of money he'd gone back. Although he'd left saying, "Don't be too down-hearted. I'm sure I'll come out here again," Ko Tut knew very well that if his friend left Burma again, it would only be to go to Singapore or Japan. It occurred to him that as the mere mention of the country their son was in was enough to reveal how much his parents could afford, his own parents too would most likely want to send him not just to Japan but to the USA, if they possibly could.

However, given his current situation, Ko Tut would just have to continue making his home in this country. He'd been here just over three years and had managed to send back about 450,000 *kyat* to his parents. Four months ago they had been able to buy a small Toyota, but that was all so far. His father, a government servant, was now retired. His three younger sisters were still at school, and their only interest in life was to see which one of them looked the prettiest. Whenever he imagined them using the nice pens or wearing the special makeup that he sent them from time to time, he would take comfort from thinking how popular they would be at school, and this would make him feel less tired and depressed. And then there was his mother . . .

His mother had such high hopes for her four children. Every mother wants her children to do well and to shine, but she wanted far more than this, he thought. However, her hopes had not been fulfilled. All four children were of just average ability, and though they did pass their final exams each year they had never once managed to land so much as a third prize. In talking with friends, whenever the occasion arose his mother would say things like, "My children work very hard. They move up to the next class regularly every year. We have never known the unhappiness of having them fail their exams. I must at least be thankful they are such good children."

And when, at the end of the eighth standard, her daughters only managed to pass in humanities subjects (but none on the science side), she would say, "Humanities subjects are very suitable for girls. These days everyone is always going on about science—so much so that there's a shortage of people who understand the humanities. If you study languages or history or something, then you can teach at a university. That'd make me really happy."

Ko Tut still remembered how, when he had jokingly remarked that if official prizes were awarded to parents for extolling the virtues of their own children, Mother would certainly get one, his middle sister, Khin Sanda Aung, had quickly retorted, "You aren't envious, are you brother? If Mother didn't speak up for us herself, I just don't like to think what the neighbors would say about us."

And his eldest sister, Khin Thawda Aung, who had just moved up into the tenth standard, had chimed in, saying, "Yes, sure I'd like to be a teacher at a university but not an ordinary schoolteacher, that's too much like hard work."

His youngest sister, Khin Ta-ya Aung, who was still only in the fourth standard at the time, hadn't joined in this exchange, but Ko Tut couldn't help wondering what she might have to say by the time she was a little older.

His full name was Nay Myo Aung (Descendent of the Sun's Victorious Race), but because he was born with a rather red complexion he had been nicknamed Atut—"Young Ginger"—which is why he was now called Ko Tut (Ginger). It had been his mother's wish to give her four children such grand, "heavenly sounding" names. She used to say, "I have given you these names because I want you all to do better than other people. You know the saying 'Your name determines your destiny,' don't you? Well, you know what you should do if you want to get a good position and stay in it—prepare generous amounts of *kya-zan* noodles with sauce and offer it to monks and friends so as to acquire merit; and if you want peace of mind and a happy life you should make offerings of the cooling drink *shwe-yin-aye*."

During Ko Tut's third year at university his father had been promoted, but it was his mother who had been beside herself with joy. She had invited five monks to the house and in addition fed a meal of *kya-zan* noodles to more than a hundred friends. Father, who was usually one for a quiet life, seemed to think that she had done well and hadn't interfered in any way. On that occasion, thanks to his mother's loquacity, everyone left the house well aware that his father had been promoted. Just one or two close friends said, "But, Daw Nwe Nwe Aung, can an offering like this of *kya-zan* noodles really be good enough to celebrate a promotion?"

"Well, if you think it's not enough, tell me where else would you want to eat? I've never stinted in any way at all." At these words of his mother's, Ko Tut recalled how she had invited three of his father's superiors and ten or so close friends to the expensive Shwe-ein-daw Restaurant and gotten into debt to the tune of five thousand *kyat*.

Time passed and there were great changes.[1] Ko Tut finally graduated when his father was just two years off retirement. As the eldest son, the time had come for him to think about taking on the responsibility of supporting the family. His first idea was to get a job in his father's office; the salary would be a little over a thousand *kyat* a month. When he tried to think how he would manage to get even this quite modest position, he quailed at the prospect; overcoming the obstacles would be like trying to find his way out of a maze. In the meantime his contemporaries were all talking endlessly about foreign countries and going abroad, and the talk reached Ko Tut's house as well.

"That girl from up the road, the daughter of Ma Lon Tin—the uneducated one who can't even spell, you know the one I mean—went off to Singapore after passing the tenth standard and now they say she's sending back fifty thousand *kyat* a month."

"The market woman who sells cloth, the fat talkative one, her young son went to Japan a month ago and now they say he's earning one *lakh* a month."

"The tuition teacher? He's not here any longer. He's gone to work in Malaysia. He's supposed to be doing pretty well." When the ripples of these and similar reports reached his mother's ears, her heart began to beat faster. More followed.

"Mummy, my friend at school, Nu Nu Htway, has a beautiful folding umbrella. She says her sister sent it from Japan."

"Oh yes, Ta-ya's story just reminded me. You know Moe Min U, don't you, that fair pretty girl? She's not poor like she used to be. When I said how super her very nice lunch box was, she said her brother had brought it back from Singapore."

It is not clear how his mother coaxed his father into it, but about a week later he took the time to come and have a talk with his son. What his father said didn't particularly surprise Ko Tut as he had already wondered himself if it mightn't be a good idea.

"I can't yet afford to send you to Singapore or Japan but I have made contact with a broker to get you to Malaysia. Apparently he charges other people about 130 to 150 thousand *kyat*, but he said that just for me he would get you there for seventy thousand *kyat*. Think it

---

1. The word used in Burmese, *hkit pyaung,* is the one that refers to the major changes in Burmese history. The reader will understand that here "change" refers to the present military rulers of Burma, SLORC, who took over in 1988. Because of the pro–democracy movement, universities were mostly closed in 1988–90.

over, son. I am soon going to retire and I've been thinking that I must make some provision for the family."

Father was a senior official in a government department where one didn't get any particularly good "extra allowances," though he did quite well out of the sixty-gallon petrol allocation that went with the old car provided for him by the office. But the elderly car was ailing, and he wasn't able to meet all the family's expenses as well as pay for the frequent treatment needed by the car. Ko Tut was well aware that the family was able to keep up appearances only through the extra money brought in on the side thanks to his mother's eloquence.

He accepted his father's plan, saying that he too was interested in going, and from that point the whole family became involved in the preparations. His mother's only pair of diamond earrings was sold off for ninety thousand *kyat* to raise the seventy thousand to pay the broker. He could still remember his mother's words when she came back with the large pair of Russian-made imitation diamond earrings which she said were good enough to make people think they were real.

"Now that I am getting on a bit I wanted some nice big earrings, so these are just fine. And my dearest wish has been granted now that my son is going abroad."

Seven or eight months after his mother had said how happy she was to be wearing paste diamonds instead of real ones, Ko Tut had said good-bye to his family and arrived in this country. On arrival, the broker had found him a job in a workshop, breaking up and repairing old cars. In Rangoon, after he had earned his Bachelor of Science degree, he had spent two months learning how to weld, as he had heard people saying, "If you know how to weld there's plenty of jobs and good money." But when it came to being interviewed at the actual workplace, things went badly wrong because of his lack of experience. The boss said he would pay him as a helper a basic rate of eighteen (Malay) dollars a day plus two hours a day overtime.

The broker busied himself for a moment with his calculator and then said persuasively, "That's not bad at all as you've only just arrived. In Burmese terms, you'll be getting over a thousand *kyat* a day." And so Ko Tut started work.

Returning from work to the house provided for him, Ko Tut wept to himself as he got into bed. All very well to call it a house! To him it looked more like a sawed-off railway carriage which had been plunked down with its wheels removed. The floor was barely a foot off the ground and the whole place was just one single room. About half a yard inside the doorway was an old TV set standing on a small rickety table. Right up against the opposite wall were three filthy bedrolls. In a corner of the room a discolored brown table fan turned slowly. And all along the wall by the foot of the sleeping area stood a motley collection of plastic buckets and bowls, pots and pans, and a large electric rice cooker pitted with patches of rust.

"Look here, Ko Tut, I know it'll be a bit cramped in here. But at least there's a fan and a TV and a rice cooker ready if you want to cook for yourself," the broker had said, trying to present the work in the best possible light. In spite of his dismay Ko Tut had no alternative but to go along with him. The sixty-five U.S. dollars of his own money that he had been allowed to bring with him were slowly running out, and realizing what difficulties he might face one day in a foreign country without any income, he had to reply, "It's okay." But he knew for sure that his expression showed the resentment he was feeling inside.

Of his three roommates, two were Burmese and the third a Malaysian from Sabah. He thought that at least he would be good friends with his fellow countrymen, but this turned out to be far from the case. The dark-skinned one who looked like an Indian came from Arakan; he could barely manage to speak Burmese and gave only short, unhelpful answers to Ko Tut's questions. The other one, who said he came from Myitkyina in Upper Burma, barely acknowledged Ko Tut's arrival and didn't give him so much as a smile. It seemed an icy welcome, but it could have been worse. At least the stranger from Sabah gave Ko Tut a few necessary explanations by means of gestures, after which he felt he could breathe more easily. They had been sharing the room for quite a few days before he found out that none of them had any proper schooling though at work they were already far ahead of him. They had been here for a whole year or even longer, and besides, they had done plenty of practical work back in Burma. Ko Tut did whatever they told him, cutting, shifting, lifting. Sometimes he lifted a weight so heavy that he felt a sharp stab of pain in his back.

The workshop was a place where old cars were repaired and renovated, so it was impossible to avoid contact with scraps of metal, dirty car parts, pots of paint, slimy oil dregs. Whatever the weather they had to keep busy, and in this country the rain was quite unpredictable. By the time he went to bed at night he felt he needed to rub his body all over with the special ointments that his mother had given him. Most depressing of all for him were the moments when he had to wash his oil-stained shirt and trousers. Ordinary soap was quite unable to shift the thick, filthy oil and grease, and waiting to wash his clothes in the thin trickle of water that came from the pipe made his back ache. At the end of each day's hard work, in the few minutes that he had to spare, he still had to prepare what he was going to eat. His workmates usually ate outside somewhere but he could save more money by cooking his own food, even if it was as little as five or ten *kyat*. Yet in every letter home to his parents he had always written, "I'm doing fine. Don't worry about me," and similar things. If he wrote and told them what he was really going through it would only make the family unhappy. He had no wish to add a minus sign to a sum total that already came out as zero.

Ko Tut had read the saying "An apple a day keeps the doctor away"— meaning that if you eat plenty of vegetables you'll be healthy—but an apple cost a dollar or more. Since the price of an egg was fifteen to twenty-five cents and a packet of dry noodles cost only thirty to forty cents, his daily sustenance was an egg and noodles and then again noodles with an egg. What's more, this was easy to cook. The day after he arrived in the country the broker had taken him to a huge and imposing shop called a supermarket. There, inside a closed glass room labeled "cold storage," filled with penetratingly cold air, he had seen packets of various types of vegetables laid out all around, wrapped in transparent plastic with small labels stuck on them saying how much they cost. At the sight of bundles of *kazun* leaves costing from sixty cents to one Malay dollar, according to size, and fist-size pieces of cauliflower costing as much as one and a half to two dollars, Ko Tut decided he would eat plenty of vegetables once he got back home again.

However hard and impoverished the life he was leading, the first time he had been able to send twenty-five thousand *kyat* home to his parents he had wept tears of joy. After this he had thought he should try to change to a new job because his present one was so hard. To do this would cost another fee to the broker of around 150 to 250 Malay dollars, in Burmese money six thousand to nine thousand *kyat*. But he couldn't be certain that he would be able to get a new job that would meet all his requirements, such as easier work, with less danger of being arrested by the police, with a good-natured boss and so on. Every foreigner working abroad is totally dependent upon luck, so for the time being, Ko Tut didn't venture to make a change. Some eight months had passed when, one day, the broker who had placed him in his job turned up and asked him if he would like to change to working in a restaurant. He wouldn't charge an extra fee, he said, and it was a job with a salary of 450 dollars a month and board and lodging thrown in. Without further hesitation, Ko Tut gratefully set out on a new stage in his life.

Even though the broker was leading the way, Ko Tut remembered, he had been annoyed with himself at feeling afraid to enter the ornate, air-conditioned restaurant with its large shining glass doors, floors carpeted in crimson, giant urns planted with flowers. The owner was Chinese with an unusually brown complexion. Ko Tut didn't particularly mind that he was assigned work at the back of the restaurant; so long as he was earning his living honestly, he felt that any job was worth doing. And it was a consolation to find among his fellow workers one who was a graduate like himself and two other university students from Burma. All the rest of those working there were Malaysians. He wondered if any of them had ever been to school, they were so rude and uncivilized. If there was a napkin or a towel that had fallen on the floor, not only did they not pick it up but they would sometimes even tread on it.

Many times he had to keep his spirits up with the thought that he had come here to earn money, and that whatever happened was of no matter so long as he didn't get arrested. Though the work here was not as exhausting as in the car workshop, washing up all the plates and cutlery used by other people left him with a feeling that his whole body stank of food. After struggling with the smells, when it came to the time for eating the sweetish and tasteless food that they were given he had to force himself to swallow it down. But however unpleasant his job, once a week, on the days when they got an extra payment for cleaning out the kitchen and scrubbing down the floors, he was able to forget his feelings of resentment.

And so the months became a year. Ko Tut's hard work and readiness to please were noticed by the restaurant owner and one day, when there was suddenly a person short in the front of the restaurant, he told him to go and do the job for the time being. This was how Ko Tut's unhappy experience began. He knew well that here in Malaysia, on important feast days and holidays, rich people sometimes invited their employees out to a meal in a smart restaurant. In the party of guests he was to serve there were three young Burmese of the same age as himself, and this sowed the seeds of his unhappiness.

"This restaurant is not bad. I wonder if there are any Burmese here." Hearing these words spoken in Burmese, Ko Moe Gyaw had warned him that if he saw any of his fellow countrymen in a party of customers he must not greet them in any way, especially if they were of his own age. At the very moment he had listened to this warning, his eyes had strayed towards the speakers, and his lingering glance seemed to have made them realize that he was Burmese.

Ko Tut was not used to being a waiter, and the fact that the party he was serving included Burmese customers made him even more flustered. In the middle of coping with all their requests, just as he was opening a bottle of wine, the bottle opener slipped out of his inexperienced hand. In an effort to catch it, he shot his arm forward and in so doing knocked a glass off the table. It fell to the ground with a crash of breaking glass.

"He's a pretty rotten waiter. These lads'll give us Burmese a bad name," came the unsympathetic comment. Ko Tut hadn't dared to look at the speaker. Were they all looking at him with contempt? Would there be mocking expressions on their faces? His thoughts in confusion, he had muttered an apologetic, "I'm sorry," and collected up the bits of glass. The three short hours that he had worked as a waiter had seemed to last longer than three eternities. He had had to pretend not to understand the sarcastic remarks of his three fellow-countrymen, sitting round the table and behaving as if they owned the place.

"I wouldn't want to come abroad just to work as a waiter. But in our factory now, that's something totally different . . ." one said. Another chimed in pointedly, "If I open a restaurant when I go back to Burma, I suppose there won't be any need to hire workers."

Inside he had been boiling with anger, and when he got home that night, it had taken him ages to get to sleep.

Ko Moe Gyaw's words of comfort—"Those people only dare to talk like that because they know that you can't retaliate. Only despicable people try to make someone more miserable when he is down. Just forget about it"—had made things a little more bearable, but all the same he had wanted to run straight back home to his parents. Two or three days later, on his day off, he happened to be sitting in front of the TV watching the news in Malay. He couldn't understand the words but he was watching the pictures. The way they presented the news was always interesting because it was so full of information. During the half-hour news bulletin, Ko Tut recalled, there had been reports of at least thirty items of national and international news interspersed with pictures of the events. As he watched, he had caught on the TV screen the mangled shapes of two corpses lying on a railway track. For a few moments the scene was shown in close up, and amidst the blood-spattered remains, he noticed a small book. "Aah! That's Saing Hti Hsaing." The popular Shan singer's name burst anxiously from his lips. The news picture that had flashed before his eyes for a few seconds had pierced deep into his brain like a rivet. Seeing Saing Hti Hsaing's songbook made him 90 percent certain that the two dead bodies were Burmese of his own age, two young men fond of music. His conjecture was confirmed when he put it to his companions. Questions raced wildly through his mind.

"Could they be young men going back home with the money they had saved?"

"It looks as if they've been run over by the train, but surely they couldn't have been sleeping so soundly that they didn't hear the train coming?"

"In that case perhaps they were robbed and then just killed and left?"

"If I'm right in thinking they're Burmese, their parents will be expecting them, longing for their return."

"Who will gather up their mutilated bodies and bury them?"

The next day, unusually, Ko Tut had gone out and bought a newspaper, eager to find out more. It was just as he had thought. The report said that two young men in their twenties had died, knocked down by a train; to judge from the possessions found near the bodies, they were Burmese. "What a tragedy!" he thought, feeling utterly miserable.

Ko Moe Gyaw had remarked somewhat jokingly as he packed his bags, "What with Burmese being arrested and being knocked down by trains, I feel quite afraid to go back." To which Ko Tut had replied, "You won't mind if I don't come with you to the bus station tomorrow, will you?" Understandingly, Ko Moe Gyaw had pretended not to notice and had changed the subject by making jokes about how rich their employers were. The following day he had left before Ko Tut came back from work.

In spite of feeling homesick and unhappy, Ko Tut just went on going to work as usual; he went on plunging the piles of dirty cups and plates left by well-fed customers into the soapy water in the dirty kitchen behind the restaurant. That was his job, after all, and it was safe. Though he kept telling himself that he could save more money this way, his resolve was weakening, and thinking of home made him feel he hadn't enough courage to continue.

One day he came back home from work at midday as usual for a short break and found a letter on his bed. He picked it up and recognized his mother's handwriting. His hand shook as he opened the letter and a newspaper cutting fell out. Only then did he glance over at the calendar and remember that it had been his birthday some time ago. He opened the greetings his mother had sent him for his birthday, one that he had tried to forget because there had been so many unhappy things on his mind. And then it came back to him that he had received a similar letter last year as well.

> To a son who is so especially mindful of his gratitude to
>> his parents,
>> ## Maung Nay Myo Aung (Ko Tut),
>> temporarily in Kuala Lumpur, in Malaysia,
>> on 18th May 1995, your birthday
>>> wishing you
>> health and prosperity for the next 120 years.
>> To our son who is caring and working for us,
>> in a distant land, far from his mother and father,
>> we wish you the best of health and a long life,
>>> and may you hold your head high.
>
> Father U Htaik Aung, B.Sc., B.A. (retired)
> Mother Daw Khin Nwe Nwe Aung, B.A.
> Eldest sister Khin Thawda Aung, Burmese Third Year, Rangoon
>> University, Hlaing Campus
> Middle sister Khin Sanda Aung, passed tenth standard with a
>> distinction in history
> Youngest sister Khin Ta-ya Aung, ninth standard, passed first part

"Is that what you wish for me, Mother—to hold my head high for a hundred years?" Ko Tut wondered to himself. "Do I have anything left to hold my head high about?"

He read the accompanying letter. On his birthday, monks had been invited to the house and offered food; friends and relations had gathered and talked of his devotion to his family till his parents glowed with pride; the little car that he had paid for was most convenient for taking his sisters to school; and more in a similar vein.

He put the two pages of the letter on the nearby table and threw himself down on his bed. Feeling oppressed by the heat, he pushed open the window above his head. The rain beat in. It was always raining in this country. Just as it seemed to him that the draft of air was making him feel cooler and a little less miserable, he noticed that it was blowing the pages of his mother's letter about. Before he finished telling himself that the wind was strong enough to blow it right away, a further sudden gust swept the letter down onto the concrete floor. As he made to pick it up, the Chinaman Alin who shared the room with them walked in from having a shower and trod on the letter. As his eye followed the newspaper cutting, now stuck underneath Alin's wet flip-flop, he couldn't think what to say to the Chinaman. After all, in this country newspaper was something that one threw away once it had been read. He tried out some words in his mind but then, as he imagined the likely response—"What's the matter? It's just a piece of paper"—in a thick Chinese accent accompanied by an insolent look, he just gazed at the scene, keeping his thoughts to himself.

Closing his eyes, he asked himself if he would manage to go on being such a devoted son—devoted enough to be able to receive the same sort of birthday wishes again next year? He found no answer to the question and for a long time sleep eluded him.

1996

Translation by Anna Allott

Cambodia

The development of modern literature in Cambodia has experienced severe vicissitudes since 1863. In that year King Norodom, buffeted by the territorial excursions of his neighbors, signed a treaty with France for protection. In 1887 France established the Union Indochinoise, incorporating Cambodia and Vietnam. The French, who were interested in traditional manuscripts, sought to revive "classical" Cambodian literature through the preservation and translation of texts. The French were in control of the printing presses until the early twentieth century. Private presses were established in Phnom Penh, and modern writers finally overcame the vociferous opposition of Cambodian traditionalists who wished to maintain control of the "sacred" scribal word.

Cambodian literature was completely transformed within a few decades, between 1910 and 1930. During this period, "traditional" literature—consisting mostly of verse with content dominated by the palace and monastic cultures—was replaced with more modern prose genres. The successful writers during this transitional era were urban intellectuals who were not the products of the traditional pagoda schools. After 1921 Cambodian authorities allied with the French to promote literary creativity and the publication of works in the Cambodian language. The first Cambodian newspaper was organized in 1925, and by the end of the 1930s, Cambodia had entered an age of modern journalism, with newspapers providing an important venue for short stories in later decades.

With the diminishing French presence in the 1940s, issues of national identity became an important theme in new literature, and a literary audience developed as Cambodia was confronted with national and international tensions. The first modern Cambodian short stories finally developed in the 1960s, later than in other Southeast Asian countries, with the exception of Laos. In 1963, then–chief of state Norodom Sihanouk sought to achieve international recognition of

Cambodia's neutrality in the Vietnam War. Nevertheless, U.S. bombing spilled over into Cambodia during the late 1960s.

Until 1970 there were periods of comparatively high literary output, often thematically critical of the government, followed by waves of censorship. Subjects for fiction included love, broken friendships, adventure, and didactic moralism, often written about in the form of novellas or short stories. The market was now shifting toward the tastes of women and young people.

In 1970, while on a trip abroad, Sihanouk was overthrown by General Lon Nol. Literary activity was brought to a halt as political instability increased. In April 1975, Pol Pot and the Khmer Rouge overthrew the Lon Nol regime. All traditional and modern literature was banned. In fact, the ability to write, if discovered, could be grounds for execution. Over the next four years between one and two million people were executed, were worked to death in concentration camps, or died from disease and malnutrition as the country was turned into a prison camp.

On 8 January 1979, Pol Pot was ousted by Vietnamese forces who established a pro-Vietnamese government under the leadership of Heng Samrin, leading to a controlled revival of literature under the People's Republic of Kampuchea (PRK) government. Two consistent themes in literature of this period are the atrocities experienced by Cambodians under the Pol Pot regime and the tragedy of life.

As the proposed deadline for the Vietnamese to leave Cambodia became protracted, a United Nations–brokered agreement between the two countries was finally signed in 1992, leading to free elections in May 1993. With the advent of the United Nations Transitional Authority in Cambodia (UNTAC) era, from October 1991 to September 1993, newspapers proliferated along with nominal freedom of the press, providing a venue for the modern short story and a return to more creative expression. A major theme for newspaper short stories now is didactic reflection of social and political issues, including prostitution, political corruption, and violence. There is still no major literary magazine in Cambodia devoted to the short-story genre. The stories provided in this section represent contemporary Cambodian short fiction published in newspapers during the 1990s.

"Just a Human Being"

*The author of this story, published in a daily newspaper, remains
anonymous, as do many writers in Cambodia, where literary art is
heavily politicized. In "Just a Human Being," the author criticizes the
inhumanity of bureaucracy unless you happen to be an "important"
person. A system of patron-client privilege is an institutionalized aspect
of the Cambodian social structure. The ballpoint pens mentioned in the
story allude to the practice of members of important Khmer Rouge
cadres, who used such pens as a sign of their higher status during the
Pol Pot era (1975–79), when unauthorized writing was essentially prohibited. This short story's form is experimental, reminiscent of a short
play or scene from a television drama.*

*The theme of the common man manipulated and outmaneuvered
by those above in the social or political hierarchy is also found in Atsiri
Thammachoti's "And the Grass Is Trampled" (Thailand) and Vo
Phien's "Unsettled" (Vietnam).*

Chief: Who's making such a commotion outside the door? What is that
racket?
Assistant: There's a visitor demanding to meet you in person, sir.
Chief: How's that? Doesn't he know that I only receive visitors on
Thursdays?
Assistant: Yes, he knows. But he says he has a matter of urgency, sir.
Chief: Then does he know that it's necessary to put his name down a
month in advance?
Assistant: Yes. He more than knows; but he keeps pushing to come in.
Chief: God! What kind of person is this?
Assistant: He says he's just a human being.
Chief: But who is he? Who is he?
Assistant: All I can say is that he's just some person.

"Just a Human Being," by an anonymous author, first published in the newspaper *Nokorbal Pracheachon/Nokorbal Cheat* (1993). Permission to republish granted by the publisher,
Chhay Sinarith, and the translator, John Marston.

Chief: Very well. Then what does he look like, this variety of human being?

Assistant: There's nothing very special about him. He's wearing a gray shirt and trousers and has black shoes and a ragged captain's hat.

Chief: Ragged? And a captain's hat, no less? There's something unusual about that. What does he want, then? He doesn't say?

Assistant: No sir. He only insists on saying one thing: "I have an urgent matter; I'm just a human being who asks to meet with . . ."

Chief: He's not a little drunk and fuzzy, is he?

Assistant: No. His demeanor is quite focused and clear, sir.

Chief: Well, this is very strange. Certainly very strange. Hey, what do you think? Who is he?

Assistant: God in heaven knows. Shall I chase him away?

Chief: Don't rush things, now . . . just in case he might not just be a human being, but someone from the inspection committee.

Assistant: Could be or could not. The sleeves of his shirt are all worn through.

Chief: Why are you telling me about his worn-through sleeves, then? *Focused and clear demeanor*—right on the day I don't receive visitors—*shirt sleeves worn through; just a human being.* I am very suspicious! There's something out of the ordinary here. Try to remember if you saw anything else.

Assistant: Anything else? In his pocket were clearly visible two ball-point pens.

Chief: Two pens! Why didn't you tell me that right away?

(He unbuttons his shirt collar.)

Look at this clearly. Isn't this someone coming here under a pretext? And what reason is he coming here for?

Assistant: Here under a pretext? For what reason?

Chief: In order to inspect our way of working with the people, that's why.

Assistant: In that case, let me invite him to enter.

Chief: Wait a minute. We've got to do this right. Tell the secretary to make some coffee quickly and to bring out some cognac and other things like that as well. Pull the chairs together a little here. And you can push the flower pot away a little, there. Now go and invite him in and don't forget that you have to treat him very warmly and intimately, like a member of the family.

(The assistant comes back into the room soon after he has left.)

Chief: How's that? You're back already? Didn't you see him?

Assistant: He's there, sir. But there's one matter which I thought I should come back and ask you about. He's weeping . . .

Chief: What? How do you mean, "He's weeping"?

Assistant: In the usual miserable way, with tears pouring from his eyes like drops of rain.

Chief: Is that so? Weeping. Then he must be just a human being after all. So then we try to . . . Ho, ho. Then everything is already quite in order. You can go kick his ass out of here, and you don't need to say anything to anybody. Tell the secretary that it's not necessary to make the coffee. As for the cognac, though . . . a stressful situation does strap one's energies. A human being, then . . . It's a problem we can handle by ourselves.

1993

Translated by John Marston

Yur Karavuth

"A Khmer Policeman's Story: A Goddamn Rich Man of the New Era"

Yur Karavuth was a staff writer for the Pracheachon *newspaper when this story was published in 1991. For the past few years he has worked as a freelance journalist in Phnom Penh. His short story illustrates the satirical use of fiction in Cambodian (Khmer) newspapers, the main venue of publication for this genre. Since the UNTAC era, freedom of the press and free speech have become important issues for some Cambodians. In a climate of violence, it seems safer to criticize political, military, and police corruption through the medium of fiction, especially if it is in the form of satirical humor. This technique is used by many*

"A Khmer Policeman's Story: A Goddamn Rich Man of the New Era," by Yur Karavuth, first published in the newspaper *Nokorbal Pracheachon/Nokorbal Cheat* (1991). Permission to reprint granted by the publisher, Chhay Sinarith. Published in English translation in the *Phnom Penh Post*, vol. I.2 (24 July 1992). Permission to reprint granted by the editor, Michael Hayes, and the translators, John Marston and Kheang Un.

Southeast Asian writers, for example, the Indonesian writer Yudhistira ANM Massardi in "Interview with Ravana."

"A Khmer Policeman's Story: A Goddamn Rich Man of the New Era" also illustrates the culture of dubious acquisition and speculation that continues to plague the social development of contemporary Cambodia. Compare this to Outhine Bounyavong's story "Death Price" (Laos).

Don't laugh or cry at my story: it is merely the way the hand of fate has marked my present incarnation. Here in the police department, I have many friends who like to joke around with me. They have all given me a nickname: "the goddamn rich man of the new era." Well, of course, it's very appropriate.

In 1988 I sold a small villa of mine for forty *domlong*. My god! As you know already, at that time forty *domlong* was quite a sum of money. When my wife and children heard, their faces blossomed like a mint seed in water.

Once we had the forty *domlong* in our hands, my wife and I began thinking hard—like the boy in the Cambodian story who thinks so hard that he falls out of the sugar palm tree.

We thought about it during the day as we rested and dreamt about it at night while we slept. It was truly thinking on a major scale because we realized there would be a portion of money left over after buying an apartment which we could use as capital for doing business with the best of them.

So, dreaming of this and dreaming of that, we bought an apartment for twenty-five *domlong,* leaving fifteen *domlong*. Then after giving some to various relatives—all told, five *domlong*—there was ten *domlong* left to put in the pot of the *tong tin* lending-group schemes at the Orasey Market.

My choice of this course of action was in part motivated by thinking that I didn't want to trouble my wife by setting up a business where she would have to work—better to keep her white, soft, and lovely for her husband, right?

I put in two *domlong* here and one *domlong* there. I started out putting in five *chi* in four places and ended up putting five *chi* in ten places. It was great fun spending it from day to day, just waiting for the interest to roll in.

It was a delicious way of life for almost a year—until the guy holding the pot skipped town and the *tong tin* house went bust, creating a very sorry situation indeed.

Whoever I talked to—the *tong tin* head or the other members of the lending group—repeated the same story, one version like another all stuck together like shrimp in a glob of shrimp paste. The sum of money, every bit of it—more than ten *domlong*—had been thrown away neatly!

Suddenly not only my mother-in-law, but my *own* mother and all my other relatives in chorus, laid the blame 100 percent on me! They said, "How were you playing *tong tin* so that you ended up losing the money?" When I was doing well by the scheme, I thought to myself, I never heard a word of criticism. Only when misfortune falls do they band together and blame me.

Nonetheless, by the middle of 1989—oh my god, a goddamn rich man of the new era like myself was still getting along in high style. That year someone came by who wanted to buy my twenty-five-*domlong* apartment and was so bold as to offer thirty-five *domlong*. I discussed the offer with my wife.

"Shall we sell it again, sweetheart?" I asked her.

"It's *completely* up to you, dear," she said.

I love my wife because when I ask her about something, she always says it's up to me. It's things like this that mean I could never be false to her love.

Sometimes, when it is her time of month—what we call her "vacation time"—she will say to me straightforwardly: "Dear, when I have to behave modestly like this, I'm afraid it leaves you bored and restless, doesn't it?" Well, this is what they call a wife who understands her husband . . . Let me make something clear at this point. Having been on the police force for thirteen or fourteen years, I can boast a little. When it comes to "being on the take"—a present here for a favor there, skimming a little off the top or skimming a little off the bottom, tucking something away for a rainy day—there hasn't been any of that.

For a goddamn rich man of the new era like myself, the only source of wealth is selling houses. So when I talk about my wife's willingness to do what I decide, you should understand that she agrees because she knows that whatever I do will be honest.

I decided to sell the apartment for the price offered to me. I lost no time in buying another house for twenty *domlong*, leaving fifteen *domlong* to buy a Toyota Corona for my wife and children to drive, with a little left over for the pleasures of life.

It is a human thing that when you have a car you want to show off. And it is precisely because of this car that they gave me the nickname, "the goddamn rich man of the new era." My wife and children were truly happy: a car to drive like the best of them!

But by the end of 1990 the money was gone, my wife was sick, and the car had broken down. Health gone, peace of mind gone, and no money to boot! I decided to sell the car. Since I needed the money quickly, I sold the car for five *domlong*, losing two *domlong*. I used most of the money for the medical bills; the rest went for family expenses.

By the time New Year's rolled by in 1991, the economic situation was beginning to bubble and boil. A playboy type came by offering to buy my apartment. This time the offer was thirty *domlong*. I decided to sell. Wealth again! I went out with my wife and got a fifteen-*domlong* apartment. With the money left over, we bought a piece of land just east of the city. It was great! Having bought the land, there was enough money to buy a car, too! Every Sunday I would go with my wife and the kids to look at the land.

As luck would have it, one of the suburbanites there got the mistaken idea that I was a rich businessman. Suddenly, at the end of 1991, the lid blew off of things, and the guy said I had bought land that belonged to him. He would not allow it. Well, since the other guy was higher up than me, and I was afraid, also, because I heard he had connections in even higher places, I surrendered pretty quickly—losing the match before I'd even entered the ring.

My wife cried a lot at that time, as though she were in great pain. She consoled me, saying, "Oh, sweetheart, don't be angry about fate: don't complain about what has been allotted in life. Don't struggle with a piece of rock; you'll only end up wounding yourself."

I did at least get two *domlong* out of the settlement. In the end, I decided to sell that last apartment, too, for twenty-five *domlong*. This is as far as I can go, I thought to myself—the only course left for me is to buy land in the country so I will have the means of earning a living.

My wife and I decided that she and the kids would go live in a wood house on a medium-sized piece of farmland. We sold the car to meet the needs of my wife, and especially, of the kids, who were bigger by now.

So this is my story—from living in a stone house with brick columns on its own plot of land, I progressed to a spacious apartment. And from there I moved on to a small, rather crowded apartment. Finally, I ended up in the sticks enjoying the fresh air.

I do know, though, that it's not just me, a poor policeman, who has a story like this. I suspect there are others who've received the nickname "a goddamn rich man of the new era," because of experiences like my own.

1991

Translated by John Marston and Kheang Un

༄༅

Mey Son Sotheary
"My Sister"

Mey Son Sotheary, born in 1977, lives in Phnom Penh, where she works at Channel 3, TV Broadcasting of Phnom Penh City. In 1993, she started to contribute her short fiction to the daily newspaper Reasmey Kampuchea, *which has the largest number of subscribers in Cambodia. Her interest in women's social problems is reflected in "My Sister." The main protagonist, San, is a young man with two sisters who has moved from a rural area into the city life of Phnom Penh.*

The sometimes unfortunate fate of rural migrants seeking a better life in the city is a common theme for many Southeast Asian writers. The tension between urban and rural cultures is also seen in Alfred A. Yuson's "The Music Child" (the Philippines) and Shahnon Ahmad's "Delirium" (Malaysia). Stories about prostitutes are common among modern Southeast Asian writers, unless that subject is censored.

It was already 7 P.M. We'd been strolling happily along the boulevards of Phnom Penh, my younger sister Moum and I, oblivious to time. Nightlife in the big city especially intrigued me. Modern cars were parked around big restaurants frequented by fashionably dressed customers. We were overwhelmed by it all.

I must confess that I'm from the countryside. My village is in Prey

---

"My Sister," by Mey Son Sotheary, published in the newspaper *Reasmey Kampuchea*, 754–57 (12–18 November 1995). Permission to publish granted by the translators, Tomoko Okada, Vuth Reth, and Teri Shaffer Yamada, with the author's consent. Rendition by Teri Shaffer Yamada.

Veng province. When my parents were alive, my dad worked for the provincial office of cultural affairs and my mother was a respected seamstress. Due to their efforts, we three children had an easy life. When my elder sister finished high school, a relative took her to continue her studies in Phnom Penh.

In Prey Veng, my younger sister Moum and I had just finished junior high school when our parents died. We would have to quit school without their financial support. Fortunately, Elder Sister insisted on our education and gave us money for school whenever she came to visit. Personally, I was delighted with the chance to continue my studies.

Elder Sister often told us about her Phnom Penh job working for a foreign investment firm. With such a good job she could finance our high-school education, so I felt motivated and never neglected my schoolwork. My dream was to graduate from high school, then to continue my education at any university in Phnom Penh. Finally, I passed the entrance exam for the Literature Faculty at the Royal University of Phnom Penh and Moum passed the exam for the Faculty of Law, thus fulfilling her own dream.

We moved to our aunt and uncle's home in Phnom Penh to prepare for the new school year at the university. Elder Sister explained why she couldn't live there. She was very busy with company business, working long hours on site, so she stayed in company housing. After all, she explained, our relative's house wasn't near her company. If she stayed with us, she would waste a lot of time commuting.

Elder Sister only came to visit us on the weekends. I remember how the three of us were so happy then. She'd become a big city girl, the way she talked and acted. What I completely adored about her was the financial support. She made our lives so easy.

It was still exciting to stroll along the streets of Phnom Penh at night. One evening, Moum and I were out fairly late when I remembered I'd better take her back home. I worried about our aunt, who probably would be waiting up for us. I called to my younger sister, and we walked toward my motorcycle parked nearby. It was a gift from Elder Sister so we would have some transportation to school. Just as I approached it, I noticed a group of bargirls across the street. Wearing heavy makeup, those ladies of the night were arriving and departing on motorbike-taxis in front of a bar, gaily laughing and teasing each other. I turned to look at Moum. She was frowning at those girls.

I said, "Moum. Don't look at them!"

She glanced away. Later, on the motorcycle, she asked: "San! Why are there so many girls like that in Phnom Penh?"

I knew that Moum wanted to talk about those prostitutes.

"It's the city. You'd better ignore it. It's like that in the city . . ."

Moum was silent. When we arrived home, I went to bed exhausted yet obsessed with the image of those bargirls. It's right, what Moum said, that kind of girl creates a bad impression, one that slowly destroys Cambodian values and tradition. I don't understand them, I thought. What I do know is that kind of business is a big mistake for Cambodian girls. Even if they say it's for survival, that kind of work is still completely wrong. They could clean floors, or wash noodle dishes, or sell vegetables. They could survive that way too. But that's my idea; those girls don't think like me. Anyway, I'd better forget it and get some sleep. I need my energy to study so I won't disappoint Elder Sister, who is working so hard to support me.

A whole year passed before I found out about it.

By then I'd grown used to city life. I'd been studying foreign languages at a private school where I did well. This encouraged me to study even harder in anticipation that after graduation I could work for a foreign company. That would enable me to help Elder Sister financially. She still provided everything, so I never worried about the money required for my education, and my academic performance continued to improve.

Soon my fluency in several foreign languages enabled me to get a job in radio broadcasting. I translated foreign news and received quite a good salary for it. I was very happy and satisfied with this job although it meant I wouldn't finish my university studies. This job gave me hope that I would be able to support myself in the future. Now I could use part of my salary to help my older sister Keo pay for our younger sister's education.

It was the last night of the month when I found out. We had just been paid. Some of my friends and I went to a party at a restaurant. We had a grand time there until about 9 P.M., when we decided to go home. I walked along with one of my friends who had become quite drunk.

I chided him, "Hey, come on! All of us are fine except you!"

While my friends were getting their vehicles, I walked him over to mine. My drunken friend murmured, "Hey, San, look at that girl! She's really neat! Too bad she's already in somebody else's car. I'd pay anything for her!"

I was really disgusted with his nonsense, such inconsiderate talk about those ladies of the night. I laughed uncomfortably and looked at the girl he'd admired as she got into a car across the street. I chided him again.

"Such a guy, aren't you! Whenever you get drunk, you say anything. Let me take you home."

My friend kept mumbling, "San! She's so beautiful. Wow!"

I was really bored with him now. Since I had to steady him as he walked ahead, I just glanced surreptitiously at the bargirl. I was stunned when she turned her face toward me. Why did she look like my sister?

I immediately dropped my friend and rushed across the street through a path of oncoming vehicles. When I got there, I noticed she had turned to look at me in astonishment. I was shocked, feeling I'd received a death sentence. It was my sister, definitely my sister. I stood silently under her sad gaze. Then I saw two men pulling her hand so she'd get into their car. They drove off leaving me standing there alone. I couldn't even cry.

I went back home in grief. I felt both betrayed and terribly insulted. My aunt was watching TV in the living room when I arrived. I didn't speak to her but went directly to my room. I passed Moum's room where she was writing something. This distressed me even more and then I noticed she was wearing the necklace Elder Sister had just given her last week. I was pondering whether to tell Moum what I'd seen when she noticed me and stopped writing.

"San! Why so late? Did you have dinner yet?"

I tried to remain calm. The truth would devastate her. I entered my room, slammed the door and took off my shirt, throwing it on the bed. I just wanted to take a shower and to forget everything I'd previously seen. But that horrible scene appeared every time I closed my eyes. Why *my* sister? Why had she chosen such a stupid path? Turning, I noticed the computer she'd purchased for my studies. I knocked it off the desk in a rage. It broke with a loud crash on the floor. I was obsessed with the scene of my sister being pulled into some car. I kicked the computer hard so it rolled across the tile floor.

My uncle, aunt, and sister opened the door to my room. They looked at me with amazement. I sat down on the bed, tears streaming down my face like I was a little child. Moum noticed and approached me.

"San! What's the matter with you? What's wrong, San?" she asked in a choked voice.

I wanted to answer but didn't know what to say. Crying, I shook my head childishly. This was the worst moment of my entire life. I felt so hurt. I didn't understand how my sister could let herself be so degraded like that.

Having spent a sleepless night, the next morning I went to the living room exhausted. Gloomily, I sat down on the sofa, picked up the newspaper, and started to read. Then Moum appeared.

"Aren't you going to work?"

"No," I murmured.

Next I heard Moum's happy voice as the front door opened.

"Keo! Don't you work today?"

I knew my elder sister would come. I suddenly blew up when I heard her quietly say: "Moum, here's some food. Eat, then go to school!"

I got up from the sofa and saw the food from Elder Sister in Moum's hand. I rushed to grab it, then hurled the snacks on the floor, shouting: "Stop bringing that filthy stuff!"

Moum looked at me incredulously. I glanced at Elder Sister's disheartened face as she stood in the doorway. She pushed the door closed, not wanting anyone outside the house to hear.

"Look at you!" I said. "How cheap you are. What a role model for our younger sister!" I was suffering and out of control. Right or wrong had no meaning. I just had to scold her. But suddenly Moum cut me short.

"San! Don't do that to Keo."

I looked at Moum and angrily told her to shut up: "From now you don't take anything from her, understand! If you need something, tell me. Stop using her indecent money. You hear me?"

I saw her hesitate. My elder sister looked down and started to gather the snacks scattered around the floor. Moum sat down to help her. I pulled her hand shouting, "Go to school, now!"

Moum jerked free of my grasp and angrily started to walk out while loudly shouting: "Don't be so unreasonable! What about your rudeness to Keo?"

Frowning, I retorted: "So go ahead. Ask her what kind of work she does."

Moum answered bravely, "Whatever she does, she's still our sister. You've no right to despise her!"

I was so mad. I turned and pointed at Elder Sister, who was still gathering the scattered food.

"Say it; say it now! Tell her what you've been doing. Are you good enough to be our sister?"

Moum furiously yelled at me: "San! Be careful. If you keep this up, I'll tell aunt and uncle when they get home from work. Don't be so unreasonable!"

I was still angry. Then Elder Sister slowly stood up and carefully articulated each word: "All right. I'll tell you if you want me to."

I turned away when I heard her sobbing.

"I am an indecent bargirl. Not only that, I sell my body. I have sex with anyone who pays me well."

Before Keo had finished speaking, Moum was leaning dejectedly against the wall, her eyes wide with astonishment. I knew this would be devastating.

Elder Sister continued speaking: "I know how much this hurts you. But both of you should realize I'm the one who hurts the most. Brother works for a famous company and younger sister studies law with a bright future ahead of her. But I understand. From now on don't regard me as your sister. Even if by chance we meet along the road somewhere, let's pretend not to know each other. Okay? I'll just discard these snacks. From now on, I won't dare buy anything for you since I've lost the right to be your sister."

I was looking at the plastic bag full of snacks my elder sister had just thrown into the trash. She turned and left. I forced back my tears since I didn't want to cry while Moum was sobbing.

Night arrived. I was sitting at a bar angrily drinking beer when a prostitute approached me. I told her to sit down then gave her ten dollars. Seeing her delighted smile, I decided to ask some questions.

"Can I ask you something?"

She laughed and answered: "I'm sitting here for you to ask, darling. For ten dollars you can ask a lot."

I was clueless about her values. Feeling awful, I asked her: "Why do you do this kind of work?"

She laughed cynically while waving the ten-dollar bill. I understood so I asked the next question.

"For money, huh? Is this the only way you can get money? With so many decent jobs available, why not find one?"

She blushed and then forced a smile.

"I'm not educated; I have no skills. What can I do? Even if I found another job, the most I could make is thirty or forty dollars a month."

I felt irritated and thought of Keo. I asked her again: "Why do you need so much money? It's true you'll earn just a small salary with an unskilled job, but it's enough for one person to survive."

Now she seemed angry and answered rudely: "Right. I can survive, just me by myself. What about you? Do you survive just for yourself and that's it? I have brothers and sisters, and they have to go to school. How can I pay for their education? You just want them to be illiterate and then get a job like me? Young man, why don't you just go back home and ask all your sisters if there is a woman happy being a bar-girl."

I was appalled at her demeanor as she switching from calling me "darling" to "young man." Now I felt embarrassed.

That night my uncle and aunt were waiting up for me when I arrived home. My uncle spoke as soon as I entered the house.

"It's so late. Where have you been?"

I answered with the usual response: "My friends invited me to a party."

He spoke louder. "You're an adult now, uh? You work, get a salary, and spend it on dancing and drinking almost every night. I'm becoming increasingly annoyed with you."

I remained silent. Actually, I couldn't comprehend the reason for uncle's anger. Then my aunt spoke.

"I heard that you scolded Elder Sister Keo. Is that right?"

When she reminded me about Keo, I glanced down at the floor and said nothing. Then my aunt, approaching me with fiery eyes, said: "Are you an animal or a human being? You have a job and a good salary. You dare to bum around and then despise your sister, uh?"

I answered her without admitting anything: "Aunt, do you know what Keo does in public?"

She replied, eyes filled with tears: "I know! But just think. Don't you realize whom she prostitutes herself for? Is she some goddess with magical powers to conjure money for you to spend frivolously? Could you and Moum have financed your university education alone? Could you have acquired the money to procure the necessary training needed for your great broadcasting job without her doing this? I don't think so."

I finally realized what Keo had done for Moum and me. The depth of her sacrifice shocked me, but I was still stubbornly insistent.

"You already knew about this? Our family used to have a good reputation. Everyone loved us, got along with us. Why didn't you stop her? Don't you know Moum and I don't want her doing this for us? Don't you realize how much we suffer from this shame?"

She continued loudly: "You suffer! Don't I suffer? Doesn't Keo suffer? I couldn't get the money you needed for school. But your sister . . . she wanted you to study so you could have a great future. Do I have the right to stop her? You are her brother and sister. She does this for you, and then you say she's wrong. Please ask the bargirls around town if they have any problems. Do you think they are carefree? Did you ever hear Keo grumbling about her problems when she gave you money to spend heedlessly?"

Irritated, I walked to my room and slammed the door. I noticed the broken computer lying in the corner. I slowly sat down next to it, touching it gently, then felt some incipient emotion. In sorrow I remembered the day she had purchased this computer for me. She had brought it over with a beautiful smile and asked if it made me happy. I didn't realize what she'd had to do to buy it. Why did I get so angry yesterday and break it?

Actually, my aunt is right. Whatever Keo did was for us. She didn't do anything wrong. I was the brute who dared to scold her.

I remembered the bag of snacks she had brought for us yesterday as she had done for many years. I pondered why, only yesterday, I demanded she throw them in the trash, and then I decided to find her.

I know self-forgiveness will be difficult. I just feel compelled to find her, to let her know she's a great person regardless of that profession. She is still noble, I still respect her. One day I hope to find Keo, to beg forgiveness for my cruelty. If I don't succeed, I may blame myself forever.

1995

Translation by Tomoko Okada, Vuth Reth, and Teri Shaffer Yamada

Indonesia

Indonesia is a culturally and linguistically complex archipelago of around seventeen thousand islands. Because of its lucrative spice trade, Indonesia attracted Hindu, Buddhist, and Muslim traders, who subsequently influenced the traditional literature of the islands. Europeans also became interested in the spice trade beginning in the late fifteenth century. In 1602, Dutch traders formed the United East India Company (VOC), which gradually colonized the area. Under Dutch rule, a system that suppressed free speech was legislated through the "Haatzai artikelen" (Hate articles). These articles, used to justify political surveillance, also enabled the colonial regime to monitor and control intellectual life. Post-independence governments have maintained this pattern of censorship, seriously affecting some modern writers.

In the twentieth century the modern Indonesian short story developed along with the proliferation of printing presses and public education. Support for modern literature came with the establishment of the Bureau for Popular Literature in 1908, and by the 1920s, the "New Writers"—mostly modern, educated writers in Minangkabau (west-central Sumatra)—had created a new style of socially critical literature. Advocates of a national language—*bahasa Indonesia*—emerged in 1928 as writers working for independence.

Literary activity exploring identity and changing value systems developed alongside growing nationalism until 1942. Japan stifled this development when it terminated Dutch colonial rule in Indonesia during World War II. Writing literature during this grim period was difficult, as the romanticism and idealism of the previous era faded into cynical realism and anarchism. After Japan's surrender, the nationalists Sukarno and Mohammad Hatta proclaimed Indonesian independence on 17 August 1945 but would fight Dutch troops for independence until 1949.

The late 1940s and 1950s saw intense nationalism in Indonesia. The concise and trenchant style of the writers some critics refer to as the

Generation of 1945 replaced the more ornate style of the prewar writers, some writers reacting to acute changes in society and the grueling conflict of war with a style described as "photographic realism." Other literary concerns included the uniqueness of native culture in contrast to the culture of colonial domination and the evaluation of indigenous culture in an attempt to suggest areas of renovation. After 1945, the short story exploded as a popular literary form, partly in response to the demand of the numerous magazines and journals that had begun to flourish. Writers pressured the government to establish the National Language and Literature Agency (Dewan Bahasa dan Pustaka) in 1957 to support literary development.

Political disagreements grew between 1945 and 1965 as contradictions between the needs of state power and the search for national identity increased. In 1959 Sukarno and other national leaders attempted to resolve this conflict through the establishment of "Guided Democracy," later referred to as the "Old Order." Guided Democracy attempted to end volatility by restoring Indonesia's original 1945 constitution and by insisting on an ideological orthodoxy (Pancasila) defined by Sukarno. It undermined investigative journalism and restricted literary freedom of expression. In opposition to this policy, members of the Institute of People's Culture, with their socialist slogan of "art for the people," became known during this period as the LEKRA (Lembaga Kebudajaan Rakjat) writers. Their fiction would be banned after 1965.

In the aftermath of an alleged communist coup attempt, the so-called Gestapu affair of 30 September–1 October 1965, army units and civilian vigilante gangs killed at least several hundred thousand suspected communists through March 1966. President Sukarno was compelled to sign the Instruction of 11 March, marking a violent transition to a military-dominated oligarchy—the "New Order" state, which was headed by Suharto, who was ultimately appointed acting president of Indonesia.

The deliberate control and manipulation of violence were consistent features of New Order Indonesia. Publications deemed disruptive to the social order were confiscated; even the possession of banned books was criminalized. Some critics refer to writers from this era as the Generation of 1966, the first year of publication for the important literary magazine *Horizon*. The literary themes of writers under the New Order are described as being subtler and more diverse than those of earlier writers, often relayed in experimental styles. By the 1970s more women writers had emerged on the literary landscape, assisted by the popularization of women's magazines and issues. More newspapers were devoting space to literature. Themes of life in an absurd world, corruption, political crises, inner conflict, and alienation are seen in serious literature of the 1970s.

During the 1980s and 1990s, short stories often dealt with social criticism or social protest. Class issues and the convergence of tradition and modernity became more apparent themes in the 1990s. Realism is a literary movement that still dominates both popular and serious literature, although some writers experiment with different literary styles.

Suharto was forced to step down in 1998 after Indonesia suffered a major economic setback in 1997, ending his thirty-two-year rule. On 7 June 1999 Indonesia held its first free parliamentary election since 1955. Some opening for the creative right of literary expression has been experienced by writers now able to publish stories that address sexuality and political activism, two censored subjects in previous decades. Most of the short stories included in this section were published during the New Order period.

Pramoedya Ananta Toer

"The Silent Center of Life's Day"

Pramoedya Ananta Toer, one of Indonesia's most distinguished writers, was born in 1926 in the small town of Blora, surrounded by rice fields and teak forests on the northern coast of East Java. He began publishing short-story collections and novels in the 1950s. His earliest collection, Pertjikan Revolusi *(Flashes of the Revolution), was written during his imprisonment by the Dutch and explores that experience linked to the universality of human suffering. Known as one of the strongest LEKRA writers, he spent fourteen years in confinement because of socialist-leftist political leanings. His works were banned in Indonesia after 1965. In 2000 part of his prison notes,* The Mute's Soliloquy: A Memoir, *was published in the United States.*

"The Silent Center of Life's Day" is a lyrical, self-reflective exploration of life's lingering disappointments and adumbrated possibilities. Replete with autobiographical content, this story encourages us to imagine that Toer is the writer-protagonist, emanating an existential sensibility about the absurdity of life and the frailty of love. Other Southeast Asian writers—such as Cristina Pantoja Hidalgo in "The Painting" (the Philippines), Shahnon Ahmad in "Delirium" (Malaysia), and Duong Thu Huong in "The Story of an Actress" (Vietnam)—also reflect a culturally nuanced existentialism in their fiction.

He always tries to be friendly. So do I. Always. But here we are, thought the writer.

He was silent, staring at the book by Gorki in front of him.

"You should read it," said his friend. "*Artamanov's Family.* The title's worn off, illegible. It's one of my favorites."

This, thought the writer, *is his way of showing his friendship.*

"The Silent Center of Life's Day" (Sunjisenjap Disiang Hidup), by Pramoedya Ananta Toer, first published in the magazine *Indonesia* (June 1956). Published in *A Heap of Ashes* (New Zealand: University of Queensland Press, 1975). Permission to reprint granted by the translator, Harry Aveling.

"Read the book. You and Artamanov are both arrogant men. Arrogance plays an important role in the book."

"Arrogance!" The word describes me, and our relationship. If one's arrogance is powerful enough, dominates one's environment, and is supported by great creative powers, then perhaps one could give birth to something useful, even monumental. But our efforts to be friendly are useless when he and I are as arrogant as each other, as fiercely and as intently arrogant.

"Read it!" the friend said.

The writer got up and put the book under his arm. He sipped at what was left of his tea, took a few steps, nodded at his friend and said, "I'll try to."

His host stood. Clapped him on the shoulder. And said, "I don't guarantee it will do anything for your restlessness. But at least it will be a good comparison."

"Thank you."

"Where are you living now?"

"Don't ask. The thought of it revolts me."

"I know. You did try to . . ."

"Don't talk about that. We understand each other."

"All right. When are you coming again?"

"I'll come and see you, bring your book back, before death gets me."

"Death? People like you don't commit suicide."

He did not reply but quickly turned and left. The traffic passed by him in rhythmless waves. He would have liked to waltz. He wanted to drink port. He wanted to kiss his children. He wanted to go into a shop and buy them toys and clothes, to buy something for their mother, whose arrogance equaled his own. He felt in his pockets. They were empty. He thought of the honorarium he had received yesterday, now gone into the hands of other people whom he didn't even know. Perhaps there'll be another tomorrow, he prayed.

He wiped his muddy shoes on the edge of the asphalt. There was a tram coming in the distance. He moved aside. When a bus—the small sort, carrying eight passengers—stopped in front of him, he got in. It was empty. He threw his body into a corner, turned up the collar of his jacket to keep out the cold night wind. It was a dark night covered in a thick mist.

If I had a thousand rupiah, he thought . . . He would go to the country, leave the city that had offered him so many stories of failure.

He wanted to live with peasants and write a novel about them. He thought about their life a little. It was the wet season now. They couldn't farm or collect wood. Their children would be in the forests, gathering the leaves long-fallen on the loose earth and carrying them to the teak villages to be sold on the sides of the roads—a pittance until the rice season began.

But where would he get a thousand *rupiah* from! If he finished a book there was no guarantee that anyone would publish it. And if they did he would only get two thousand. For a whole year's work. And the tax was three hundred. There was a tax on writing, yet there was no investment tax. Who would support his children? The government? A government which only cared about taxing? The bus stopped at Senin to pick up more passengers, three faded women who had been waiting a long time.

A horse-like laugh drew his attention towards the red lamps scattered along the road's edges. Jakarta was often beautiful at night. Red lights on shop awnings too, pointing straight at the sky. His mind flew with the lights to Chinatown in the docksides of Amsterdam, to houses with red lights, brothels, to black water and motor boats, to the shining roads covered with a thin layer of water becoming ice, to the Chinese restaurant in a cellar, and how homesick he had been for Jakarta, this Jakarta, which sent him sprawling with new failure.

He said I was arrogant. Maybe I am.

And he remembered again how his own father hated him. Even before they knew him properly his friends were calling him arrogant.

What's wrong? I have to grow my own way! I have a right to do as I want! Even when I was a child nobody put out a hand to help me. And when I made my own life in my own way, they tried to stop me.

Horse-like laughter.

"Bugger!" said the driver.

The bus plunged on.

He had started riding buses only the last few days. He found the square boxes romantic. People from various birthplaces, various occupations, various interests, from various departure points going to various destinations. Sometimes they talked together like intimates, sometimes one person grew aggressive and everyone else left him and got out to walk.

He smiled. Dramatic material for a novel, he thought. Hell. There was so much to write about in Jakarta but most writers were busy with themselves, their tiny thoughts and feelings. *So am I.*

He thought of the fire in Poncol. Thousands of shanties destroyed, tens of thousands without a place to hide.

But I didn't want to go and see them. Damn. A damn writer. This was arrogance. No one ever comes to help me, so I don't care about anyone else either. I should have gone to see how they lived, the tumult as they fought for their land, piece by piece. Their anguished cries as their faith collapsed: the fight between God and the fire. And between the individual and the city council.

"We're here."

He was conscious again, got out of the bus and paid a *rupiah,* then leapt on to a trishaw and called softly but firmly: "In there." The trishaw, its driver and himself vanished into a lane shaped like a curving black cave. A soft wind blew. He coughed and swallowed phlegm. A few noodle vendors were busy beating their bells. Yellow chicken legs and claws stuck up out of a porcelain Japanese bowl. He wanted to try the chicken. "No!" he whispered and struck his own thigh. He remembered last week's failure.

There can be no justification for living like this all the time! he told himself. He often told himself that, but he insisted on his total freedom. And what secular results came from such freedom? These: crawling from one cliff to another; falling into the ravine again, still followed by spies who dragged offers of work before his eyes.

The chance to be a director, the front-man for a Chinese firm, so that it looked Indonesian. He sighed. Three thousand a month, a car and a house. No work and no responsibilities. He shook his head. No. He rejected the offers.

Then came the final offer and he had decided to accept it, so as to be near the work he enjoyed, advertising. First he would have to have a medical examination.

He failed the blood, stomach and kidney examination. Was it his TB? No. "Your blood pressure is too high, sir. Your stomach and kidneys have been destroyed by malaria. You are not very healthy."

"Is this your final verdict, doctor?"

"Let's have another look."

And he was refused the work he had decided to accept. His life expectancy was too short, and the firm would lose on pension funds; insurance would be too expensive; and the cost of training him would be wasted.

He placed the thick book by Gorki carefully on his lap. The road was empty. After ordering the trishaw driver to stop, he leapt out, paid him and hurried into the dark alley. When he stopped beneath an old tree he heard the sound of flooding water. When he walked it disappeared. He walked holding on to the fences. The clay path beneath his feet was too slippery for his shoes. He wasn't strong enough, so he couldn't earn enough, he thought to himself. This was modern business. He smiled, amused.

His feet carried him to a lane which belonged to a *haji,* a narrow descending lane, and before he reached the bottom he fell with a thud. He swore, swore at himself. He couldn't blame anyone else for this. No one.

He crawled and stood up, felt his trousers which were thick with mud, then groped for the road again—and arrived at his hut. He turned up the weak oil lamp. From within the main house he heard a voice cough "Is that you?" Then: "Have you eaten?" This was followed by the creak of a wooden bed.

It was night on the edge of the city and more silent than usual. The song of the frogs in the mud-puddles near the house made the silence more intense—and intensified his own silence, his own life. He prayed, as numerous times before: "May my children not have to go through what I have been through."

The prisons, the battles, loves at the front and at various bases, periods of hunger, and the tortures, the chance to study torn away by unsettled conditions . . . The hopes he had had in the distant past had all narrowed to this solitary one.

My children will never have to eat rice porridge with diced potato leaves and unripe tomatoes. They will never need to steal as I have done. They will never have to bring themselves to cheat to live a human life. They will never need to cry until they could cry no more as I have done, nor go out and kill for their wages. They will grow as citizens of an independent nation. They will learn the lessons each acre of their own land owes them.

Tiredly he took his notebook from the book rack on the wall in front of him. He opened it and read a few pieces written in a special shorthand: "How sweet the world is, when one's heart is full of hope. Hope, however, occasionally dies, as other creatures do. For the rest of my life I will live without it. I only want to work, work, work. The others would laugh if I told them that work was my main refuge in which I forget the past and the corpse of hope. The past, the sweet past, is gone. The others would abuse me mercilessly and say: 'coward!', 'can't face it!' "

He closed his notebook slowly, thinking. All he could think of was a character in a book of Saint-Exupéry's, who was very ugly and who lost himself in his work and associated studies, finally becoming a successful pilot.

I don't want to be like him! the writer's heart screamed. *The others would only mock me, cover their bitterness with politeness, wait with pleasure for the ammunition-store to explode. They've always been against me.*

His grandmother had even said, "Your father's a scoundrel." She made him feel like the son of a scoundrel. Once she wanted to take him out, and he agreed, but she had a heart attack first, after a fight with his uncle. At this dark point in his life's day, even nonsense came crowding in upon him. Everyone wanted to dominate him, or at least part of him, even his toes!

But they can't dominate me! Not even my toes! I will keep dedicating myself to my work, to the future of my children. Let that damn poet, Chairil, "refuse to share himself," I've divided myself three times!

Thunder and a flash of lightening stamped on the ground. The frogs in the mud-puddles at the side of the house stopped croaking. He was startled. He stood, took his typewriter from on top of the cupboard and began to type, to pour out his feelings. Word by word, sentence by sentence. In the middle of the fifth sentence, a baby in a compartment at the side of the house began to cry. His fingers stopped dancing.

You bastard. He was angry with himself. *You're not the only one in the world.* "Poor baby. Go to sleep."

He threw his shoes into a corner, took off his muddy trousers and threw himself on to his bed. All he could now hear was his own breathing, gradually swallowed up in the rustle of the rain on the roof. The rain leaked slowly on the bed. He thought how nice it was to sleep on a new mattress, how peaceful life would be with spirit, spirit filled with hope, like Dini—Dini who had bought him the bed a week ago—Dini who had tried to appreciate him, who believed she could understand a writer's life and, therefore, was ready to be his wife.

The young, he shouted to himself, *still have hopes. When the hopes come to nothing, she'll realize, and remember my warnings. No woman ought to marry a writer, especially an Indonesian writer. She wouldn't be of any benefit to him. To actually do something for a writer is instant death.*

He took the oil lamp down and hung it on a nail above his head. Then he took *Artamanov's Family* and read it until his eyes stung. Then he turned the lamp down until it died. He sighed: *Gorki was a god. He could shake an entire house with one hand, and replace the rotted fragments which fell off with new pieces. Even so, it was still an old house, just as each man is always the same man, although each generation brings humanity new appetites, new ideals and new madnesses.*

He was asleep.

His sleep was disturbed several times. The roof tore and scattered rain and dust on the bed. He remembered Bisma, the friend he had just visited. In the wet season, Bisma used a raincoat as a blanket. How pleased he was to have enough for a raincoat.

He remembered his children and their mother. Slowly he prayed that they might sleep peacefully without rain and dust.

He rolled up the sodden mattress Dini had given him and formed a makeshift bed from two chairs, reading again after he put the light back on. He wanted to work, he wanted to finish an essay, a collection of foreign short stories, a discussion of foreign poetry, an outline of literary theory, a literary dictionary—he wanted to do them and finish them all at the same time. But the baby! And his eyes were sore now. He threw Gorki onto the bedroll. He looked up and closed his eyes. Perhaps Bisma was happy because he never wanted to do much, except participate in the organization in which he was one of the important men. He had no children! He paid no taxes! Not even when he went abroad. He had friends in Prague, Moscow and Peking, because he knew one tune: "The Red Flower," "Kembang Beureum," a sentimental West Javanese folk song.

He smiled. Imagine conquering hearts across the seas and continents with just one song!

And "The Red Flower" flowed from his lips. He had known the melody for twelve years and never learnt the words. *Kembang beureum, nu bareureum* . . . "The red flower blooms . . ." Nice, beautiful, like the mountain and valley women over whom the song daily flowed, with their shy and sudden laughter: mocking history. As Bisma had once said, walking with him, waiting for the bus at Jatinegara, "I know how hard things are. But you must think them through and provide for your children. Much will be required of them. They must be strong!" Bisma's voice was pleasant, but it mocked him as well.

The writer always gave everything he had, leaving nothing for the next day, for posterity. He did all he could and all he was able to do. He wondered what would remain in ten years. A heap of useless flesh and bone, his childhood songs trampled on by the war.

From time to time it was right to think about himself. The thought was consoling.

He wanted to do something that quiet evening. He wanted to do something new. But he couldn't think of anything. He opened the cupboard—another present from Dini, almost a month ago, with very fine glass which was already beginning to crack—and took out a dagger wrapped in white cloth: his only heirloom from his parents. The dagger always troubled him. He was supposed to bathe it during the Javanese month of Sura and he never knew when it was, or who—in Jakarta, a city devoid of regional traditions—could do it. A pinch of superstition, and materialistic living, had divided his soul into two parts, each drawn in different directions, sometimes with absolutely no connection with each other.

And as night took increasing possession of him, he fell asleep on the chairs. He was tired, physically and spiritually tired. He had wanted many things in his life, but his life had been like a shady coconut tree bearing fruit every year, before being hit by pestilence. He was his own battlefield.

When he woke, his breathing was constricted and his chest tight. The sun's rays filtered through the cheap wooden slats of the door of the room. The children in the nearby compartments were beginning to scream, and there was a hot cup of tea on the table beside him. He was not allowed coffee, on doctors' orders. He stopped thinking of his chest and turned to the day's program: the routine journey to magazine editors to see if they had any payment for any of his short pieces they had used. Each day since becoming a writer, morning had forced him to consider which of the routine circuits he would follow.

The cough grew deeper. He wiped the sleep from his eyes, and staggered to the common bathroom. The water trough was full of thick yellow-mud water! He had given up bathing in the mornings and contented himself by wiping his eyes. The men and women of the neighboring compartments were ready to go to work, later today than usual because the *haji*'s "mountain," his private road, was slippery. No one minded if office work were left for a few hours more.

For several days he went nowhere and did nothing. His inner torment left him crushed. The typewriter was dumb.

"A sentimental writer!" someone had once written of him. "An emotional writer!" someone else claimed.

The final word, however, was his. *How and where I go are my own problems, to be solved my own way.* His soul was like a chemical-stained negative in a camera, over-sensitive to everything outside of himself, and even more so to things eternal.

His room was nothing more than a rotunda, fenced in with cheap palings. And on the wall hung a door, divided into an upper and lower half. You could close the bottom half and use the top as a window. Between the door and the proper window stretched a wall, partly reworked to provide a place for his books, a meter high and a meter wide. He had had the same done on the other side of the window too, surrounding it with two tightly packed shelves of books.

The room was too small. The bed Dini had given him used up more than half of it, then there was the cupboard and the table at which he typed, and the chair from which he worked each day. Sometimes he thought that the room was as crowded as his heart and that not one item was dispensable, not one emotion. A full heart was necessary before he could write.

This was an obsession. He needed a way out. If he didn't have it, he would collapse. None of the forces known to man were of any use if there was no way to channel them. The thought drove him hurriedly to take his typewriter from its box and begin typing. A few lines, then he stalled. He couldn't work.

Perhaps I'm finished.

Perhaps it's time to become a civil servant, or a laborer, keep regular hours, keep my dreams alive. To believe that my wage or salary, no matter how large, is always too small. To believe that my dreams are always larger, more powerful, more valid than productivity and money, or than my superiors, the leaders of the government, or even their friends whom they respect for working out the same complicated things they themselves have just realized.

The sun was beginning to shine on the side of the house, from behind the kitchen. He left his typewriter and stood bent over the bottom door, his eyes gazing at the sky, the oceanic primal source of the world's greatness. The sky was a shining, sparkling blue. Hawks, children's kites, doves, crisscrossed each other like tiny speckles. He heard various noises and voices, vague elements at the base of the eternal silence. For a moment a siren roared its pain. It was either from the prison or the printers: he had never known which. Looking down, his gaze spread over a broad rice field, fenced in by prison buildings and the printers, by huts with grass roofs, by the spreading cassava grass which was fed each day with human excreta brought in carts. Men he had never met walked on the banks of the rice field. Because of the size of the field, they were of no consequence. He was aware of this, of how inconsequential man was in nature's bounty. But the walking creatures had, as he had, their own arrogances, their own desires, and their own conviction that they were better than other men, yes, them, pockmarks on the anvil of the field, nothing compared to the size of the cassava spreading dark-green because of human excreta brought in carts. He laughed, laughed at them, and at himself.

And he decided that a writer should not be bitter when he was criticized, for he always criticized himself more than others did. He was immune to bourgeois tilts, without foundation or content, meaningless attacks arising out of the futility of life's emptiness.

Once again he looked at the field—saw it surrounded by the city. He remembered what men had said of it: "Useless thing!" He remembered that. A hundred and fifty thousand people sold it to one firm. The wolves in the Jakarta undergrowth made sure that they didn't get much of what was theirs. Later, when the main road tore its edge off, the field would vanish, turn into a white building, a factory, which the newspapers would proudly declare "the largest in Southeast Asia." The breadth, greatness and glory of nature, of which this was part, would then be pillaged from his gaze. And again he would live like the others: city men, playing hide-and-seek in the spaces between the buildings. And because of the intensity of economic and political problems, he would be like all other city people, besieged, driven back into their homes, happy to receive a packet of foreign cigarettes as a present, proud to know a managing director, or a regent, or a district chief, or a politician. He smiled broadly, then smiled at himself.

The field reminded him of the diary he had kept for ten years, and lost during the Revolution. He remembered the part of his life in the faded past which had given him the greatest pleasure. During the Japanese Occupation he had a broad field of five, possibly ten, hectares, with fishponds in it, which he traveled over in a jeep, scattering bundles of plants in the corners to plant along with the fish. He wanted to farm one day, a piece of land which would free him from all complications. He shook his head. Even a four-paddock field in the middle of a city yielded two hundred *rupiah* every week for each paddock of spinach. The same as he got for a short story built of the bitterness of his own life. The owner only had to weed it a few hours a week after the vegetable sellers had picked the spinach. And he? A short story often took up a month, sometimes two, sometimes he wrote nothing in six months. The spinach grew all year as long as water came to it in carts. Eight hundred *rupiah* a month, regularly: part-time work.

He was jealous. And revolted by his jealousy.

As he sat before his typewriter to compose his thoughts, the bottom half of the door moved. And when he stopped thinking, he saw Dini standing beside him.

"You've come," he said.

She laughed. "Didn't you think I'd come this early?"

"Sit down."

She sat on the chair beside him. He looked at her. Her skin was so fine. He remembered another woman, the mother of his children, and was sad, and lonely. He had hoped for a happy, peaceful home with her, but his love for his work had created tensions. Without thinking, he said: "Dini, could you possibly be happy with me? Your father's rich, he gives you eight hundred just for pocket money each month."

"I don't need anything from you, dear."

"How odd. What do you want then?"

"I like you. You're so miserable! I've been miserable."

"Is that all?"

"No! That isn't all."

How was it possible? How? Again he looked at her. She was a stranger, she didn't really know him. She never read literature. She didn't even know his name. Those who said she was attracted to him because of his writings were mistaken. She knew nothing about them. She was a cluster of atoms bound together by God, brought to fruition in humanity, a classic Eve created too late, unsuited to the age of anxiety.

"Are you worried?"

"Of course I am. I haven't got any money."

"Money's easy."

He remembered what she told him as she sat sewing. A seamstress got much more than a writer. And it was tax-free.

She looked at the bed she had bought, looked at him and asked, "Did you dream about me last night?"

"No."

"A pity. I dreamt about you. I'm not disturbing you, am I? You look tired."

"Of course not." The words were honest. Dini's arrival had made him forget his confusion, the conflict of emotions stabbing into his heart. He could not tell her this, only show her, by embracing her and giving her a brief kiss. "What have you brought, Dini?"

She looked at her bag. "Some porridge. You look so pale. And two large Balinese limes. You haven't forgotten what I told you, have you? You have to eat a salad every day. It's good for your blood pressure."

She's afraid I'll have a stroke, he thought. *She is afraid that I'll die. I gave up worrying about dying a long time ago.*

"Don't forget," he said, "I don't know what love is."

"That's all right. I don't know either."

He felt happier when she was around. This was how he had wanted to feel with the mother of his children. But all that had happened was that things became worse, more embittered, and he had become less confident of his own abilities.

This woman wanted little more than to serve him. He saw her smile distantly. He didn't know why, perhaps she was thinking of something splendid in the future. The mother of his children, at first, threw out suggestions of how little she would need. Even offered, quite genuinely, to live under a bridge with him, with no fuss or quarrel. Was that a pose? Who knows what the future brings. In taking a second wife, he would be surrendering the answer to time.

"I don't want you to spoil me," Dini suddenly said.

No woman, he thought to himself, *ought to be spoiled. The husband might have good intentions at first, but after a few months, or after a few years, he is a carthorse, only good for dragging his money home.*

How did he know?

From experience. From watching my mother. She sacrificed everything to be a beast of burden and spoil father. And in the end he was the source of all the trouble at home. He spoiled my stepmother and the same thing happened: he was a workhorse.

Life's bitterness played before his eyes. Unaware, he bowed his head.

"You'll suffer," he said, drawing her out. He studied her soft face, its acceptance of whatever might happen to her: pain and bitterness, joy and laughter. Finally she said, "I have to choose someone, sometime. I have to decide my fate in my own way. Some women think about it for a long time, very carefully. They often get the reverse of what they hope for: a scoundrel, a thief or a lecher."

And when they do, he continued to himself, *whether they are legally married or not, they explode. Their voices become shrill, harsh.*

Like a firecracker, leaving only charred paper, smoke disappearing into the sky, memories. He coughed.

"You've still got a cold," she said.

"It's the wind off the wet field."

She looked out at the spinach field.

"Would you like to live near a field, with no plumbing, no electricity, no water and bad roads?" he said.

"Don't try to spoil me. I'm more used to poverty than you are."

"Because of him? The one you used to dream about?"

She was silent. It was obvious she hated to think of her distant past. Almost whispering to herself she continued, as if grateful for her freedom, "I was confined as a divorced woman for two years."

"Two years!"

"Two years," she repeated slowly. "I never left the house. The first time I did I met you. I don't know why I liked you or came to love you. You were so thin, so pale and unhealthy looking. I thought to myself, something extraordinary might have happened to you." Her eyes glazed. "The same as happened to me."

"Something to drink, Dini?"

"No thank you."

"Let me get you something."

"No."

"Shall we walk?"

"No, thanks. I have to help cook. There's to be a wedding at . . . Oh, you wouldn't want to know, would you? The ceremony's today. This afternoon at half-past four. I'd like it if you wanted to come."

"I wouldn't know anyone!"

"You have to learn to mix."

"I can't!"

"You don't have to suffer alone if you have friends," she said. Then, pouring out what she had so long held back: "We're lonely when we suffer, alone in a world growing smaller. We want sympathy in our suffering. So we have to mix, to divide up the suffering and to receive sympathy in return."

"Where did you learn to talk like that?" he asked in wonder.

She answered in tears. Tears are the only language and words possible for a woman. He was silent.

"I have to go." And she went.

He grabbed his notebook and wrote: "The tranquility she gives me is only superficial. Damn sex. Everyone says how beautiful it is. But eventually it becomes a boring routine, and you start thinking about things you'd never imagined you could think about. Why should I keep on with her?"

His mind continued: *Perhaps I am weak. Perhaps I'm greedy. A writer should stay a bachelor, in total command of his own history. His own ruin. Without involving anyone else, without dragging a family into poverty.* He thought of Zola, Edgar Allan Poe, Jalalludin Rumi, Hafiz, Samsi Tabriz, Gogol, even Gorki, whose book lay on the pillow beside him. Finally he continued in his notebook: "Writing is a compulsion. One does it because one has no other available choice. I do not like being a writer but I accept it. I want to be a farmer, I want to be as Saint-Exupéry was, not a pilot, but a gardener.

"If the writer is really a reflection of his society, my confusion reflects that of my society: the first stage of the explosive admixture of East and West. One ought to aspire to Western achievements but our Eastern heritage cannot yet allow that. The East makes continual concessions, the West increasingly demands more room within it, in its soul, but I do not know the West. All I can finally know is a space opened as a field of conflict, unceasingly, explosion by explosion, myself."

There was a knock at the front door. At first all he could see was a row of large teeth, shining in the light from the back door of the kitchen, then tightly combed hair, then: "Oh, here you are." It was an editor. The man sat down, again flashing his large teeth. "Look, I'm leaving for America. I want to handle your work. Get it published quickly. Have you got something I can take with me? Have you?"

The writer reflected on the pressure from all sides for him to continue in the role of author. But he said, "All right, take this one. I'll wait for whatever advance you want to send."

The manuscript vanished from his narrow room, off into the wide world. He had spent four years on it, devoting patience, care, and all that he knew. It was still not perfect. For a while he would wait for the advance, to help him exist. The editor would leave for America. He would hear nothing of an advance the next year. Perhaps he never would.

The writer sipped his cold tea.

1956
Translated by Harry Aveling

Yudhistira ANM Massardi

"Interview with Ravana"

Yudhistira ANM Massardi, the pen name of Yudhistira Ardi Noegraha, was born in 1954 in Subang. He is a novelist, short-story writer, and playwright. "Interview with Ravana" is a short story from his 1982 collection, Wawancara dengan Rahwana.

The characters in this short story are taken from the two Hindu epics, the Ramayana *and the* Mahabharata, *familiar to Indonesians. Ravana (Rahwana in Indonesian) is the villainous demon king in the* Ramayana *who kidnaps Sita, the wife of Rama. After abducting her to his kingdom in Lanka, Ravana is defeated in battle by Rama with the aid of the magical white monkey Hanuman. Sanjaya, currently recast in the role of a news reporter, is the prince in the* Mahabharata *who tells the story of the great battle at Kurukshetra between the Pandavas and the Kauravas, two feuding branches of the Bharata family. The term "warrior" (*kshatriya) *in the short story refers to the second caste in the* varna, *or four-caste system, which originated in India. Kshatriyas are the warriors and rulers whose dharma, or duty, includes violence and killing in the context of a righteous war.*

At the end of this short story, Semar, who is the grotesquely fat clown servant in Javanese wayang *shadow theater, is introduced as the next reporter, his subject Marilyn Monroe. This clues the reader in to the allegorical nature of the short story, which can be decoded as a political satire of New Order Indonesia. Perhaps Ravana, while symbolizing the archetypal evil present in the cosmic view of the epics, also represents the political corruption and arrogance of Suharto's regime. The need to conceal political critique in a satirical guise to slip work past the government censor is also seen in modern Burmese writing, such as Ne Win Myint's "Thadun."*

"Interview with Ravana" (Wawancara dengan Rahwana), by Yudhistira ANM Massardi, published in *Wawancara dengan Rahwana* (Jakarta: Grafiti Pers, 1982). Permission to publish granted by the translator, Patricia B. Henry, with the author's consent.

In the moment before Hanuman threw him headfirst into the earth, Ravana had time to curse: "It may be that my physical body will disappear after this, but the essence of my being will live on. It will soak into the soul of every human being. For centuries to come . . ."

The earth held him tight, then swallowed him and crushed him to bits. The sky reverberated with thunder. Then it grew dark. From the deep crack in the earth into which the tragic figure of Lanka's ruler had disappeared, millions of black bubbles came forth and swiftly spread over the entire world.

Sanjaya—the world's first war correspondent, who had previously been the eyewitness reporter for the huge battle of the Bharata family on the field of Kurukshetra, and who had then had the opportunity to witness the death of this major scoundrel—immediately went in pursuit. He asked for the assistance of Hanuman so that he could follow Ravana's soul into the earth as it headed for the hereafter.

What follows are excerpts from Sanjaya's interview with that Fountainhead of all Evil.

Sanjaya (S): "Do you agree with the occurrence and the manner of the death that you have just experienced?"

Ravana (R): "Death, or even life, is not a matter to be agreed to or not. Both of them are very simple matters, such that they needn't be considered a problem. As for the 'manner,' is it really all that important? Humans certainly have all kinds of nasty habits. Just like you, they always have a passion to ask about how somebody died and how somebody lived. Those kinds of 'tragic' questions only have importance for the dramatic concerns of the plot that is being acted out.

"The manner of my death that you just witnessed was indeed dramatic. How could a person who had so much power, who had been given the boon of invulnerability, and who was rich beyond imagining, come to an end so miserable and helpless? That contrast is the particular stipulation that has been highlighted. But you may be certain: I am not dead in the usual sense of the word because fundamentally I continue to live. My death is the instrument that will bring about the eternal existence of my essence in the world.

"The disintegration of my physical body serves to strengthen my essence. You'll be able to prove it when as a result of this event the world will fill with black bubbles—you saw them just now? (Sanjaya nodded.) That is the form of my new power. A truly tenacious evil.

"So, should I really protest against my death and the way it happened? I shouldn't, right? (Sanjaya nodded again.) And, as for the way I lived while I was Lanka's ruler, will you sensationalize it for the sake of those dramatic concerns I was talking about? Oh, and by the way, where will this interview be aired? Oh, never mind, never mind. If it's aired or not, it's no concern of mine. But the way I lived, the way in which I managed authority, the way I indulged family members far and near, I suppose it is important to have all that expressed in your report. By all means, write down your views of all that. Expose whatever scandal you think has been going on. Go ahead and smash everything up, if the smashing is sufficiently dramatic. I won't be sorry. Because I'll be there inside the soul of every person who wants to ransack whatever remains of my power and property. It is the job of my essence to encourage all of this."

S: "Can you describe in concrete terms how large that power is?"

R: "As large as the cosmos."

S: "Do you control every human being?"

R: "Every human being has the instinct for evil."

S: "What profit do you get from power like that?"

R: "That's always how it is. Everybody always thinks about profit and loss. What's the big deal with profit and loss? And surely you know, I'm no tradesman. However wicked, I am of the warrior caste. A warrior never thinks like a tradesman. Profit and loss have no meaning to us. What's important to me is consistency in the ideals of struggle. I must nurture fatalism and the destruction of human dignity. It is my task and duty to cultivate ruthless greed on the face of this earth."

S: "Doesn't this duty of yours make you sick at heart?"

R: "Oh, please! What is it with you, anyway? Grief, happiness, and all those things that sound so emotional—like profit and loss, they have no meaning for me. Warriors are not such crybabies. A prince who grasps in his fist a substantial power cannot be overcome with melancholy. He must resolutely carry out his task. The kind of sentimental claptrap you speak of is something only for slaves. For the peasants. Because once a prince lets himself be swept away by feelings, he will become shaken and uncertain. Power will slip away from his hand. After that comes his downfall. Do you understand? A prince is prohibited from losing that which has become his possession. That which he possesses must be held onto until the last drop of blood has been shed. There is no compromise."

S: "And this is true even if the people who are under your authority are suffering?"

R: "The suffering and pain of underlings is the most important part of absolute power. Without suffering, a given power has no meaning. In fact, without the pain of many people, it isn't possible for a given power to maintain itself with firmness."

S: "If there are critics who say that you don't want to hear or pay attention to the complaints of your underlings . . . ?"

R: "Critics? That is the most beautiful part of holding on to a powerful position. Critics are important from a dramatic standpoint. The sobs and complaints of underlings are sweet and gentle background music for the dream-filled night."

S: "Truly you are sadistic."

R: "A person in authority who is any good has to be sadistic. And the power that is in my grasp is sadism. Because of that, lots of victims are needed—as sacrificial offerings—also as a sign of the perpetuity of that power."

S: "Do you have power over all the power-holders in this world?"

R: "Why not? Every power-holder, every authority that exists on earth, is an instrument that reverberates with the song of each and every black bubble that diffused from the place where my physical body was hurled down just now."

S: "What is your commitment to those power-holders?"

R: "Eh? That's a secret . . ."

S: "Very well. As for your future plans, will you be choosing heaven or hell?"

R: "Oh, bullshit. What kind of stupid question is that? Of course I'll choose hell. I suggest that you do the same when your turn comes. There are lots of problems there that you need to look into. I think that a bit of reporting from hell would be quite interesting. Because, as I said before, human beings prefer things to be dramatic, don't they? Heaven is too calm, too peaceful, to the point that there are no more problems. But in hell, every minute there is a huge fuss and excitement, and all manner of troublesome people coming together there. You can interview them. All the pain and regret that they bring forward will surely make excellent reminders for those who still live, right? For that, certainly you will earn a suitable karmic reward. Also, in that place you will be able to meet all the power-holders of the earth who were slaves to their own greediness."

S: "A final question. What is your opinion of Devi Sita, the wife of Sri
   Rama, whom you once kidnapped?"
R: "Oh, excellent! Excellent!"[1]
S: "Thank you."

(Coming up, an interview by Semar of Marilyn Monroe)
Translated by Patricia B. Henry, 1982

Seno Gumira Ajidarma

"The Mysterious Shooter Trilogy"

*Seno Gumira Ajidarma was born in Boston, Massachusetts, in 1958
but grew up in Yogyakarta. He became a journalist when he was nine-
teen years old and now works as an editor for the newsmagazine*
Jakarta-Jakarta. *In 1992, when he was barred from publishing first-
hand accounts of the Indonesian military's massacre of several hundred
people the previous year in Dili, East Timor, he fictionalized a number
of these accounts and embedded them as segments in his 1996 novel*
Jazz, Parfum dan Insiden *(Jazz, Perfume and the Incident).*

*"The Mysterious Shooter Trilogy" is a collection of three episodes
inspired by the "Petrus killings," which took place in Indonesia pri-
marily during the 1980s in response to a sharply rising crime rate in the
cities. ("Petrus" is an Indonesian acronym formed from* Penembakan
Misterius, *or "Mysterious Killings.") It is widely believed that some
groups within the Indonesian armed forces, which include the police,
were involved in eliminating criminals, some of whom had previously
been used by these same groups for political ends.*

---

1. This is in English in the original.
"Killing Song" (Keroncong Pembunuhan) was first published in *Kompas* daily newspaper
on 3 February 1985. "The Sound of Rain on Roof Tiles" (Bunyi Hujan di Atas Genting)
was first published in *Kompas* on 28 July 1985 and "Grrrr!" in *Kompas* on 18 January
1987. The three stories were reprinted together as "The Mysterious Shooter Trilogy" (Penembakan Misterius: Trilogi) in *Penembak Misterius: Kumpulan Cerita Pendek* (The Mysterious Shooter: A Collection of Short Stories) by Seno Gumira Ajidarma (Jakarta: Pustaka
Utama Grafiti, 1993). Permission to publish granted by the translator, Patricia B. Henry,
with the author's consent.

The first episode in the trilogy, "Killing Song," indirectly addresses the issue of political assassination through the character of a hit-man protagonist who suddenly questions the intent of his employer. In the second episode, "The Sound of Rain on Roof Tiles," the female protagonist, Sawitri, wonders whether any of the tattooed corpses mysteriously appearing at the entrance of the lane near her home on rainy nights may be her missing lover, Pamuji. In the final story, "Grrrr!," hundreds of these assassinated criminals rise from the dead as rotting zombies, taking over the city.

Writing about tense political events in Indonesia, with its draconian censorship laws, requires both circumspection and imagination. Many other Southeast Asian nations—for example, Vietnam, Laos, and Burma—have censorship laws that may seriously affect a writer's freedom of expression and personal safety. In such situations, the ability to mask political commentary in fiction becomes part of a writer's repertoire of literary techniques, as also illustrated by Ne Win Myint's "Thadun" (Burma), and Yudhistira ANM Massardi's "Interview with Ravana" (Indonesia).

∾

(1) "Killing Song"

almost night in Jogja
as my train arrived

The *keroncong* song made me sleepy, despite the fact that tonight I had to kill someone. Of course, old people always like *keroncong* songs; they bring to mind the good old days.

They were scattered around down there, around the swimming pool, but apparently not many of them were really listening to the *keroncong* music. They talked among themselves, noisy chatter and laughter from time to time breaking out of each group.

Indeed, not all of them were old; in fact, there were many young women. At the very least, that was enough to attract my attention. Through the telescopic gunsight, I watched them one by one, as if I were in amongst them. A lively party. There was goat roasted on a spit. Mmm . . .

The crosshairs on the telescopic sight continued to wander. Once in a while it rested on the brow of a person and followed him. If I were to squeeze my index finger, obviously that forehead would get a hole. And the body of that person would collapse. It might collapse slowly, like a large tree falling to earth, or it might suddenly jerk and drop, causing great consternation among the groups of laughing people, causing the glasses to spill all over the trays borne by the waiters. Certainly it would be more interesting if the body fell sprawling into the swimming pool with a reverberating splash, so that the water would spurt out wetting the clothes of the guests, the swimming pool quickly redden from the blood, and the women scream "Oooow!"

But I hadn't yet found the person I was supposed to kill. Indeed, it was not yet time. He would arrive momentarily. And as a matter of fact, I really didn't need to be too concerned about finding him because the communication device in my ear would alert me to him.

"Are you ready?" asked a sweet and soothing voice from my headphone.

"I've been ready for some time; which one is he?"

"Take it easy, just a bit longer."

From the terrace on the seventh floor of the hotel, I continued to peer through the telescopic sight. The damp sea breeze tasted salty on my lips. To pass the time while waiting for my target, I looked for the person who had spoken to me. And I gazed on the passing faces through the gunsight. Women were dressed in elegant evening gowns. Some with bare backs. Very beautiful. The woman whose soft voice commanded me was also beautiful, I was sure. I had never thought a woman would be involved in a killing like this.

"Who is my target?" I had asked last week when she ordered this shooting. Since the transaction was done by telephone, of course I could only guess at her appearance.

"You don't need to know; this is part of our contract."

Indeed, contracts like this were often the way things happened. I was just paid to shoot; the target's identity was none of my business.

"But one thing you are allowed to know."

"What?"

"The person is a traitor."

"A traitor?"

"Yes, a traitor to his people and country."

So, my target was a traitor to people and country. Would I be considered a hero for killing him? I moved my rifle again. From behind the telescopic sight, I studied the people who were arriving in increasing numbers. There was an uncomfortable feeling every time I focused on one of the people down below.

Of course, their faces were the faces of perfectly fine people. I really didn't know what was making me uncomfortable. Was it because so many of them wore formal clothes, the uniform that I hated? Or was it just a feeling I had? Whatever it was, I swore to God I would feel truly happy if my victim, this time, were someone loathsome. A traitor to people and country is certainly a loathsome person.

I swung my rifle around again. Spying on people's actions without them knowing I was watching gave me a pleasant feeling.

a pair of flashing eyes
from behind the window

It still hadn't come to an end, that *keroncong* song. It felt as if it had been going on a long time. Like the people down there, I didn't really need to listen to it attentively. *Keroncong* music nowadays was like something preserved in a museum; those who performed it lacked the genius to develop it. Where was the woman with the gentle voice?

Everywhere, people were chewing food, sucking down drinks, smiling and laughing. There were wives standing stiffly beside their husbands who were busily talking with their hands gesticulating in all directions—men whose appearance revealed the souls of civil servants, respectfully keeping themselves inconspicuous, but eating greedily. Plainclothes officers could be seen walking back and forth carrying walkie-talkies. It would seem that the goat-roast party by the swimming pool at this seaside hotel was being attended by important people.

The night was clear and the sky was full of stars. In fact, the moon was full. I put down my rifle to rest my aching muscles. I walked into the room, getting some peanuts from the table. I turned on the television, but quickly turned it off again. Television programs were always awful. It felt terribly quiet in the hotel room. I wanted to shoot my target quickly, then go home and have a beer.

"Hey, are you still there?" Suddenly the voice was heard again.

"Yes, what's up?"

"Don't play games! I know you aren't in position!"

I hurriedly went back to the terrace.

"How about it? Has he shown up yet?"

"He's wearing a red batik shirt, as it happens the only red one here, so it's easy for you."

I looked below. They were milling around like little animals. It certainly was not clear which one was wearing a red batik shirt from seven stories up like this. I raised my rifle again and tried to find a comfortable position. While chewing the peanuts, I peeped again through the telescopic sight. The crosshairs went back to wandering from face to face. They were still laughing and smiling. I also smiled. In another minute your face will be overwhelmed with unabashed terror. I could shoot you all from here just as I please. But I won't do that. I only work based on a contract.

"On which side is he?" I asked via the mike which hung below my chin.

"He's by the corner of the swimming pool, on the south side, near the green umbrella."

I swung my rifle to the right. Again I surveyed the greasy, shiny, glistening faces. The beautiful women I just had to pass by. And, there! That was him, a man wearing a red batik shirt.

He was a man with regular features and an authoritative bearing. He was middle-aged, but didn't appear to be over the hill. His hair was combed neatly to the back. He wasn't laughing or smiling excessively. People crowded around him respectfully. There were also those who looked like they were fawning on him. The crosshairs of my gunsight stopped exactly between his eyes.

"Do I do it now?"

"Just a minute, wait for the command."

And I studied his face. Did he feel any presentiment of his fate? From behind the gunsight, faces bring forth their own particular enchantment, which is different if compared to that which we experience when meeting the person face to face. He didn't talk much, but apparently he had to answer many questions. And I felt that he answered very carefully. His countenance displayed an intention of courteousness without resentment. What was going to happen shortly when I shot him? I remembered the death of Ninoy[1] in the Philippines . . .

But I knew nothing of politics. So while staring at the face that would soon have a hole in it, I thought about other matters. Perhaps he had a wife, had children. In fact, I thought it quite likely that he would have grandchildren. They would be wailing after hearing about the death of this person, and their weeping would be even more intense

---

1. "Ninoy" refers to Benigno S. Aquino, assassinated by military police at Manila International Airport in 1983.

when they heard about how he had died. Let it be. Wasn't he a traitor to his people and country? He had to get his punishment.

Somewhat tensely, I waited for the order to shoot. That was always the trouble with working according to a contract. I couldn't do as I pleased. I was being paid to point the crosshairs of my gunsight towards the point where a shot would cause death most efficiently, and then to pull the trigger. I always told myself that I didn't kill people, I just aimed and squeezed the trigger.

I stared at the face again, it felt so close—even the pores could be seen clearly. It was as if I were studying the imagination of God, of divine fate. Who in fact will stop the life of this person, me or You? He is completely unaware that the angel of death is brushing against the back of his neck.

"How about it? Now?"

"I said, wait for the order!"

To hell with this little bitch, she really had her nerve, bossing around a paid hit man. My hand moved by itself, rubbing the gun. Relying on instinct, I searched for her among the crowded groups of people. One after another, beautiful faces filled my telescopic sight. I had to coax her into speaking.

"What are we waiting for?"

"You don't need to know; the point is: wait!"

"This wasn't in the agreement."

"Yes, it was! Don't act like an idiot!"

a silken sca-arf
a keepsake from you

Bullshit! That *keroncong* song again, now very clear in my ear. For certain she was near the orchestra. I looked all around the orchestra. My scope alighted on the swelling bosom of the *keroncong* singer. There were several groups of people milling about. I could also hear the clinking of glasses and plates through my headphone. Maybe she was behind the orchestra, near the buffet table. There were several women, as well as plainclothesmen. Which one? I carefully looked them over one by one. Several among them were clearly only workers for the catering business. There was one woman who looked like she was in charge. Maybe the one next to her. Her hair was straight and black, with bangs covering her brow. Her eyes stared in the direction of the red batik shirt!

"Shoot him now," she said softly in my headphone, and I saw through the scope she was indeed talking to herself. It looked like she was the one. She was listening by means of an ear piece and spoke to me through a microphone that was hidden in the strands of her necklace. A beautiful pendant, displayed on her slight chest.

"What?" I asked again, because I wanted to be certain that she was indeed the person.

"Shoot now!"

So this is how all the killings are carried out; just a link in a chain without end or starting point. This woman certainly was only one link in that chain. I turned my rifle back to its target. The middle-aged man was patiently listening to the story of someone who was standing in front of him. The person telling the story seemed to be aflame with excitement, but the man apparently was holding himself back from catching on fire. He nodded, while stealing glances at those around him. As if he was worried that someone would hear.

I was ready to shoot. One squeeze of my index finger would end that man's life story. I shifted the crosshairs of the scope slightly to the side, so that the bullet hole in his head wouldn't make too symmetrical a division. The bullet would pierce his left eye. And I stared at the man's eyes. Good God. Was it true that he was a traitor?

"You're not mistaken? Is it true that he's a traitor?"

"There's no need to ask all these questions, shoot now!" I looked into his eyes again, wondering what kind of traitor he was.

"What kind of traitor? Why wasn't he just put on trial?"

"What business is it of yours, fool? Shoot him now, or I'll cancel the contract!"

A strange feeling suddenly came over me. I pointed the rifle at the woman instead.

"The barrel of my rifle is now pointing at you, sweetie," I said coldly.

"What the hell is this?" In my scope I saw her face jerk up in surprise toward me.

"Tell me," I repeated, "what wrong did this person do?"

"Shoot him now, you fool, or you will die!"

"In fact, you're the one who's just about to die."

"Empty threats! You don't know where I am."

"You're wearing a *cheongsam* with a slit to the thigh, and you're behind the orchestra." And I saw her face turn pale.

"You've broken the contract."

"I don't want to shoot an innocent person."

"That's none of your business; last year you shot thousands of innocent people."

"That's my own affair. Tell me quickly what this person did wrong."

The woman looked as if she was making a move to run away.

"Don't run, there's no use. Nobody will know who shot you. This rifle is equipped with a silencer. You know I never miss my shot, and I can disappear immediately."

Her face looked up in my direction. I saw she was in a cold sweat. Full of anxiety.

"What do you want?"

"Tell me his wrongdoing."

"He's a traitor, he blackened the name of our people and country abroad."

"Only that?"

"He stirred up society with statements that weren't true."

"And then?"

"What do you want? I don't know that much."

"I want to know, does all that constitute a sufficient reason to kill him?"

"That's not your business. This is politics."

"My business is your necklace, sweetie; it could break into pieces from my bullet, and the bullet wouldn't stop there."

Her face once again stared in my direction, with a pleading look.

"Don't shoot me! I don't know anything!"

"Who gives you orders?"

"I don't know anything."

"Your necklace, sweetie . . ."

"Oh, don't, don't shoot! *Please* . . ."

"Who?"

"I . . . I can get in trouble."

"Right now you can get in trouble. I'll count to three. One . . ."

"You're crazy, you're ruining everything."

"Two . . ." Mmm, how panicked she was.

"He's in front of the person you're supposed to shoot."

"Wearing glasses?"

"Yes."

I pointed the rifle there. And I saw that person. He was telling a story with great excitement. His hands gestured all around, clenching his fist and hitting it into the palm of his other hand. His face was cunning and full of trickery. Very loathsome. And to make it worse, he was quite old.

I aimed the crosshairs of my scope at his heart, while in my ear the high nasal voice of the singer whined, starting up another *keroncong* song, a song pleasing to old people. This will indeed make them remember the good old days.

This is a keroncong fantasy-y . . .

(2) "The Sound of Rain on Roof Tiles"

"Tell me a story about fear," said Alina to the storyteller. And thus the storyteller told the tale of Sawitri:

Every time the rain let up, a tattooed corpse would be found sprawled at the entrance of the lane. That was the reason Sawitri always felt a trembling in her heart every time she heard the sound of rain starting to tap on the roof tiles.

Her house, in fact, was situated on the corner, where the lane joined the main road. Sometimes at night, she could hear sounds like gunshots, and the sounds of car engines disappearing into the distance. But even on those frequent nights when she heard nothing, whenever the rain let up, tattooed corpses always appeared, sprawled at the entrance to the lane. Indeed, perhaps she hadn't heard anything because of the sound of the rain coming down so hard. A heavy rain, you know, can often be very scary. Especially if your house isn't a sturdy building, has a lot of leaks, can get flooded, and could be crushed if even a small tree fell on it.

Then too, Sawitri might not have heard anything because she'd been sleepy and might have nodded off. Perhaps the radio was turned on too loudly. She liked to listen to Indonesian pop songs while she sewed. Her eyes often stung from squinting at the eye of a needle in the light of a fifteen-watt bulb. When her eyes stung and watered, she would shut them for a moment. Shutting her eyes for a moment like that, she would listen to a fragment of song from the radio. And while she listened, sometimes she nodded off. But without fail, every time the rain let up, a tattooed corpse would be sprawled at the entrance to the lane.

In order to see the tattooed corpse, Sawitri only needed to open the side window of her house and look to the right. She had to lean over if she wanted to see the corpse clearly; otherwise the shutter would obstruct her gaze. She had to lean over until her stomach pressed against the window sill, and the spatters of the remains of the rain dripped onto her hair and also on part of her face.

Her chest was always tight and her heart pounded hard every time the rain ended and the sound of the last raindrops was like a song ending. But Sawitri still kept on opening the window and looking to the right while leaning over to see the corpse. Even if she had nodded off while the rain came down in the middle of the night with its gentle rhythm that invited people to forget about this impermanent world, Sawitri always woke up the moment the rain let up. She would immediately open the window, then look over to the right while leaning out.

She always felt fear, but she still always wanted to look closely at the faces of the tattooed corpses. If the corpse had already drawn a crowd of her neighbors, Sawitri, too, would take the opportunity to go out of the house and make her way through the crowd until she could see the corpse. She didn't always succeed in seeing its face because sometimes it was too late and the corpse had already been covered with a cloth. But Sawitri was relieved if she'd been able to see any part of the corpse at all, be it the foot, the hand, or at the very least its tattoo.

Sawitri had on occasion lifted the cloth covering the corpse in order to see its face, but she didn't want to do it again. A couple of times when she'd lifted the cloth, what she'd seen was a face twisted into a grimace, with staring eyes wide open and teeth showing in a grin, as if it were still alive. A face to make your hair stand on end.

However, as it turned out, Sawitri usually did not join in crowding around with her neighbors. She was almost always the first person who saw the tattooed corpses. When the rain hadn't quite stopped, so that it hung like a glittering screen in the yellowish glow of the mercury street-lights, the shape of the sprawled body really looked like an animal carcass. Sawitri would only look for a second, but it was enough for her to keep the mental picture of how the blood had spattered on the wet cement, and how the shape itself also quickly became wet, and how the person's hair and whiskers and drawstring shorts were wet too.

Not all the faces of the tattooed corpses were horrible. Sometimes Sawitri had the impression that the tattooed corpse was like a person sleeping soundly, or a person smiling. The tattooed people slept soundly and smiled in the soothing embrace of the gentle rain which, in Sawitri's eyes, sometimes looked like the curtain of a theater stage. The pale, yellowish light of the mercury street lamps sometimes made the color of blood on the person's chest and back look black instead of red. It was the blood that distinguished the tattooed corpses from sleeping people.

Sometimes the eyes of the tattooed corpse stared straight at Sawitri when she turned to the right after opening the window, leaning out after the rain had let up. And Sawitri often felt that she was observing them right at the moment their lives were ending. The eyes were still alive at the moment when they met hers. And Sawitri could feel how those eyes in their final gaze had so much to tell. So often had Sawitri locked eyes with those tattooed bodies, she felt she could tell with only a glance whether the person still lived or had already died. She could also sense immediately whether the soul of the person was still in his body, or had just left, or had long since flown, who knew whether to heaven or to hell.

Sawitri felt she had seen many stories in those eyes, but that the retelling of them would be extremely difficult. She sometimes felt that the person wanted to scream that he didn't want to die, that he still wanted to live, that he had a wife and children. Sometimes also Sawitri saw eyes that were questioning. Eyes that demanded. Eyes that rejected their fate.

But the well-built tattooed bodies just remained wet, wet from blood and rain. Flashes of lightning made the blood and the wet body shine, and the blood and rainwater on the cement also shone. The heads drooped forward or back, as decreed by their individual fates. It might happen that the head faced downwards, kissing the earth, or it might gaze upward at the sky, with eyes wide open and mouth gaping. And at those times when the rain hadn't stopped completely, Sawitri saw how the gaping mouth filled up with rainwater.

Sawitri felt that her neighbors had gotten used to the tattooed corpses. In fact, she thought that the neighbors were delighted every time they saw a tattooed corpse sprawled at the entrance to the lane, whenever the rain let up and the corpse lay bathed in the light from the yellowish mercury lamps. From inside her house, which was situated at the corner of the lane, Sawitri heard everything they talked about. They screamed and yelled while crowding around the sprawling corpse, even though sometimes the rain hadn't completely ended; and the children shouted gleefully.

"Look! Another one!"

"Dead as a doornail!"

"Smashed like a damn bug!"

"Now he knows what it feels like!"

"Right, now he knows what it feels like!"

"The filthy dog!"

"Right, the filthy dog!"

Sometimes they kicked the corpse around, too, and stomped on its face. Sometimes they just dragged the corpse the length of the road to the office of the subdistrict chief, so that the face of the tattooed person was smeared with mud because the neighborhood folks had dragged him by the legs. Sawitri never went along with the procession of cheering happy people. It was enough for her to open her window every time the rain let up, to look to the right while leaning over, and then to close it again after seeing a tattooed corpse.

Sawitri would take a deep breath once it was clear that the corpse wasn't Pamuji. Didn't Pamuji also have a tattoo like those corpses, and wasn't it also true that some of the corpses that lay sprawled at the entrance to the lane every time the rain let up were friends of Pamuji? Once in a while, Sawitri recognized those friends among tattooed corpses, like Kandang Jinongkeng (Jail Dodger), Pentung Pinanggul (Club on the Shoulder) . . .

The corpses were sprawled there, really like rat carcasses that had been tossed into the road. Sawitri felt their fate was worse than that of slaughtered animals. The corpses were sprawled there with their hands and feet tied together. Sometimes their hands were tied behind their backs with plastic string. Sometimes only their two thumbs were tied together with wire. Sometimes, in fact, their feet weren't tied. Indeed there were some who weren't tied up at all. However, those corpses who were not tied up usually had more bullet holes in them. The bullet holes formed a line on the back and chest, so that the beautiful tattooed drawings were ruined.

Sawitri sometimes thought that the shooters of the tattooed people had in fact purposely ruined the pictures. Actually, they shot them in all sorts of unnecessary places, although they could just shoot them in the fatal spots. Did they shoot at those non-fatal places only because they wanted to make the tattooed people feel pain? Sometimes a tattooed picture was destroyed because of bullet holes in those non-fatal places.

She always looked carefully at the tattoos of the people who were sprawled at the entrance to the lane every time the rain let up. That was the way Sawitri recognized Kandang Jinongkeng. He was face down, but the light of the mercury street lamp was strong enough for Sawitri to recognize the tattoo on his back which was now full of holes—a piece of writing, MAMA DEAR, and a picture of a cross on his left arm. Sawitri could remember clearly the drawings on those corpses: anchors, hearts, roses, skulls, women's names, various writings, all sorts of large letters . . .

Sawitri always looked carefully at the tattoos because Pamuji also had a tattoo. She had once tattooed her own name on Pamuji's chest. She had written on the chest of that man: SAWITRI. Further, a picture of a heart as a sign of love surrounded the writing. Sawitri remembered she needed two days to perforate Pamuji's skin with a needle.

But it wasn't just Sawitri's name that was tattooed on Pamuji's chest. She always remembered that on his left arm there was a picture of a beautiful rose. Beneath the rose was the word *Nungki*. According to Pamuji, that was his first sweetheart. And then there was a drawing of a nude woman. On the chest of the naked woman there was the word *Asih*. According to Pamuji, again, he had once fallen in love with Asih, but it hadn't come to anything. Sawitri knew Asih. In earlier times they had been prostitutes together in the Greater Mango district. It was because of Asih that Sawitri had gotten to know Pamuji in the first place. Ah, the dear old days gone by!

And so the rain kept coming down, as if in a bad dream. For the past few years, since the tattooed corpses had been showing up sprawled out on every corner, life itself had become like a bad dream for Sawitri. From that time on, Pamuji had vanished without a trace.

At first, the sprawled-out corpses turned up almost constantly. Morning, noon and night, there were corpses sprawled in the corners of the market, floating by in the river, lying sunk in the ditches or scattered along the toll roads. Every day the newspapers carried pictures of tattooed corpses with bullet wounds at the base of the skull, in the forehead, the heart, or between the eyes. Sometimes the tattooed corpses had even been tossed, in broad daylight, onto the main roads, from cars that swiftly disappeared. Those corpses that fell into the midst of a crowd of people caused quite a commotion. People crowded around the corpse screaming and creating a traffic jam. Sawitri had seen this with her own eyes while out shopping one day. She saw the dust rise up in a cloud after the corpse had hit the ground. The billowing dust had made it difficult for her to breathe. Pamuji, oh Pamuji, where could you be?

The pictures of the corpses eventually disappeared from the newspapers, but the tattooed corpses still turned up with the same characteristic signs. Their hands and feet were tied. They had fatal gunshot wounds, but there were still other bullet holes in places that would not cause death. If they had been shot in those non-fatal places first, surely the pain had been awful, Sawitri thought to herself. How much more so with hands and feet tied like that.

Had Pamuji already turned up sprawled out someplace, like the corpses at the entrance to the lane? Sawitri had received a letter from Pamuji with no return address, but only once. Sawitri in fact was certain that Pamuji wouldn't be caught. Pamuji was very clever. And if the shooters gave Pamuji a chance to fight, it was by no means certain that he would lose. Sawitri knew that Pamuji was very good at fighting. But, if every time the rain stopped, there was always a corpse sprawled at the end of the lane, who could guarantee that Pamuji wasn't going to suffer the same fate?

This was the reason Sawitri always trembled every time the sound of the rain was heard tapping on the roof tiles. Every time the rain ended, at the entrance to the lane there would be a sprawled-out tattooed corpse. Their eyes always stared in Sawitri's direction, as if they knew that Sawitri would open the window and then look to the right . . .

"At the end of the story will Sawitri meet again with Pamuji?" Alina asked the storyteller.

And thus the storyteller answered: "I cannot as yet answer you, Alina. The story still isn't over."

Jakarta, 15 July 1985

∾

(3) *"Grrrr!"*

Detective Sarman was still intensely slurping up his coffee in Markonah's roadside stall, when the irritating sound of his walkie-talkie started calling him over and over. It was late at night. The remnants of a drizzling rain reflected the light of the pressure lantern.

"Officer Sarman?"

"Here, sir!"

"Get to First Street, on the double! There's a disturbance!"

"Right away, sir!"

His coffee was still steaming, but even so Detective Sarman had to rush off. The momentary relaxation he was enjoying at the coffee stall would have to wait for another time. Markonah's smiles, which had been poking holes in his heart for some time, would have to be forgotten for now. Ah well, that was the way it was, Detective Sarman said to himself. Scrambling to keep up with things from one moment to the next, and every time you had a chance to come up for air and catch your breath, you immediately found yourself drowning in problems again. In the jitney cab on his way to the place of the incident, he felt for his pistol under his jacket. It was still there.

Nimbly, he jumped out of the cab without paying. People were still crowding around by the side of the road. From behind the crowd, Detective Sarman craned his neck to see. And straight away his eyes took in a bloodcurdling sight.

In the moonlight, a hulking form stood in the intersection. Every once in a while its head jerked up and out of its mouth came a hoarse growl. *Grrrr! Grrrr!* No one dared to come near. Its fist clenched a golden necklace that sparkled as the light from the street lamps fell on it.

Detective Sarman pushed his way forward. Now it was increasingly clear just how horrifying the thing was. In form it was tall and large. Its feet trampled on its already half-dead victim.

Grrrr! It growled again. And Detective Sarman saw how thick, soupy spittle was dripping from its mouth. Its lips looked sticky, as if they could only be opened by force. One side of its face was already liquefied. Its left eye was gouged out; and out of the socket, worms came crawling, *creepity-creepity*. The flesh from its whole body was half-rotten and the stench was truly awful. Detective Sarman was used to seeing corpses—from those who had died in accidents to those who had been tortured. Those corpses very often were horrible and disgusting, but they didn't terrify Detective Sarman at all.

Now Detective Sarman looked upon a sight that he had never in his whole life seen before. In the stinking body he could see gaping holes that were crawling with worms. Every time the worms fell out and went *creepity-creepity* along the road, more worms came pouring out from inside the torso of the body and went *creepity-creepity* some more and *creepity-creepity* some more and *creepity-creepity* some more. *Grrrr!*

The thing made a threatening move towards the victim that was underfoot. Detective Sarman quickly took action. He aimed his gun at the body's head. He shot.

An explosion was heard. The body jerked to a stop. But it didn't become still. Its forehead had a hole because of Detective Sarman's bullet, but no blood came gushing out. It was as though the bullet had pierced a banana trunk. But out of the bullet hole emerged more worms which immediately began going *creepity-creepity,* tumbling down onto the asphalt.

Detective Sarman shot several more times with suppressed rage. But his bullets only made more impact holes. And from every hole came forth worms that went *creepity-creepity* so that the thing became even more horrible. And it started moving closer to Detective Sarman. Its steps were slow but sure. It lurched forward stiffly but with certainty. Both its hands were held up in front as if heavily waving. People scattered like mice. Detective Sarman quickly reached for his walkie-talkie.

"Missiles! Missiles! Send guided missiles immediately!"

"What for?"

"To shoot a monster! Hurry up! Twenty-two-caliber bullets won't do it! Quick! The monster's chasing me! Quick!"

"Monster? What monster?"

"Never mind that now! We can talk about it later! Hurry up!"

"What missiles are you requesting?"

"Don't be stupid! Anti-tank missiles, of course!"

Because the streets were deserted by now, the delivery of TOW missiles arrived quickly. The foul-smelling body that strode with heavy feet was still some distance from Detective Sarman. It was immediately smashed to a pulp. In the blink of an eye, a forty-pound missile had been launched with all its awesome power. The rotten body was destroyed without a trace. Only the worms, which had just picked up the pace of their *creepity-creepity,* were still going *creepity-creepity* everywhere. *Creepity-creepity. Creepity-creepity. Creepity-creepity.*

A reporter who up until then had been quietly taking pictures of the event immediately hailed a cab.

"To Palmerah! On the double!"

The morning papers came out the next day like something in a nightmare. LIVING CORPSES WANDER THROUGHOUT THE CITY. An excerpt of the news:

. . . and our reporters in various parts of the capital report that in every gathering place, living corpses are emerging. Their bodies are extremely rotten. Their flesh has partially liquefied, and bullets from pistols or rifles have no effect. Even firearms that have been given magical powers by shamans are still useless. The living corpse can only be destroyed with a missile. And even that doesn't mean it's dead. Shreds of its flesh continue twitching. And the worms that fall from its body flourish and multiply at an awesome rate.

In general, our reporters have reported almost identical events. The living corpses, alias zombies, behave like criminals. They pickpocket wallets, snatch necklaces, demand money, or rob people at gunpoint. But because of their rotten bodies and their slow, awkward movements, they can't run away like criminals. They can only hold up whatever they've stolen while emitting a hoarse sound: Grrrr! Grrrr! They appear suddenly from out of nowhere. Perhaps directly from the graveyard. But there are no reports of graveyards that have been broken open.

Now the doctors are examining the shreds of flesh, which are still writhing around. We hope that the proper authorities, whose responsibility it is to take care of this truly weird situation, will immediately do so. It's true that in the everyday life of this country plenty of unbelievable and shocking things happen all the time, and people somehow manage to just accept them. However, it is to be hoped that this particular situation will quickly pass. Living corpses wandering around is just too appalling.

Detective Sarman read the news while shaking his head.

"Too much. How come my name isn't given even a mention? The press nowadays always blows up unimportant things out of all proportion, while covering up the real issue. Just look, where is there any mention of the hard work being done by the authorities? Here I've been working day and night without rest, and it's the picture of the stupid living corpse that gets put in the paper! I could see the point if the thing were at least good-looking! And the damned public, too—invariably insulting the police. Meanwhile, they always love the cops in Western movies. To hell with them all!"

At Markonah's food stall he ranted on while chewing on a slice of tempeh.

"And now the newspapers are joining in. Making a big fat deal of the news of the living corpses. The community is being frightened out of its wits. And the upshot of it is, at the very least, that the police will be blamed again! Once more the police! The higher-ups will get all pissed off, and then we're the ones who catch hell! No way is the salary enough to get anyone through a week! Damn! Who knows, if I'd passed the college entrance exam way back when, maybe my luck would be a little better? What the hell do reporters know about anything? Bunch of show-off smart asses!"

He was still cursing enthusiastically when his walkie-talkie called him to attention again. He jumped up, all energetic efficiency.

"Here, sir!"

And in a flash, Detective Sarman vanished.

"Hey, what about paying the check?" Markonah yelled after him, aggrieved. But she didn't grumble long. She knew that Detective Sarman would always come back to her. Even though he had a wife and four children. Always, he would come back to her.

Once more, Detective Sarman was face to face with a living corpse. Its head was hairless, its body reeked, and it was crawling with worms. It stood in the intersection with its hands in front of it. Its putrefying mouth looked like it was melting, but out of it still came the hoarse voice: *Grrrr! Grrrr!* The street was jammed with traffic. Cars were abandoned by their passengers. The rotting body strode over the roofs of the cars. Every so often it would lose its balance because the soles of its feet were also starting to rot away.

Detective Sarman contemplated the situation more calmly now. He knew that even if this one could be taken care of, others would immediately come forth. There had to be a reason why all these rotten bodies were coming back from the grave. Surely it was the same reason for all of them. If not, what were they up to, creating such chaos?

Probably they were criminals during their lifetimes, thought Detective Sarman. They looked like petty thugs and crooks, small fry. The kind of crooks that depended on their weapons and their strength, not on their brains. Detective Sarman had noticed that on the bodies that were beginning to rot away there were still traces of tattoos. And in the bodies there were always holes, from which the worms started spreading to the outside, falling *creepity-creepity-creepity.* Detective Sarman felt there was something he could almost remember, but then he forgot it again.

Grrrr! The voice brought him out of his deep thought. He looked closely at the body again, and sure enough, it had a tattoo. The form of a naked woman could still be made out faintly on its chest. And the holes. Yes, the holes were always in the same places. At the back of the head, on the left side of the chest, or in the forehead. To be sure, sometimes there were lines of holes from the chest to the stomach. Or along the length of the back. But not often. Suddenly Detective Sarman was reminded of something. But the voice intruded again: *Grrrr!*

He had already ordered the TOW missiles. The most effective weapon for immobilizing zombies. While waiting he lit a cigarette, watching the monster fall and pick itself up as it lurched around on the tops of the cars. It was truly disgusting. Detective Sarman could smell its rotten stench even from where he was standing. Good God, who would believe it—a corpse coming to life again. What evil spirit possessed it?

If you counted them all up, there had been more than twenty living corpses popping up on various street corners. Detective Sarman's colleagues had run themselves ragged keeping track of them all. Every time, they had to use a TOW missile to destroy them. Unfortunately, the TOW missiles didn't confine themselves to smashing to smithereens only the living corpses. The corpses' surroundings were also smashed up along with them. The Minister for Protecting the Environment was getting angry.

"Just why is it we have to use missiles? Isn't it a shame to squander all those expensive missiles? Can't you snare them in a net? Chop them down with a machete? Or pour gasoline all over them?" he asked in a televised statement.

But while the polemics were going on, the living corpses continued to show up conspicuously all over the place. The authorities wanted to take care of this matter quickly. For that, missiles really were the most effective means.

Nevertheless, in only a few days, there had been so many incidents. What would happen if we ran out of missiles? This is what Detective Sarman was thinking. His brain was reeling. The United States had just said they were sick and tired of selling missiles. To buy them from Israel was tantamount to treason. There had to be another way. We have no way of knowing how many more living corpses will be terrorizing us. Where in hell are all these stinking corpses coming from? Detective Sarman was truly at his wit's end, trying to figure it out. He reached for his walkie-talkie.

"Check out the graveyards in all corners of the land. Report back on which graves have been broken into!" ordered Detective Sarman.

At that very moment the missile delivery arrived. The missile specialists set it up carefully. The zombie was standing firmly on top of a car. *Grrrr! Grrrr!* Detective Sarman looked closely at the half-dissolved face. He had the feeling he had seen it before. Who was it, anyway? *Grrrr! Grrrr!* Worms were falling out of its mouth. And as usual, they were going *creepity-creepity* in their disgusting way, rapidly spreading over everything. Creeping over the car windows, so that the pretty women who hadn't been able to escape were screaming like crazy people. The zombie was now looking more ferocious.

"Shoot it, quick!" yelled Detective Sarman.

"OK, Boss!" And the TOW missile was off in a flash. *Ka-POW!*

The capital was like a war zone. Smashed-up ruins lay scattered all around everywhere. This was the result of the missiles that had been shot off with such abandon. Nonetheless, the zombies continued to emerge. Worms were infesting everything like a plague. Worms were going *creepity-creepity* on top of tables, chairs, windows, toilets, in bathrooms, shirt pockets, shoes, dishes, glasses, and bottles. People were busy every day, flicking off worms that were crawling all over their shirts, their hair, their nostrils; they even had worms dangling from their eyeglasses.

Zombies were raging around increasingly. Daily life was disrupted. Now they weren't just snatching cheap things, but they'd also started gobbling up all kinds of food. Their very existence was an act of terrorism. The supply of missiles was getting lower and lower. Keep in mind, this was a calm and peaceful country, fertile and prosperous, like a kingdom in a shadow play. What the hell! Who would have dreamed they'd have to fight a war against zombies?

Detective Sarman's walkie-talkie squealed.

"Officer Sarman?"

"Here, sir!"

"Get to Fifth Street on the double! There's another zombie!"

"Right away, sir!"

But Detective Sarman didn't budge. He put both his feet up on top of his desk in the office. His head drooped. His walkie-talkie went on squealing. He could hear there was a lot of yapping back and forth.

Lazily he reached for some of the reports that had been filed.

. . . our informants from every corner of the land report that there are a certain number of grave sites that have been broken open. The coffins within them have been opened and whatever was in them is not there anymore. The data shows that these graves are in fact those of criminals of the "small fry" class. However, not all the graves have names or dates. The result of the research we've been able to do up to now also shows that some of the living corpses come from the Mass Grave . . .

Detective Sarman felt more and more as if he should be remembering something. He hadn't yet gotten the answer to the puzzle when he heard a knocking on the glass window behind him. He turned, and felt a stab of terror: zombies!

His heart pounded hard. The horrible face had suddenly appeared just like that in the window. At a glance, even though this face too had begun to rot away, Detective Sarman recognized it.

"Ngadul!" he screamed.[1] But Ngadul, who had become a zombie, didn't recognize him anymore. The zombies crept inside. *Grrrr! Grrrr!*

Detective Sarman leapt on top of the table, grabbing for his walkie-talkie. Now he felt that he was on to something.

"Commander! One of the zombies is Ngadul! One of the victims of the legendary mysterious slaughter of the Mass Grave! I recognize him, sir! He's turned up at the station!"

"Shoot him quick with a missile!"

"Forgive me, Commander, but that won't solve the problem!"

The zombies approached and knocked over Detective Sarman's desk. The Honorable Detective jumped like a hunted rabbit and ran into another room. The zombies kept on coming after him. Worms swarmed over the walls.

"Officer Sarman! Are you disobeying your commander's orders?"

"It's not that, sir! We don't have enough missiles to get rid of all the zombies!"

"What are you talking about, Officer Sarman? Those zombies are disrupting our lives!"

The zombies were kicking at the door and breaking it down. Detective Sarman jumped out of a window with his walkie-talkie.

"Don't you remember, sir? Along with Ngadul there were six thousand criminals of the 'small fry' class who were slaughtered mysteriously! Do you still remember, sir?"

"Yes, yes! What about it?"

"Most of the corpses were buried in the Mass Grave, Commander, sir!"

"I know! So what then?"

---

1. "Ngadul" means "Squealer"; this is the name of an informant.

"There was a report, it seemed that many among them weren't active criminals anymore, sir! Among those mysteriously slaughtered, there were many who had seen the error of their ways, sir! And all of them were buried without religious rites, sir! At the time, nobody dared mention it! They were scared they'd get slaughtered, too, sir! The fact is, at that time anybody at all could be killed mysteriously, sir!"

Grrrr! The zombies jumped from the window. Detective Sarman started climbing the wall of the outside fence.

"So, have you come to some conclusion, Officer Sarman?"

"That slaughter was a big mistake, sir! Our generation is suffering the consequences! Those people weren't ready to die, sir! They're taking their revenge!"

"What should we do?"

"Perform rites for them, sir! There has to be a mass funeral service, sir! We only have a hundred missiles left! It isn't enough to wipe them out! Perform rites for them, sir! So that their souls will find rest!"

"You're dreaming, right, Officer Sarman? You're babbling in your sleep! That's all utter nonsense! We're importing missiles from overseas even now! Do you hear that? Six thousand missiles are being shipped here! The zombies will be butchered!"

A zombie caught hold of Detective Sarman's foot, which was still half in the station compound.

"Help! They've got me! Help!" Detective Sarman screamed in horror. The zombie was starting to swallow his leg. Detective Sarman's shrieks pierced the heavens. His walkie-talkie fell into the ditch.

From various quarters of town, zombies appeared, more and more of them, moving faster and faster, becoming more and more ferocious. They crept along like worms, filling the streets, skulking in the supermarkets, and entering the campuses. They wandered about in every nook and cranny. They climbed up on top of multistoried buildings and roared hoarsely: *Grrrr! Grrrr! Revenge! Revenge!* They growled in unison like a choir from hell: *Grrrr! Grrrr! Revenge unto death! Revenge unto death! Grrrr!*

In the intervals between that horrible chorus that made the entire town quake with fear could be heard the shrill, heartrending wails of Detective Sarman: "He-e-e-elp! My leg is being eaten by zombi-e-e-es! He-e-e-elp! Commander-r-r-r-r! He-e-e-e-e-e-e-e-elp!!!!!"

Jakarta—Yogya, December 1986
Translated by Patricia B. Henry

Leila S. Chudori

"The Purification of Sita"

Leila S. Chudori was born in 1962 in Jakarta, where she lived until 1982, the year she left to study in Canada for six years. Considered one of Indonesia's important new writers, she worked as a reporter in Jakarta for the newsmagazine Tempo, until Suharto's New Order government banned it in 1994.

In 1974 the Indonesian government promoted a conservative social policy (Panca Dharma Wanita) that reemphasized the value of a domestic role for women. "The Purification of Sita" reflects Chudori's interest in women's issues and the cultural double standard. She causes readers to reflect on social inconsistencies through Indonesian characters living in the West. This juxtaposition is seen in "The Purification of Sita," whose protagonist, from the Ramayana, now lives in contemporary Peterborough, waiting stoically for her fiancé, Rama. Her physical condition, an experience of intense heat, is both a flashback and premonition of the fire ordeal that she did and will have to undergo to prove her chastity to Rama. This sense of intertwined realities—a melding of past, present, and future—gives the reader insight into how social conventions, like sexual norms, never really seem to change. The modern Sita questions why she is still unable to ask Rama about his affairs.

Since Sita's passivity has traditionally exemplified the "ideal" woman, it is no wonder that other Southeast Asian writers, including Sri Daoruang in "Sita Puts Out the Fire" (Thailand), deploy her as a character in their fiction. Many Southeast Asian writers take up the subject of a gender-based double standard, including Marianne Villanueva in "The Mayor of the Roses" (the Philippines) and Mary Loh in "Sex, Size and Ginseng" (Singapore).

"The Purification of Sita" (Air Suci Sita), by Leila S. Chudori, from *Malam Terakhir* (Jakarta: Grafiti Pers, 1988). Reprinted from John H. McGlynn, ed. *Menagerie, 1: Indonesian Fiction, Poetry, Photographs, Essays* (Jakarta: The Lontar Foundation, 1992). Permission to republish granted by John H. McGlynn.

Night broke on her so suddenly. Flung into the darkness surrounding her, she scanned the scene, wide-eyed, stunned, and anxious. And so night did finally arrive, though hardly, she thought bitterly, with the nobility befitting a warrior. Indeed, the proper way for night to fall is gently, in a feminine sort of way, gradually replacing the twilight, which merely mediates between day and night. And because of its gentleness, the creatures of the world would be able to feel the nuances of freshness that the change of day should bring. But because the night vented such fury, she faltered, unsure how to react. For the first few moments she was held captive by the mugginess which had presented itself uninvited. The air felt so close, so uncomfortable, she thought as she tried to suck back into herself the beads of sweat even then beginning to dampen her clothes.

Agitated, she took a deep breath. The power that was evident in the long letter from her fiancé seemed to pursue her; the chase had left her completely winded. She couldn't imagine how she might react if he were there with her now.

Amidst the unrelenting and restless heat of an unfriendly Peterborough summer, she could hardly interpret the arrival of his letter as a joyous occasion.

Four frozen years, she mused as her mind suddenly filled with the image of knee-deep Canadian snow. For four years she had to steel herself, had to guard her defenses . . .

Beads of sweat, a continuous flow, moistened her temples and brows. He, her fiancé, would be unable to fathom how she had managed to maintain her good health and her sanity through the onslaught of sixteen changes in seasons. He would not understand. He won't believe it! He'll refuse to pull back his blinders when judging me, she thought, stung by paranoia.

Her entire body grappled with the stifling heat. God, it's hot, she thought, as she wrestled with the flames that were about to consume her.

She got herself a glass of cold water. Through one gulp and then another she panned the world outside her window. Even though the sun was still round in the sky, the thought of the darkness that lay ahead made her skin crawl. She seemed oblivious to the screams of the neighbor's children as they played in the water outside. She heard a different sound, a loving but authoritative voice. Then she beheld the image of Vishnu, the Great King, in one of his reincarnations . . .

"My dear wife . . . I know you have no reason to doubt my love for you. We have been separated by a vast and raging sea, one so vast that a legion of faithful soldiers was needed to build a bridge to reunite us . . . But you know, my darling, even without that bridge, the fact remains that you have spent time in this evil, foreign kingdom . . ."

The Great King loved his wife . . . However, after she had been abducted by the ten-headed giant, he spoke no more of his undying devotion to her. Instead, he questioned her as to what had taken place during the long period she was held captive in that alien land. And as his concern about her fidelity grew, her obstinacy in answering his questions perturbed him all the more.

It was so hot. The woman sighed irritably, replaying in her mind the scene that only moments before had chilled her to the marrow. They were husband and wife, yet they still did not trust each other!

She ran to the shower and frantically turned the cold water tap on full blast. And there she stood, eyes closed, completely motionless, beneath a flood of water pouring over her body. She emerged from the bathroom a few minutes later, her sopping clothes clinging to her body.

Looking out the window she smiled at the sight of the neighbor's children playing naked in the water. Their stark white flesh glistened in the sunlight. Yelling and screaming, they took turns splashing each other until their mother shouted for them to stop. What? She was surprised. It was not yet dark after all . . .

"Will you sleep with me?" A slight tremble heightened the intimacy of the man's voice.

Strangely enough, contrary to the way one might have presumed she would react, the man's overture left her indifferent. She walked to the door, opened it and stood there smiling disparagingly.

"Are you asking me to leave?"

"Well, there's nothing more to be said," she replied calmly.

"So this is what they mean when they rave about the chastity of Asian women?"

The woman shook her head. "I like you, really, I do. But I'm not going to sleep with you."

"Why?"

"Why? Because I'm not going to sleep with a man who is not my husband . . . How many times do I have to tell you that?"

"Even though we love each other? Even though we've been seeing each other for nearly two years?"

The woman opened the door wider. The man just stood there, miserable, shaking his head.

"Good night," she said, kissing his cheek.

God, she moaned as she leaned against the door. It was so incredibly muggy! And those insidious flames keep coming back to torture me, she wailed to herself. She pictured the giant approaching the beautiful goddess. Was he, the ten-headed beast, really so evil? Was he, the creature portrayed in the ancient Hindu epic, really so horrible? In what manner had he approached the goddess whom he abducted? Had he been aggressive or had he been gentle? If he really was as cruel as all that, would it not have been a simple matter for him to subdue the goddess? Yet, in the end, she had proved her purity, had she not?

The woman was seized by paranoia. Although her lover, if that is what he could be called, had never so much as laid a finger on her, she still felt that she had entered the realm of the ten-headed giant. God, she thought, suppose that out of the blue my fiancé were to show up at my door and find me with him. What would happen? She let her imagination run wild . . . Her fiancé would kill him; that's the first thing he'd do. And after that, assuming the worst of her, he would launch into a series of accusations . . . Just like the reincarnation of the Great King Vishnu, he too would scatter pearls of wisdom about undying love and affection. Comparing love to the endless sea, the open sky and so on and so forth, and so forth and so on. But then, like a saint from some hallowed land— her fiancé did, in fact, have a strong religious background—he would say to her: "Even so, my love, given my position and my prestige as a man held in esteem by the religious community, it is only natural that I ask you about your faithfulness, your purity and your self-restraint. In the permissive West, where physical relations are as easy to come by as cabbage at the market, it is not without justification that I ask you about the four years that we have been apart . . ."

The words would roll from his tongue as swiftly as water courses through a broken dam. And his accusations, thinly veiled as innocent questions, would flow with equal speed, drowning her in her inability to maintain her defense. Her defense? Must she prepare some kind of testimony? Or submit proof that, even though she and the Canadian man had become close friends, he had never touched so much as a hair on her head? Wouldn't the truth of their relationship provide its own defense? But would her fiancé be perceptive enough to sense the truth and to realize her commitment to him? . . . But even the Great King Vishnu had demanded that his wife immolate herself in the sea of fire to prove that the ten-headed monster had never touched her.

She felt herself consumed by the flames. The clock struck three times. The other occupants of the building must have melted into oblivion. The morning was so quiet and still. She could take it no longer and ran into the bathroom once again to let the flood of water pour over her. Fully clothed, she drenched her entire body till her clothes clung to her. Behind her eyelids, the image of her fiancé alternated with that of the Great King. "Darling, for the sake of the community, for the sake of my reputation as a man, for the sake of . . ."

"Pardon me, but were you the one taking the shower last night?" the old woman whose flat shared a wall with her bathroom inquired.

The younger woman nodded slowly. "I was hot. I'm sorry. I hope I didn't disturb you . . ."

"Oh, no, not at all. I was just wondering . . . Um, what's happening with your fiancé? Isn't he planning to visit?"

The young woman steadied herself against the hallway wall and drew in a deep breath.

"You look pale, dear," the old woman ventured. "Are you all right?"

She shook her head vigorously, "I'm fine, really. He's supposed to arrive this evening. I guess I'm just excited, that's all . . ." she said, hastily slipping behind the door.

Outside the door, the old woman chuckled and shook her head. "Young ladies always get so nervous when their prince is about to come . . ."

And indeed, inside her room, the young woman was anxious. Darkness crashed down on her once more, leaving her utterly bewildered. Night had fallen impulsively and arbitrarily overthrew her day. "I can't take another minute of this heat!" she screamed as she ran towards the bathroom and the refuge of the rushing water.

She stood there for hours, and hours . . .

"You look so pale and worn out," her fiancé observed, embracing her tightly. "Didn't you sleep last night?"

The woman shook her head weakly. "I just feel so hot . . ."

"But your body feels cold. And look at your fingers—they're all wrinkled! Do you have a fever?"

She shook her head and quickly changed the subject. "Would you like some tea or coffee?"

"That can wait. Let's sit down. I want to feast my eyes on you . . ." Her fiancé's eyes studied her from head to toe. "I guess we have a lot of gaps to fill in for these last four years," he added, gently taking her two hands in his.

Her hands suddenly felt frozen. So, she thought bleakly, the trial is about to commence.

"Four years away from each other probably isn't the most ideal way for future newlyweds to live," he began. "We've both had obstacles to deal with, I'm sure, like hills and valleys on a road. But the important thing is to ascertain how low the valleys were and how high the hills have been . . ."

A sweet and diplomatic beginning, the woman thought to herself as she fixed her gaze on her fiancé's face, which seemed ever so much to resemble that of the reincarnation of the Great King Vishnu.

"We both have had ample occasion to run into—and to search for ways around—hazards along the way. Now we have to fill in and smooth over some of the potholes. We have to deal with the realities of the last four years, head-on and honestly . . . What's wrong? Aren't you going to say anything?"

"Well I don't know about the hills and valleys that I've had to pass, but . . ."

"Don't say it, please. I know, you're too good for me. I know that you are pure. It's me . . . I'm the one who can't match your loyalty . . ." Her fiancé paused. His eyes were glassy as he caressed her cheek. "What I mean is that we have to deal with the barriers that have come between us by expressing ourselves honestly . . ."

The woman frowned.

"I'm sure you had no problem in conquering all the hills and valleys during our time apart. But you are a woman and women seem to be more capable of exercising self-control. In a typhoon a woman somehow manages to stay dry. Even after climbing the highest mountain, a woman somehow manages to remain strong."

The woman sat, spellbound.

"But I'm a man . . . and you know what they say: that the die have been cast and men are damned to be less adept than women in coping with the hills, which are not really so high, and those valleys, which are not really as low as they seem. When it comes to dealing with temptations of the flesh, men for some reason don't seem willing to be rational or to keep a level head. We've been spoiled by what is accepted as the man's prerogative. Society grants us complete freedom to give free rein to our desires, without need of having to feel treachery or shame. Maybe I'm a fool but I'm one of those rare men who do feel deceitful and contemptible. I feel so small knowing that you have remained true. I don't know what came over me when I was away from you these last four years. I'll never be able to forgive myself . . ."

The woman focused on the movement of her fiancé's lips. Yet in his eyes lurked the image of King Vishnu beside Queen Sita as she prepared to purify herself in the sea of flames. She suddenly remembered that the queen had never been given the opportunity to question her husband. Supposing that she had asked, "During the time that we were separated, my husband, were you tempted to involve yourself with another woman . . . ?" But, no, that sort of question was not raised. And never would be allowed to be raised. How strange . . .

And now the evening, stooped low, crawled slowly and politely forward.

1988
Translated by Claire Siverson

Laos

M odern literature in Laos emerged from a colonial legacy similar to Cambodia's. At the end of the nineteenth century, Thailand—known then as Siam—was forced to cede Laos to the French. In 1893, France incorporated the area into its Union Indochinoise, already including Cambodia and Vietnam. Laos would remain under French colonial administration until 1954.

Traditional Lao literature, dating from the fourteenth century, reflects a strong Buddhist influence. It is composed largely of poetic works. Creativity in traditional literature was measured by the verbal skill and poetic aesthetics of the storyteller, not by plot development.

Since the French were more preoccupied with Vietnam and to a lesser extent Cambodia, traditional Lao culture did not begin the process of modernization until the 1930s. One major factor in the development of modern literature was the state institutionalization of secular education with a Western-oriented curriculum, which only took place in the late 1940s. The introduction of French literature stimulated an emerging modern literature, developed initially by Lao nobility trained in French schools and writing in French. The development of modern literature in Lao was also delayed by the comparatively slow integration of modern print technology. The first Lao-language newspaper did not appear on a regular basis until the early 1940s.

During World War II a strong nationalist movement gained impetus, leading to full independence for Laos within the French union by 1950. After World War II, Lao language and literature were politically promoted for the construction of a distinct Lao national identity. Over the next twenty years, the country would fall into intermittent civil war. Between Laos's independence from France in 1954 and 1975, modern literature was highly politicized due to civil war. A few monthly magazines, some with literary content, were published during the 1950s. By the mid-1960s, however, short stories were being regularly published in newspapers and literary journals under the supervision of the Lao

Royal Government in Vientiane. By 1965, the Lao Patriotic Front, located in the rural areas, was publishing short stories in their newspaper and in collections. These stories often portrayed heroic revolutionary characters in the style of straightforward reports.

In 1975 the communist Pathet Lao seized power under a one-party system, abolished the monarchy, and brought an end to decades of civil war. The revolutionary-story style became more developed under the new government. Writers were frequently employed as civil servants with the State Printing House, where their duties included translation projects and fiction writing.

Beginning in the late 1980s, the Lao government began a process of openness, following the lead of the former Soviet Union's policy of *glasnost*. In 1991 the Lao Supreme Peoples' Assembly adopted a new constitution that retained a one-party state. For a short period of time, under the state policy of "New Imagination," writers were allowed more freedom to deploy political and cultural criticism through the medium of fiction.

During the late 1990s, the Lao government focused on economic reforms and modernization, although its policy toward literary freedom became more conservative. Writers are now often employed as reporters for government newspapers and magazines, where writing fiction is part of their job description. The themes for modern stories have shifted toward romance and general entertainment as the public demand for popular fiction has grown. The stories in this section are examples of serious short fiction by two contemporary Lao writers.

Outhine Bounyavong
"Death Price"

Outhine Bounyavong, born in 1942, currently resides in Vientiane. A prominent contemporary writer in Laos, he has authored four collections of short stories while working as a journalist, editor, and translator. During the 1990s, he served in the Ministry of Information and Culture, with responsibility for contemporary literature and children's books.

"Death Price" reflects a snapshot-style of experiential realism. It deals with a number of themes that are recurrent in Outhine's fiction, which is often concerned with contemporary Lao culture, village mores, and the complexities of fate. Another satirical critique of bureaucratic indifference is found in the anonymous "Just a Human Being" (Cambodia). The subject of patron-client relationships and the abusiveness of such a system is also taken up in Atsiri Thammachoti's "And the Grass Is Trampled" (Thailand) and Yur Karavuth's "A Khmer Policeman's Story" (Cambodia).

Everybody said they hated the way he stood. Thanks to his certificate from the elementary school exam, which he barely passed, he became a corporal as soon as he enlisted in the army. And thanks to his ability to "sweet-talk" and be a good lackey, he rose rapidly to the rank of lieutenant. In fact, he had been promoted so recently to his new grade that he looked dreadfully unfit to wear brass on his epaulettes.

He was in charge of the Army Transport Division, a service provided to transport military officials and their families from Viengchan to other provinces within the country. The passengers knew him only by the name of Mister The Lieutenant.

He was standing there, right at the bottom of the steps of the air-

"Death Price," by Outhine Bounyavong, published in *Mother's Beloved: Stories from Laos* (Seattle: University of Washington Press, 1999). Reprinted by permission of University of Washington Press.

plane, calling out names from the passenger manifest with authority and grandeur as if he were the mightiest of the mighty. All eyes were focused anxiously on him, all afraid that their names might be forgotten.

Thongsy was one of many passengers waiting to board the plane. Two of her children hung in her arms, one on each side, and the third clung to her waist. She was married to an army officer who was posted in Muong Sui.[1] She had tried many times to get passes to visit her husband and each time her name had been bypassed.

Once again, she began waiting at daybreak to board the plane. Earlier, Mister The Lieutenant had taken her name and told her to be patient for a while. She waited to be called for the first flight, but that did not happen. Instead, Mister The Lieutenant announced: "The plane is full. You'll have to wait for the second flight at twelve o'clock."

So she waited a little longer at the airport, and went without food or water.

Twelve o'clock came. Thongsy saw a car drive up full of cargo, and a woman got out and went straight to Mister The Lieutenant. She was the wife of some high-ranking army officer and was able to do business between the provinces, using the army airplanes to send her merchandise without paying shipping fees.

"The bosses are sending goods to the soldiers, so the plane is quite heavy and no more than ten passengers are allowed. You must wait for the next flight."

The hot May sun radiated down on the cement airfield; seen from afar, it shimmered like hot flames. Thongsy sat under a shade tree by the edge of the airfield facing Luang Prabang Road, holding her six-month-old baby with one hand, while fanning herself slowly with the other. Her other two young children were eating rice wrapped in banana leaves, which she'd bought at the market that morning. The children looked unkempt. Their clothes were old, dirty, and torn. She had borrowed five thousand *kip* from a relative to prepare for this journey. But the fruitless trips to the airport and the money spent to buy food for each day of waiting had cost her a good deal. Now she had only two thousand *kip* left. She was trying as best she could to be frugal.

She was thinking of selling her ring so she could bribe Mister The Lieutenant to let her onto the airplane, but because the ring was the last bit of wealth she'd inherited from her parents, she hesitated. She

---

1. Muong Sui, near the Plain of Jars, is a former base of the Royalist army.

decided to continue waiting, hoping she'd be able to leave any day now. A lot of other people were waiting, too, most of them, like herself, the wives of low-ranking army officers. They knew that, in order to depart promptly, it was necessary to bribe Mister The Lieutenant. But since they didn't have enough money, they waited patiently for their luck to change, even though the situation seemed hopeless.

It was widely known that Mister The Lieutenant took bribes from the passengers. He was certainly friendlier when greeting the merchants. He'd been posted to the airport about six months ago, and he already had a big motorcycle that he liked to show off by veering left and right on the road. He smoked the most expensive cigarettes, ate out at restaurants, and got drunk almost every night.

The third flight of the day was canceled because of engine trouble. All travel plans had to be postponed till tomorrow. Disappointed, Thongsy returned home once again.

The next day, Thongsy entered the office of Mister The Lieutenant and begged for his compassion. She asked if he could please put her on the plane as a special favor, then she pulled out five hundred *kip* and offered it to Mister The Lieutenant. He refused the money and told Thongsy that he would do his best for her. No doubt, the amount offered was "peanuts," and simply not worth his trouble.

At eight o'clock that morning, Thongsy and her children were the last passengers boarding the plane. She was overjoyed that she was finally going to see her husband. All the passengers were in their seats. They were just waiting for the pilot. At that moment, Thongsy saw a jeep drive up and stop next to the plane. Three men got out and went to speak to Mister The Lieutenant. The three men looked as if they were big shots of some kind, and one of them greeted Mister The Lieutenant casually: "Hi, mate! How are things?"

A long discussion followed. Then Mister The Lieutenant boarded the plane, removed Thongsy, her children, and another unlucky passenger, and replaced them with those three men.

"You have too many children. You must wait for the next flight. The bosses have important business to attend to," Mister The Lieutenant explained briefly, in a matter-of-fact way.

That day, Thongsy waited until late afternoon, and she noticed that the plane had not returned. Maybe it would never return.

She was furious with Mister The Lieutenant for the way he had treated her. But her anger suddenly dissipated when she heard that the plane she'd hoped to take to Muong Sui had had engine trouble. It had crashed and exploded in the middle of a jungle.

She felt so sorry for all the passengers meeting their death in such an unfortunate way. But she was also thankful that Mister The Lieutenant had taken her children and herself off the death list.

After this accident, Mister The Lieutenant was roundly criticized and later court-martialed because many of the people who had died were not on the manifest. Thongsy and her children had been spared despite the fact that their names were on the list. She knew then that five hundred *kip* could not buy death.

1972

Bunthanaung Somsaiphon

"A Bar at the Edge of a Cemetery"

Bunthanaung Somsaiphon was born in 1953 in Champasak in Southern Laos. Since the mid-1970s, he has been a prolific writer of stories, poetry, and songs and has played an active role as both editor and contributor to various Lao literary magazines. His writings are highly regarded as outspoken, insightful accounts of contemporary Lao society. He represents the post-1975 new generation of Lao writers.

"A Bar at the Edge of a Cemetery" reflects the hard economic reality of postwar Laos. The residual effects of the Indochinese War years on the peoples and economies of Laos, Vietnam, and Cambodia are the subject of many writers from these countries. The lingering impact of war on human relationships is an underlying theme in Vo Phien's "Unsettled" (Vietnam) and Mey Son Sotheary's "My Sister" (Cambodia). Life at the bottom of the socioeconomic hierarchy is also a concern in Khai Hung's "You Must Live" (Vietnam).

"A Bar at the Edge of a Cemetery," by Bunthanaung Somsaiphon. Permission to publish granted by the translator, Peter Koret, with the author's consent.

I poured the bottle of beer into my glass, lifted it, and drank slowly. I gazed at the crosses in the cemetery, which were scattered in front of me, illuminated by the light of the full moon. Dark shadows were cast from rows of aging pine trees standing along the fences that surrounded the cemetery on all four sides. Their blackness contrasted with the overall whiteness of the cemetery and the chalky color of its plastered walls. Although the warmer dry season had recently arrived, the area around the cemetery remained cold as a result of the wind that swept across the fields and forest beyond.

It was not the first time I had stopped to drink beer. The open-air whiskey shop where I sat consisted of two tables for customers, and a third table that was used to store bottles of beer, whiskey, and a glass container filled with cartons of cigarettes. An oil lantern hung from the wall, its light competing with that of the moon and stars. The back wall that ran between the bar and the cemetery was no different than the white cloth that a traveling Mau Lam musical performer would use for the backdrop to his stage, so that people driving by could see the performers only from the front side.

The back of this particular stage was filled with graves and crosses, cold and quiet. The pale yellow light cast a wide enough circle of radiance to allow the drunks, who sat around both of the tables, to see the plates of food that were eaten with the whiskey. I sat on a bench at the table that was used for selling merchandise. I was not obliged, therefore, to get involved with anyone else and could simply play the role of an observer. A middle-aged woman, older than myself, walked back and forth between the table reserved for the store's merchandise and a stove used to grill cattle tendons and innards. They were sold for fifty *kip* per skewer. The teenage daughter of the middle-aged woman had powdered her face so that it appeared white and soft. Observing only her face, it would be impossible to tell that her skin was coarse and as dark as a cup of coffee with cream.

The young woman worked as a waitress. She both poured beer and drank with the customers. When the middle-aged woman had a free moment, she came to sit down in a chair in front of mine.

"When you're in the neighborhood, please stop by and give us your business. Our shop has been open for less than month, and we still don't have many regular customers."

"Where did you set up your store in the past?"

"Nowhere. All we did was farm. Our fields are behind this cemetery. For a long time we did not sell whiskey or cigarettes because we thought there were plenty of shops selling similar goods. We couldn't compete with the others. We are poor, and my daughter is not as pretty as the other girls are. After there was a big roundup and arrest of prostitutes last month and most of the bars were shut down, we saw our opportunity."

"Aren't you afraid that the officials are going to shut down the bars again?"

"Why should I be afraid? We sell whiskey, not women."

"I've heard that many of the stores that were closed did not sell women. It was only that they refused to give free whiskey to government officials out of uniform. That in itself can be a problem."

"Well, if we don't do it, we'll starve to death. Whatever you do, you take a chance."

Our conversation ended in silence. The only sound that remained was music from a tape recorder with a single speaker and the continuous back and forth arguing of the drunks.

"Would you like another beer?" the woman asked.

"Sounds like a good idea."

The woman stood up, took out a bottle of beer that was chilled in ice in a bucket, and returned to sit down as before.

"God, am I tired. There is not a day when I'm not drunk. I don't want to drink but the customers force me. I have to please them. I want their money."

I poured beer into a glass and handed it to the pitiable middle-aged woman.

"Expenses are high," she said, "wages are low. I don't make as much as I have to pay out. As for you younger people, you have no problems. You are government workers and bosses. You have money left over to save."

"Government workers," I responded, "now they are the problem-makers. Their salary is less than a child makes selling grilled bananas at the side of the road. Some work for three months and still smell not a scent or cent of their salary. Their work is inefficient. They have no respect for discipline. Orders from their bosses have no meaning to them. Shameless corruption is rampant throughout government circles."

"There is truth in what you say. Look at my daughter. After graduating from a teacher's college, she taught nursery children. After several years of work, she could not afford even a single pretty silk dress. I couldn't bear to watch any longer, so I had her resign to sell whiskey.

It is better for her to do up her face than work like that when her salary couldn't even pay for half a sack of rice."

"How much land do you own?"

"Only four or five hectares. But it's fortunate that we can farm during the rice season and also with the help of irrigation."

"Is it your own private field?"

"No, it's owned by the state. In the past, nobody was interested in the land around here because it's next to the cemetery. Our family was the first to move in and build a house here. At the time, my husband had a small cart that carried merchandise in the market. As the number of our children grew, however, such work was not enough to make ends meet. We had to rent our house and buy our rice. My husband decided to move out here to the outskirts of the town to make a living."

"You must have been much better off after you moved."

"What do you mean, better off? Government officials have come here on many occasions to tell us to leave and make our living elsewhere. Where will they have us go? The officials have said that they have plans to expand the cemetery. However, that is not the truth. We have seen them come and stake claim to every inch of land around here and start their own gardens and rice fields. The more difficult the times become, the more people lack kindness and compassion. The greater a man's power and destiny, the more heartless he becomes to other people. I am honestly worried for the dead that sleep peacefully in the cemetery. It won't be long before they will have to pay rent on their plots."

What the old woman said was, in fact, the truth. No longer was true peace and tranquility to be found inside of the cemetery, as people have believed for ages.

I did not hurry to drink my beer. The middle-aged woman stood up, brought snacks over to another table, and sat with the people there. The faces of the drinkers were as slimy as the faces of grilled pigs and their eyes as blurred as pig's eyes scalded with hot water. What a task, to lift up such heavy tongues and carry on continuously about such pointless topics. Most of their conversation was centered on the struggle for money, family conflicts, and the various obstacles presented by the environment that invariably thwarted personal happiness. The table where the young woman drank had a livelier atmosphere with flirtation and humor concerning what goes on under the mosquito net and inside of women's dresses. Such humor was followed by the thunderous laughter of people who showed not the slightest fear or deference to any ghosts. Some of the drunks stumbled off to vomit in dark shadows before they laid themselves out on their rickshaw, their life companion. Some people sprawled themselves out on the tables. Those who remained functional continued in the struggle with ears that buzzed, eyes that blurred, and mouths that no longer made human-like sounds.

"Pour another round of whiskey, young woman. My liver is dry." A drunk with a *lao* flower in his hair started to speak, causing an eruption of laughter among his friends.

"Old man with the head of a snake, do you still want to eat turtle eggs?" the middle-aged woman scolded.[1]

The commotion and laughter suddenly fell silent. The old man with the *lao* flowers in his hair spoke up to defend himself: "Happiness . . . just a little happiness . . . We are all human beings. All of us are the same. Couldn't you share, if just a little bit? Is what I am saying not true, young girl?"

"What are you saying? Is it just a little happiness then, to deceive a young child so that you can deflower her?"

The middle-aged woman stood up and showed signs that she was taking offense at the man's words.

"Who said that I was deceptive? I asked her in a polite and straightforward manner."

"This type of merchandise is expensive. How can you ask for it free?"

Another drunk interrupted, saying: "We can't find one to borrow. If we wish to buy one, it's not available. What else can we do but ask for it free?"

The man's supporters let out a great laugh.

"Everyone keeps one at home so that they can eat it for a long time. And yet you're still not full." The middle-aged woman continued, reluctant to sit down.

"The one you're talking about is already dead. We've eaten it so much that we're bored. We want to try something new."

The young woman showed no signs of being upset. She continued to pour their whiskey and listen to them speak. When she had the opportunity, however, she turned in my direction.

---

1. A "snake-headed man" refers to an old man with a propensity for women of a much younger age. The conversation is filled with sexual imagery. "Turtle eggs" refers to a young virgin.

"What? Is he your husband?"

"No. I have only come here to sit and drink beer," I excused myself.

"Really? Is that the case?" The man with the *lao* flower in his hair was suspicious.

"Don't take offense at words spoken by people who drink whiskey. They are said in jest. Sometimes they are a little bit filthy." The drunk who was less drunk than all of the other drunks attempted to speak with formality and politeness.

"Relax," I said with sincerity in my voice. "Don't feel uncomfortable."

From that moment onwards, I could feel that the surroundings had suddenly become silent. Some of the drunks invited their friends to leave. I felt uncomfortable that I had brought about this change in atmosphere, and had ruined the slight happiness of others. I especially felt badly because I had observed from the very beginning that these three drunks were in fact nothing more than corpses that could breathe. They were leftover bones and fragments of skin who hadn't the slightest interest or concern about the problems that encompassed their lives, but whose only agitation lay in whether or not the whiskey had evaporated from their glasses.

Or could it be said that true tranquility was contained in each bottle of whiskey?

I lifted my glass and drank the beer slowly.

The full moon spread its soft white light, bathing the tops of the pine trees and the cheeks of the young woman who sat in front of me. The woman's hazy black hair was tied in a rose-colored bow shaped like rabbit's ears; her bushy eyebrows, her face, and deep dark eyes spoke of her innocence. There was so much she still had to learn from life, which is as confusing and convoluted as a tornado.

"Did your wife run away with her lover? Is that why you're sitting sad and lonely, putting on such a long face?"

"No," I replied. "It's the young woman who sells whiskey that runs away."

"But I am still here."

"I'm afraid that you will also leave."

As the young woman poured beer into my glass, I noticed a suggestive glance from her that was aimed in my direction.

I allowed the country music from the tape recorder to interrupt our conversation for a moment, then spoke to her directly: "Do you realize that you have made the other people afraid of me?"

"Well then, that's good. It'll make them hurry home to their wives and kids."

"But I have no wish for people to misunderstand me. I am not a fly that travels around collecting news of other people, reporting to the powerful in the hope of collecting a reward. And what is truly important, I have no wish for this land to have any more cowards than it already has."

The young woman sat quietly and listened to all that I said. I did not know how much she actually understood. It is a pity that I could not explain any more than I already had. She may even think that I myself am just another coward.

"Let's talk about other things," I changed the topic.

"Will you have another beer?"

She stood up and left the table. I glanced at her well-rounded hips, which she moved gracefully as she walked, creating in me a feeling of desire. Her skin, however, was coarse and black, and her body rather stout and muscular. She was not well proportioned.

"Mother, the beer is all finished. I'll have this man take me home to get some more."

Before the middle-aged woman gave a response, the young woman nodded her head as a sign that I should follow her out of the bar.

At the edge of the northern wall there was a gravel path that traveled deep inside the village. Along the way, at regular intervals, pine trees threw shadows on the ground. It was the night of a full moon and an orchestra of crickets resounded throughout the forest.

"Are you afraid of ghosts?" she whispered.

"There is plenty more to fear than ghosts," I replied.

There were many places behind the cemetery where the wall was dilapidated and fallen down. We could see white gravestones spread thickly throughout the cemetery. Crosses were scattered helter-skelter, giving the graveyard the appearance of a rice field that had only recently been pummeled and pounded by the fury of a storm.

The atmosphere inside of the cemetery was colder than that of the surrounding area. I never would have imagined that this young woman would have invited me here to sit and watch the full moon. The graveyard was spotlessly clean as if it were swept several times each day.

"What do you think is more frightening than the ghosts that sleep in this cemetery?" the young woman asked.

I sincerely did not wish to answer this kind of question.

"Dead people that breathe are more frightening than ghosts."

She turned her head and stared at me. The same suggestive hint shone from her deep black eyes with their thick eyebrows.

I answered her question: "The type of person who remains indifferent and merely lives his life day to day, lacking in commitment and concern. In all that he does, his sole motivation is survival. Never will this type of person make a choice between good or bad, right or wrong. He merely clings to rank, status, and power, bags of money, and the handle of a gun. He is no different than a parasite, living off rotten decomposing matter, and destroying all that is decent in the human body."

I turned to look at the young woman. I wanted to know if she was interested in what I had to say. She was lying down happily, watching the light of the full moon. One might say that she was giving up her body to be caressed by the light of the moon.

"Have I spoken too much?"

"We don't have much time," she whispered.

"Get up. I don't have any money to give you."

"What do you mean? I'll have you know that I am not a girl who sells herself."

"Let's go then. I'm so drunk that I can't lift up my own head."

We returned to the bar with four bottles of beer.

The young woman did not come near my table again. I poured my own beer, filling my glass with most of the bottle. I lifted it and drank slowly, gazing out at the crosses in the cemetery that was spread out before me. I drank from my beer, feeling nothing at all.

1990s

Translated by Peter Koret

Malaysia

British involvement led to the development of modern Malaysian literature. The Malay Peninsula has been an important trade region for over a thousand years. British trade in the peninsula intensified with the founding of Penang in 1786. Within forty years colonial influence had extended to the island of Singapore and the city of Malacca, which were grouped together in 1826 to become the Straits Settlements. In the 1880s Britain formally established protectorates in the area, and by the 1920s the entire peninsula was under British rule. Malaya finally gained its independence in 1957.

Traditional written literature was court centered, focusing on records of the mythical origins of the ruler, genealogies, and epics, whereas literature among the subjects was largely oral. With colonization, English education became a vehicle for economic success. The first modern writers to produce short stories about the area were British.

During the 1920s, Malay writers formed a didactic definition for the short story—the *cerita Pendek,* or *cerpen.* These early short-story writers, influenced by a pre-British, didactic, oral tradition of Malay storytelling, created moralistic plots with stereotypical characters to incite Malays toward self-improvement and a national identity.

During the 1930s, printing presses became available. Issues of family life and problems of racial intermarriage found their way into Malay short stories published in newspapers. Some Malay writers presented the town as a place of ruin and moral degradation since the basis of Malay culture was considered to be rural. The correct use of Malay language, felt to have fallen into neglect under the British, became an important issue for modern Malay fiction writers.

With the advent of World War II and the Japanese occupation (1942–45), short-story output declined due to strict Japanese censorship. Nevertheless, writers during this period formed the basis of the new experimental writing that would emerge after 1945. Social justice and the fate of the Malay peasantry continued to be important subjects of fiction after the Japanese occupation had ended.

To quell nationalist opposition to its control after World War II, Britain established the semiautonomous Federation of Malaya in 1948. This led to a declaration of emergency when resistance erupted. As opposition to the Malayan union increased, heroes in Malay short stories were portrayed as patriots ready to sacrifice personal happiness for the nation. Leading writers of the 1950s and many members of the socially engaged Angkatan Sasterawan 50 (the Literary Generation of 1950), whose slogan was "art for the people," infused modernist themes and Western social critique into their fiction, while other writers continued to write didactic fiction.

Newspapers and literary journals, which flourished after Malaya achieved complete independence in 1957, provided a venue for short stories. Prior to 1957, stories written by Malayans in Malay, Chinese, and Tamil had rarely been read outside their specific language communities. In 1959, the Malayan Parliament reconstituted the Language and Literary Agency (Dewan Bahasa dan Pustaka) and enjoined it to promote literary talent and enrichment of the Malay language.

A national debate over what constitutes Malay literature gained momentum in the early 1960s. Along with the rise of "the nation" arose the question of how to establish a national literature and a national language for an ethnically and linguistically diverse country. During the 1960s, Malaysian writers in English emerged while short-story writers in Malay began to revitalize Malay literature. Some constructed an idealized vision of a communal, rural village society while other Malay writers sought to achieve a more innovative and thematically diverse fiction.

In 1963 Malaysia came into existence as a federation of Malaya, Singapore, Sabah (North Borneo), and Sarawak. Singapore withdrew from this federation in 1965, leaving an East and a West Malaysia. The Malay center of culture shifted from Singapore to the new national capital of Kuala Lumpur. Although English continued to be the language of education and administration after independence, Bahasa Malaysia was adopted as the national language after the 13 May 1969 ethnic riots. In 1971, the Malaysian Parliament prohibited any further discussion or debate about "national language." Today, a more multiethnic audience reads Malay.

During the 1970s, as the debate continued over what constitutes a national literature, a number of Malay short-story writers returned to Islamic ethics to shape their social vision while others experimented with psychological realism. Governmental funds were used to develop Malay literature and culture in the "art for society" mode as the basis of a "national" culture. With more women writers emerging during the 1970s, women's issues became increasingly popular. During the 1980s, many fiction writers shifted to global issues and the world of urban Malay intellectuals as they continued to develop protagonists with greater psychological depth.

Throughout the 1990s, Malaysian writers in English presented a fragmented view of Malaysian culture, undercutting the government's advocacy of modernization. Economic transformation has occurred along with more social divisions, changing gender relations, and the rise of a new Muslim fundamentalism. Current themes include upper-class corruption, mendacity, and "transgressive" sexuality. Writers in Bahasa Malaysia continue to develop a more experimental psychological realism that remains socially engaged. The short stories in this section represent the diversity of contemporary fiction on Malaysia by Southeast Asian writers.

K. S. Maniam

"The Kling-Kling Woman"

K. S. Maniam, born in Bedong, Kedah, in 1942, was educated in both Tamil and English. A playwright, novelist, and short-story writer, he has won a number of literary awards. He is currently at work on his third novel, Delayed Passage. *In the literary history of modern Malaysia, he represents a group of creative writers in English who emerged out of the 1960s.*

In "The Kling-Kling Woman" we are transported into the British colonial past, when immigrant labor from China, India, and other parts of Southeast Asia was imported as "more controllable" than the indigenous Malay. Here the exploitation of manual laborers on the railroad and the sexual objectification of women are portrayed through the experience of an Indian woman worker. Another glimpse into the Malay colonial past, but through a Chinese lens, is found in Suchen Christine Lim's "Two Brothers" (Malaysia). Recapturing the past through the eyes of indigenous writers is an important theme in modern Southeast Asian fiction.

Modern Malay literature has been criticized for its representation of weak female protagonists. The heroine of Maniam's story, however, is a powerful woman who paradoxically takes control of her own destiny within the confines of tradition. Female protagonists in modern Southeast Asian fiction are often portrayed as being in a weakened position because of a traditional double standard—for example, in Ma Sandar's "An Umbrella" (Burma) and in Marianne Villanueva's "The Mayor of the Roses" (the Philippines).

It was that evening, when sitting on the steps looking out towards the laterite road and then looking at her mother's face, that she made the pact with herself. She would never be like her mother! She would never wear the *pottu* dot on her forehead. She wouldn't sit in that dumb way,

---

waiting for *her* husband to come back; sit there hoping he would come back to her, and finally praying he would come back to the family. She wouldn't get up in the small hours of the night to let in a drunk, unfamiliar man whom custom had dictated she accept as her husband. She would refuse to pretend she wasn't starving in order to keep her husband's name clean in the eyes of society. She wouldn't wait, like a slave, for any handouts he might make towards the household expenses. Instead, for the rest of her life, she would follow her mother about, working or resting, to taunt her away from subservience.

Sumathi looked at her mother's face as if to store in her mind all that it stood for. She didn't know why, but she saw that it was beginning to resemble her great-grandmother's face she had been shown in a faded sepia photograph. The eyes were beginning to darken and become unfathomable, eyes that had turned away from the light of the world. Her mother had taken the velvet-lined box that she always kept at the family shrine and showed Sumathi, as she would a holy object, the silver anklet with its pair of bells. Then, for the thousandth time, she told Sumathi some of the stories that were lodged deep in her memories about great-grandmother.

Remembering the stories her mother and others had told about her great-grandmother, Sumathi found herself bringing a new, critical awareness to the recollection. The most popular story was called "The Kling-Kling Woman." They had even turned it into a kind of play. When relatives, far and near, met at Sumathi's grandmother's house on the outskirts of the town, about thirty kilometers from Kuala Lumpur, they played this silly game. Some of the older girls put on anklets with bells and ran about noisily, pursued by those young male relatives who would be reaching or had already reached marriageable age. This part of her great-grandmother's life had become a ritual for matchmaking eligible young girls and men among the relatives.

Her great-grandmother was one of those rare young women who, country-born and country-raised, suddenly realized that there was more to life than following the time-honored tradition of being given in marriage to some young man, bearing children, serving her lord and master, bringing up her children, worrying about sickness and death, and receiving in return for the fulfillment of her last days on earth, the tidings of the marriages of her grandsons and granddaughters.

She wanted to and did break out. (The storyteller never mentioned how she got to this new country, but the next thing Sumathi knew was that her great-grandmother was already a railroad worker here.) Her descendants were awestruck by the magical leap from one station to another. "An ordinary house girl become a railroad builder? How many of you could have done that?" they asked.

From the time she arrived in this country and until she died, she was never spared this admiration. A comely and full-bosomed young woman, she had, from the beginning, refused to discard the sari for a more protective and practical garment.

"The sari is good for anything!" she declared. "I wore the sari to the rice fields. It didn't stop me from ploughing and planting! And not one tear anywhere on it!"

"*Amma,* there are all kinds of tearing," her dumpily dressed companions said, giggling and sniggering.

She had a mile-long stubborn streak; she went her graceful, provocative way, carrying loads of granite stones to the gangs of men who laid the sleepers. In all that dazzling heat, white dust clouds and flash of metal, she was a soft, desirable dream, and the men often paused in their work to gaze at her.

"Not yet rest time!" the foreman shouted at them, and they picked up their tools as they would in an elusive, sensual dream.

"You've to look after yourself," the women warned her.

"I was born in a sari!" she sang out.

"Some man will tear it off you!" they said.

They were jealous, she thought, for the men would often offer her a cold drink from the stone bottles they stored in cool places. They were not offended when she didn't accept; they only laughed with pleasure. Even the white supervisor, in khaki shorts and shirt, the pot-like brown hat on his head, extended only to her the flat flask he drank from. She sniffed at the sharp sour smell, and throwing the basket at his feet, stumbled away smiling to herself. He gazed thoughtfully at her broad rump and thin waist, gulping thirstily from the flask.

The workers lived in rows of small, terrace brick houses; lorries picked them up every morning and brought them back in the evenings. Those railway quarters, usually on the fringe of small towns, came to life as the lamps were lit. The men would have gotten together at a toddy shop, if there was one, or at some Chinese sundry shop, where at the back, they could drink cheap *samsu* or some other brew and celebrate their release from work. The younger men loitered at the other shops or on street corners, bought some food and returned to their quarters. The married and single women would be preparing the evening meal, listening to a common, battery-powered valve radio.

Though Sumathi's great-grandmother shared a house with seven other women, she kept to herself and made sure no one trespassed into her corner of the living space. The first chore she did when she returned from work was to wash and spread out her sari to dry. Then she shared the cooking duties with the other women, ate her meal and went to sleep, ignoring the strange, nocturnal rituals of courtship that went on all around her.

Lying in that corner, so the succession of storytellers claimed, she must have entered her dream-self. For what else could have made her not see or hear the things that were going on around her? In that dreamland, she saw what she would be one day. She wouldn't always be working; she would have money in her pouch—she was already embroidering one—and there would be a caring family around her. Her brothers' and sisters' faces appeared briefly in that dreamland, cruel and malicious. She had gone to the rice fields, though women weren't needed there, to show them that she was as good as any of them. But they had always made difficulties for her. Sometimes she couldn't find the plough; sometimes the plough bull would have strayed away though she had tied it by its tether to a tree the previous evening. Once, her brothers had stood in her way and said, "No woman does this kind of work!" and spat on her. Now in this new land, she would make good; she would have a husband she could respect, a house that answered her needs. She would be the woman she was born to be.

She began saving from the time she joined the railroad gang; she stored her meager hoard in some inaccessible fold of her sari. And she kept her distance from the other workers.

The young men kept away from her or made jokes about lonely birds who didn't know about the warmth of a nest. The common compound, with the houses for the married and unmarried built around it, seemed to give them some sense of restraint. The housewives, who swept it in the absence of the workers, brushed it with some sense of law and order. The eldest married man, acting as a moral guide, cast severe glances in the young men's direction.

But as the tracks moved farther and farther away from their usual quarters, their behavior became less predictable. They were housed in makeshift huts, and as the tracks cut through the country, they were taken apart and put up again in the new work sites. Both the married and the unmarried men were somehow getting in her way; she couldn't load her basket without some man watching her from the bushes. She couldn't get to the sleeper site without another brushing past her. The foreman didn't do anything at first; hardly any of the men were absent from his task for a noticeable length of time. Some of the other women too, felt their gaze and their hands.

"I didn't see you coming," one man said, when a woman accused him of molesting her.

"Don't you have ears?"

"In all this noise?"

They were laying tracks far away from any town or other habitation, the unpredictable jungle all around them. The women had heard many, many stories about the dangers that lurked there. They had heard about all kinds of snakes: one-bite poisonous ones, the sharp-fanged slow killer, and the body-crushing monsters. But they kept their minds on their work, and when they went into the bushes to relieve themselves, they went in pairs or even in groups. They kept their eyes peeled for tigers. The tiger, for them, was the most fearsome of the animals that roamed the jungle.

"Can you see your limbs being torn apart?" they asked. "Like a *rakshasa* tearing you to pieces!"

They gave the tiger all kinds of power. It was the silent watcher, a benevolent protector, and an arbiter of justice.

"You don't molest it, it won't molest you," the women said, almost like a prayer.

Some of the women went hunting for a pestle-like stone and planted it at the foot of a tree. They wrapped a piece of red cloth around it, made three white strokes across the rounded head and placed a yellow-and-red dot on the middle line. They prayed at this simple shrine before and after work. The more pious among them struck their heads before it, saying, "Shiva! Shiva! Protect us from all harm!"

Sumathi's great-grandmother, wrapping the sari more tightly around her body, knelt before the stone Shiva and mumbled a private prayer. No one knew what boon she wanted from the gods, but she went about her work with renewed confidence. Her self-assurance only provoked more taunts and not-so-subtle assaults upon her person. The men stood in her way; they sat on the mound of stones beside the sleepers so she couldn't empty her basket. She could never bring herself to plead with them. She waited patiently, silently, for the man to stop making lewd remarks at her and move away. The other women were also taunted and abused but not so persistently.

"It's the sari. Wear something else," her fellow workers said.

"I'll wear what I want," she replied.

The men became more demanding, more hard hearted. They sent this or that woman for their bottles of sun-warmed coffee or containers of water.

"Just up the track," the man said. "I'm fixing this steel thing."

Some woman went to do his bidding, grudgingly.

Then they sat outside their huts, in the evenings, and grumbled among themselves. The men went to the nearest one-street town to drink some brew.

"A slave's slave!"

"They'll come back drunk," one woman said, "and the peace will go."

"Something must be done."

"We must tell the foreman," Sumathi's great-grandmother said.

The other women laughed.

"He's looking for a poultice," one of the women said, "for the swelling between his legs!"

The women laughed again, but bitterly.

"We must go to someone higher then," Sumathi's great-grandmother said.

The women went back to their grumbling.

"I can't go to the bushes," one young woman said, "some man is always behind me."

"I've seen bushes shaking," another said. "Winds don't shake them like that!"

"We must do something," Sumathi's great-grandmother said. "We can't keep back our water forever."

"You tell us what to do."

"We must keep together as a group," she said, "in spirit."

"She's a thinker, I tell you. But where to get the spirit?"

"Why make fun of yourselves? So others can make fun of you? Get their fun from you?"

The women fell silent, staring into the frightening darkness around them. They hadn't heard her speak so strongly before. The kerosene lamplight seemed to fall on her for the first time, and they saw a face bright with thought.

"Bells," she said. "We need bells. Small ones. On our ankles. There are temple bells to call people to prayer. We'll have ankle bells!"

"Ankle bells! Ankle bells!"

"So we can hear ourselves," she said. "So they can hear us. Move out of our way."

"So we can hear where we're going."

"To the bushes."

"To the stone heap."

"To the foreman!"

"To the white man!" she said. "If the foreman won't listen, the white man will."

They heard the men coming back, drunk and noisy; they put out their lights and went to sleep.

"Bells? Anklets?" the foreman said.

"Don't you see? The men are not working like before," Sumathi's great-grandmother said.

"When they're out here too long," the foreman said, "their minds go wild."

"The women will go out of their minds because of them," she said. "We must wear anklets. You won't let us? Take us to the white man!"

"Bells? Anklets?" the white man said, his face reddened by the sun and drink. "Jolly good idea! Something to hear them by! No more mutes in the midday sun!"

"We can go now," the foreman said. "The *tuan* has agreed."

"Belling the cat!" the white man said, laughing at the retreating sensuous hips.

The work went on smoothly after the women began wearing the anklets. Their sounds mingled with the breaking of stones and the hammering of metal into place.

"Kling-Kling!"

The men moved out of their way.

"Kling-Kling-Kling!"

The women stood guard over their sisters who had gone to the bushes.

"Kling-Kling-Kling-Kling!"

The women came to the aid of a sister about to be molested by a man.

"Sisters in belldom!" the white man said approvingly, from a distance.

The track kling-klinged its way through the country. The workers forged past *kampungs* and small towns, hills and valleys, slopes and scrubland. Where they cut into mountain sides, the land stood exposed, inviting cries of excitement and wonder. Where they dug into the earth to lay the foundations for the rails, black, brown or red soil covered the men's and women's feet and hands and, sometimes, their faces. Sumathi's great-grandmother felt, as the tracks opened up the country and connected the various towns and ports, that she, too, was part of a great and awesome design.

As more of the Shiva stones sprang up under the trees, the more the women saw themselves drawn into the land. A different mood came over the men; the inescapable jingling of the ankle bells drove them into sensual fantasies and frenzies. They stopped moving out of the way of the bells.

"Kling-Kling!" the men mimicked, the words becoming licks that caressed.

"Kling-Kling," another said, reaching out and fingering the bells as he would the intimate parts of the woman's body.

"Kling-Kling-Kling!" he said, rattling the bells, as the other women came to huddle around their sister.

The foreman strode up with his rattan stick; he waved it with the authority he thought he had gained from the white man.

"Have you all become children?" he shouted. "Get back to work!"

"We must stop work," Sumathi's great-grandmother said when the women gathered outside the huts in the evenings.

"Children! Children!" the foreman shouted sarcastically when the women put down their baskets in their on-the-spot strikes. "Get back to work!"

The bells that were meant to protect led the men to the women. Now and then shrieks were heard from the bushes and a man would come out buttoning up his shorts.

"Went there first," he said. "She followed me."

"Why can't she go farther inside?" another said. "Wants to show her backside to the whole world!"

The foreman's silence gained the weight of suppressed laughter; he winked at the men.

The women kept their anklets on. When a sister was assaulted, they made a ring around her and raised a clamor that sounded like a whole temple of bells. Even the men paused in their derision to listen to something that rang deep inside them: the memory of cows grazing on thick grass, sugar-cane harvests and offerings, camphor flames and incense smoke, a child's innocent cry. When they came out of their trance, they were more brutal to the women.

The men betrayed them. When they went into a town, they kept ahead of them. The kling-kling of the anklets seemed an insult to them.

"The klings are here!" a shopkeeper warned. "Klings don't buy! Klings only look!"

The women in their frugal fineries attracted and repelled the townsfolk. They hung together fiercely, their nose-rings and plaited or coiled hair binding them into a unique sisterhood. The townsfolk had never seen such unashamed curiosity. The women trooped through the various shops, testing pots and pans, admiring necklaces and bangles; they flung folds of textiles across their breasts and waists, imagining the blouses and saris that could come from them.

At one time, they found themselves in a Chinese shop and were amazed by the display of antiques and figurines. Sumathi's great-grandmother sat on a throne-like chair and played the queen to her sisters. The proprietor rushed up to her.

"Kling can't sit there!" he said.

He grabbed her by the shoulder and tried to push her away, but she shook him off and returned to her seat.

"I sit where I like!"

Her sisters laughed, but the man advanced menacingly towards her.

"Klings don't know where to sit! Klings don't know where to shit!"

He lunged for her, but she slapped his hands away. Her sisters grew alarmed; they stood in a knot, watching, not knowing what to do. The man's pale face turned a muddy color. He threw himself at her again.

"Come away!" one of the women said. "He looks like a money spider!"

"Spider or snake," Sumathi's great-grandmother said, "I don't care! He can't put his hands on a woman!"

His hands shot again and caught hold of her sari border.

"Kling! Kling!" he said. "No shame! Sitting on other people's chairs. Let's see your shame!"

He tugged brutally at her sari and began to loosen its folds.

"Run! Run!" the woman who had spoken earlier said. "Go and fetch the men!"

A woman ran out of the shop.

The Chinese continued to tug at the sari, muttering, "Kling! Kling!" She resisted him, her face dark with anger and humiliation.

By the time the woman returned with the men, she had somehow got hold of her sandal and was waving it before her, while with the other hand, she held on to her sari. The Chinese continued to pull at the sari until it was a tight band over her breasts.

The men who had followed the woman back swayed on their feet.

"Kling! Kling!" one of them said, suddenly. "There kling-kling; here nothing!"

"Showing this stranger what you won't show us!" another shouted.

"Think you know everything!"

The Chinese gave a final wrench at the sari and then flung the ends in her face.

"Next time don't sit on other people's property!" he said, and turning to the men, "You smell too much of drink. Get out of here!"

Sumathi's great-grandmother, rewrapping the sari around her body, took her time to move away from the chair.

Sumathi thought that the sight of her great-grandmother, her sari down to her waist, had ravished whatever reason was left to the men. Word went down the line to the rest of the workers, the foreman, and even the white man. The kling-kling of the women's anklets roused more than an abusive sense in them. The women were confronted by a mystifying savagery; they were assaulted by looks, words and actions. Now they couldn't go anywhere without brushing against a leering or a mocking man. The foreman wielded his stick with a great show of authority, but he didn't care whether the men obeyed him or not.

Sumathi's great-grandmother jingled her anklets fiercely wherever she went, but she couldn't keep the men out of her sari. Their lascivious remarks crawled into its nooks and folds and stayed there like dirt long after the workers had put down their tools. The women turned resentful gazes on her. A few of them even used the anklets to lure the men into the bushes.

Sumathi's great-grandmother got tired of them all. She withdrew into herself and didn't even come out to talk to the women after work. She went to sleep early and in the mornings prayed long and fervently at the Shiva shrine. She trod carefully at work, hoping not to attract unnecessary attention, but the men never left her alone.

Her silence was soon taken for submission. The men began to

abuse her even more ruthlessly. The few women who still respected her tried to draw her out of her self-absorption.

"We need women like you," they said. "Otherwise the men will walk all over us."

But something seemed to have run down inside her; she merely smiled at them and returned to her brooding.

She had trudged off one midmorning—she had earlier been trailed by the foreman—to find some calm for herself, when she heard someone following her. She stopped and listened; she only heard a slight wind among the trees. When she moved on again, jingling her anklets noisily, she heard someone call out to her.

"Let me take off that sari!"

She lost her mind and began to run, the voice coming at her from various directions. Remembering the incident many years later, she said she wasn't sure if the voice had come from inside her or from some desperate man. All she knew was that she was suddenly inside a deep and singing silence.

She had just sat down on a large, jutting root to recover her breath when she heard some animal at hand. Instead of the tiger of the stories, there stood the white man in the morning shadows, almost camouflaged by his work clothes. He seemed to growl at her in a strange way.

She got up and began to run again, the sari proving to be, for the first time in her life, a handicap; that was the only time she cursed it.

"Stop! Stop! Nobody's going to eat you!" the man shouted, panting after her.

Then she tripped and fell, and he upon her.

What followed was turned into a ritual by generations of her relatives. She ran, the bells jingled; she stopped, the bells fell silent. She heard the man cursing and thrashing through the bushes and plants. Suddenly, she lost all her fear. She stamped her foot, the bells jingled more boisterously, and the man cursed and thrashed about more desperately in the bushes. She remembered his words "belling the cat," but this time he was going to be the cat. She ran about here and there, weaving a bell-trail of seduction; he followed, growling and swearing and panting. At last she got tired of the game; she held herself stiffly behind a huge tree trunk and slipped off the anklet with its bells. She managed to steal back to the shacks, dig up her tin of savings, and tucking the embroidered pouch into her bundle of clothes, she fled past the newly laid and gleaming tracks.

The following day, she found herself in the estate where she would also find her husband. She seemed content to help him run the small sundry shop business; she put the anklets away in a velvet-covered box. When, after her husband's death, she was forced to move out with her children to a shop in a small town, she never let the box out of her sight. She kept it on the small table beside her bed, where she spent her last days telling her stories to whomever wanted to listen to them. Now and then she would mutter, "The klings are coming! The klings are coming!"

When Sumathi went to bed, fully resolved to haunt her mother out of her subservience, she didn't, as she had expected, fall asleep straight away. The memory of the anklet with its bells, stored away in its velvet-lined box, kept coming to her throughout the night. Then towards morning, it seemed to come floating out of its furry hiding place and hang before Sumathi, the silence of the years of suppression bursting into a blood-rich clamor.

1997

Suchen Christine Lim

"Two Brothers"

Suchen Christine Lim was born in Malaysia in 1948 but was sent to a convent in Singapore at age fifteen for an English education. A graduate of the University of Singapore, she describes herself as a Singaporean writer and a third-generation descendant of illiterate Chinese immigrants. In 1993 she was awarded the Singapore Literature Prize for her novel Fistful of Colours. *She currently serves as a curriculum specialist in the Ministry of Education, Singapore.*

"Two Brothers" questions British colonial practices and stereo-

"Two Brothers " extracted from *A Bit of Earth* by Suchen Christine Lim. ISBN 981 232 123 3, © 2001 Times Media Pte. Ltd. Published by Times Books International, an imprint of Times Media Pte. Ltd. E-mail: te@tpl.comsg. Website: http://www.timesone.com.sg/te.

types during the Straits Settlements period, when the British carried out their economic infiltration of the Malay Peninsula through the Chinese entrepreneurial class. It illustrates the power and divisiveness of English-language privilege in a Straits Chinese family caught up in this colonial process. Other Southeast Asian writers, such as K. S. Maniam in "The Kling-Kling Woman" (Malaysia) and Cristina Pantoja Hidalgo in "The Painting" (the Philippines), also feel compelled to reconstruct the past from the perspective of the colonized.

THE HUMBLE ADDRESS OF THE STRAITS CHINESE BRITISH ASSOCIATION, PENANG, S.S., PRESENTED TO HIS MOST GRACIOUS MAJESTY, EDWARD, KING OF GREAT BRITAIN AND IRELAND, DEFENDER OF THE FAITH AND EMPEROR OF INDIA, ON THE OCCASION OF HIS ACCESSION TO THE THRONE OF GREAT BRITAIN AND IRELAND, 1901.

May it please Your Majesty,

We the members of the Chinese community of Penang venture to approach Your Majesty and to offer our humble but earnest and heartfelt congratulations on Your Majesty's accession to the Throne of Great Britain and Ireland.

Many of us have the great fortune to be the subjects of Your Majesty while others have come from far and wide to make a home in this colony. We venture to say that no class or section of the inhabitants of Your Majesty's widespread dominions have greater reason to rejoice on this occasion than we who live under Your Majesty's wise and enlightened rule.

As the representatives of the British subjects of Chinese descent in British Malaya, we rejoice in the opportunity which is now afforded us, of giving expression to the strong feelings of loyalty, devotion and attachment to Your Majesty's throne, as well as gratitude for the security and prosperity we enjoy under the aegis of the British flag.

We pray the God who is Lord of all nations upon the Earth, that He may in His mercy bless Your Majesty's reign, and may your loyal subjects of all races and creeds continue to live in peace and prosperity!

And we, as in duty bound, will ever pray,

Ong Boon Leong, L.L.B. (Cambridge)
President, Straits Chinese British Association

Looking elegant in his formal attire of dark coat and dark gray trousers, Ong Boon Leong waited for the applause to die down before handing over to the governor the slim silver casket with its declaration of loyalty to the newly crowned British monarch. His speech in English had been impeccable, delivered with a distinctly Oxbridge accent, of which he was extremely proud, for none in the colony could speak as well as he.

"But only so among Asians; only among us, Asians," he was usually quick to add in a soft self-deprecating murmur whenever he was praised by a member of the English community. His modesty added to his charm, so he was generally well liked.

The Right Honorable Ong Boon Leong was a man of his time in a world that had been tilting westwards ever since the signing of the Pangkor Treaty at the end of the Perak wars, a quarter of a century ago. He was not only English-educated, but also the first Straits-born Chinese to cut off his queue and have his hair styled like an English gentleman.

Like most boys from wealthy Straits Chinese families, he and his two brothers had been educated by English schoolmasters who were the elite staff of the first English-language school in Southeast Asia, known ironically as the Penang Free School. The young Boon Leong, a keen student with an excellent ear for the nuances of the language of the empire builders, was one of the very few boys in the colony awarded a Queen's scholarship to read law in Cambridge University. While at Cambridge, he stayed with the Reverend Dr. James Graves and his family, and under the tutelage of Dr. Graves, Boon Leong was inducted into the finer aspects of being an English gentleman.

Upon his return from England six years later, he had set up a law firm to help steer his Chinese clients through the maze of English laws and colonial regulations. He soon gained the confidence of the influential Straits Chinese and they chose him to be their leader and spokesman. This brought him to the notice of the governor. He was invited to serve in the colony's Legislative Council and became a well-known figure in public and civic affairs.

"Thank you, gentlemen, thank you! A splendid gift and a most gratifying display of your loyalty!" The governor was effusive in his thanks. The Straits Chinese British Association had paid for the celebrations to mark the accession of Edward VII and had organized a garden party for Penang's leading citizens.

"Thank you for your kind words, Your Excellency," Boon Leong bowed. Then he led his delegation of English-educated lawyers and merchants to the red-carpeted area, gratified that they were to stand next to the representatives of the European community. It shows the world how highly we Straits Chinese are regarded, he thought.

Watching him, Inspector Ian Thomson was reminded of Boon Leong's grandfather. That old Baba was a gentleman, he thought. Never before had he witnessed a grander funeral than the one Baba Wee's family had arranged for him. As the inspector-in-charge, he had rendered invaluable service during that funeral. Well, let's hope the Right Honorable grandson would remember that and find him a suitable position after his retirement from the police force.

The stocky man heaved a sigh as he mopped his shiny brow. Stout and red with too much beer and sun, he was no longer the young and dashing sergeant who had rushed headlong into a riot to save Baba Wee's life twenty years ago. Neither was he the courageous officer who had led his police forces upriver to attack the Malay rebels in Bandong.

Now he longed for ease and comfort, preferring to let the young officers take charge while he busied himself with schemes to increase the size of his retirement fund. Officers in the colonial service were grossly underpaid; once a man was retired from the service, all his years of loyalty to the empire, his citations and decorations would count for nothing. A smart fellow had best look out for himself rather than depend on the big boys who ran the empire from London. A year or two in one of the rich Malay States would add a few more hundred pounds to his miserable pension, he calculated. And he would be able to provide for poor Molly in her twilight years and buy his long-suffering wife a comfortable cottage in Moreton Heath. That would be something to look forward to. He dreaded the empty existence of a retired officer from the colonies. On his last visit home, he had found the London clubs full of lonely gray men living in genteel poverty.

A roll of drums made him return to the festivities on the Padang. The huge lawn was thronged with loyal subjects of all races who had gathered to watch the royal regiments trooping their colors. Amid the gaiety and sunshine, the sudden realization that he was going to miss such pomp and ceremony back home in the gray Midlands clouded his vision and dampened his pride. He blamed it on the heat that he was beginning to find unbearable. He took out a neatly folded handkerchief to soak up the beads of sweat gathering on his forehead.

The sun had dissipated the morning's coolness and the ladies were shielding their faces with their lace parasols. No one was listening to the governor's speech. He glowered at the shoving throng. Every goddamn race under the sun is fidgeting behind the rope, he thought. A good thing we used a thick rope. It wouldn't do to have them jostle round the governor like so many heads of cattle.

"Damn this blasted heat!" he muttered to the young subaltern next to him. "Look at those Asiatics. No idea of orderly behavior. A good thing we got the cordon up. Self-restraint is not in their blood, you know."

He twisted the ends of his mustache and exchanged brief nods with the officials from the Colonial Office and the Federated Malay States who were standing stiffly in the red-carpeted area. Next to them were the colony's European lawyers, bankers, insurers, merchants and representatives of the major European trading houses. No cordon of rope kept this elite group away from the red carpet, and if anyone had asked why, Ian Thomson would have muttered, "Simply wasn't done, don't need to," by way of an explanation if at all. However, since no European would have noticed it anyway and no Asian would have challenged such disparity of treatment, Inspector Ian Thomson was allowed to go on thinking that his cordoning off of the Asians, with the exception of the English-educated Straits Chinese, was entirely natural and in keeping with the scheme of things out in the East. Like thousands of his kind in the colonies, he subscribed to the use of ropes and canes for Asians and believed that these, together with red carpets, guns, drums and gold braids, were the essence of power, vital to maintaining public order in a colonial society.

"Carry a big stick and use it if you have to. The cane is something that all coolies understand."

"That so, sir?"

"Why, Hennings, none of them speaks a known tongue."

"I did pick up a few words of Mandarin before coming out here."

Thomson chortled, "Old chap! Trouble is, these fellows don't speak it. It's mostly gibberish with them."

"Look over there, sir. Who might that be?"

"Why, that's Sir Hugh Low, Resident of the state of Perak. This man single-handedly tamed the Malays."

"Those Malays beside him must be nobles. They're splendid-looking in their rich *baju* and sarong."

"Indeed they are! Look at them now. Wealthy beyond their wildest dreams. Pax Britannia did it."

"I heard that these fellows are going with his excellency to a conference in Kuala Lumpur."

"The poor sods! They wouldn't understand a thing. If not for chaps like Sir Hugh Low, none of these royal buzzards would've known the meaning of conference! Why, they'd still be slitting each other's throats."

"But sir, shouldn't we teach the natives to govern themselves?"

"Good lord, Hennings! What made you say a thing like that? It's contrary to their race and history!"

He stopped when he saw the Honorable Ong Boon Leong coming towards them.

"Good morning, Inspector Thomson."

"Good morning, Mr. Ong. This is Sergeant Hennings."

"Pleased to meet you, Sergeant."

"Any news on the Exchange, sir?"

"The price of tin is showing signs of rising even higher on the London Exchange. It's good news all round, gentlemen. Have a good day."

"Same to you, Mr. Ong."

They watched him walk over to the Straits Chinese delegation of traders and compradors. Like him, they were smartly attired in dark morning coats and silk cravats, looking much like their English counterparts from the Chamber of Commerce.

"Now that's a civilized Western oriental gentleman," Thomson chuckled. His lobster-red face shone like a grotesque mask in the sunshine.

Tuck Heng, squeezed behind the rope cordon amongst the Asian traders, tried to catch the eye of the inspector. Clasping his hands together, he bowed several times. To his great mortification, Thomson did not acknowledge him with so much as a nod.

He was filled with shame. Dressed in the traditional robes of a Chinese mandarin, he had been conscious of his high rank. He had observed the ease with which Boon Leong had greeted the Englishman, as though they were equals. Self-contempt followed by resentment against his brother swept through him. Outwardly he remained a picture of calm and dignity. He glanced at his companions from the White Crane and wondered if any of them had noticed his humiliation. Fool! he berated himself. Only a fool would stoop so low as to bow to a low-ranking red-faced foreign devil such as Thomson! And just so that he could keep up the pretence that he was doing as well if not better than that English-speaking swine! Brothers in name and by adoption, they were like a chicken and a duck, each strutting in his own corner of the farmyard pretending the other did not exist.

He'd snorted before at the sycophancy of the likes of Boon Leong and his Straits Chinese British Association. He'd laughed at their ridiculous foreign attire, but he had also half-wished, especially on public occasions such as this, that he could speak the foreign devil's tongue as fluently as Boon Leong and move among them with ease. He realized with a deep sense of failure that, despite his wealth, he could never speak like a high-ranking English gentleman. His English was that of a foul-mouthed sailor's. A member of the lower classes. The riffraff despised by those of high rank. Boon Leong had told him in a moment of unthinking derision years ago. That barb had remained lodged in his heart to this day.

His ship-chandling business had brought him into constant contact with English seamen and masters of vessels. In due course, he'd acquired a sailor's rough speech. In those days, due to his ignorance of English society and manners, he'd been very proud of his achievement, uttering the seamen's words in a clipped Cantonese accent.

He recalled with agony the day when he, like a vainglorious cockerel, had crowed in his newly acquired tongue in an attempt to impress Boon Leong and his brothers. Oh, how they had choked and doubled up in laughter when they heard his sailor's talk! That was when he realized with intense shame that his speech was of such a low kind, no English gentleman would have uttered it. His shame was all the more heartwounding because he'd always prided himself on being the son of a gentleman and a poet. From that day onwards, he'd studiously avoided Boon Leong and his brothers. "River water shouldn't mix with well water," he told his wife, and they stopped visiting Roseville, Boon Leong's mansion.

That was years before. But his heart had never stopped yearning for recognition as a gentleman and not as the trader and shop proprietor he had become. The mandarin robes, the silk hat with its peacock feather and the jade beads he had donned for this occasion demonstrated the high rank he had attained, unfortunately not by a scholar's learning. Merchant's gold had turned him outwardly into a scholar-mandarin.

The band of the infantry regiment struck up. The governor was making his way through the crowd to receive their gifts and good wishes on behalf of the British monarch. Heart thumping, his excitement and expectation mounting by the minute as his excellency drew nearer, he stood stiffly at attention, eyes fixed on the representative of the British Crown, and waited like hundreds of others in the tropical blaze for his turn to touch the white god's hand.

2000

Shahnon Ahmad
"Delirium"

Shahnon Ahmad, born in 1933, has been involved with the "art for society" movement since the 1960s, continuing the tradition of "engaged writing" that typifies the roots of modern Malaysian literature. He is considered to be one of Malaysia's greatest national writers, signified by his ability to express a Malay sense of place and people with literary innovation. With over thirty novels and six collections of short stories to his credit, he has won a number of distinguished literary awards. For a number of years, he served as Dean of the School of Humanities at the University of Science, Penang. Recently he has been serving as a member of the Malaysian Parliament.

    "Delirium" represents a form of psychological realism that Ahmad and several other writers began experimenting with in the 1970s. It also reflects an approach prominent among Malay writers: establishing an urban-rural dichotomy with rural values privileged over the decadent yet economically seductive pull of the modern city. The psyche of the protagonist in "Delirium" is a theater of contradiction, where the dilemmas posed by conflicting values defy any sense of stable resolution. There is a tone of despair, an existential quality to this dilemma, as the meaning of the individual's existence in a conflicted reality is called into question. A similar resonance of despair is found in Pramoedya Ananta Toer's "The Silent Center of Life's Day" (Indonesia) and Daw Ohn Khin's "An Unanswerable Question" (Burma).

A thousand eyes seem to blink in every curve of my skull. Damn them all! I have told you, over and over again: I am not a slave. I am not a slave. I am not a slave. But those damn eyes keep blinking at me. They demand to know: "Well then, who are you?"

"Delirium" (Tak Keruan) by Shahnon Ahmad was originally published in *Dewan Sastera* (April 1973), then published in an English translation in *The Third Notch and Other Stories* (Kuala Lumpur: Heinemann Educational Books, 1980). Reprinted by permission of the translator, Harry Aveling, with the author's consent.

The sky is full of black clouds.

I think of our village. With its spreading rice fields. The carp catching insects. The water rippling around the brown-stained tops of the weeds. The trees growing dark green to the right and left of our hut. I can hear someone shouting in the distance; the voice rolls against the slopes of Srengenge Mountain and finally disappears. Mother busy with her coconut milk and glutinous rice. The thick bamboo trunks are behind the house. Cut them down, Dad. That's all that's needed. Rub the fine threads off with coconut husk. And in the morning, when the sun rises and the chickens chirp, the children will come rushing out of their houses with their eyes shining. Firecrackers will bang and boom so loudly that the geese and duck will crane their necks to see what is happening.

I rub my eyes.

Just look around you. At that. And this. You have eyes, haven't you? And ears as well? Our brick house is surrounded by other brick houses, tens and thousands of them. And surrounded by squabbling people. And dogs, rubbish tins, cars, bottles, smoke, churches, pubs, sex, demons, devils and death.

The thousand eyes in my skull shine more fiercely. The number changes from one thousand to two thousand, to four thousand, to a million. The eyes fight each other, they run, collide and fall in a struggling mass. A confused, tangled heap.

"Anti-Christ! Damn you! Ha, ha, ha!"

I stamp out the stub of my still-burning cigarette and stare out of the window at a young couple petting on the verandah of the house across the road.

"Anti-Christ! Damn you! Ha, ha!"

"What's wrong?"

I am aware of my wife's lovely face. And her clear eyes. She is peering into my study, waiting for an answer to her question. My oldest child comes. Then another. And another.

"Anything wrong?"

They have bright eyes. I love them all. The million flickering eyes in my skull vanish, replaced by five pairs of beautiful eyes. There is love in their eyes.

There are black clouds in the sky.

"Daddy, where are you taking us today?"

Choking back a sob, I turn away and wipe my eye. The tear falls from my eyelash. Turning back, I try to face those five pairs of bright eyes. I stand up and take my youngest child's hand. We call him "Little Brother." I embrace him.

It might rain.

"Let's just stay home."

The expression in four of those pairs of eyes changes. I'm not exactly sure how it changes, but I know one thing: they don't want to stay home on a day like today. I can tell that much. Little Brother struggles in my arms. Even though I can't see his eyes, I know. He doesn't want to stay locked up like an animal on a day as fine as this one.

But where can we all go? Be serious—look outside. At the tens, hundreds and thousands of brick homes. And we know no one. The color of our skin is different. We are neither white nor black. And the world recognizes no other color these days but those two. Look at the traffic roaring along the highway, screaming past night and day. Satan and death waiting at every intersection.

The million burning eyes reappear inside my skull. They all have trailing, twisting intestines attached, like banshees. Damn them! I've already told them I'm neither a slave nor a king. But who are you if you're neither slave nor king? You and your family, who are you?

"Anti-Christ! Damn! Ha, ha!"

"Anything wrong?"

My wife keeps on asking the same question. The children gathered about the door try to look happy. The child in my arms looks up; his eyes are shining brightly. I look into his clear black pupils and see myself reflected there. Bowing slightly, I kiss his forehead.

Again the million burning eyes in my head vanish. I turn away. The young couple are still kissing, across the road. They are using their hands to arouse each other.

I stand up. My wife and the other children rush towards me. We hug each other and weep, feeling absolutely rootless, neither part of that world nor of this. Not knowing who we are. Divided, with our hearts in one country and our bodies in another.

"All right. Let's go home to our village and celebrate the end of the fasting month with all our relatives."

. . . and the whole family went home.

Oh! What beautiful clothes Mother is wearing! Won't Father feel proud on his way to the mosque? And why shouldn't he? Ah, go and kiss Grandmother's knee. Her knee, I said. Knee. Not her nose. Not her cheek. Ha, ha, ha, ha. Yati, cut the rice cakes. Careful now. The bamboo is very sharp. Aimi, open the *ketupat* cakes. Oh, Uncle. Come on in. What's that? Fine. Drop in after you've prayed. I ask your pardon for all my conscious and unconscious offences towards you, Uncle. Is Aunty still in a state of ritual transition after giving birth? Praise be to Allah. What did you call the child? Why, that's a marvelous name. The same as one of the holy Prophet's companions. Ah! Here come the boys now. Nusi! Get me some ten-cent coins from my purse. Ah. Here's ten cents. Here's ten cents. Here's ten cents. Bow to them, Yati. Now go and get the rice cakes. Feed them until they can't eat any more. Bring two or three different curries. Yes, that's right. Watch out for the fireworks. Don't scorch the sleeve of your blouse. Oh, Little Uncle! Come in! I ask your pardon for all my conscious and unconscious offences towards you, Little Uncle. Where is Aunty? Good gracious, we'll come over this afternoon. Don't bother catching any hens for our sake. Whatever you've got will be fine. Is Dollah married yet? Thanks be to Allah. Who will the lucky parents-in-law be? Excellent. He's a fortunate lad. How many water buffalo will you need? That doesn't matter. How many hens? Mix the meat with banana stem and palm pith, it will all taste like curried beef. That's the best way. Hey! Senior Uncle and Aunt. Gosh, you look like newlyweds! Pardon . . . Pardon . . . Pardon . . . And what's this? Thank you. Father is inside. He's not so well. I doubt he'll be at the mosque this year, Uncle. Mother! Senior Uncle and Aunt are here. They want you to go to the mosque with them. Please . . . Please . . . . Ah! Here come more boys. Bow first. Fine. Here's ten cents. Here's ten cents. Here's ten cents. I ask your pardon . . . I ask your pardon . . . I ask . . .

Suddenly I glance out of the window again. The young couple are writhing in each other's arms. In the distance, I see a cute young woman walking quickly. Her miniskirt is so short that I am forced to concentrate on Allah to avoid the thought of sin. I watch her, step by step, until she is level with my window. I can feel my pulses throbbing.

"Do you want me to rape you?" my heart silently screams at her.

"Yes."

The black clouds hang heavy in the sky.

The million burning eyes in my skull have answered my question at once. The demons and anti-christs return. The corners of my mind shake and tremble. Hard, upright fingers probe in the crevices between the eyes. A misshapen mouth gapes next to them. I can see the tongue hopping about, waving at something. Suddenly the crooked mouth and the dancing tongue fasten onto the fingers and eat them.

"Yes! She wants to be raped."

. . . I rape her violently. I lift her and carry her running to the church. The naked bowed figure of Jesus Christ smiles at me from His crucifix. I rip the eighteen inches of miniskirt off her. I rip her sleeveless blouse off. I rip her brassiere off. I rip her pants off. I pull her hand and knock her down. Then I fall to the ground. Ah! There it is. The million blinking eyes in my head scream encouragement at me. The noise is incredible. Something turns, twists, and coarsens in the cavities of my head. Clashes. I look up. The naked Jesus on the cross is laughing at me. I scream with delight. And between the screaming and the laughter I can hear the faint sound of many people crying . . .

"Daddy! Daddy!"

I am still hugging and weeping with my family.

"Where can we go to celebrate Hari Raya, Daddy?"

"Anywhere you like."

"Can we go to Lake Birley Griffin to see the yachts?"

"If you want to."

"To Tibbinvilla, to see the kangaroos and kookaburras?"

"Sure."

"Can we go horse-riding at Western Creek, Pop?"

"Anywhere you want. Now go and put your new clothes on."

I kiss them on top of their heads and they go to take their turn in the bathroom, leaving my wife beside me. Her eyes are wet. I gaze into her wet eyes.

"We'll go anywhere they want, as long as the weather is fine."

Without saying a word, she stands looking at me. I can hear the water running in the bathroom. My wife goes to the bedroom. I can hear her opening the wardrobe. I follow her.

"It isn't."

Gazing out, I can see how unsettled the sky is. Large drops of rain are already starting to fall. The weather here is frightful. You can never rely on it. It is worst of all early in summer.

"Let them put their new clothes on." The water is still running. The young couple across the street have gone inside, probably to bed. The wind is beginning to howl and breaks into an occasional shriek. I grab a piece of paper and the pen next to it and write: "Slave."

The wind howls and sighs. The rain falls in drops. My eyes follow a piece of newspaper which has suddenly appeared from somewhere or other. It soars into the air, opens, and slams into the fence of the cuddling couple. The wind blows again and the ragged sheet lifts, landing on the side of Mrs. Furlonger's rubbish tin, where it sticks tight.

I turn from the newspaper to the piece of paper in front of me.
"Slave."
That's the title.
We are all slaves. Morning, noon and night, our only task is to suck up to others.
Then I quickly strike the whole lot out. We are not all slaves. Nor do we spend all our time sucking up to others. I cross the sentences out a second time, covering the first lines I drew.
The word "Slave" remains.
Thunder and lightning break through the wind and rain. The sky is pitch black. Rain pours down, beating against the earth. I try to see through the rain, to the torn newspaper lying dead against the side of Mrs. Furlonger's rubbish bin. The paper is soaked. It disintegrates.
I can't hear water running in the bathroom now.
With one stroke, I cross out the word "Slave." Then I write it again. "Slave."
We are all noble slaves. But who decides what is noble?
I run a wavy line through the sentences, for no reason at all.
The word "Slave" remains.
There is a sudden flash of lightning and burst of thunder. A small child screams. Or perhaps it is not a small child. How could Mrs. Furlonger let her child play in the yard when it is raining like this? She must be crazy. Another scream pierces my ears. I stand and peer out of the window. Mrs. Furlonger's front yard is flooded. For some reason, she is standing bent over near her garbage can. What is she doing? She looks like the old hunchback, Nyang Limah . . .
I've forgotten what day it was exactly. But I swear it wasn't Friday. Today is Friday. I'm sure it wasn't. The caretaker wasn't beating the big mosque drum. A torrential downpour attacked the village, helped along by a fierce wind. Long ropes of rain beat against the earth, trailing like the intestines of a banshee set on destroying every creature of Allah. Great-grandmother Limah sat in the middle room singing a lullaby to my child in its cradle:

> *Ayun lambut-lambut,*
> *Sampai kubang babi;*
> *Takut keling janggut,*
> *Lari patah kaki.*
> (Swing the baby in his cradle,
> See the pig wallowing in its sty;

Frightened by the Indian's big black beard,
  Baby runs away and breaks his leg.)

The child was stubborn. It blinked at Great-grandmother's face, which was wrapped in innumerable layers of wrinkles. Over and over she sang:

Ayun lambut-lambut,
Sampai kubang babi;
Takut keling janggut,
Lari patah kaki.

The blinking eyes were gradually lost under the baby's eyelids. The child was asleep. Nyang stopped singing. But the rain and fierce wind raged on. Lightning swooped. She stood up and hobbled to the door. She was still strong on her feet.

"Where do you think you're going?"

I wasn't sure who had spoken. Perhaps it was my mother, in the kitchen. Or my father, on the kitchen verandah. Perhaps my wife. Or myself.

"I want to see if I've caught a carp or a catfish in my trap in the rice field."

"But it's pouring!" I think I said.

Great-grandmother had a will of iron. It was impossible to stop her doing what she wanted. Who cared about the rain? Or the storm? She hobbled out towards the rice fields.

"Nyang! Nyang! Nyang!"

There was a roar of thunder. Great-grandmother fell to the ground. Dead, in the middle of the yard. Perhaps a carp or catfish was nibbling at the bait in her fishtrap . . . perhaps . . .

"Mrs. Furlonger! Mrs. Furlonger!"

The heavy rain muffled my voice. Oh! Let her be. Let her be.

I looked at the piece of paper in front of me. The word "Slave."

"Daddy!"

I turn to the open door. My gosh! Aren't the children beautiful! The girls are wearing long tops and skirts. My three sons look very grand. They have Malay shirts, light green—the color of banana leaf. The same colored trousers. The same colored wraps around their waists. Three black *songkok* slightly sloping to the right. Come here! Ah. Here's ten cents. Here's ten cents. Here's ten cents. Here's ten cents.

"Happy Hari Raya, Daddy."

We bow to each other. I kiss them on top of their heads.

"Where's your mother?"

My wife appears. She is dressed in a long blouse too. Her skirt covers her ankles. Her hair is carefully tied in a bun. To me, she is the most beautiful woman in the world. She comes forward, kneels, and holds her hands out to me. I take her hands and hold them tight. She kisses my knee.

"I ask your pardon for all my conscious and unconscious offences towards you."

"I ask your pardon for all my conscious and unconscious offences towards you."

Four pairs of childish eyes stare at us. I can feel my knee is wet. I hear someone crying. I cry. For some reason, I feel very sad. There is a tear on my cheek, my tear. As I raise my wife's face, her crying intensifies. She is openly weeping.

Outside, it is still raining. Fortunately Mrs. Furlonger hasn't been struck by lightning, as was Great-grandmother Limah. The shreds of newspaper have blown away. I turn to my desk. The word "Slave" remains.

"We'll go out when it stops raining."

"Where can we go, daddy?"

"Anywhere you like."

"Can we go to somebody's house?"

I am dumb. My wife goes to the lounge room, followed by the children. I turn back to the humble, miserable, insignificant word "Slave."

. . . the village is silent. Where is everybody?

"Mother!" The echoes of my voice are mysteriously swallowed by Srengenge Mountain.

"Father! Uncle! Aunty!"

The sun shines in the sky, giving off a gentle warmth. The breeze moves over the leaves around me.

"Mother!" I scream as loudly as I can. The roar of my voice is swallowed by Srengenge.

The village is dead.

We are dressed in beautiful clothes. My family walks up and down excitedly in the front yard. We run through the village. We light firecrackers. We breathe in the fresh country air.

"Mother! Father!"

The village is still dead.

We jump up and down, run around the village and light firecrackers one by one.

"Ooooooi!" we all shout.

The sound echoes and is swallowed by Srengenge.

"Mother! Father! Ooooooooi!"

Suddenly we are under attack. We are surrounded by thousands of brick homes, interspersed with wooden thatched houses. White and brown-skinned people mingle together. They all scream and blink. Dogs bark. Horses whinny. Water buffalo, hens, ducks, appear from nowhere. Churches stand side by side with mosques. The pubs are filled with bottles of palm wine. There are cars everywhere. Teenagers kiss on the steps of the churches and the mosques. I can see an old *haji* leaning quietly against the cross of Christ. And in the very front of everything else is an attractive, naked girl, next to Mother, Father, Senior Uncle and Aunt, Middle Uncle and Aunt, Little Uncle and Aunt.

"Mother! Father!"

They all slowly move forward, pressing in on us. We hug each other affectionately . . .

"Daddy! It's stopped raining!"

I turn my face to the right. Little Brother looks best of all, in his light green Malay costume. His eyes are so bright. Outside, it really has stopped raining. There are puddles in the yard. Holding my forehead in my hand, I stare at the piece of paper on my desk. "Slave, slave."

I stand, go to my room and change into my new clothes.

"Come on! We're going out to celebrate Hari Raya."

"Where are we going, Daddy?"

"Back to the village to celebrate with your grandmothers."

We all painfully smile.

1973
Translated by Harry Aveling

Noraini Md. Yusof

"Dance of the Bees"

Noraini Md. Yusof, born in 1962, has a master's degree in linguistics from California State University, Fresno, where she won a prize for best fiction in 1985 for her short story "The Monsoon." Now living in Malaysia, she teaches literature and is currently the Deputy Dean at the Faculty of Language Studies, Universiti Kebangsaan.

In "Dance of the Bees," Yusof explores the psychological contradictions generated by the different values and educational systems associated with Christianity and Islam in Malaysia. We poignantly feel the consequences of these contradictions in the lives of both the parents and their child Sal in this story. The theme of psychological instability as the inexorable consequence of conflicting value systems that defy emotional resolution is an important subject in modern Southeast Asian fiction. It also appears in Shahnon Ahmad's "Delirium" (Malaysia) and Daw Ohn Khin's "An Unanswerable Question" (Burma).

The building overwhelmed her. Tilting her head back, she gazed at the tip of a looming tower where a metallic "t" pierced the blue sky. Another huge one, the biggest one she had ever seen, was engraved on the wall. She wondered who had carved it into the stone. What she feared most was the man hanging on it. His arms and shoulders were stretched tight across the bar, forming a human "t" over the cold, concrete one. There at the top of the front door, with blood running down his face, arms and legs, he looked like he was crying; only they were not tears but rivulets of blood. What seemed like nails pinned him up, and the skin on his torso strained under his weight. Through the wide-gaping mouth of the front door, she saw a huge hall with seats facing the altar like wooden rows of teeth. There was another of those huge "t"s on the wall behind the altar. She wanted to cry when she saw the same man hanging there; only now, he seemed even bigger from the distance.

Sal was so scared, she felt like crying aloud. She couldn't restrain a sob from escaping her lips.

"Remember what I told you, Sal? Now, don't cry."

"Yes . . . yes, father. I speak English. Thank you, hello, my name is Salmah. What is yours? Please, teacher, may I go out? I do what others do. Do what teacher tell us, and wait for you," she recited, sniffing.

"Good girl. I'll see you later. You won't cry, will you?"

"No . . . no, father."

"Good. Now, kiss me good-bye."

The little girl obliged. Her father's words were the only familiar sounds to her ears. She put her plump arms around her father's neck and gave a tight hug. He was crouched opposite her; and as he held her close, he was not eager to let go. Like a little mongoose squirming in the coils of a snake, she was already wriggling to escape his clutch. A final squeeze, and he let the child go. As he stood, he realized how towering the church spire was behind her. Other parents, who were registering their children in the kindergarten, filled the front yard of the church grounds. Many began to enter the chapel. Voices hummed like bees in search of the molten cores of flowers; when one bee caught a whiff of a sweet scent, the message was passed to the next; and a few seconds later, bees converged on the spot and buzzed an excited dance. This group of people danced to a similar tune, coming together and separating at intervals as they greeted each other. Heads nodded, hands touched, hugs and smiles were exchanged as friends met friends. Only the father and his child stood slightly apart from the rest. A little hand crept into his when he smiled a warm welcome to the approaching figure.

"Mrs. Wong, it's a pleasure meeting you again," he greeted in Malay.

"It's always my pleasure to meet you, Encik Supyan. How are you?" Mrs. Wong responded.

"Good, good, and I wish you that too."

"Thank you. And who is this sweet little girl? Hello, what's your name?" The last question was posed in English.

"Sal, *jawablah*. Go on, answer your teacher."

"Hello, my name is Salmah, and what is yours?"

"Oh, how sweet. She speaks very well. Hello, I'm Mrs. Wong, your teacher. Who taught you English? Your father? This is really good, Encik Supyan. You must be really proud of her."

"I'm afraid that's about all she knows. I taught her two weeks ago, after I received the letter confirming her attendance here. I'm not so good myself."

"No, no, it's great."

"She's going to need some time to get used to this place. I just hope she won't have many problems fitting in."

"That's what we're here for, to ease her into the school system. I'll look out for her. Don't worry, I'm sure she'll be fine."

"Thank you, Mrs. Wong. You're very kind. I'm sorry, but I have to go now. I only got an hour off from the school to do the registration here."

"I understand that you must have classes today. Leave Salmah with us. She'll make friends in a couple of days. Good day, Encik Supyan."

"Good day. Bye, Sal. Listen to your teacher. *Jangan nakal,* behave."

Thus began Sal's first day at kindergarten. She watched her father's retreating back, but was too nervous to cry. She wanted to run after him. Mrs. Wong looked down at her, smiled and took hold of her arm. She started to speak. Sal stared in fascination at the moving red lips.

"Sal, don't cry. Your father will be back soon in the afternoon. Meanwhile I'm here and we'll make friends. Don't be shy, come, let's go meet the rest. Come on, sweetheart." She tugged at the little hand.

Sal started crying when she saw that she was being pulled toward the door and the man. The wide mouth swallowed her into its cavernous depths. It was dark and hollow inside, like moist and musty sweet breath. She was pulled closer to him, that man who was hanging and bleeding at the back of the throat. Other people were already seated on rows of teeth, with children sitting gingerly on the wooden edges. The hum of murmuring voices vibrated in the huge room. Mrs. Wong slid into the front seat, pulling Sal after her, and they sat and waited. Sal squirmed beneath the bleeding man's stare. Her fear dried her tears.

A woman in a black robe approached the altar and started speaking. Another person, also robed, but this one male and in white, joined her and faced the crowd. The woman sat down beside Sal. The man talked for a long time, and when he stopped, music came suddenly from an organ behind him. Sal was surprised when the whole crowd, as if on secret cue, rose and started singing from a small black book. She saw one on the bench beside her. The song vibrated through the whole room, causing the hairs on Sal's arms to rise in reaction. She wished she were home. When she closed her eyes tightly, the choral voices and piano music reverberated in her brain.

"Are you very sure?"

"To tell you the truth, no. But, there is truth in what has been said. Sending the children to English schools will provide them with more opportunities in the future. That means Sal will have to go to an all-girls school and not be with the boys."

Supyan looked at his wife. They sat facing each other on the prayer mat. She was still in her *telekong,* the all-white robe donned by the women for prayers. Every part of her was covered, except for her face and hands. It was evening and they had just finished praying together, the whole family. The children had gone off to watch TV after kissing their parents' hands, which they did after every prayer time. He studied the face before him and sensed troubled thoughts.

"I don't like it. She'll be alone. At least the boys have each other. Imagine the problems she has to face alone."

Niah was distressed. She remembered her own first day of school; she had cried when her parents left her in class. And she was among the familiar faces of the children in her village.

"I know, I know. But English schools are either all boys or all girls. The two years at kindergarten will help them adjust. Even then, when Sal goes there, the boys will already be in school. I know what you mean, but we can't send the boys and not Sal. How will we explain to them later if they ask?"

"I don't know. Are we doing the right thing? A church runs the kindergarten. A school run by nuns and priests! What will the neighbors say?" Niah asked quietly.

"Why care? We do this for the children. If they follow the neighborhood children to the nearby school, what will they become? At best, if they do well, they will get to enter the Teacher Training College. Like me. If not, they end up working the land. Like my father, and yours too. Look at Haji Salleh. He sent Abdullah to the English school in town, and look at Abdullah now. He's in England with a scholarship, and when he comes back, he'll be an Assistant District Officer. And that is just the beginning for him. We went to school together, Niah. I got better results, but my father could not pay for an English education. Why worry about what the neighbors will say? It's the children's future. They'll win scholarships, study overseas. Don't you want that for them?"

Supyan knew his arguments were sound. Yet he wondered why, somehow sometimes, the same arguments could not convince him. When he talked to the other teachers at school, it seemed easy. It was just a choice of pedagogy for the children. It was not like he was planning their conversion to Christianity. The only way for the children to have an English education was for them to attend missionary schools. Now, more Malay parents were doing this. But Supyan knew that it was his being a Malay language teacher that was the issue here. Some of his Malay colleagues were already calling him a traitor. They said he should have shown more loyalty to their cause; theirs was to fight for the dignity of their mother tongue, this newly accepted national language for this newborn nation. Yet, they claimed he was now joining the long queue of many Malay parents who craved an English education for their children. The queue of parents who wanted children who could speak English, who could work alongside the English, who could dress like them, wearing shirts, ties, black blazers (even under the sweltering equatorial sun) and matching pants and shoes. The women wore dresses, short and flared, barely covering their kneecaps, and matching high-heeled pumps. They talked like the English, but their skin belied the fact. Supyan knew he was taking a risk in allowing that educational system to mold his children. But the opportunities that he knew would come along with it tugged at his heart.

In the evenings after *maghrib,* the fourth daily prayer, Supyan sat in front of the three children: Kamal, Khalil and Salmah. A Quran, splayed across the small crossed-plank stand, was in front of each one. Their shrill, singsong voices chanted the Arabic verses. Little palms cupped against small ears helped to improve the tone of their voices, as cleaned turkey feathers clutched in warm fists flitted across the pages. Once in a while Sal fumbled, and Supyan corrected her pronunciation. The two boys barely needed help. The children had started their Quranic lessons early, at the age of four. At six now, Sal was already twenty pages into the holy book, while the boys were about to end their first round of reading. Niah and Supyan had argued about the lessons. She had wanted them to have daily lessons with Haji Mail, the *imam* at the small mosque near the house.

The neighborhood children thronged the small building where the villagers performed their prayers together every evening; and a few minutes later, the cherubim choir beckoned the coming of night. The sound droned on for a couple of hours until lanterns illuminated the darkness. Insects, finding the lights irresistible, killed themselves, dropping on the heads below. Once in a while, a sharp crack interrupted the choral song. Voices momentarily stopped in midair, while one deep voice snapped rebuke; then the choir resumed in volume and energy. Haji Mail had just caned a slow learner, which was the reason why

Supyan had decided to teach his own children. He had survived the old man's quick arm and temper as a young boy; thus he could not bear the thought of the cane slicing the soft skin of his children's palms.

His decision angered the neighbors. They accused Supyan of humiliating Haji Mail and of rejecting tradition. Haji Mail had taught all the children in Kampung Pokok Mangga to read the Quran, and his father before him. What Supyan was doing was just not right. When Supyan started his children's prayer lessons, the neighbors buzzed with anger. Niah cried but Supyan was adamant. It soothed his heart to see the boys in their miniature sarongs and Sal's little form enveloped in a *telekung*, miming his every action on the prayer mat. He cherished every *amin* they chorused after his own.

"Dear Lord, bless this food we are about to have. *Amin.*"

A chorus of young voices echoed, "*Amin . . .*" Heads were bowed, eyes clenched tight and fingers clasped in prayers at the table. Sandwiches were piled on the plate in front of them; tea steamed from little colorful cups. Each table sat eight little children dressed in pink organdy shirts or dresses. Sister Claire smiled. She turned when she heard a commotion from a table in one corner of the hall.

"That's wrong!"

Sal just stared at him.

"You hold your hand this way." He waved his entwined fingers in her face.

Sal looked down at her hands, palms cupped in prayers, just as her father had taught her at home. She shook her head and pulled her hands away from the boy's prying fingers.

"Like this!" Another fist jabbed her face.

Sal turned away.

"Sister Claire, she did it wrong!" the boy cried to the black-robed woman. Sister Claire approached the table. She recognized the new girl Mrs. Wong had told her about. She looked at the bristling boy next to her.

"Richard Tan, why aren't you eating?"

"Sister, she didn't want me to show her the right way to pray," he announced, a little frown etched into his forehead.

"Salmah, go on. You may eat." She gestured towards Sal. Turning she continued, "Richard, it's all right. Salmah prays differently from us. She doesn't have to follow your way. Now, go on and have your meal before it's too late. Lessons will start again in a few minutes." She walked around the other tables, stopping once in a while to talk to some children.

"Why you different?" A probing pair of eyes questioned.

"No." Sal stammered back, not knowing what to say. She could not understand all his words, but she instinctively knew they had something to do with the way she had said blessings. She grasped at the unfamiliar word. "Different? What different?"

"You do this; we do this." The boy acted out his words. "Different."

Sal nodded. She now began to understand the looks thrown in her direction, the different way the teachers talked to her as compared to the other students. She was still having problems with the language, and she thought that was why they had looked at and talked to her differently. She studied the boy sitting beside her: his needle-black hairs cropped close to the skin of his head; eyes, charcoal black, peered from flat lids, slanted at an angle toward his temple; a flat nose and a huge grin spread across his round face.

After two weeks at the kindergarten, she began to grasp new words, expanding her once very limited vocabulary. The teachers helped by speaking very slowly to her, allowing her to hear each syllable and on many occasions prompting her to repeat them. Words were also acted out in class. The little children hooted in glee to see the antics of their teachers. While not really comprehending every word, Sal was able to grasp the message by combining the words with the action. She, too, smiled in class but was still too intimidated by the others to participate. The other children could already speak the language. Many of them were Chinese, and some were Indian and expatriate children, who jumped and skipped and chattered in breathless English. Sal stood apart from them during game hour, craving to join in the chanting games, but her silent tongue was a barrier.

"What's your name? Me, Richard." Mr. Right beside her asked.

"Sal," came a shy response.

"Is it short for Sally?"

A shake of the head.

"It's okay. I call you Sally. You want to eat?"

A sandwich, squeezed in a grubby hand, was shoved into her face. Sal accepted the friendly offer gratefully. She smiled at Richard, her heart going out to this first friend. If a change in name would win her one, she would accept any.

"Sally" and Richard were inseparable after that day. His little shoulders swelled as he took on the responsibility of being her spokesperson, advisor and guide. With his hand tightly clutching hers, he dragged her into the little games played during the breaks. Richard was a self-appointed leader, bullying the other children into letting Sal play. He vehemently refused to join any game unless Sal did too. Sal was pressured into mimicking every action in the game, memorizing every sound in the little songs, and her heart burst when one day other hands started to clutch at hers too. She looked forward to these sessions. From marching in giggling lines to the London Bridge and being caught in its falling arms to trekking round mountains, Sal never stopped being amazed at the wealth of games to play. Besides her classmates, she found new friends in funny characters like Judy, Miss Muffet, Little Jack, and Humpty Dumpty. She treasured all of them, but Richard was her favorite. After all the games and songs were played and chanted, the two of them sat together in one corner away from the rest and giggled. And when she reached home, tales of these adventures were recounted to her parents.

One day during lunch hour, Sister Claire asked the usual question. "And who would like to say prayers before we eat today?"

Little arms waved to volunteer.

Richard stood and said aloud, "Sally."

Sal's heart stopped. All eyes swerved to hers.

Sister Claire smiled, "Sal? Yes, would you like to say the prayers?"

A bony elbow poked her waist repeatedly. A few other voices chirped up, "Sally . . . Sally . . ."

"Children, hush . . . Sal?"

Another nudge and a hiss. Sal nodded, her heart beating too fast. Sister Claire gave her a smile. She sat upright and cupped her palms. A quick look at Richard's consternation made her change to clasp her hands together on the table. She could not breathe. Richard nodded, his face flushed red. Her voice trembled, "Dear Lord, please bless the food that we're about to have. *Amin.*"

A chorus repeated, "*Amin.*"

Another smile from Sister Claire, "That was very good, Sal."

Richard grinned. He crowed. Sounds of eating in the hall drowned Sal's heartbeats.

Supyan watched Sal's progress with pride. He saw her stumbled reading quickly improve to a more confident pace. She read aloud more, often now at home. The two boys sometimes helped to correct her pronunciation. Supyan had even caught her going through their schoolbooks and reading their storybooks from the library. She had adapted very well to the kindergarten, better than he had expected. He bought more storybooks for her. She became an avid reader, preferring to read rather than play with the boys in the evening. Her sixth birthday was approaching fast and he looked forward to giving her the present she had been begging him for.

"Happy birthday, *sayang*. Kiss me." Supyan hugged the little girl.

He got a little peck and with a quick wriggle she was out of his arms.

"Present? Present?" Sal jumped up and down.

With a laugh, Supyan handed her the package that was wrapped in multicolored hearts. Frantic fingers tore at the paper and revealed a doll, upright in a box with a plastic window on the front. Her limbs were pink and plump, her dress dark blue and laced at the collar. She had black wavy hair that was sculptured onto her plastic head. The smile on her lips was plastered in a frozen friendless gesture. Sal's lips wobbled in disappointment.

"I don't want. This is not Sally."

"Eh, why Sal? You said you wanted a doll. Isn't this pretty?" Supyan answered her in Malay.

"No!"

"Why?"

"No hair. Sally must have hair."

"No, no, she has got hair. This is her hair. It's just stuck to her head, see?"

"No, I want hair. Real pretty hair, gold color. Real curls. Not this . . . this ugly black head!" The offending doll was hurled. Tears accompanied the action. Feet stamped in anger.

Supyan frowned. Niah bit her lips. The boys chuckled, grabbed the doll, pulled off the plastic head and started kicking it around the room.

"Sally . . . Sally . . ." Khalil chanted. The head was kicked.

"Sally has black hair. Ugly head! Black hair! Sal has ugly hair!" Kamal kicked back. Laughed.

"Sal wants gold hair," Khalil howled. Another kick.

The plastic head bounced on the floor and hit Sal's head. She screamed.

One morning all the children were huddled and made to line up in pairs facing the chapel. There was talk about a celebration and a feast. This was the first time since her initial experience that Sal found herself looking at the hanged man again. She had always avoided going near the chapel, pulling back whenever Richard moved towards it. She had never told anyone about her fears; she did not even talk about it at home. For the past months she had managed to avoid looking at him. There were pictures of him that she sometimes saw in the books the teachers used, but she would always look away or just close her eyes. By now she knew his name: Jesus. Even his name mentioned aloud caused the hairs on her neck to rise. Goose pimples rose like little mountains on her arms and legs. Now, she felt the same panic coming again.

"Richard, I don't want to go in." Sal tugged at the hand in hers.

"Don't be silly. This is Easter, we sing songs."

"No." Sal hung back. Obstinate.

"Sally, quick!"

Hands pulled her arm in the direction of the chapel door. Jesus looked down at them sadly. Sal started to whimper and desperately tugged her hand back. Other hands pushed her from the back. The door yawned open; Jesus was still crying blood. His cuts were still not healed and the blood still red. The eternal pained sadness on his face remained. Sal began crying.

"Sister, look at Sally," Richard called out.

Some teachers approached the little commotion in the line. Other children crowded around and Sal cried louder. Richard made another attempt to push her forward. Sal refused to budge; her sobs caused her little chest to heave and a warm trickle of urine flowed down her leg. The children gasped in shock. Mrs. Wong quickly pulled Sal away from Richard and hurried her to the classroom across the grounds. Sister Claire got the children to line up again and the procession continued into the chapel amidst an excited buzz. Richard hung back, but after some urging from Sister Claire, he walked in with a long face.

"Sal, talk to me, dear."

Sal burrowed her head in her lap; she was still crying hard. She was shivering in the hot room, and Mrs. Wong fanned the child with a book taken from a nearby table. Sal pulled away from the kind gesture.

"Dear, tell me."

The truth was Sal feared her own answer. Many things terrified her: the dim solemnity of the chapel, the hanged man's silent pain, Richard's high expectations of her, rejection from the other children, the shame of not comprehending the teachers and making mistakes in class, the confusion of being different and the pain of wanting to belong. She shook her head, unsure of Mrs. Wong's reaction to her fears. She clamped her mouth shut, dried her tears, and remained silent the rest of the day. The teachers discussed the matter and decided upon the best solution: to inform En. Supyan of the incident and let him talk to his daughter to find the root of the matter. Hence, he was made aware of the situation when he came to pick Sal up. Sal realized her father knew when she saw Mrs. Wong whispering to him and the concerned looks he threw in her direction. She resented the fact that they were talking about it in front of her. The trip home was stony quiet and the whisperings continued with her mother.

Everything else that happened after that was a blur. That night, the boys were solemn. Her father prayed and recited a longer blessing than usual. Sal's hands shook when she chorused her silent *amin*. A sob choked her. Every few minutes, eyes turned to her. She refused to look at them and her lips remained clamped until bedtime.

She broke into cold sweat. She dreaded opening her eyes, knowing that he was still hanging onto the "t"-bar. She could hear his agonized breathing—the heaving chest inhaled deeply until the chest cavity was filled to capacity and then exhaled with a hissing sound as the air passed through his narrow nostrils. She could hear the stretch of his muscles pulled tight by the bar. She could hear little droplets of blood seeping through the tiny pores on his skin; and when they clotted into a bigger drop, the blood-tear rolled down his face, engulfing the little hairs for one second and then leaving them behind, drenched and neglected. Bees, she knew not from where, buzzed a busy dance around her head. She felt sharp stings on her arms and legs. A slow moan started deep in his chest and crept slowly up his throat and escaped from his lips. The pained sound grasped at her, ripped her lips apart, and forced its way into her heart. Strong fingers of sound clenched the muscular walls of her heart, constricting her breath, and squeezing out the last particles of air. Pain shot through her body, droplets of blood seeped from the stings, and another moan started deep inside, only this time from her. She clawed at her chest, choking back the moan. Pray, pray for help, ease all the pain. She cupped her palms together, praying; droplets of blood dripped into the clammy cup. More and more drops. The small cup spilled and blood overflowed. She screamed.

1998

Negara Brunei Darussalam

Brunei is an independent sultanate on the northwest coast of the island of Borneo in the South China Sea. An important entrepôt along the spice-trade route, it conducted commerce with China in the sixth century A.D. It was subsequently influenced by Indian traditions through the Javanese Majapahit kingdom and later, in the fifteenth century, came under the sway of Islam. It was a powerful state from the sixteenth century until the middle of the nineteenth century. The site of the rich Seria oilfield, Brunei became a British protectorate in 1888 and a British dependency in 1905. Japan occupied Brunei during World War II, and in 1945 Australia liberated it. In 1984 the sultanate became fully independent from Britain. The five-hundred-year-old monarchy remains in existence today, currently plagued by issues involving the appropriateness of certain state expenditures. It is one of the wealthiest nations in Asia.

Very little has been written about the development of modern literature in Brunei. Writers were undoubtedly influenced by trends in Malay-language literature from Malaysia and Indonesia. Themes associated with a rural and urban dichotomy, the tension between Islamic values and modernization, and changing gender roles are represented in this fiction. Writers associated with the Language and Literature Bureau in Berakas, which publishes the literary magazine *Bahana,* contributed the contemporary short stories in this section.

P. H. Muhammad Abdul Aziz
"The Plankway"

*P. H. Muhammad Abdul Aziz (Pengiran Haji Aji), born in 1948, began
writing as a teenager. He worked as a teacher for more than ten years,
until 1986, when he joined Brunei Darussalam's Language and Literature Bureau as an author. He is now editor of* Bahana, *a magazine published by the bureau. Over the last thirty years Aziz has received
numerous literary awards, including the South East Asia Write Award
(SEA Write Award) in 1995.*

*"The Plankway" exemplifies an important theme for many Malay
writers, that of Malay rural life and traditional culture. It paints a scene
of village life along the coast of the South China Sea and the relationships of interdependency that unfold there. Humanistic in intent, it
reveals the foibles of human nature and the importance of* adat *(traditional custom and morality), pride, and expediency. Note that forms of
address, such as* liao, dang, *and* chikgu, *are used before personal
names.*

*Marriage, with its quixotic uncertainty, is a popular theme for
modern writers, including many of those represented in this anthology.
Compare Khai Hung's "You Must Live" (Vietnam), Sila Khomchai's
"The Family in the Street" (Thailand), and Ma Sandar's "An
Umbrella" (Burma).*

The stumps of *kulimpapa* trees that line the way to Liau Bakar's house
are still green, although the branches have been wildly hacked with an
axe. If you look closely, it seems like some demented person must have
cut them. A few wooden planks are still nailed to the toppled plankway
built across the muddy riverbed, while others lie strewn about.

"Ooi, Liau! Aren't you working today?" Budin called out while
plodding along the riverbed near the collapsed plankway. His son, in

"The Plankway," by P. H. Muhammad Abdul Aziz. Permission to publish granted by the
author. English rendition by the author and the editor.

school uniform, was riding on his back. Budin's trouser legs had been rolled up to his thighs. With their combined weight, his legs sank knee-deep into the mud. A basket of the day's provisions was held in his right hand while his son's school bag was clasped under his left arm. Plodding through the mud made him sway like a scarecrow in the wind.

"Aa, n . . . no, Din. My boat is stuck in the low tide," he explained, stuttering a bit. Now Budin had already arrived at the lowest rung of Liau Bakar's house-ladder. He washed his muddy feet in a puddle of water, then climbed up the ladder. Relying on the strength of his two feet, both hands full, he was almost strangled by his son's hold while using his knees to balance his body weight at each rung. Should one give way, both father and son would face the consequences. But Budin was so used to living in the Water Village that he displayed complete confidence.

"Excuse me, Liau . . . !" called Budin, smiling faintly on his way to the main bridge of the Water Village with his son.

"Damn me!" Liau Tangah cursed silently. Budin's smile seemed to be mocking his hasty action. He had this feeling despite the sincerity of Budin's smile and his consistent generosity. "Damn," Liau Tangah continued to curse.

Saman, Samsu and Bahar appeared soon after this. All of them were like Budin, nonplussed while plodding and swaying in the mud. Saman, among them the king-of-comedians, joked along the way. All three of them, victims of the collapsed plankway, were coughing and laughing. What they were joking about wasn't clear.

Cikgu Ahmad, a schoolteacher, then appeared. He was swaying more than anyone else and looking rather disgusted by the mud, sticky like *ambuyat*. Nonetheless, he too was smiling at Saman's jokes, even though he couldn't hear them clearly.

"Ooi, Cikgu," called Saman, who was now on the veranda of Liau Bakar's house. "No need to be disgusted by that sticky mud. The mud of our graves will be worse—squeezing us until our bones break!"

"Eh, no dead man is going to be buried in any mud," interjected Samsu, who had just reached the ladder, his slight smile barely revealing his teeth.

"Gooey, firm or hard—it's all earth, just earth!" Saman jokingly defended his view while helping Samsu, who was having difficulty negotiating the sticky mud with his bag and basket of the day's provisions.

Cikgu Ahmad, smiling and smirking, plodded sluggishly in the sticky mud until he finally reached the lowest rung of the ladder to Liau Bakar's house. Sweat was flowing down the curves of his face. His formerly nicely pressed Van Houghton shirt was now damp with perspiration. Saman and Samsu quickly took the James Bond bag and Bally shoes he was holding in his outstretched hands even before he began climbing the ladder.

At last the four of them continued on, joking all the way. It made Liau Tangah uneasy to see his neighbors—victims of the collapsed plankway, victims of his rash action—with their antics joking like that. He felt deeply guilty. The event that had caused this destruction having happened only a few days ago, it still burned his conscience. If only he could undo it, turn back time to prevent it so the terrible event could be avoided altogether. But what was done could not be undone. He was neither a prophet nor an angel. He was just an ordinary man not free of imperfections. Recalling the event, he felt an injustice had been done to both himself and others.

"Those who sever ties of friendship will be denied heaven!" Those words were with him now giving him no peace. If heaven were denied to him, what would happen to his salvation? Surely he would be thrown into the deepest hell! "Merciful God, deliver me from my bad deeds. Don't make me dwell in hell!" Liau Tangah cried inwardly.

Only now did he realize that the twenty-meter plankway was a bridge of friendship. His neighbors' children could use it to go to school; parents, too. Villagers could use it to attend social functions or to visit one another. That narrow plankway played an important role in many events. Wouldn't it be wonderful for his faith if the plankway were still standing sturdily erect serving each footstep of every user? "Damn me!" he cursed continuously. "Why was I so stupid! So stubborn!"

Of course he had every right to demolish that plankway. It was all his property. The wooden planks, the beams, the supports, even the nails belonged to him. He built it himself, with his own sweat. So, if he ever wanted to pull it down, it was up to him. Any natural law, any human court, would take his side.

But that was not the question now. The question confronting him was the question of faith: his religious belief. Judged by the values of his own culture, he would be considered to possess low moral character now. The collapse of the plankway symbolized the collapse of his morality. That twenty-meter plankway had been the path connecting his neighbors' houses in the west to the main bridge of the Water Village. Now he realized it was the bridge of friendship that should be the courtesy of any religious man like him on the edge of his own grave. But he had selfishly severed that link of friendship. Only now did he feel the event as a deep loss, a loss caused by his own evil temper. Why was it that such a trivial matter could make him capable of axing the supports of the plankway until the whole thing collapsed? "Stupid! Idiot!" He cursed himself again.

He had decided now. Even if his decision was against Dang Piah's will, he didn't care anymore. Let there be war in his house as long as the war in his heart ceased.

"Ooii! Dang!" His call echoed through the house like a ship's siren piercing early morning silence. No answer. The clang of crockery could be heard from the kitchen. He called again.

"Ah? Whatzit . . . ?" Dang Piah's high-pitched voice pierced his ears as her tired face appeared in the kitchen doorway. There were traces of soapy water on her arms.

"The axe!" he commanded. Dang Piah, who understood the significance of that kind of command, went immediately to get the axe located in a kitchen corner and took it to the doorway of the veranda. Her slight figure looked even thinner holding the axe, whose width was wider than her arm.

He grabbed the axe from Piah and wordlessly headed away. Piah was still standing confused, gawking at the timber strewn about already cut into one-meter lengths. Sawdust covered the entire area. Now she felt even more confused.

Liau Tangah's face was serious and stiff. The veins on his hard arms protruded as he leveled the ends of the *kulimpapa* trees for the plank holders.

"*Astaghfirullah*, God forgive me . . . !" Piah sighed regretfully. Tangah's face hardened. He looked even more serious now with his lips pursed and eyes squinting in focused concentration on leveling the timber supports and plank holders arrayed in front of him. Now he was determined that nothing would stop him.

"Eh, old man! Aren't those timbers for the new kitchen beams? Why cut them to pieces?" Piah tensely accosted him in a loud voice. Ready to pounce on her victim, she glared furiously.

Liau Tangah had already anticipated this. He remained nonplussed, knowing that a fight would break out at any time. Piah's loud and piercing voice was a sign that a war was imminent. This time, however, he was determined to fight back. He would be henpecked no longer. No more would he let her undermine his authority and public image. Her big mouth would have to be stopped somehow, by being quiet, fighting back, or by physically punishing her. Let her taste her own consequences. It was because of her big mouth that he had demolished the plankway in the first place and, along with it, his status as a respectable old man in the village.

"Shut up!" he snapped, while violently striking the stump of the *kulimpapa* tree with his axe. It sank halfway into the stump. "This is all your fault. I should stuff your big mouth!" he shouted at her, his voice loud with anger now. Piah did not expect this. Her big vociferous mouth had started to quiver. This change was so sudden.

"Why . . . ?" Piah's voice had turned nervous and almost inaudible. For a while she tried to control herself. "But . . . ," she continued disjointedly, swallowing her saliva now. "You acted right in demolishing that plankway. Look, our son's arm is still in a sling! Have you forgotten that?" Her lips were still quivering, although less now, and her voice was getting louder. Despite her attempts at emotional restraint, her eyes still filled with tears that coursed down the wrinkled paths of her face. Seeing this, Liau Tangah's tension relaxed. His anger was gone.

"I should not have demolished the plankway just because of the children's fight," he said regretfully but softly, still blaming Piah. "Luckily, Liau Bakar didn't answer back," he continued, "or there would have been a terrible fight, and I . . . I would have been so shamed!"

"So now you want to rebuild the plankway?" Piah slightly raised her voice in the midst of her sobbing. She wiped away the tears with her shirtsleeve. "Yes! God forbid . . . !" Piah sighed regretfully.

Tangah's face hardened. He looked even more serious now with his lips pursed and eyes squinting in focused concentration on leveling the timber supports and plank holders arrayed in front of him. He was determined, now, that nothing would stop him. Tangah answered. With his short and determined body he was dragging the *kulimpapa* poles to the side of the veranda then sliding them down the riverbank. Buurr! The *kulimpapa* poles hit the muddy riverbed now flooding with the quickly rising tide. "It was the worst low tide, now it will be the worst high tide," he grudgingly thought as though venting his wrath on the muddy riverbed and the incoming tide. It would not be long now until the tide would be level to his breast. It would be hard for an old man like him to erect the five-meter-high poles.

"I won't allow you to rebuild the plankway!" Suddenly Piah's anger exploded after a brief silence. Her formerly teary eyes were even more hostile then before. "Coward! You just demolished it. Now you want to rebuild it? Licking your own spit! Coward! Senile old man!"

Piah's sharp words provoked Tangah. His face became taut and serious once more. He glared at Piah. He would really like to stuff something in that old woman's mouth but, fortunately, he was not that kind of person. All this time he controlled his anger, which could only be seen on his taut and serious face. Perhaps his gentle nature had encouraged Piah's big mouth.

"Go in! Inside!" He snapped at her while pointing his finger at their house. Piah was again confounded by Tangah's serious face, but not as much as before, since she continued protesting, if only with loud grumbling. As a wife, she had to obey her husband. She sulked back into the kitchen, her stomping feet making sounds as though the *bakau* tree poles that held up the house would be driven down and shatter in the muddy riverbed. A little later, loud sounds of clanging crockery could be heard from the kitchen. Liau Tangah pretended not to hear. One by one he slid the poles down to the muddy riverbed, leaning them on the side of the veranda.

On the main bridge of the Water Village, Mahri, a child with his left arm in a sling, could be seen glancing up and down, walking in small steps, his free hand holding a basket of kitchen items. He had just returned from Haji Damit's retail shop in the nearby village. From afar, he called out to inform his father of his presence, showing him the goods.

Tangah only nodded at his son, traces of anger still present in his heart. "Climb down carefully!" he called out to Mahri, who was now at the topmost rung of the ladder to Liau Bakar's house.

Agilely the boy climbed down the ladder and started wading through the rising tides. Liau Tangah felt uneasy. Usually at high tide like this, there were stinging fish—*tuka-tuka* or baby *lapu*—creeping beneath the muddy waters. Halfway to their house, Mahri suddenly screamed and collapsed. His scream traveled with the wavelets caused by the water taxis traveling the waterway to the west.

Tangah was now very worried. As though flying, he jumped off the ladder to the riverbed, unconcerned about hidden shards of broken glass and sharp metal cans strewn among the stumps of the former plankway. He rushed to Mahri, who was now rather weak. The boy's quivering lips were pale, his eyes heavy, half his body submerged in muddy water, the shopping goods gone.

Liau Tangah supported the slight body of his son up to the house, calling loudly for Piah. The distress in his voice startled her. Seeing Mahri's condition, she was even more perplexed. She would certainly be frantic, crying and screaming for help, without him there.

"Call a water taxi," Tangah urgently ordered Piah, who was now acting like a mother cat with a long-lost kitten. Piah ran outside looking all around for a water taxi passing by. In the meantime, he was doing his best to suck the poison out of Mahri's foot. Tangah's face was also getting pale, as though he, too, was fighting the pain in his own leg. Mahri had to be saved. The wound on the sole of Mahri's foot was now beginning to spurt blood. He tied a piece of cloth tightly around the boy's thigh to stop the *tuka-tuka*'s poison from flowing into the rest of his body. Meanwhile, the gash on his own foot was bleeding profusely and becoming critical. He slumped for a while, dizzy at the redness of his own gushing blood.

"Liau Bakarrr! Help! Help! Si Mahriii! Si Mahriii! Help! Tangah's injured! Help!" Piah was shouting in every direction. There was no water taxi passing by. Even if there were one, nobody would want to brave the water, still shallow with the incoming tide. Piah continued to call relentlessly, now to Liau Bakar's house, then to her neighbors' houses to the west—calling the names of all those people she had so resented: Budin, Saman, Samsu, and maybe even Cikgu Ahmad. She didn't care anymore. Weeping, all she could see was Tangah's muddy footprints, red with blood, all over the veranda.

Soon the sounds of a water taxi could be heard coming from Liau Bakar's house, a house whose inhabitants she had always considered as incarnations of the devil. The engine of the motorboat could be heard howling over the sound of the incoming tide, struggling through the shallow muddy water—coming nearer and nearer.

1976

Aminah Haji Momin

"Foolish"

Aminah Haji Momin, born in 1959, currently works as a language officer at the Language and Literature Bureau in Brunei Darussalam. She is a prolific writer in many genres. Her first children's book, Dang Katak Dan Dang Belalang, *was published in 1997 and her first novel,* Liku-Liku Hidup, *in 1999.*

"Foolish" is written in a clipped, fast-paced narrative style, perhaps emulating the assiduous urban lifestyle of its sophisticated Islamic couple, who seem to plan their busy professional lives around work. Some Islamic countries, such as Saudi Arabia, grant driver's licenses only to men. The pretty, pregnant protagonist of this story seems pleased with her driver's license and the independence it brings. Ultimately, however modern this couple may seem, a traditional double standard overtakes her in the end. The gender-based double standard is also a theme of Sri Daoruang's "Sita Puts Out the Fire" (Thailand), Leila S. Chudori's "The Purification of Sita" (Indonesia), and Marianne Villanueva's "The Mayor of the Roses" (the Philippines).

Today the pretty-face pregnant woman has reached the age of 13,350 days, a most significant day. It is her four-thousand-day anniversary of obtaining a valid driver's license. The pretty-face pregnant woman is satisfied about driving a car by herself. She can drive by herself to work. Drive by herself to shop. Drive by herself to the women's association meetings. Drive by herself to the beauty salon. She does not trouble her husband. He also drives a car by himself. Basically they each drive alone. They never complain to each other.

Four thousand days is a large amount. Maybe as large and as many as the curses of this pretty-face pregnant woman to the foolish people on the road. The more people with valid driver's licenses, the more

---

"Foolish," by Aminah Haji Momin, first published in Malay in *Bahana* (1996). Permission to publish granted by the author. English rendition by the author and the editor.

people acting foolish on the road. The more sophisticated the road, the more foolish the unchecked people on the road. Each day the number increases. From one person, it becomes two, ten, then hundreds and thousands. *Foolish, really foolish!* snarls the pretty-face pregnant woman driving on the road. *Silly, stupid, foolish—doesn't know the laws!* These are the words that usually erupted from the thin lips of the pretty-face pregnant woman.

Am I wrong? Am I sinful for cursing foolish people on the road? But they are wrong. The pretty-face pregnant woman keeps on asking herself this question. Her right hand is clutching the steering wheel. Her left hand sometimes helps. It is always relaxed, except to shift gears or to search for some radio channel. The pretty-face pregnant woman is restless. There is a traffic jam.

It's 4:30, time to return home from the office. The situation around Berakas Road is usually like this. At present, moreover, there are excavation projects dotting the road here and there in order to widen and beautify it. *But all these are for the comfort and benefit of the people,* whispers the pretty-face pregnant woman. However, her heart protests. Today the contractor is filling in the road; tomorrow he will dig it up again. Warning signs are placed near the work area. If foolish people drive 160 kilometers per hour, it will endanger the road-workers themselves. On several occasions, both the foolish and not foolish people on the road have suffered consequences.

The foolish people on the road do not concern themselves with road signs. Today the pretty-face pregnant woman is cursing once again. The curse is still directed to the foolish people on the road. She is uneasy. Suddenly two cars accelerate past her. The pretty-face pregnant woman quickly swerves to one side. Fortunately, there was a small space to swerve into along the side of the road. The pretty-face pregnant woman shouts angrily: Fool! *You don't respect other drivers. You don't own the road. Foolish. These people are really foolish. I'd better not follow him.* She is both furious and annoyed, yet her angry voice is heard only by herself. The pretty-face pregnant woman does not press the car horn. She does not like to sound the horn, even though once she was nearly hit by a car darting out unexpectedly at the junction. Only her curses are abundant.

The pretty-face pregnant woman is trembling. Her car almost fell into the drain gutter. The pretty-face pregnant woman is sure those two cars are racing. One, a white luxury car, is driven by a foolish man and the other, a black-metallic luxury car, is driven by a foolish woman. *We all pay road taxes,* the pretty-face pregnant woman is murmuring.

What irritates her is that both those foolish drivers do not see that the road is being repaired. Although it has two lanes, one is impassable. Many barriers have been put there to close the uncompleted highway. The white luxury car, driven by the foolish man, manages to pass through. But the black-metallic luxury car, driven by the foolish woman who failed to transform herself into a stunt driver, crashes against them. All the barriers are wrecked. She is lucky. Nothing has happened to her. Only the front part of her car is crushed.

The pretty-face pregnant woman is terrified. She stops for a moment. Several other cars also stop. Some help out while others act as onlookers, including the pretty-face pregnant woman. Since she is frightened and because of her bulging stomach, the pretty-face pregnant woman returns to her car.

The pretty-face pregnant woman continues her journey. She drives leisurely while listening to the radio station 91.4 as if nothing had happened. Even though her heart is pounding now, the pretty-face pregnant woman quickly settles down. She does not let this recently experienced incident overwhelm her. *All praises to Allah. Luckily I do not suffer from a heart attack or high blood pressure; otherwise, it would be disastrous for me.* She massages her bulging stomach.

The pretty-face pregnant woman drives slowly. She wants to arrive safely at her destination. Her guiding principle is that the house will not run away; only time passes. Time always goes by. It will not wait. The evening prayer should be performed before its time ends. Afternoon tea, together with the husband and children, should not be left out. We will suffer some loss if these activities are neglected. This is what the pretty-face pregnant woman usually wants to achieve, unlike the foolish woman she just saw a moment ago. The pretty-face pregnant woman strokes her bulging stomach. *What a waste! An expensive car is wrecked. That woman doesn't care for the lives of others. If she alone is affected, it doesn't matter. But if it involves other people, children and husband at home will mourn.*

The pretty-face pregnant woman is driving again. Yesterday, she cursed. Yesterday, the tragedy occurred at this same place. Now there is a long queue of cars. In front of her are two impatient ones. The two drivers get out. The pretty-face pregnant woman wonders about this. She questions it and thinks that one foolish man wants to jog. But what is happening? God forbid! The pretty-face pregnant woman can't believe it. *There are really so many foolish people,* she thinks to herself. *They shouldn't move the road sign "No Entry" to the side of the road.* The foolish man removes three barriers—enough space for his car to pass through. Then his car darts forward with great speed. This action is followed by yet another foolish man. He doesn't bother to queue up since he wants to reach his destination as soon as possible. *Foolish, stupid! As if you don't know the rules. Even though you are in a hurry, don't risk your life! It doesn't matter if it doesn't affect other innocent people.*

Today, July 13, the pretty-face pregnant woman is fetching her child from a religious school on Berakas Road. The pretty-face pregnant woman is taking over for her husband. Usually he fetches their children. But today, the husband of the pretty-face pregnant woman is too busy. *Please fetch the children for me, honey. I am very busy.* That is the message he left for her.

The pretty-face pregnant woman looks at the wall clock at her office. It's 4:30; the children finish their religious class at 5:15. The pretty-face pregnant woman carries on with her work, even though the office hours have already ended. Usually the pretty-face pregnant woman leaves her office at 4:50 when there is a lot of work to be done. But today she needs to leave by 4:45 to avoid the traffic and get a good parking space. At exactly 4:45, the pretty-face pregnant woman tidies up her desk. Every once in a while, she holds her bulging stomach. Her desk must be tidied up before leaving the office. The pretty-face pregnant woman wants her mind to be calmed by the clean room when she returns to work the next morning, so she can do her work smoothly.

The pretty-face pregnant woman goes to her car. She prays and entrusts herself to Allah three times. Then she starts her journey when she feels secure. As usual, the pretty-face pregnant woman drives calmly to the school. Suddenly, the car of a foolish driver darts out of the junction. The pretty-face pregnant woman is startled and jams on the car brake. But it is too late. Her car hits the one in front. Boooom-mmmm. The pretty-face pregnant woman is shivering in panic. The pretty-face pregnant woman holds her bulging stomach.

The foolish driver emerges from his car. *Hey, don't you have eyes?* His finger is pointing at the pretty-face pregnant woman, who emerges from the car holding her stomach. Bewildered and in tears she says, *It's your fault. You didn't stop.*

Come on lady. Don't you have a driver's license? If you can't drive right, don't get behind the wheel. The comments of the foolish driver are very sarcastic. He has lost his temper and does not realize that the pretty-face pregnant woman is holding her stomach.

The pretty-face pregnant woman is irritated. *Why blame me? I'm not stupid. I know right from wrong. It is your fault. I won't tolerate this and you must pay for it.* The voice of the pretty-face pregnant woman is trembling while she presses her stomach.

Let's settle it, darling. It's our fault. Luckily nothing bad happened, persuades the wife of the foolish driver.

Oh, you think nothing happened. Don't you realize my stomach is aching? And I am insured. The foolish driver's eyes protrude upon hearing about the insurance of the pretty-face pregnant woman. He finally looks at her stomach. He is scared and trembling. Only then does the pretty-face pregnant woman remember her husband. She takes out her cell phone from the car. Her fingers dial her husband's office number. *Darling, I have had an accident at Kebangsaan Road. Can you come here? Yes, I'm all right, except my stomach is aching.*

Shortly, the husband of the pretty-face woman arrives. He negotiates with the foolish driver. The husband of the pretty-face pregnant woman knows well how to settle the matter, how to claim the insurance. The foolish driver smiles bluntly. *In that case we will settle the matter between ourselves. I will pay for the damage to your wife's car.* Finally the foolish driver admits his mistake.

It is not possible to settle it between ourselves, as claiming insurance may be difficult later. Not like in the past. The hoarse voice of the pretty-face pregnant woman penetrates the ears of the foolish diver.

Then we report it to the police, he laments.

The pretty-face pregnant woman is sad. Her beloved car of which she is so proud is no longer great. Her left eye and cheek are injured. *Even if you go for an operation and plastic surgery, you will not be attractive anymore. You are no longer original,* she comments to herself while holding her bulging stomach, which is growing more and more painful. The pain becomes more intense. *Ahhhh!!!!* The pretty-face pregnant woman suddenly collapses. Luckily her husband could catch her.

My dear, my dear! What's happened? The husband of the pretty-face pregnant woman is getting worried. *It is not due yet,* he whispers to himself. *This is all because of you.*

Let's get her to the hospital and settle this matter later, persuades the wife of the foolish driver.

The pretty-face pregnant woman is immediately lifted into her husband's car. He puts on the emergency signal. The husband of the pretty-face pregnant woman speeds rapidly. He does not care about other people. He acts just like the other foolish drivers. *May you be all right, darling,* he prays over and over again.

1996

Singapore

Modern literature in Singapore emerged from the colonial legacy and the desire for national identity. As in Malaysia, Western influence began with the Portuguese and Dutch during the fifteenth century. British involvement intensified with their establishment of the entrepôt Penang in 1786. Within forty years, British influence had extended to the island of Singapore, which was founded as a trading post in 1819 by Sir Thomas Stamford Raffles to counter Dutch influence in the region. In 1826, the British consolidated Penang, Singapore, and Malacca into the Straits Settlements. Singapore ultimately became a separate crown colony of Britain with the dissolution of the Straits Settlements in 1946.

The Straits Chinese, with their pro-English stance, generated the first modern forms of literature in Singapore through their publication of the English-language *Straits Chinese Magazine* from 1897 to 1907. This publication became an important venue for short fiction concerned with Peranakan (Straits Chinese) culture and identity. Beginning in the 1920s, partly in reaction to the British colonists' hegemonic use of the English language, writers working in the medium of the Malay language felt the need to use literature to promote social progress for Malays. Over the next several decades, many writers in Malay would strive to create a renovated Malay language for modern literature.

Following a declaration of emergency in 1948, when Britain established the semiautonomous Federation of Malaya and communist guerillas in the jungles began a war of national liberation, Singapore became the assembly place of Malay writers. In 1950, the writers' association Angkatan Sasterawan 50 (the Literary Generation of 1950) was founded in Singapore, advocating "art for the people." With its flourishing print industry, Singapore played the role of a Malay cultural center until withdrawing from the independent Federation of Malaysia in 1965. Short-story writing developed faster than other literary genres during this period as the form of stories shifted from longer works or novellas to shorter fiction.

In 1959 Singapore attained full self-government under the leadership of Prime Minister Lee Kuan Yew. In 1965 Singapore became a republic, ending its brief period (1963–65) as a member of the Federation of Malaysia. At this juncture, the center of Malay culture shifted to Kuala Lumpur, the capital of Malaysia.

Singapore's independence in 1965 and its need to establish a separate national identity gave rise to its modern fiction. Although the government promoted the four major language groups spoken in the city, it established English as the national language. The first English-language writers after independence came out of the former University of Singapore, where English was the medium of education. Their writing did not reflect a Singaporean sensibility but European and American literary influences. Other ethnic communities reacted to English as an outsider's language and wanted to produce fiction in the vernacular. Gradually, a greater effort was made to develop the popular short-story genre into a reflection of the Singaporean life and locale.

A seminal year for the recognition of the modern Singaporean short story was marked in 1978 with the publication of *Singapore Short Stories,* edited by Robert Yeo. During the 1980s, writers explored Singaporean identity and the quest for self-fulfillment, often with an aftertaste of disillusionment. The urbanization of Singaporean society left a feeling of isolation along with an increased sense of individuality. Characters in short stories became more eccentric and self-absorbed. Rapidly changing gender roles caught women in the double bind of modern work and traditional culture. This subject became a preoccupation for a number of short-story writers, who often portrayed male characters as disempowered husbands. A sense of entrapment and materialism, fragmentation and alienation, pervades the short story of this era and continues to this day.

Lee Kuan Yew maintained authority as prime minister of Singapore until 1990, when he became a senior advisor to Goh Chok Tong, who took his place. Singapore currently has a majority Chinese population (76.4 percent) and a minority population of Malay, Tamil, and other ethnic groups. The capital city of Singapore has become one of the most prosperous and efficiently run cities in Southeast Asia, a high-tech capital of world commerce and investment. Singapore has drawn criticism because of its strict rules of civil obedience, which may come at the price of individual freedom and creativity. Some contemporary writers reflect these conflicts between the individual and conventional society by creating antisocial protagonists. Other writers explore more universal themes and try to establish the Singaporean individual within the scope of a larger world community. The short stories in this section represent contemporary Singapore writers.

Gopal Baratham

"A Personal History of an Island"

Gopal Baratham, born in 1935, is a Singaporean neurosurgeon and writer. Two of his novels, A Candle or the Sun *and* Moonrise, Sunset, *have been published internationally. In 1991, he was awarded the SEA Write Award for his short story collection* Memories that Glow in the Dark *(Singapore: PipalTree Publishings, 1995). He is currently working on his autobiography,* Beads in a Sutra.

"A Personal History of an Island" takes us swiftly through a psychological panorama of Gopal Baratham's Singapore—from a child's viewpoint of colonial history through a young adult's wonderment at the miracle of modernization to a father's despair at the impact of overzealous policy controls on the minds of his own children. Poignant reflections on social change are found in the fiction of many Southeast Asian writers, such as Shahnon Ahmad's "Delirium" (Malaysia), Alfred A. Yuson's "The Music Child" (the Philippines), and Vo Phien's "Unsettled" (Vietnam).

Once upon a time, there was an island. It was founded, my teacher told me, by an Englishman.

"Why founded?" I asked my teacher. "Find is today, found is yesterday. Is founded the day before yesterday?"

My teacher laughed. "Found has nothing to do with finding. The island was always here. When the British say they have 'founded' something, they are merely telling us that they have taken it over and consider it their own."

I asked if the island belonged to anyone before the British "founded" it.

"Yes," my teacher replied. "It belonged to a Malay Sultan, and I

"A Personal History of an Island," by Gopal Baratham, first published in *Memories that Glow in the Dark* (Singapore: PipalTree Publishings, 1995). Reprinted by permission of the author.

believe they paid him something for it. But much less than it was really worth."

"Is that not cheating?" I asked. "Paying less for something than it's worth?"

"There are worse things than cheating, my boy," said my teacher. "And, to be fair, this man did not want the island for himself. He wanted it for his country. He wanted it for England."

"Is it all right to cheat if you are not doing it for yourself?"

"Ah, my innocent," said the old man. "It is not right to do wrong for any reason at all, but men persuade themselves that it is. And there are worse things."

He showed me a picture of the Englishman who had founded the island on which I happened to be born. He was a tall man with a long nose. A proud man, he looked. Haughty, I think, was the expression used to describe him. He didn't look the sort of man who liked answering questions. My teacher told me that this haughty person was a man of vision, a man who saw what the island could become. I wasn't too sure. He seemed to be looking over our heads. Perhaps, he was looking into the future. Perhaps, he adopted a lofty gaze to avoid looking into the eyes of the Malays he had cheated.

However, all this had happened a long time ago. When I came to be born on the island, the British no longer approved of cheating, or gunboats, or taking advantage of the weak. Now they talked of honor and the rights of men. They told us of truth which it was our duty to speak.

I thought it strange that men who had but recently enforced bargains with canon and cunning should talk this way.

I asked my teacher and he said, "It does not matter why they say it. It matters that what they say is true. And you, my innocent, must always be prepared to fight for the rights of other men and to speak what you see as the truth."

I believed him. I had reason to. Honesty and fair play, justice and honor, must be good things, for they have made the British masters of the land, rulers of the waves.

I came also to believe two things: first, that the British were invincible; second, that they always played by the rules that I had come to hold so dear. I was wrong about both.

Far to the north of our island, in the mindless darkness of the China Sea, several thuds were heard. They were Japanese bombs hitting the decks of the *Prince of Wales* and the *Repulse,* battleships which we had come to believe no power on earth could sink.

More thuds were heard. The air was filled with smoke and fire.

Unfamiliar aircraft crowded the skies and rained bombs on our island. Everything was on fire: houses, ships, people. The smell of burning invaded your nose and stayed there.

Soon, we saw them: the conquerors, the giants who had defeated the British. But they were not giants. They were little men with bandy-legs and flat faces. Men who spoke in grunts and smelled of the swamp from which they had just emerged. These were men who didn't play by our rules. They raped women, hit children, kicked the old out of their way. Justice was whatever they said it was. The torture chamber replaced the courtroom; confessions, the truth.

Hungry and sick, we forgot truth and justice and decency. We cheated the unwary, robbed the weak. I was troubled. Everything I held so dear seemed no longer to be true.

I asked my teacher, "Are all the things I believed in false? Do truth and justice cease to exist as soon as the going gets rough?"

My teacher said, "You cheat because you are hungry, but do you not feel that you are doing wrong? Do you not feel ashamed? Surely that tells you that what you believed in is not destroyed."

"Yes," I said. "But what should I do now?"

"Write down, my innocent one, all the wrong you have seen, all the wrong you have done. Let it be burned in your brain so you never forget. Someday, things will get better and you will make atonement."

And things got better. The little yellow men were beaten and the British came back. Things returned to normal. But with one difference. The British had told us that all men were equal and that injustice to one threatened justice for all. We asked them merely to live up to what they had taught us and to allow us to shape our destinies. Events had shown me that the British were not invincible but I held on to my other belief: that they would play the game by the rules.

I was wrong again.

When we asked for freedom of speech, they gave us censorship. When more than two or three gathered, they called them subversives. In the dead of night, men were taken from their homes. They told us that political prisoners were not tortured as they were in the days of the Kempeti, but who knows what the Special Branch did to you in that dark, high building whose entrance was its only exit? Especially if you were poor, and especially if you could not speak English.

"What now?" I asked my teacher.

He said, "Fight for freedom, my innocent one. Fight with words whose wounds are more mortal than those produced by weapons. Injustice and bondage must not be allowed to win."

"Will injustice and bondage cease to exist when we rule ourselves?"

"Perhaps," he replied. "Perhaps."

So we took to the streets with barricades and boards, books and banners. We shouted slogans to raise the consciousness of the people . . . and to bolster our own confidence. Finally, shaking hands like gentlemen, their equity secure, their profits guaranteed, the British left. We had our freedom.

But the new freedom was worse than the old bondage. More than ever was it necessary to contain expression, restrict liberty.

The laws of repression, fashioned by the British, were not wide enough to contain the new reality. They had to be made more comprehensive, more versatile. There were good reasons for repression. There always are. We were a tiny island threatened by colonialists, communists, chauvinists, communalists . . . and god knows who else. We had to stand as one or die. Dissent was counterproductive; disagreement, treason. Oneness was all: one chieftain, one party, one point of view.

Yet again, men were taken. Yet again, in the dead of night. Where we knew not, and why we dared not ask. When they emerged, they humiliated themselves in the newspapers, on the radio, on television, offering us the anticlimax of a confession for which no absolution seemed necessary.

I was afraid and asked my teacher, now a very old man, what I should do.

"Speak the truth," he advised.

"I am afraid to," I replied.

"Then write it down," he said. "These things must not be forgotten. A people without a memory are a race of zombies."

So I scribbled and watched. Watched families move from hovels to high-rises; watched boys grow straight-legged and strong; girls, bright-eyed and full-breasted. Watched as our GNP grew and we happily extinguished the light of self-determination as we did our cigarettes, swallowed our self-respect as we did our chewing gum. I watched but was silent.

Time passed. Our island prospered. Communism died. Enemies became friends. Over a tired world freedom's dawn was breaking, warming limbs stiff from the cold of repression, lighting the road so people could again walk on their own. Could we, too, not sing, speak our minds, shape our destinies?

Oh no, our masters told us. Freedom and justice were Western ideas and alien to our Asian genes. We, on our little island, would have our own form of freedom, our own brand of justice.

For the first time in my life, I was afraid. Truly afraid. Words, the signpost of truth, were being made to lie.

Too weak-kneed to stand up on our own, we talked of "consensus." Too cowardly to disagree, we became "nonconfrontational." "Feedback" was where we voiced minor disagreements, even when we knew what we were discussing was a load of shit. Yes, we were now free to speak; but only if we first raised our hands, and only if the bossman thought that we had been good boys for long enough.

My teacher was dead and I turned to my sons. Like other children of their generation, they had "mind-sets" instead of views, "role models" instead of heroes.

I asked what they felt about justice.

"Justice," they replied, "is something lawyers are concerned with; and if you are so interested in what is right and what is wrong, you can easily find out by consulting the statute books."

"Of course we have freedom," they assured me. "We vote every four years, don't we, and the vote is free, if not exactly secret."

I dared not ask them what truth was.

I remember what my teacher said and still write down my thoughts.

When I do, I weep. Sometimes I weep a lot, but I hope not enough for my tears to wash away my words.

1995

Mary Loh

"Sex, Size and Ginseng"

Mary Loh (Mary Loh Chieu Kwuan), born in 1959, obtained her master's degree in literature from the National University of Singapore with her thesis entitled Structure, Style and Strategy in the Singapore Short Story. *In 1989, she collaborated with two other local Singapore writers to produce the anthology* Mistress and Other Creative Take-Offs *and in the same year won the Shell Short Play Competition. Currently she is working on a full-length novel on the theater in early Singapore.*

"Sex, Size and Ginseng" humorously reveals a changing world of Chinese gender roles and shifting double standards. The subservient position of women in society is an important theme for many Southeast Asian writers, such as Leila S. Chudori in "The Purification of Sita" (Indonesia), Sri Daoruang in "Sita Puts Out the Fire" (Thailand), Marianne Villanueva in "The Mayor of the Roses" (the Philippines), and K. S. Maniam in "The Kling-Kling Woman" (Malaysia).

Night. She goes to the cupboard and takes out a small glass bottle. Inside it, there is a small, pink, paper-wrapped packet. She takes out the packet and unfolds it carefully and shakes the precious golden flakes into the waiting mug. Going over to the stove, she heaves the heavy black kettle over to the table and pours. The hot clean water rushes from the spout and sends the gold swirling in the white mug. The bitter root-smell rises and wafts through the kitchen. She returns the kettle to the stove and then brings a cover for the mug. She leaves the tea to infuse for a few minutes and then carefully carries it into the study where the old man sits reading.

Daily rituals. We all have them. Sometimes our lives are measured, not by minutes, but by the little carefully attended duties we each have to perform. For Ah Lan, it is the making of ginseng tea for her Master. Ah Lan marks her days by it. Every night, night after night, before she

---

"Sex, Size and Ginseng," by Mary Loh. Permission to publish granted by the author.

goes to sleep, it is Ah Lan's last duty of the day. This was the first duty she was entrusted with, and one which she has carried out for more than a quarter of a century. Ah Lan remembers.

The old man smells of ginseng. How much ginseng has he drunk already in his lifetime? More than a quarter of a century? More than half a lifetime? Night after night and yet he still has no male heir to carry on his name. The Big Mistress has accepted that the fault is hers. She has given him no children, neither male nor female. She has failed in her duty. Hence Mistress Number Two.

Mistress Number Two had two beautiful daughters by him, but they say that her womb is also dried up. It cannot fulfill a wife's first duty, which is to produce sons to carry on the family name. The man was in a dilemma. That's when they told him that he should drink ginseng. It would not only purify the lungs but increase the secretions of the hormones which would urge fertility, especially those which helped to produce sons. Ginseng has been tried and tested. After all, the little roots were shaped like little men. Surely, drinking ginseng would help to produce little men. So convinced, the man went to a medicine shop in the heart of Chinatown.

The medicine shop was a small, cramped and dingy room, lined with walls of little drawers carved with the names of the different herbs etched in gold. The smell of dried roots and bark pervaded the air. Here and there, on open shelving, were bottles of preserved snakes and squirrels with their insides gutted and stretched out. Black beetles, specially bred and bottled, stood on the open counter, ready to be mixed with other elements for coughs and catarrh. In another bottle, they kept the precious rhinoceros horns. These were all guaranteed health tonics brought straight from Mainland China and their quality was never in dispute. The *sinseh* was there and he backed up the recommendation that ginseng be consumed regularly to achieve the desired result and, for proof, quoted many different examples of those who had taken the brew and produced many male offspring.

So the old man bought a large quantity. Expense was no object. He brought it gleefully home, handed it to young Ah Lan, and instructed her as he had been instructed. He drank the potion that night and half imagined that it took effect immediately for he could feel it in his system. He took the ginseng regularly and persuaded Mistress Number Two to do the same. Then she conceived and her stomach grew big and round and her eyes shone with health and everyone predicted that the next child would be a son. The great day arrived. After the relatively short period of birthing, two children were born, the fruit of her labor: two beautiful bouncing twin girls.

The man groaned and covered his face in dismay. What would put an end to this great shame? Four children. All girls. Disgusting. Much as he loved his first and second wives, he knew that he had to take another. There was no other solution to his dilemma. A man of his standing in the business community could not very well take the ignominy of having no sons.

The matchmaker was summoned. He commended her choice of the second mistress, but shaking his head with an exaggerated gesture of disappointment, he told her that Mistress Number Two was also unable to produce sons. The matchmaker felt responsible, of course. It was her duty to make sure that the marriages made on earth were blessed by heaven with beautiful children. For this purpose, she had checked the genealogy of each candidate, read their faces, and then looked at the size of their hips to see that they would produce children. Her method had been foolproof until now.

The man shook his head again. Again he explained. His quarrel was not that Mistress Number Two couldn't produce children. After all, he had four beautiful daughters, but he wanted sons and the matchmaker was assigned the task of making sure that Wife Number Three was a son-bearer. Matchmaker agreed to help but it was not going to be an easy task. One could safely assess the potential fertility, but how could one guarantee sons?

Wife Number Three-to-be was ugly, fat, and coarse. She looked more like a man than a woman. Her face was riddled with large pock-marks and her thick arms hung by her sides, testament to having come from a family that toiled. No one in their right mind would marry her. But, according to the matchmaker, she came from a family of eight sons. She was the only daughter. If she descended from such a mother, would she not also be capable of such a feat, the matchmaker reasoned. Further, her physical structure and the matchmaker's reading of her fortune foretold that she would bear many sons. The man agreed to see her.

When the man met his potential bride, he shuddered. She was almost as tall as he was and was large and grotesque. He had been warned, but it was almost a great shock to see this man-woman before him. Her appearance was made all the more incongruous by the fact that she had a thin, high-pitched voice.

The matchmaker reiterated all the woman's positive points, and once again the man's desire to see his line continue was fueled. He was prepared to make this small sacrifice. He would endure.

And endure, he did. Night after night, night after night, he suffered Wife Number Three's heavy presence. Meanwhile he continued his visits to Mistress Number Two and she conceived. Ginseng was consumed in large quantities. Wife Number Three also conceived. The man looked forward expectantly to the days when both his wives would deliver. Surely the gods could not be so unfair? Surely of the two, at least one could produce a boy?

Again the day arrived for Mistress Number Two to deliver. Damp from the perspiration of exertion, she lay on the bed and watched the midwife as she carried the little baby, swabbed it clean, and placed it in her arms. The little diaper cloth was undone. It was a girl. The midwife was consolatory. There was still Wife Number Three.

The man was not daunted. He had faith. He had to have faith. The matchmaker, midwife and the *sinseh* could not be wrong. Or could they? Daily he went to the temple and implored the gods for their blessing and their mercy. He brought the gods fruit and gave large donations so that the gods could have larger dwellings. He promised them more. Then every day he went home to wait and drink ginseng.

There was a sudden shout. "Labor, labor, Mistress Number Three is in labor. Call the midwife!! Quick!!" The whole household sprang into action. Everywhere, there was the frenzy of activity. The midwife arrived along with the matchmaker who was all ready to crown her success and perhaps receive an *angpow* gift.

The midwife stood at the doorway. One look at her face told him the truth. Girls again. Twins again. Now seven daughters in all.

I do not have to continue this story. The cup of ginseng tea sits on the table, its aroma wafting up to me. Ah Lan has placed another small cup at my elbow. But I'm sure you are curious about how the story ends. How does it all end? Did the man take another wife? Did he go crazy from grief? No. The old man resigned himself to his fate and added another few more daughters to his line. The old man became known as the "Keeper of Beautiful Jade" because all of his daughters were named Jade-something; and, yes, they were all beautiful and sought after. The daughters married well and his sons-in-law, well-chosen, reinforced his business connections, and he was now aligned with many powerful people in the community. They added to his wealth by big contributions. His daughters, in turn, produced sons—all sons, surprisingly.

The old man was pleased at least that he had grandsons, even if they did not carry his surname. The three wives were treated well, and they all lived happily as one large and happy family. All his daughters did well in marriage, except for one.

And that is me.

I did not marry. I did not bear him a grandson. I live in his house and every night, when Ah Lan brews his ginseng tea, she brews me mine. It doesn't do him much good. I know from my science degree that it is a matter of genetics and chromosomes. It doesn't matter, of course. It is a special quality of ginseng. The Cantonese describe its unique flavor as being like *kum*—gold and glinting in a transparent glass. It is the color of pale gold; the best ginseng, of course. I should know because I own the ginseng farm and the best roots come from it. After all, someone must maintain the duty of managing the family business empire.

1997

Philip Jeyaretnam

"Painting the Eye"

Philip Jeyaretnam, born in 1964, is married with two children. He won second prize in the 1983 National Short Story Writing Competition and first place in the same competition in 1985 for his short-story collection First Loves, *which was on the best-seller list for fiction in Singapore for over forty weeks, a record. He was named Young Artist of the Year in 1993 by Singapore's National Arts Council. His most recent novel is* Abraham's Promise *(Honolulu: University of Hawai'i Press, 1995). Currently he works as a lawyer in private practice.*

Jeyaretnam's writing signifies an important shift during the 1980s toward an acceptance of Singapore itself as the subject of writing. "Painting the Eye" conveys a sense of the modern cosmopolitan cityscape of an ethnically polychromatic Singapore through the eyes of the protagonist Ah Leong, an artistically talented insurance salesman with a penchant for mystery. Stories that have an urban landscape as a backdrop for action, often from a critical perspective, include Sila Khomchai's "The Family in the Street" (Thailand) and Mey Son Sotheary's "My Sister" (Cambodia).

Now that Song Jiang was abroad doing his doctoral thesis on some obscure branch of Chinese literature, Ah Leong suddenly felt his absence keenly. They had not really been together for a long time, eight or nine years, and especially once Song Jiang had entered the National University of Singapore, they had seen one another not more than once a month. Yet Song Jiang's being overseas, almost on the other side of the world at Harvard University, seemed to create a hole in Ah Leong's picture of his nation. He wondered why it was necessary for Song Jiang to disappear across half the world in order to study something that ought to be at the center of our lives, right here, and yet wasn't. He wondered whether all these scholars, streaming outwards from Singapore, brought more back when they returned than they took when they departed.

He worked as an insurance salesman, not a very good one, for just as he reached the crescendo of a sales pitch, his mind would wander. He'd wonder why his target, or victim, had chosen to paint the walls of her flat that luminous blue color; and drifting skywards, his thoughts would fly. And he'd see a thousand salesmen just like himself, all across the island, trying to convince people to buy, and then doubt would strike—was this policy really the best for her, could she really afford the policy—and he'd end up stumbling towards the door, mumbling apologies.

Of course, in the evenings there was his painting; he'd signed up for all the courses he could, wondering why they were termed extra-mural, imagining a course for vandals, spray-painting walls, and then finding himself squirming in his seat, as if the *rotan* were already making contact. But the instructors were always pedestrian, teaching skills as if their purpose were merely to pass the time, and for his course-mates, often housewives, perhaps that was true. After all, what meaning could be found in the constant repetition of black branches and red blossoms? After a while though, he found his facility with ink and brush growing, and then with watercolors and oils. Then one day at the Substation, he came face to face with a collage, scraps of *The Straits Times,* and *peranakan* fabrics, and lurking behind them, a face—smoldering, a big Indian face, eyes deep-set and burning—that at first he thought was male, and only later when he saw the artist, large and silent in the middle of the gallery, did he realize was female.

From that moment on, he started painting only faces, and to do so observed everyone he came across, from passersby in the street to each and every one of his clients or potential clients, studying their eyes especially: were they calm or shifty, clear or clouded, profound or shallow, icy or warm? And then the same day or as soon as possible after, the canvas stretched tight across his easel, he would struggle to recapture the face, to fix himself with its remembered gaze. It was strange how different they all were—not just a young undergraduate girl's from that of the old *char kuay teow* man, or a middle-aged Indian doctor's from a Malay housewife's—but all of them. And he began to believe that all of the traditional classifications of faces (young or old, Chinese or Indian, happy or sad) helped not one bit in determining the true essence of faces, of people. Not that he could find new classifications to take their place. No pattern was discernible. Each face seemed to exist entirely unto itself, constituting its own universe. And in the course of a single observation, he would see a face transform itself a hundred times, as if to tell him that it contained at least in memory or in anticipation, all possible experiences of the human animal.

And then the faces began to speak to him and he to listen, rapt. He visited the woman in the house with the sky-blue walls again; and she told him of her husband, who used to visit prostitutes in Indonesia and Thailand but had now found a second wife in China, and her son away at the University, who hardly telephoned, even though she had made her husband buy a Telecom calling-card number that made calling from overseas cheap and convenient. He looked at the sky-blue walls and understood her desire to escape, and when he saw another prospect of his—a shy, timid teacher whom he imagined was bullied every day by students such as he had been ten years earlier—he put them in touch with one another. They both bought insurance and recommended him to others. And when she divorced and married the retiring teacher, he painted them both on their wedding day: two faces separate but together, their gazes joined. And suddenly Ah Léong was looking at his work differently, as something that brought him into contact with a thousand different unique individuals: people who talked to him, to whom he listened, people who sometimes helped him and whom sometimes he helped. And suddenly he was making a lot of money (from insurance that is, he had not yet sold a single painting), and wondering why the world had so intimidated him, why getting a good job had always seemed so hard, why he had seen people as a hurrying scurrying mass with no time or need for him.

A client of his, one day, told him that he had a friend who required life insurance. Could Ah Leong call him? Of course. The next day he did so, and although the man sounded less than friendly over the phone, Ah Leong was not surprised. It was often like that, the assumption being that a salesman was always out to con or cheat, that to be guarded and noncommittal was simple prudence. At least the man agreed to see him, so that his options could be explained further. It appeared Mr. Wee (for that was his name) worked from home, because the appointment, even though it was for 3 P.M., was at a residential address in Queenstown.

It was an ordinary enough, if somewhat old, HDB block with a lift that seemed to take forever, shuddering from one level to the next. The window to the flat was shuttered, and the door, not the HDB original but a sturdy, almost armored-looking replacement, was further protected by a padlocked metal grille. Ah Leong took a deep breath and knocked. The door resonated, but nothing stirred within. Again he knocked, and again without response until, just as he was ready to give up, he heard metal grate on metal; and after a while, the door opened just an inch. At first Ah Leong could see nothing through the crack, and then lowering his gaze, he espied an eye and addressed it. "My name is Ah Leong. Are you Mr. Wee?" There was no reply, but the eye remained. Ah Leong tried again. "We spoke yesterday. About insurance. Your friend Mr. Lim recommended me."

The door swung open, and a man of half his height, dressed in a white cotton body suit, such as Ah Leong had only previously seen on babies, stood before him. "Identification please." Ah Leong fumbled in his wallet for his IC, and a name card, and then handed them to the man. The man held them up, one after the other, close to his face, and studied them intently. Then he held them back out towards Ah Leong. Ah Leong retrieved his IC and told the man in a hurried nervous stammer that he could keep the business card.

"Thank you," the man muttered as he unlocked the padlock. Ah Leong hesitated over whether to pull open the grille, for the man made no attempt to do so and was already turning back into the flat. Then he remembered what he had been taught ("A foot in the door is half the battle won") and pulled it open. He stepped into the dark interior, his eyes struggling to adjust after the sunlit corridor.

"Lock the grille after you."

Ah Leong flinched. A quick getaway would be impossible if he obeyed the man, whom he was still not certain was even Mr. Wee. But if he refused, he could forget about the sale. Focus on the face, he thought, but the man's back was towards him, and all he could remember was the eye: large, round, and opaque. An eye whose size was concentrated on seeing, and kept its owner's soul quite hidden. "Are you Mr. Wee?" he stammered, one hand on the grille.

"Yes."

Ah Leong's relief was so complete that he closed the grille and fastened the padlock in one short fluid motion.

"Sit."

The man was sitting in an armchair and gesturing towards the sofa. Ah Leong obeyed, noting that a dusty TV was the only presence in the room other than the man.

"Now I've worked out a couple of possibilities, based on the age you told me over the phone, thirty-six wasn't it? And you're a non-smoker, right?" Ah Leong removed the plans from his folder. "Perhaps a light would help you see?"

"No. Tell me the difference between the plans."

"Well, I know you wanted just insurance payable on death, but I've taken the liberty to work one out that also pays an assured sum at age sixty-five, as well as providing for certain partial payments in the event of certain illnesses . . ."

"No, just death."

"I see." Ah Leong was struck by the suspicion that something lay behind Mr. Wee's obstinacy.

"May I ask why, sir?"

"No."

"Suicide in the first year is an excluded event." The words had rushed out as they formed in his brain, before his tongue could restrain them. Now he waited trembling as the man stared at him, his eyes seeming to bulge threateningly. How he regretted padlocking the grille! But surely he could fend off this pint-sized fellow, if the worst came to the . . .

"I understand. No question of suicide. Have you brought the proposal form?"

"Yes. Now the insured amount is only $100,000, am I right?"

"That's the maximum without a medical, isn't it?"

"Yes, but you know the policy won't pay out if death occurs from any preexisting medical condition."

"Understood."

Ah Leong went through the form with him and was relieved when the man's doctor turned out to be on the company's panel anyway, and that the man was happy to authorize the doctor to release his medical history.

But in bed that night, he puzzled over Mr. Wee. The beneficiary of the policy was to be his mother, a choice Ah Leong had vainly cautioned against, suggesting someone younger, someone more certain of outliving him. Although Mr. Wee never said so, it was obvious that he was sure of an imminent demise. Yet a planned suicide did not, judging by Mr. Wee's rejoinder, seem the explanation, unless the man thought he could disguise it as something else, some natural cause. Nor did he seem to be ill. Anyway, it wasn't his job to rate the risk. That was for the girls in the backroom, who had suddenly become a good deal more friendly, even respectful, now that his business was booming. One of them was particularly cute, Lee Hua, and his mind turned to the question of whether she might or might not agree to go out with him. Someone as pretty as her must surely have a boyfriend already. But then she always worked late . . . never seemed in a hurry to rush off . . . no indication at all that she was attached . . .

He woke the next morning with a headache and a pounding conviction that Mr. Wee was in grave danger. He wanted the insurance because he expected to be murdered. Gambling . . . that was the answer. Poor Mr. Wee must owe too much money to one of the betting syndicates. He knew he would be rubbed out, and so for the first time was taking a sure bet: insurance on his life.

But what could Ah Leong do? Persuade the man to seek protection from the police? Would that help? There was so much betting money around these days that one could never tell. The syndicate had probably covered that angle already. Or could he protect Mr. Wee? No, he could hardly stake out the place night and day, even if he could persuade Selvam or anyone else to help. And to be honest, he didn't really fancy a life-and-death struggle with a couple of knife-wielding hoodlums. But could he just sit back and do nothing? He thought of the man's eye and how unyielding his gaze had been. He could not leave him to his fate.

That day and the days that followed, he found himself chasing Lee

Hua for the company's acceptance of Mr. Wee's proposal, and for the insurance policy. He felt if he could only talk to the man again, he could offer his help, and together they might find a solution. But first, he needed the policy to provide an occasion for his returning to the flat. He comforted himself that Mr. Wee would only have troubled to obtain insurance if he knew he had enough time for the policy to be issued. And sure enough, when policy in hand he returned to Mr. Wee's apartment a week later, it was to a familiar unflinching scrutiny that the door opened a crack. Moments later he was within, and after a stuttering presentation of the policy, he knew it was now or never.

"I believe you are in danger . . . I want to help."

"Danger . . . how? What do you mean?"

"The betting syndicate. The gangsters."

"Betting . . . what do you mean?" The man stood up . . . Ah Leong imagined the man's heart pounding faster and faster as he realized that at last someone had arrived to help him.

"I understand, sir. I know why you need insurance for death only . . . someone's going to kill you, right?"

"You're mad. From the moment you first came in here, I thought there was something wrong with you. Get out of here now."

Ah Leong left, confused and ashamed. His imagination had run away with him again. Interfering, nosy, insensitive—his mind raced to find the appropriate condemnation of his flawed character. Yet he had only been trying to help. What surely could be wrong with that? And if his concern had been ill-founded, then what explained the man's distrust of anyone who came knocking at his door? At home he began a painting of an eye peering through a door opened no more than an inch. He made the door the standard HDB fitting, but the eye, just as he had seen it, larger than life, and lower than one would ordinarily expect. He filled the eye with fear and suspicion, with all the things that make a man turn in upon himself and away from his neighbors. It was the city, this city that he loved so much, that made men like that. His reaching out to face after face could make no difference, if the faces turned away, if the eyes were shuttered. This city would make him the freak, the one who poked his nose into other people's business. And his own rage and helplessness filled the painting, till it was saturated with the hues of his emotions.

The painting took him a week. Its creation so consumed him that he took time off work, postponed his follow-up of contracts and clients until his anger, channeled into this painting, left him. When it was finished, he went downstairs to the coffee shop, where he liked to sit and watch the faces of others. Today, however, he was still too demoralized for such observation, and he kept his eyes upon the floor as he walked. Thus it so happened that he came across the front page of a several-days-old *New Paper* and its sensational brazen headline: "You Bet You'll Die." There was the man, those same eyes staring up from a blown-up passport photograph. The report was on page three, and there was no page three.

Weariness descended upon him. He no longer wished to solve the mystery. It was as if all his curiosity had been extinguished by the realization that the distance between two individuals was sometimes too great for anyone, even Ah Leong, to overcome. It was almost worse that the man had not been irrationally afraid and suspicious and that he had good cause for his locks and caution. Ah Leong had correctly understood the man's fears, and yet those fears had been so great that his offer of help had been rejected, as if the man thought Ah Leong, even Ah Leong, might be another of his enemies.

It was only much later, months later, after the painting of "The Eye" had been bought for a deliciously large sum of money at an exhibition of young artists he participated in at Boat Quay, that Ah Leong realized it was possible that the man might have been motivated by concern, the desire not to involve him in a problem that in all honesty he would not have solved. And then, with more money in his pocket than he'd ever had before, Ah Leong returned to walking the streets and studying the faces of the city that he loved.

1997

Thailand

Thailand, formerly known as Siam, has the distinction of being the only Southeast Asian country to have avoided direct colonial rule. Traditional literature, composed of verse, is still deeply respected in Thai society and continues to overshadow appreciation of modern genres.

Modern Thai literature developed synergistically with print technology, journalism, and public education, a pattern similar to that in many other Southeast Asian countries. In the first part of the nineteenth century, Protestant missionaries from the United States started a press for the publication of periodicals and religious books. Thailand was the earliest country in Southeast Asia to develop the modern short-story genre, even before the novel. In the 1880s, the traditional term for didactic Buddhist stories, *nithan* (tale), was used to describe an idealistic short-story genre developed by Thai aristocracy for the first Thai magazines.

Nationalism emerged as part of the country's political discourse between 1900 and 1925. This era also marked the growth of a newspaper and magazine industry that encouraged writers to produce authentically Thai stories. A coup in 1932, organized by a group of young Western-oriented political elites, changed the political system to one of a constitutional monarchy with a representational government and universal suffrage. A rift quickly developed between the civilian bureaucrats and the military, a tension that continues today.

During the early 1930s, some emerging writers began to critique the Thai social concept of *sakdina*, which privileged the upper class over commoners and maintained a patron-client system. After 1932, the royal court was no longer the center of Thai culture, and social realism became important for a few writers who depicted commoners as protagonists in their fiction. Although romance continued to be the predominant subject of many short stories, these authors focused on more socially critical subjects, such as the status of women and the superficial adoption of Western values. But class differences were generally rationalized as the result of personal karma. During the late 1930s, nationalism became equated with Westernization, which really meant "economic modernization" and the privileging of Thai ethnicity. When Field Marshal Phibun Songkhram acquired power in 1938, his cultural reforms and strict censorship deterred writers from creative expression. In 1939 the name of the country was officially changed to Muang Thai (Land of the Free), or Thailand.

On 8 December 1941, at the beginning of World War II, Phibun acceded to Japan's demand to use Thailand as a staging area against Malaya and Burma. His government was ousted in June 1944. Between 1944 and 1947, factionalism developed under Thailand's civilian regime. A new upper class of well-educated government officials and businessmen emerged as a powerful civic force after World War II. Their political machinations, sometimes resulting in tragedy, became the subject of fiction in the following decades. The abolition of Phibun's cultural law increased literary freedom. However, in 1947 Phibun's faction overthrew the civilian government. Phibun promoted secondary education, which would expand the audience for new literature. He also used anticommunist propaganda to oppose and jail socialist writers critical of his regime.

In November 1951, the military and police, declaring a communist threat, took over the government and abolished the 1949 constitution. In the early 1950s, a few writers, like Kulap, took advantage of relaxed censorship and wrote about social and political injustice, only to be arrested. To regain power, Phibun became an advocate for democracy. He then gave the press more freedom and began to encourage public criticism of the regime. Although free elections were held in 1957, Phibun declared a state of emergency after students organized protests against the government's handling of the election. In 1958, under the leadership of Field Marshal Sarit Thanarat, a new policy of "national discipline" was imposed under Article 17 of the interim constitution, which led to the jailing of around two hundred writers and intellectuals critical of the regime. The period between 1958 and 1963 is considered to have been a "dark age" for Thai writers and intellectuals. Many shifted to love and sex as safe subjects for fiction. A dozen or more newspapers were shut down. Writers who survived the censors developed a form of subtle and indirect social critique, often employing an allegorical style.

During the 1960s, the "development era," economic modernization aided by U.S. investment and the Second Indochina War began to positively impact the economy. Sarit attempted to mobilize the nation under a revived motto: "Nation-Religion-King." Literature became a medium for discontent as the public became more critical of military involvement in the government. "New Wave" writers rediscovered the socially critical fiction of the 1940s and 1950s. They criticized the negative impact of the government's development plans on people's lives and explored the significance of traditional Thai versus modern values.

Although Thanom Kittikachorn, Sarit's successor, had been duly elected under the new constitution, he led a coup in 1971 against his own parliamentary democracy. On 13/14 October 1973 the military fired on student and civilian protestors, killing seventy-five people. Following this political upheaval, the slogan "literature for life" became the rallying cry for writers opposing social and political injustice. They addressed issues of social inequalities, interethnic tensions, social problems caused by the American military presence, and the gender-based double standard. They also criticized the literature curriculum in Thai schools, which emphasized classical texts and ignored modern Thai literature.

Press and censorship restrictions were lifted in 1973, and political factions flourished. Tension again came to a head on 6 October 1976 when a student sit-in at Thammasat University in Bangkok led to a fight with police, resulting in several hundred deaths. That evening a military coup replaced three years of civilian government with the National Administrative Reform Council (NARC). Censorship was again imposed upon writers. Regional problems became one subject of fiction during this period, along with popular romance for general entertainment.

In 1980 limited freedom was granted to political parties, and an election was held. In February 1991 General Suchinda overthrew the democratic government on charges of corruption. Martial law was declared and the constitution abolished. A scandal over the land-reform program caused the fall of Suchinda's military government in May 1995.

The 1980s had seen the growth of an educated and economically successful middle class, along with a widening gap between the rural poor and the urban rich. During this period, several literary magazines helped to promote a deeper understanding of Thai and international literature. Several of the short stories in this section illustrate the keen sense of satirical humor that has become a sophisticated staple of literary art in serious Thai fiction. Please note that different transliteration systems are used for a number of Southeast Asian languages, including Thai. For example, among the authors represented in this section, Atsiri Thammachoti's name has also been transliterated as Atsiri Thammachot and Ussiri Dhammachot; and Sri Daoruang's as Sri Dao Ruang and Sidaoru'ang.

Atsiri Thammachoti

"And the Grass Is Trampled"

Atsiri Thammachoti was born the son of a fisherman in 1947 in the sea-side town of Hua Hin, Prachuapkhirikhan Province. After graduating from Chulalongkorn University, he worked as a journalist for a number of major newspapers. For the past several years he has been the editor in chief of Thailand's leading newspaper, Siam Rath, *while continuing to write and publish fiction. He has published many novels and collections of short stories, including* Khun Thong *(You Will Return at Dawn), which was awarded the 1981 SEAWrite Award for best short-story collection.*

"And the Grass Is Trampled" has been anthologized in many Thai short-story collections since it was first published in 1970 in Phay *magazine. It is a story of two bodyguards, best friends with rural backgrounds, who are ordered to kill each other by rival "big-city" bosses who also happen to be brothers. Conflicting values—urban and rural, traditional and modern—form a critical subtext to the drama of this story. It can also be viewed as an allegory of the patron-client system. Some other Southeast Asian writers who explore the impact of society on the individual include Khai Hung in "You Must Live" (Vietnam), Shahnon Ahmad in "Delirium" (Malaysia), and Daw Ohn Khin in "An Unanswerable Question" (Burma).*

> *When elephants fight, the grass gets trampled.*
>
> —Thai saying

"You have to leave. The boss said. He'll be out here tomorrow about the house. And the land." The visitor speaks rapidly, standing in the middle of the yard before the house.

"And the Grass Is Trampled," by Atsiri Thammachoti, first published in the magazine *Phay* (1970). Permission to publish granted by the translator, Susan F. Kepner, with the author's consent. Another translation of this story, under the title "Bondage," is found in *Kun Thong* (You Will Return at Dawn), edited and translated by Chammongsri Rutnin (Bangkok: Lo Kai Publishers, 1987).

"Yeah, well I have to stay. *My* boss said, you know? Guard the place, and the land. With my life." The man who has replied from the top of the stairs speaks in the same rapid manner.

"Your boss is in the city. He's no help to you. If you die, he'll never even see your corpse."

"So? This kind of thing . . . Nak, you know. Our lives belong to them."

The man called Nak stretches his shoulders, does not move his feet. He stands like a post that has been driven into the earth. He wears loose black pants and a matching shirt. A *pakomah* cloth is knotted about his waist, its ends fluttering like a flag. He is tall, a commanding figure. His shadow leans far across the grass, which like the ends of his *pakomah* moves faintly with the breeze of late afternoon.

Fine dust swirls in the hot, sultry air. The sun floats high above, as if trying to escape the strength of its own flames.

"We have to do it, Hern. This is the last day. He told me, if you're not out of here, my wife, my children, they won't have the life they have now." As he speaks, Nak pulls at the knot of his *pakomah* with both hands, tightening it, stands a little straighter, lifts his chest.

Hern sits on his knees on the porch above. He wears the same kind of loose black pants, but his *pakomah* rests on broad, naked shoulders. He, too, is sturdily built. These men look much alike; they have the same thick, tough bodies, the identical resolute air. Hern, on his knees, resembles the stump of some great tree. He looks down at his visitor with unblinking eyes.

"I know. It's our duty. They tell us what to do, and we do it."

Nak chuckles quietly, looks down at the clumps of dry grass, scrapes a pattern in the dust with his foot, looks up again and says, "You're here by yourself, Hern."

"How many are with you?"

"I came alone. There are others who would have come. But I didn't want them. Kids . . . Besides, it wouldn't give you a fair chance."

"Thanks. Gun or sword?" Now Hern rises to his feet.

"Sword. Quieter." Nak swallows a chuckle.

Hern is silent for a moment; then he laughs too and says, "You gonna go to jail if you kill somebody?"

"Nah. He'll fix it. You?"

"Same. It's their business."

The two stand quietly, one in the center of the yard, the other at the top of the stairs.

"That's all," Nak says. "I'll be back before dawn."

Hern nods, and Nak turns and walks off, his arms swinging, heading for the gate. He could be a man going out to admire his fields. His ordinary manner has returned. And this is true also of Hern, who slowly sits down, lights a cigarette and blows a puff of smoke with perfect indifference.

The fiery sun climbs a little further in the sky, scorching the desolate house and the fields that lie all about it. Hern's eyes follow the retreating figure of his visitor as he sits with his cigarette, and he sees Nak vanish into the distance like the smoke he expels with each breath.

"Oh, Nak," he says quietly. "So this is our duty." Nak has disappeared from sight but is all the more visible in Hern's memory. He has gone out through the gate where Hern first saw him on a night long ago. Nak was just a boy, and so was he. The boss and his older brother had brought Nak to the house. As Hern rushed to open the gate, his boss introduced the boys.

"Hern, this is Nak. He's my big brother's man."

They had smiled at each other. The first time they met, it was friendship. They understood each other's job perfectly, and why not? Their duties were identical. They knew each other's feelings. The importance of their position. The two young men belonged to the two bosses, who were brothers.

The bosses went ahead, up into the house. Hern turned to Nak and asked, "You drink booze?"

"Some." Nak grinned and added, "Maybe we could have a little celebration tonight."

The friendship progressed. They were like two trees whose roots had grown together, strengthening both. Many times, Hern had reflected that he and Nak were exactly alike: fearless, dogged, and tough. They were the same age. Each had been given by his family to this boss. Eventually, and at the same time, each had been provided a wife and a home by the boss. It was their shared duty to follow and protect the brothers. Not a tuft of grass was trodden by their great benefactors, but Nak and Hern stepped on that tuft of grass in the next moment.

If the bosses were brothers, Nak and Hern were like twins. If Hern thought that his boss was greater than life, more important than anyone or anything, Nak was of exactly the same opinion. "We are men," he said. "Everything we have, our bosses have given us, and if we must, we will die in their place." Hern agreed, and meant it.

Hern does not know even how to think about what has happened. How could two brothers, who as infants crawled on the floor of their father's house together, who grew up together—how could brothers have come to this? They had turned their backs on each other, a parting as bitter and as final as death.

One day the younger brother, Hern's boss, had left this farm and taken his family to the city. Of course, Hern's own family had packed their things and gone too. All the boss told him was, "My brother has betrayed me. We have to get out of here for awhile, and stay in town." Not long after, the boss came to Hern and said, "You have to go back, Hern. Alone. Stay in the house, and don't let anybody on the property. My brother's going to try and take it all. My house, the farm. But I know you won't let that happen, Hern. You'll defend what is mine, with your life. You do understand?"

Hern knelt before his boss, placed his palms together before his face, bent forward and touched his forehead to the floor. Of course he understood. He said good-bye to his wife and children and went back to the farm, moved into the house from which he had not moved until this day.

Hern was home again, but everything was different. Nak had become a person to be kept out. He belonged to the enemy. Hern had not seen his face since the events that had parted them. Fear, caution, and suspicion had twisted his thoughts about his old friend. Nak's boss was a stranger now, and Nak belonged to the stranger. He knew that Nak must feel exactly as he did, that he owed his loyalty and his life to the boss.

"This is our duty," Hern muttered to himself, "this is our job."

Nak turns quickly, and with rapid strides passes the gate, his heart heavy. "Hern, why don't you go?" he thinks. "Please, get out of here . . ."

Some of the truth is that he is thinking of himself. But he knows that Hern is a man. Hern will never walk away, never refuse an order from his boss, any more than he would. How well he knows Hern. He thinks again of the night they met, of all the days they followed the brothers over their wide fields. "When the brothers worked for the same things," Nak thought, "when they loved each other. That's what brought Hern and me together, and we loved each other, too. Now that the bosses have broken with each other, turned their backs on each other, Nak and I have to turn our backs, too. It is a very ordinary thing. Our lives do not belong to ourselves. Even though our friendship was born with the bosses . . . No, that doesn't matter. Everything we have, Hern and me, the bosses gave us, and he was right. They come before us, before our wives and children."

The bosses have split up over—what? Nak has no idea, cannot imagine. The business of the bosses, and the things Nak and Hern think about—it's like the sky above, the dirt below. Things Nak doesn't understand. But he does understand what he's supposed to do, what his duties are. What it is to be a man, one who has been given to serve one master. The boss's orders are sacred. He knows that Hern would say the same thing.

"My younger brother has betrayed me," the boss had told Nak. "That piece of land, that house—they are mine. It's time for you to get rid of Hern. Tomorrow I will be there, and take care of things—before then, you take care of Hern."

Remnants of tales his mother had told him flare in Nak's mind as he trudges past the huts of farmers, between the tangles of brush on either side of the dusty road. She had told him many stories, when he was just a little boy, about the sacredness of the bonds, the loyalty between a good master and a faithful servant.

The words of a good master, one who has provided all things for his servant, are sacred. And the honorable servant, the one who does all that is expected of him without question, is a fine example to instruct the hearts of men. "Mother, know that I am like the servants in your stories," Nak says within his heart, then turns his face straight up to the sun, which is about to begin its journey toward the west, and evening. He cannot help but feel sorry that he must destroy his great friendship, at the next dawn, and in the most ultimate manner. "Although it is true," he thinks, "that our break came long before this day." The break had come, had to come, on the day the brothers separated, and Hern became the enemy's man. Of course, the break was not nearly so final as the one at dawn would be.

Who will be defeated? Who will be the victor? Nak has not thought about it, and he is sure that Hern has not thought about it either. As if it were not their own matter at all, but the business of time, of sky and earth, nothing about which they should be making any decision, or having any opinion, before the event even began.

"Hern, please get out of here, please go . . ." Nak cannot help the selfish thoughts from coming again.

When he realizes his confusion, Nak shakes his head, pulls himself a little straighter, deepens his stride, walks on.

It is nearly dawn when Nak ascends the stairs, enters the house where Hern has lit a lamp and waits for him. He holds a sword in his hand. Its blade gleams against the dark wooden walls in the lamplight, and at once metal joins metal, the flame of the lamp flickers and surges like so many final leaps of falling stars. The men's breath is harsh, rapid; the house itself resounds, metal clamoring against the thin wooden walls, floorboards creaking and groaning beneath the stomping of swift bare feet. The house shudders with the tumult, while outside all is dark and silent.

With each gust of wind through the door, the light flares momentarily, illuminating the creatures now locked in mortal combat, alone in a desolate house in the midst of bleak fields. Their eyes are flecked with red: the eyes of animals. Shining rivulets of sweat stand on their upper lips, gleaming wetly in the lamplight; they are like demons hungry for blood. Blood streaks their faces, courses down their naked chests and sturdy arms, drips from the tips of the pale blades of their swords. All is light and shadow, sweat and blood. Dreadful scenes are illuminated, disappearing with the rise and fall of the night wind, the rise and fall of the flame. With every new gust and each new gleam of light, there is more blood, more noise, fiercer and more desperate breath. The sound of crashing blades never ceases, nor the bellowing of the walls and floor that enclose the battle.

All is quiet, now. The dawn has arrived, the moon hides behind treetops at the far edge of the field. A rooster crows, impatient for the dawn.

Nak stands at the head of the stairs, struggling to keep his balance. He listens to the rooster, he can barely see—all the world is blurred. Mustering his strength, with shaking arms he brings the sword above his head, then drives the tip hard into the floor. Behind the swaying sword lies Hern's still body. The sun is gaining strength, the lamplight is barely visible.

Nak stands exactly where Hern had stood this afternoon. The *pakomah* about his waist and his black pants are soaked with blood that continues to run down his arms and his bare chest, to spill from the wounds on his head and face.

He descends the stairs very slowly, with empty hands. The sword fixed to the floor above still sways. He takes a cautious step, then another, then falls, his body crashing to the ground. He rolls over the stiff tufts of dry grass, seizes at them as if to stop himself. "Hern is gone . . ."

Nak feels the swift faint beating of his heart. "Tomorrow the boss can come out here, he can deal with the farm, with—everything . . . Whatever he wants to do. My job is finished."

And in this moment, Nak knows that the friendship, despite all that has happened, has not ended at all. Hern's breath is no more, but all that they had—understanding each other, being men together—doesn't end, not even in this moment. At the instant Hern's life ends and Nak knows that his own life is about to end also, he feels his tears flow hotly through his drying blood and sweat.

His mother's old stories float into his mind once again. Those old tales of master and servant that he had never forgotten. She had told him that he must never forget them. They were the key to a good life for his family. He sees the faces of his boss, his wife, his children, and of course Hern so clearly, even though his face is buried deep in the dry grass. He sees the face of his mother, who has long been dead. She is telling stories.

"Mother, I know that you were right. But—I think it is fortunate that you have not told your stories to my children, stories which have brought me so much pain." Nak weeps, the pain suffusing his body and also reaching into his soul. Not only is he losing his life, which now steadily flows from his body; he is losing also his children, his wife. Already he has lost his friend, Hern. He is also losing his boss, but his pain somehow does not encompass that loss. Now that the last day of Nak's life has arrived, he is glad of one thing, that he is losing the boss. Hern, when his death grew near, had felt exactly this; Nak is sure of it. Nak feels the ultimate obligation that has ruled his life begin to loosen and fall away. He will soon be free of all bonds, free of the great pledge of his life. There will be nothing, from this moment forward, no one to control Nak or Hern. No bosses.

With all the strength that remains in his hands, Nak seizes two clumps of grass stiff with blood, hangs on, clutches them with his fists until, at last, his body relaxes and his last breath escapes.

1970
Translated by Susan F. Kepner

Sri Daoruang

"Sita Puts Out the Fire"

Sri Daoruang (pen name Wanna Thappananon) was born in 1943 in Phitsanulok Province to a working-class family. After her employment as a maid and factory laborer in Bangkok, her first short story was published by the editor Suchat Sawatsi, whom she later married. Her early short stories were influenced by the "literature for life" movement, their subject matter taken from her own experience as a low-paid worker. During the 1980s and 1990s her writing has become more experimental, with controversial and uncompromising depictions of contemporary Thai life.

"Sita Puts Out the Fire" is a satirical sketch on the gender-based double standard in contemporary Thai society, cleverly depicted through well-known characters in the Ramayana, *who now have busy lives in modern Bangkok. But unlike the original epic, in which Sita and Rama are married, Sita now chooses Ravana (Tosakan), the demon king, as her husband. Although the time frame of the story is the 1980s, the same male privilege seems to have prevailed over the last two thousand years, whether Sita's husband is Rama or Ravana. In "Sita Puts Out the Fire" our heroine experiences jealousy over Monto, the chief consort of Ravana in the* Ramayana, *whose telephone number she now finds listed in Ravana's private, little black notebook. How she solves her despair gives cause for reflection.*

Another author who uses a similar technique of transposing traditional literary characters into a modern setting is Leila S. Chudori in "The Purification of Sita" (Indonesia). The issue of a gender-based double standard troubles many Southeast Asian writers. It appears in

"Sita Puts Out the Fire," by Sri Daoruang, first published in the magazine *Lalana* (1984) and later included in the collection *Demon Folk/The Friday Club* (1996). Permission to publish granted by the translator, Susan F. Kepner, with the author's consent. Another translation of this story, under the title "Sida Extinguishes the Flames," translated by David Smyth and Manas Chitrakasem, is found in *The Sergeant's Garland and Other Stories* (Kuala Lumpur: Oxford University Press, 1998).

Mary Loh's "Sex, Size and Ginseng" (Singapore), Marianne Vil-
lanueva's "The Mayor of the Roses" (the Philippines), and K. S.
Maniam's "The Kling-Kling Woman" (Malaysia).

"Sita, I'll be late tonight."

Truly, Sita had been preparing herself to hear these words from him. The only thing she had not been able to guess was the exact nature of the ruse he would employ. She cast a glance at her beloved demon, and her heart pounded. She tried to suppress the feelings that surged within her, to speak in a perfectly normal tone of voice, for she herself had a thing or two to conceal, and thus had to lower her head and avoid his eyes as she asked, "Will you be home in time for dinner?"

"Probably not. A friend invited me out. You and the boy had better go ahead and eat. No need to wait for me."

When it came to loving and deeply caring for one's wife and child, Tosakan was in a class by himself. Not once had he come home in the dark of night with no explanation for his behavior. And before going out the door each morning, he would always hug his wife and give her a smacking kiss on the cheek.

Today was no exception. He called out to his son, "Hey, Hanuman, Papa's boy—whose mama am I kissing here, eh?"

The son was like the father. At his papa's words, he came tumbling onto the scene like an actor in a Chinese movie, landing between his parents in the attitude of a Ninja set to strike. Sita got up and left the jokesters to their tricks. Those two! As usual, the moment they perceived that no one was admiring their performance, it ended. Tosakan sent Hanuman out to buy him a pack of cigarettes, and hurried into the bathroom to finish getting ready.

While her husband bathed, Sita was able to quell the heat in her heart sufficiently to be sure that her voice would not tremble, and that the tears would stay in her eyes where they belonged. "I must not seem any different from usual," she said to herself, and forced herself to smile when her beloved husband emerged fully dressed from the bathroom. She even teased him.

"My, how handsome you look," she said with a sweet smile. But she was unable to resist adding, "This 'friend' wouldn't happen to be a woman friend, would it?"

"A m-a-n friend," he replied, drawing out the letters as he picked up his shoes. He carried his shoes from the bedroom, and then returned to the bathroom once again. He shook a little cologne over his hair, patted some on his throat, and then reached inside his shirt and dabbed some into his armpits. He combed his hair again, and also his mustache. "Why do you ask?"

"I don't know."

"Do you suspect something, is that it?"

"No."

He smiled at her reflection in the mirror. "Tosakan is old, my dear. Nobody wants him. Uh, where's that little comb I keep in my pants pocket? Did you wash it? If you wouldn't mind finding it for me . . ."

"Here it is."

"Ah." He planted a light kiss on Sita's forehead and, taking the comb from her hand and the pack of cigarettes from Hanuman's, went swaggering off down the path with a cigarette stuck in his mouth. And then, just as he did every day, Tosakan turned and looked back at his wife and child.

Never, since they began to share their lives with each other, had there been a hint that Tosakan might have other women. If it was true . . . if this, the thing that she suspected, turned out to be true, never again would his word be sacred to her. He had caused Sita to feel a great, heavy, sorrowful anger. Had he no shame, before her and their son? (Was Tosakan not only ten-faced, but two-faced as well?)

Very early this morning, while it was still dark and she had been removing things from the demon's pants pockets in order to lay out a fresh outfit for him to wear that day, she had pulled out his black pocket comb, his keys, his wallet, and his notebook, and set them before the mirror. Then she pulled out a handkerchief and tossed it into the hamper.

And then, something unusual happened. Sita turned around, looking this way and that to be sure that she was alone, and then she was seized with the desire to pick up the little black notebook . . . and open it . . . and read it. Something, some kind of a gossipy voice seemed to be talking inside her head, and it was saying, "Pick up the notebook, pick it up, read the notebook . . ." And a feeling stole from her heart out to her fingertips, an irresistible feeling that caused her to reach out, to snatch up the notebook, and to read every line of every page in the "daily diary" part.

On those narrow pages, her husband had written the telephone numbers of many people. Sita felt proud when she saw that her birthday and their son's birthday were written on the very first page. The dates of various events were jotted down, along with clever remarks that Tosakan had thought of, or heard.

Sita came to the last jotting in the notebook, Tosakan's notes for today, the fourteenth of October: "Birthday—Monto." Eh—what was this?[1]

October the fourteenth, oh marvelous day . . . Tosakan is going out, even though he doesn't have to go to work today. One of his "friends" is taking him out . . . he says. Now, Sita has no doubt of the true situation!

Suddenly, the god of the wind sent a gust through the open window, and Sita ran to close the shutters to keep the dirt of the fields from invading her home. She sank wearily onto her bed and stretched out, face down in the gloom. The good Saturday TV movies that Tosakan and his son loved would be watched by only one today. Sita behaved like the worst of mothers—one who has no interest in her child, who does not bother to amuse him. She felt irritated by the stupid roar of the soap commercial coming from the other room, which had never bothered her before.

As the day progressed, Hanuman himself wondered what was going on, because on most Saturdays he and his father would lie side by side watching TV, and his mother would bring them nice things to eat. But today, she was quiet and stayed in her room. She hadn't taken their dirty clothes out to soak in the basin yet, and there was a big pile of dirty cups, dishes, bowls, pots and pans in the kitchen. Worse, she had actually yelled at Hanuman to go in there and wash them himself as soon as the Thai film "A Man Called Horse" was over.

Sita sobbed miserably, silently into her pillow. The flames of her hurt and anger billowed and subsided, fanned by awful thoughts she could not suppress. What sort of creature did she seem to him? Oh, she knew all too well that she had no "family" (and no birthmark, either).[2] Or perhaps he was simply bored with her. Had she done anything wrong? She was forced to admit that she would have been spared these dreadful thoughts and suspicions had she not discovered his secret by

---

1. This date is associated with the Thanom government's massacre of student protesters on 14 October 1973. The use of this date indicates the extent of Sita's distress.

2. The author is making fun of Thai romances in which the heroine's true aristocratic origins are proven due to a birthmark that is remembered by someone who cared for her in infancy.

sneaking into his diary—a thing a truly good wife would never have done.

From the first moment of their life together until today, nothing in his behavior had hinted of anything but love for her and for their child. Sita was sure that this woman he had found must be beautiful—in the way women who worked out in the world were beautiful. In fact, she was probably—oh, no! She was probably—an intellectual! And what was she, Sita, by comparison? A plain old up-country factory worker, that's what! The kind of woman who washes her face and combs her hair once a day, maybe twice; a woman whose clothes have never known the heat of an iron; a woman who never, during the course of a whole day, gives one thought to "two-way powder, 280 *baht* a box"!

No, all Sita thought about was housework! She even thought that it was important; that, and helping her husband by making a little money here and there with her sewing, all of which somehow made the time disappear, day by day, almost without her knowing how, until she could not help but wonder how so much time had gone by so swiftly without her having accomplished much of anything worthwhile.

However, the hell with all that. Now is what matters, Sita thought dazedly. What is he doing? Where is he doing it? (And how, exactly?) He is in a room somewhere with this woman, and they are alone. A voluptuous scene unfolds in Sita's mind, a scene that cannot but end with Tosakan passionately embracing . . . her . . . what's-her-name— that slut, Monto!

If the woman is so beautiful, if she is such an unforgettable lover . . . Oh, Hanuman, my poor little son, will you end up living with your papa, or your mama?

After lying in her tears for a long time, painting various pictures in her mind, which only deepened her sorrow and vexation, Sita was left with even more unanswerable questions. Exhausted from running in the frantic circles of her imagination, presently she began to feel ashamed before her son, who had crept into her bedroom from time to time and then crept out again, terrified. She was determined to rouse herself, and she did.

She went to the bathroom, undressed, dipped cool water from the earthen jar, and poured it over her head. Dip and pour . . . dip and pour . . . the water streamed down her body and began to wash away her sadness. Just a little cool water, pouring down from her head all over her body, and her tension, the giddy misery of her mind, began to heal.

Her skin felt clean and fresh, her thoughts were clearing, and the answers for which she had searched for so many unhappy hours began to come.

"Aow! Aow! Come here, everybody, I'm home! Bearing gifts for both wife and son! Come and look!"

It is nine o'clock and Tosakan's voice preceded him into the house. Hanuman sprang up, abandoning the TV show "Singha Gry Pope" at once and cried, "Oh, ho-o, Mama—look at the beautiful cloth Papa brought for you! And candy for me—and a toy, too!" He turned quickly to his father, whispering, "I don't know what's wrong with Mama. She's been lying on her bed crying all day, and she even made Ninja Boy wash the dishes all by himself. It's been terrible here!"

Sita accepted her gift. Although she had firmly resolved the matter of how she would behave toward the source of her suffering, she was unable to muster the cheery smile she had planned. Tosakan, however, was smiling from ear to ear; indeed, his face looked as jolly as a bowl of popped rice. There were two things about him that Sita could hardly fail to notice: first, he was as clean and fresh as the moment he left the house that morning; and second, there was not one trace to be sniffed of the cologne that he had sprinkled over his hair, patted on his throat, and dabbed into his armpits.

"Do you want something to eat? Or perhaps you aren't—hungry, anymore . . ." She lightly shrugged off the arm with which her beloved husband would have encircled her, a gesture in which he could not but discern a trace of disgust.

"I've eaten," he replied.

"I see. You don't seem to have had anything to drink at all—how odd. You and your friend get together, and you don't have a drink?"

There was something in Sita's tone of voice, and in the studied blankness of her expression, that pushed Tosakan to the edge of his endurance.

"What is this? Do you suspect me of something?"

"No." She lifted her chin, and sniffed. "How nice. You've had your bath. Now you won't have to argue with your son about who gets to bathe first." She turned to Hanuman. "Get going, Hanuman, or did you plan to go to bed just as dirty as you are?"

Hanuman stood transfixed, his glance darting between his mother's face and his father's. He grinned nervously. "Papa, maybe you should take a bath before you come home *every* day—then we wouldn't be wasting so much water, right?" He was desperate to coax a laugh from his papa, but Tosakan was not amused. In fact, his formerly cheerful face was clouding over rapidly, and he no longer resembled a jolly bowl of popped rice. He was as silent as a grain of rice that refuses to pop, one that lies sullenly beside the fire like a pebble. He stalked out the front door and sat down on the porch by himself, taking sulky drags on his cigarette. It was what he did whenever he felt resentful at having been criticized, or picked on. Sita followed a moment later and sat beside him.

"What is this?" he asked angrily, glaring at her. "Can't I even go out to enjoy myself with my friends after working all week?"

"Absolutely. We all have the same rights, don't we?"

"And what is that supposed to mean? You want to go out? So, my little Sita is capable of jealousy after all."

"So, my demon admits that there is something to be jealous of? Yes, we all have the same 'rights'—but some of us choose not to exercise them. I never told you not to go out with your friends. I'm not angry about that—I'm angry because you lied to me."

"I lied to you?"

"I read it in your notebook."

He could not believe it. Never would he have imagined that his beloved Sita, she with the honest face, would have thought of doing such a thing! Tosakan's face turned such a deep shade of red that he began to look like Kuan U.[3] Suddenly he rose, picked up a chair, and slammed it down on the floor of the porch.

Hanuman heard the crash. He had been watching TV inside the house and listening to the argument with half an ear. Now, he crept to a good vantage point from which to view the more interesting proceedings outside.

"You are blaming me! So, my friend and I went to a massage parlor—so what? I hurry home from the massage parlor, to my wife and child—I even stop to buy gifts for my wife and child—and what do I find? A spy in my house, that's what I find. What I want to know is this: why am I now living with a spy in my house?"

Sita had expected Tosakan to be silent, not only because he was the guilty party but because he had been caught. She had not been prepared for the possibility that the tables might be turned, that she might be designated as the guilty party.

---

3. Kuan U: a general with a dark red face in the Chinese epic *Three Kingdoms*.

"Well, I know that I was wrong about that, I shouldn't have looked. Say what you like, curse me if you want to about that, and I won't argue. But I beg your indulgence to say that I never thought you would lie to me."

"So, you admit that you were wrong, and now—now what do you want from me? I'd have been better off not to come home at all."

"I'm not finished. I've said everything I have to say about you, but not everything I have to say about myself. From now on, I will never look at your notebook again, never."

"Hoy! And how will I know? Such a thing in my house—a spy in my house! I don't like it at all. After this, no matter what I do, I shall feel that I have no freedom in this life."

Sita struggled to keep her voice down, to keep the conversation from growing into a shouting match—for she, too, was becoming angrier.

"Tosakan, since the day we began with each other, have you ever caught me lying to you?"

"Have I ever caught you? You, the most perfect woman in the world? And if you hadn't been, would I have chosen you to be Hanuman's mother? No. But now—now, you are so much more than Hanuman's mother—you are my mother, too!"

"You needn't be sarcastic. You will see that you can make all the notes you like on all your love affairs—whoever you have them with, and wherever you choose to conduct them. You can fill your notebooks with them, and I will never look. Or—perhaps I will. Perhaps I will give in to temptation, and open the notebook again—in other words, perhaps I will be no better at keeping my word than my husband is."

By now, Tosakan had forgotten that it was he who had first stood accused. He ranted on until Hanuman grew so bored with hearing the words "a spy in my house" that he took himself off to bed. It was Sita, Tosakan continued to insist, who had caused all of this trouble, with her admission to being a spy in his house. But she continued to argue back that he had lied to her!

And so it went, on and on.

Since that unhappy day, Sita has felt quite proud of the way she conducted herself in the matter, and of the way in which she was able, finally, to gain control of her feelings. For in the end, she did. The "Nang Monto fire" has been extinguished—for the most part, although she is not altogether sure how she feels about some things.[4] For example, if a husband comes to a wife in all honesty to announce what she had only suspected when she looked into his notebook, will that wife be grateful for his integrity?

Sita continues to believe in the importance of expressing one's feelings. It is a matter of self-respect as far as she is concerned, both for herself and for her demon, and also a demonstration of both intimacy and sincerity. Such behavior ought to engender love and happiness between them anew, if only because it will remind them that we human beings are an imperfect lot, full of defects and weaknesses.

Today, Sita is able to touch the little notebook, the tempting object that caused so much trouble, with a sensation of victory, even though she still does not know whether she trusts her demon completely (or whether, for that matter, he trusts her). She has thought long and hard about the matter, and decided upon what she *does* know to be absolutely true: her demon loves and trusts her, no more and no less than she loves and trusts him; and there is no doubt that he is able to love her the more because she was able to put out the "fire" that had consumed her on that terrible Saturday, the fourteenth of October.

Now, she is able to take his things from his pockets, and pile them in front of the mirror. And leave them alone.

Does he lie to her face or behind her back? Either way, it is no responsibility of hers. She knows that she still loves him and that his love for her has not waned. And she laughs to herself, when she remembers how Tosakan, the picture of wounded self-righteousness, had announced, "I hurry home from the massage parlor, to my wife and child—I even stop to buy gifts for my wife and child!"

Wait and see. Another day, "Nang Monto" just might pay a call. Who can tell?

1984

Translated by Susan F. Kepner

---

4. Nang Monto: "Nang" is the prefix for the name of an adult woman. "Nang Monto" is funny because in the *Ramayana*, Monto is the Consort of the Demon King. This is sort of like referring to Queen Elizabeth as "Mrs. Windsor." Sri Daoruang brings all these characters down to her own class level with these names.

Sila Khomchai

"The Family in the Street"

Sila Khomchai is the pen name of Winai Bunchuay. A native of Nakhorn Si Thammarat Province, in southern Thailand, he was born in 1952 into a Muslim family. During the turbulent early 1970s, he worked as a political activist and singer while attending Ramkham-haeng University in Bangkok. After the 6 October 1976 massacre of student protesters and political dissidents at Thammasat University, he and thousands of other students sought refuge with groups of revolutionaries in remote rural areas. He returned to mainstream society following government amnesty in the early 1980s. Currently he is a successful journalist, editor, and fiction writer. His short-story collection The Family in the Street *won the 1993 SEAWrite Award.*

"The Family in the Street" transports the reader to the modern world of industrialized Bangkok. By the 1980s, this crowded metropolis had become a major center of the Southeast Asian "Tiger" economy. Its mushrooming automotive and computer-parts factories produced so much growth and wealth so rapidly that the city's streets became choked with legendary traffic jams. The impact of this "modern" industrialization on domestic life is satirically expressed with keen humor in "The Family in the Street." The downside of economic development is a theme taken up by other Southeast Asian writers, such as Alfred A. Yuson in "The Music Child" (the Philippines).

My wife is a thorough and wonderfully organized woman. When I remarked that I had to meet my boss for an important client meeting at three in the afternoon at a riverside hotel in Klong Saan, she said that in that case, we would have to leave the house at nine o'clock in the

"The Family in the Street," by Sila Khomchai, published in *Khrawp-krua taam thanon* (The Family in the Street) (1992). Permission to publish granted by the translator, Susan F. Kepner, with the author's consent. Another translation of this story, under the title "Middle of the Road Family," translated by David Smyth and Manas Chitrakasem, is found in *The Sergeant's Garland and Other Stories* (Kuala Lumpur: Oxford University Press, 1998).

morning so that she could make her appointment just before noon near Saphan Khwai.

But her thoroughness and organizational skill go much further. In the back seat of our automobile she has always ready a basket of *fast food,* a cooler full of iced drinks, an assortment of salty and sweet snacks, green tamarind, star gooseberries, a plastic trash bag, and a spittoon. Often there are changes of clothes hanging from the rear-view mirror. It looks as though we are going on a picnic.

Theoretically, we are middle-class people, which you would assume from our address in the northern suburb of Tambon Saimai, between Lam Luk-kaa and Bang Khen. To get into midtown, we pass housing developments one after another, turn at Kilometer 25 on Paholyothin Road, then get onto Vipavadi Rangsit Highway at the Jetchuakhot Bridge (which means "seven generations" bridge—the length of time it took to build it), and keep going. That's the convenient way.

If we were poor people, we would live in the center of town just like the rich people, who live far above the slums, enjoying, from the windows of their elegant condominiums, the golden sunset rippling and twinkling over the Chao Phraya River. But the splendid view is not so important as the glittering panorama of the visions that are ever before the eyes of the rich. The goals of the upper class are plainly visible; and we work ourselves into a frenzy devising a plan to carry us in that direction, obsessed every day with the vision of owning our own business. And while we may never achieve that goal, we can at least own a home—and a car, our very own car.

There are several reasons for owning a car. To be sure, owning a car elevates one's status; this, I do not deny. But there is a more important reason: a body that has begun protesting that it can no longer bear to stand on the bus, hanging from a strap for three or four hours, packed between the other riders while the bus inches its way forward in the midst of the scorching road. Even if one's car is stuck as if by glue to the others, one may sit comfortably, enjoying the cool breeze from the air conditioner and listening to one's favorite music. It is much, much to be preferred.

Still, I found it unsettling that upon reaching thirty-eight years of age, coming home at eleven o'clock at night I was so weak that I could barely muster the strength to haul my body, its every sinew slack, onto the bed. I, who as a lad was such a strong footballer, chosen by the coach to play *half* (or *midfield,* as they say nowadays), a *dy-na-mo* who could run on and on, ignorant of the very idea of fatigue. I might have been so tired simply from working too hard, but according to one of those mini-documentaries I heard on the car radio between songs, we are all tired because of the air pollution that poisons our organs relentlessly, and the level of stress that affects us, and of course our performance, so negatively.

Owning a car is a necessity. One spends as much time in the car as at home, or at work. And with all the food, drink and other amenities my wife provides, it also is a roving office, and in a sense it is our rolling home. It was when I arrived at this understanding that I ceased to feel the stress of being in the car, and on the road. So what if Bangkok has however many million cars, with stalls so long that one becomes almost a resident of the street. Moreover, I suspect that it was when I learned to like the conditions of my life in the car that our family began to grow closer. Luncheon on the expressway became a time for warm communion, sharing funny stories and whispered confidences. Often when we've been stuck in the same place for over an hour, we think up amusing games.

"Close your eyes," my wife commands playfully.

"Why?"

"Naa . . . naa . . . don't ask," she giggles, taking the spittoon from the back seat and placing it on the floor, for its real purpose. She hikes up her skirt, and slides down toward it. I peek through my fingers, stealing a glance at the smooth white flesh of her thigh which is, naturally, nothing new. Yet, today this not uncommon event has an astounding effect on my senses.

"Ooh, you lied and *watched*!" she says coyly when she's done, pretending to look angry and smacking me on the shoulder smartly two or three times.

We were quite grown up by the time we got married, in accordance with dictum of the Ministry of Health to wed at a mature age, and we took seriously the advice to have children only when we were completely ready. Since my wife and I are from the provinces and had to struggle to establish ourselves in the city, we were only "ready" at thirty-eight and thirty-five—and coming home at eleven o'clock every night barely able to climb into bed at midnight is not conducive to probable parenthood. Although desire occasionally surged, other aspects of the situation were weak; this, combined with the rarity of the act, gave us little hope that our dream of a family would be realized.

On the morning of which I write, the morning I peeked between my fingers and she smacked me on the shoulder, I had awakened feeling quite bright, even cheerful. Perhaps it was because I had enjoyed an unusually long sleep, the longest in some time. I greeted the caress of the sun, sucked in the fresh air of morning, and stretched my muscles with a few samba steps. I showered and washed my hair and consumed two fresh eggs and a glass of milk, feeling some of the old midfielder strength seep through me.

"Vipavadi Rangsit Road is completely stopped just beyond the Kaset intersection," came the clear and cheerful tones of Pearl, my favorite morning traffic person. "A ten-wheeler hit a utility pole, which fell into the roadway before the Thai Airways building. It is presently being cleared."

I felt pretty good. My wife was driving, and I was enjoying the scene.

In the car a little behind us and to our left, a couple of teenagers were fooling around. He reached out and tousled her hair, she pinched his arm; and when he put his arm around her shoulders and pulled her closer, she knocked him in the ribs with her elbow, but gently.

I felt a sudden jolt of energy, as though I were part of the game, too. I turned to my wife and touched her face. She looked more beautiful than usual, and my eyes traveled appreciatively from her shoulder to the plump curve of her bosom, to the rounded gleam of her thigh. She was wearing a short skirt, and for the convenience of driving she had hitched it up even further, dangerously high.

"Your legs are beautiful," I said. I could hear my voice shaking, and feel my heart beating fast.

"Are you crazy?" She lifted her hand to inspect her nails, stretching her smooth, pale neck slightly.

I swallowed hard and looked away, trying to calm myself. But the sight of her thighs remained in my mind, inflaming my imagination. The animal was running wild, that animal that longs to taste untried pleasures, that feels itself losing control. My palms began to sweat. I peered out through the tinted screens on our windows to see the tinted screens on most of the other car windows. We could not see the occupants of those cars, and they could not see us. And we had another layer of plastic, a screen which could be lowered to further discourage the rays of sunlight. The breeze from the air conditioner was cool, and a piano concerto poured from the radio speakers like the waters of a river. So quiet, so peaceful . . . I reached up and pulled down the plastic screen, and it seemed as though our world, the world of Us, floated suspended in sweetness.

I believe that after we humans destroyed the natural world around us, our own human nature was also destroyed; and here we are, stifled in the city, working, breathing poisoned air, stalled in endless traffic. The life of a family by nature has a rhythm; it is a happy song, but families must now make do, adapting themselves to harsh conditions and rapid change.

Perhaps because it had been so long—so long without touching, combined with her maternal desire to have a child to love and admire—my lovely wife's "Yaa! My clothing will be all wrinkled!" and other feeble remonstrances dwindled away to the exigencies of starting our family, right there in the middle of the street.

Oh, happy life. After that day, we returned to the pleasures of our early love together. In the car, we did crossword puzzles, and played Scrabble and other games that young men and women enjoy playing together. What did it matter that the radio reported traffic jams in every corner of Bangkok? Worse and worse: "Sukhumvit, the whole length jammed," says Pearl. "Also Paholyothin, and on Phyathai you can't wiggle a finger between the cars . . . And on Rama IV Road, nothing's moving . . ."

But I feel as though I am sitting in my own living room, curled up on my favorite sofa. I'm thinking of getting a bigger car. More room for food preparation and relieving ourselves, for playing games and catching naps.

In the street, people get out of their cars to stretch their legs and chat. I've met quite a few folks this way. We greet each other, talk about the stock market, politics, the economy, business, important sports matches. Like any other neighbors.

Khun Wichai is marketing director of a big sanitary napkin and toilet paper company. Khun Brat has a sardine factory, and Khun Phanu manufactures spray starch. I'm in advertising, and I can get along with all of them because I've learned a bit about people's preferences and values, and how they live their lives today. As a matter of fact, I've made a few customers in the street.

I'm a good worker, and close to the boss. Take today's appointment with the owner of a soft drink company. The new product is "Sato-can," which we have promoted from the very choice of the product's name.[1] A name the consumer can remember easily, one that rolls

---

1. The idea of canned *sato* (rice liquor made by farmers) is hilarious in Thai, suggesting that nothing in the modern world is beyond the reach of commercialization.

off the tongue . . . *Sato-can.* We're targeting the middle-income market. It's going to be *hard sell* all the way. For the ten million *baht* a year the client is going to pay us, we guarantee to grab the emotions of the potential Sato-can-buying public. Which means that I need to help the boss explain the details—to *"present"* the plan, in today's jargon. And I mean to *present* in a totally sincere and convincing manner.

The streets of Bangkok are as thick as molasses today, as they are every day. My meeting is at three o'clock this afternoon and it is now just eleven o'clock, so there's quite a bit of time remaining to get there. I sit thinking about the work I have to prepare and about the new car. New. More convenient. Not a hopeless dream.

Cars are slowly droning forward onto the Kaset intersection bridge. This is where it happened, the event behind the plastic screen that shut out the blazing sun and the eyes of neighbors. Ahead, I see a raft of unmoving cars, and the fact that we have been steeping here for over ten minutes does not bode well for the rest of the trip; it will be an unusually long one, without a doubt. I lean back against the seat, tip my head back and shut my eyes, and although I try to think about work my heartbeat quickens . . .

It is as though a spell hangs over this portion of the road. It happened here, that bit of hidden and intensely exciting wrongdoing, that inconveniently delightful thrashing in a small space. When had I experienced so delicious a sense of guilt? Not since as a boy I climbed the mangosteen trees in the temple grounds to steal the fruit. Although the episode in the car was, of course, inexpressibly better.

I remember how her pretty outfit was all wrinkled, and not only because of my advances—she had responded hungrily, until from our mighty breathing the car was as hot as if we had neglected to get the freon recharged. I remember how she gripped my hands so hard they hurt, reached up to my shoulders, digging her nails in . . .

I reach up to lower the plastic screen.

"No!" she says, and turns to face me. "I don't know what's wrong with me today. I feel so . . . dizzy."

I sigh and turn away, trying to gather my wits and stifle my fantasies as I haul the food basket from the back seat. Maybe a sandwich will do it. She, who is not looking too good this morning, takes a sour tamarind and begins chewing it hungrily.

When I am no longer hungry, boredom sets in. I open the car door and get out to walk around, smiling faintly at the other people walking around to relieve their stiff muscles. Back and forth we walk, my neighbors and I, like people in a housing complex out sharing their morning calisthenics. Off to our right, a middle-aged man holding a spade in his hand is digging in the middle of the traffic island. Fascinated, I approach him.

"What are you doing, sir?"

"Planting banana palms," he replies without taking his eyes from his spade, but when he has finished his task, he turns to me with a smile. "Banana palms have long, wide leaves. They absorb toxins from the air most efficiently." He sounds like a leading environmentalist. "I plant a sprout or two every day—would you care to plant one? I have more in the car. This stall will go on for some time, you know. I understand from the radio that there's a seven- or eight-car pileup at the foot of the Lad Phraw Bridge and another in front of the Maw Chit Railway Station, so we've plenty of time."

"Thank you. Before long, you'll have a banana grove here," I say as I take the spade and begin digging.

It isn't only the relief of boredom that I feel as I dig. Before I became a Bangkokian, I worked in our family's orchard, so this is familiar and pleasant work. The important thing is that as I plant one sprout after another, I feel myself carried by the motions of planting on a journey into my distant past.

"When they mature and the green leaves open," the man says cheerfully, "when we gardeners have finished our work, it will be like driving through an orchard. How pleasant it will be."

We have become friends so easily, and I feel close to him, as if this place is no longer a part of a vast, crowded street. He invites me to his car for coffee, and we exchange business cards, but I cannot stay long because by now I have been away for quite some time and have to return to my car and wife.

"I can't drive anymore. Would you, please?"

I open the door and sit down, and my wife begins moaning. Her face is pale, and great drops of sweat stand on her forehead. In her hands, she holds a plastic bucket into which she has been vomiting.

"What's wrong?" I am naturally horrified.

"Dizzy. And oooh . . . so nauseated."

"We'll stop at the doctor's—it's on our way."

"I don't think it's anything serious," she says, turning and staring at me for a long moment. "This is the second month I haven't gotten my period. I think I'm pregnant."

I gasp. Then I sit frozen for a long moment before inwardly shouting, *Victory!* to myself. The sound of her vomiting into her plastic bucket! The smell! Who cares? I want to rip open the car door and scream out over the traffic . . .

"My wife is preeeeeegnant! Pregnant in the streeeets!"

I take the driver's seat. When the traffic begins to crawl forward again, I think about the little one, the child who will make our family complete. And I think about a big car, big enough for a father, a mother, and a child. And all the things we'll need in our car, for family activities.

A new, bigger car . . . A necessity, and the greatest source of happiness for the family that lives its life in the streets of Bangkok.

1992

Translated by Susan F. Kepner

The Philippines

The Philippines is a culturally and linguistically diverse archipelago of over seven thousand islands, distinguished as an area twice colonized since the sixteenth century. In 1521 Ferdinand Magellan claimed the islands for Spain, and the archipelago was ultimately named "the Philippines" in honor of Philip II. For the next several centuries, Spain retained possession of the islands, its only colony in Asia, and left a heavy imprint on Filipino cultural development. The Spanish friars found a traditional Tagalog verse literature written on fragile palm leaf, bark, or bamboo, which they destroyed in the zeal of their conversion efforts.

An emerging modern Filipino literature in Spanish and Tagalog appeared in the last decades of the nineteenth century. By midcentury, liberal ideas from the European Enlightenment had infiltrated the Philippines through Spain. Between 1872 and 1892, exiled young educated Filipino men—the *ilustrados* (enlightened ones)—and students at European universities started the Propaganda movement and founded newspapers to promote the rights of Filipinos, writing in both Spanish and Tagalog. Among these activist-journalists were the first writers of a developing modern fiction, often in a style of political satire or realism. By the 1880s, the Spanish authorities in the Philippines suppressed "subversive" literature and in the 1890s jailed and executed influential writers like José Rizal. The revolution of 1896 and the arrival of the Americans in 1898 put an end to the Spanish regime. Meanwhile, the Filipinos had declared their independence and initiated guerrilla warfare against American troops that would last until 1901.

After 1901 there was greater freedom for writers, although the 1901 Sedition Law, enforced by the United States, prohibited Filipinos from discussing independence. Literature and information, formerly banned by Spain, entered the country and inspired young writers. The *pensionado* program was established, allowing Filipinos to study in the United States. English was declared the official language of education, and a new public-school system, with teachers imported from the United States, was promoted throughout the region, lasting until the 1970s. This second colonization, under the aegis of development toward self-rule, would significantly influence Filipino culture, language, and modern literature.

By the 1930s, the American educational system had produced young Filipino short-story writers in English. Several had started their literary careers in the 1910s through publications associated with the new University of the Philippines. Some serious writers gradually shifted from romance to depictions of life in rural settings. Beginning in the mid-1930s, more writers sought higher education in the United States through government scholarships, and a nomadic pattern of life in two countries emerged, a pattern that still persists for some Filipino writers in English.

Initially, writers in Tagalog had more freedom for political critique since the Americans could not read their language. These nationalist writers spent their creative efforts from 1902 to 1930 in the production of seditious plays and satirical musical comedies (*zarzuelas*). Writers popularized the Tagalog short story, first in the form of narrative sketches, sometimes escapist or moralist in tone or sometimes more reflective of social injustice. By the mid-1930s, a generation of young writers in Tagalog had revolted against romanticism. Influenced by French, Russian, and American realist fiction, they depicted scenes of urban despair in Manila or sketches of human desperation in a changing Tagalog medium that contained some Americanisms.

Japanese troops invaded the islands on 8 December 1941 and were ousted by the United States in February 1945. The Philippines achieved full independence on 4 July 1946, and democratic elections were held for president. From the post–World War II period through the 1950s, popular magazines preferring romantic short fiction proliferated. The more serious Tagalog short stories were relegated to publication in college papers and the magazine section of the daily *Bagong Buhay*. Writers in other languages, such as Ilocano and Visayan, continued to develop their literary art. English-language writers flourished. Some popularized a style of Filipino historical romanticism. They also wrote stories about the successful urban middle class and cosmopolitan social life or about a growing cultural gap between generations. The talent of many women writers was finally realized. Some of their subjects were war and violence, clashes between Filipino and American values, the social status of women, and romance.

The 1950s and 1960s witnessed growing disaffection with the establishment. Young writers, often university educated, were concerned with injustice in both urban and rural locales. They developed a second Propaganda movement in Filipino fiction, publishing in magazines like *Pilipino*. Difficulties became more apparent under the leadership of President Ferdinand Marcos (1965–86). Opposition to his authoritarian control broke out as civil unrest and caused him to declare martial law on 21 September 1972. This initiated more than a decade of unspoken censorship, with writers fearing interrogation and arrest. Cleverly oblique political theater became a form of protest that escaped the censors' wrath. Some writers in English, influenced by New Criticism, simply retreated into romanticism, while others became activists. A form of existentialist literature, reflecting American influence, emerged in the late 1960s. In 1973, Filipino was declared the national language as Marcos implemented his "New Society" program.

Martial law was lifted in 1981, but Marcos and his wife, Imelda, retained broad powers. Ignoring assassination warnings, opposition leader Benigno S. Aquino returned to the Philippines in 1983 from a self-imposed exile and was killed by military police at Manila International Airport. His widow, Corazon Aquino, led a "People Power" movement in opposition to Marcos, forcing him to set presidential elections in 1986. Under protests of voter fraud, Marcos fled to the United States. Elected governments have subsequently come and gone, often plagued by public concerns over crony capitalism and corruption.

Contemporary writers use the mediums of Spanish, English, Filipino, Tagalog, and other vernaculars, but English in the Philippines has lost its former popularity. In fact, serious literature in any language has keen competition from comics and other forms of popular fiction. The short stories in this section were composed in English by contemporary nomadic or cosmopolitan Filipino writers.

Cristina Pantoja Hidalgo
"The Painting"

Cristina Pantoja Hidalgo, born in 1944, began writing for Manila newspapers when she was still in high school. She has published more than a dozen books (both fiction and nonfiction), several of which have won national literary prizes. Her first novel, Recuerdo, won the Carlos Palanca Grand Prize for the Novel in 1996 and her short-story collection, Catch a Falling Star, received a National Book Award for Fiction in 2000. At present, Hidalgo is a professor at the University of the Philippines, teaching literature and creative writing, and is director of the university's Creative Writing Center.

"The Painting" resonates with a style of historical romantic fiction popularized in the 1950s. It can also be read as a subtle satire of failed past revolutionary politics that continue to haunt the present. Its layers of rich ambiguity and intertextuality and its independent female protagonist bring a new dimension to this type of romantic fiction. The story within a story in "The Painting" is narrated by a priest with a "revered" ancestor. This is probably an allusion to José Rizal, the Philippines' national hero, who was an ilustrado *and leader of the expatriate Propaganda movement in Spain. Upon his return, the Spaniards arrested him, found him guilty of treason, and executed him in 1896.*

His young sweetheart, Leonor Rivera, who had been pressured by her family into marrying another man, died in childbirth. She is believed to have been the inspiration for Maria Clara, the heroine of his first novel, who succumbs to family pressure and betrays her lover to the authorities but then chooses to go into a convent, where she becomes the victim of an unscrupulous priest. The hero returns in the second novel and, while plotting the revolution, plans also to rescue Maria Clara from the convent. She dies shortly before he gets there. In

"The Painting," by Cristina Pantoja Hidalgo, from *Tales for a Rainy Night* (Manila: De La Salle University Press, 1993). Permission to publish granted by the author.

"The Painting" we have the characters of José Rizal and Leonor Rivera possibly appearing again.

A reclaiming of the past in terms of a contemporary reinterpretation is found in the fiction of many modern writers. It is reflected in K. S. Maniam's "The Kling-Kling Woman" (Malaysia), Suchen Christine Lim's "Two Brothers" (Malaysia), and Marianne Villanueva's "The Mayor of the Roses" (the Philippines).

While they waited for the storm to spend itself, the stranded travelers had sought shelter in a small roadside noodle house. It was not particularly clean or comfortable, and its wooden shutters were such flimsy protection against the strong gusts of wind and rain that puddles had formed all along the room's walls.

But, as often happens when people find themselves in this sort of predicament, a kind of intimacy had sprung up among the travelers, and this partly made up for the inconvenience and the anxiety the storm was causing them.

The thin man with a cane had suggested that the hours would pass more quickly if they were to take turns entertaining the group with stories. And they were thus now pleasantly occupied, sitting around a long wooden table, which had been cleared of the remains of their supper.

No one had expected the young priest to speak. He had been sitting so quietly at the far end of the table, that they had forgotten he was there.

But when the laughter had died down after the tale told by the large woman in a green dress, he suddenly said, "I have a story. I think it is an interesting one, and I've often wanted to tell it."

This startled his companions, not just because his speaking out was so unexpected, but because his voice was so deep and resonant. It did not seem to come from him at all, for he was slight of build and unprepossessing of appearance.

"Have you never told it before, Father?" asked the bald dentist.

"No, I have not," the young priest admitted.

"Why not, Father?" asked the elegant old lady with the sleeping grandchild.

"I think . . . because I have never quite believed it myself," the young priest replied.

"Did it happen to you, Father?" asked the aging ballerina.

"Have not all the tales we tell somehow happened to us? And do they not happen again in the telling? But now, with your permission, I shall tell the story. I feel that it is time."

So, the young priest began his tale. And, as he spoke, complete silence fell upon the little group, for his voice was compelling, and the tale he told, stranger than any they had heard that night.

I come from a very old and distinguished family. I shall not mention its name, but I think you will recognize it as I go along. One of my ancestors is revered as a great hero of our people. Not everyone agrees that he deserves such an honor. In fact, brothers have been known to become alienated from each other as a result of such disagreements. But that is not really relevant to my story. I personally have never doubted that my ancestor was the kind of man who is born on this earth. And there are those who actually believe him to be a god.

You will understand that it is not easy to belong to a family like mine. In fact, it can be quite a burden. People expect heroism to be passed on, or at least to be reflected in some extraordinary form, like intellectual brilliance or singular talent or exceptional ambition. In fact, most of us are quite ordinary. Therefore, to save myself some embarrassment, I have made it a practice not to reveal my lineage, particularly to my illustrious ancestor's ardent admirers.

But, as it is part of the human condition to be unable to escape one's identity even while one rebels against it, I have always been drawn to those people who have made a cult of my ancestor.

There are numerous groups all over the islands. They call themselves the *kapatiran*—there is no exact translation for the word. I think I have at some time visited them all. And I have studied many of them closely. Though I have never myself become a believer (as you know, I serve another God), I think I have a little understanding of what lies at the heart of their faith. It is nationhood, which to them is simply the kingdom of God on earth. Therefore a man who gives his life to attain it is not just a hero, but a saint, or even a god.

It was at one of their rites that I first saw the woman who is the real subject of my tale.

I had gone to visit a little chapel at the foot of what believers call the sacred mountain. Perhaps some of you know the mountain of which I speak. It is a place of great beauty and enchantment. Before the white man introduced the religion that most of us now claim as our own into these islands, the mountain was the heart and soul of the land, the center of life, the wellspring of legend. Even today, it is said that it shelters deities unknown to us for whom those early creeds are lost. And there are many among our own kind who, disillusioned by what we have made of our world, seek and find sanctuary within its deep groves.

I had witnessed (you note I say "witnessed," not "participated in") the rites held in the modest wooden chapel. These rites were over, and the congregation had dispersed. But a few people still lingered, hoping for a word with the Suprema.

I wonder if any of you have ever seen these priestesses. They are impressive individuals. All have a commanding presence, and some are strikingly beautiful. This one was very tall and very fair, with strongly chiseled features in an ageless face, large penetrating eyes, and long hair drawn back in a bun. She had changed from her vestments into a loose white robe, and was sitting on a wooden bench to one side of the chapel, where she always received people who wished to consult with her.

The Suprema was speaking with someone whose appearance was a striking contrast to hers—a woman in her late forties or early fifties perhaps, of medium height, plain looking, and a little on the stout side, her hair cut short, as though she did not wish to be bothered with it. She wore thick glasses and a simple dress of some unfashionable color—I believe it was purple. One of her shoes had fallen off, and she was swinging a bare foot as she talked. They appeared to be having a good time, for their conversation was punctuated by laughter.

The woman in purple had a hearty uninhibited laugh and a rather loud voice which carried to where I sat observing them from one of the pews. When I began to pay attention, I found that I could understand quite clearly what she was saying. She was speaking of her classes, so I gathered with some surprise that she was a teacher.

At a later occasion, I learned that she was, in fact, a university professor, and moreover, held a position of responsibility in the university's administration. This was even more astonishing to me, for she did not look in the least either like an academician or a bureaucrat. I had by then known her long enough to learn that she was quite a disorganized person, the sort that always misplaces and forgets things, mixes up dates, arrives late for appointments. She was also, however, disarmingly unpretentious. And this made me like her instantly.

I do not remember now who introduced us, or when we became friends. There are persons one warms to immediately, perhaps because they are so open and trusting themselves. Consuelo was one of them. She was also truly unaware of any distinction of race or class or creed.

She was exactly the same with everyone she met, as much at ease with bishops and bankers as with beggars and bums.

At first, I took her for a very simple woman. That is, I thought she was not particularly intelligent. Later, I realized that she was indeed simple, but only in the sense of being completely honest and good hearted. I also found her to be very funny. She said comical things, she behaved in a comical manner. Later, I discovered that she had the gift of making people laugh because her own heart was so full of joy.

But I am getting ahead of my story.

I think I may say that I made a favorable impression on Consuelo myself. One of these connections was established which are difficult to explain, because they are not based on any actual experiences shared. Some people call this the meeting of kindred spirits. Others believe it is simply the picking up of a relationship begun elsewhere, perhaps in another lifetime (like the unusual bond between the young man and the beautiful woman in your story, Madame). I do not know the explanation. But I am certain that such connections occur.

When Consuelo learned I was a priest, her treatment of me changed subtly. She became at once protective and respectful, motherly and deferential. I have found that some Catholic women react this way to priests. You will probably think this presumptuous of me, but I have sometimes thought that in just such a manner must the Virgin Mary have regarded her Son, our Divine Lord.

Consuelo told me that she herself had been a nun, and somehow, this did not surprise me. She had known quite early that she had a vocation and had chosen a contemplative order. She confided to me that her happiest years had been those five years in the convent. But the sudden death of her only brother forced her to return to the world. He had left behind their elderly mother and a young widow with two children and no means of support.

Her Superior had consoled her with the thought that this was probably God's way of testing her vocation. But if trial it was, it was a long one. When I met her, Consuelo had been away from the convent many years, and there seemed no likelihood that she would return to it in the near future. Her family's needs had grown rather than diminished. She had come to think that perhaps this was God's way of telling her that she belonged in the world, that she was to serve Him in another capacity. But she had not yet discovered what this other role might be. Until she did, she was simply trying to do good in whatever way she could.

This way, I was to see, was multifarious. For aside from her work as teacher and administrator in the university, she was involved in all kinds of efforts to ease the plight of the less fortunate—the imprisoned, the insane, the bereaved, the terminally ill, the hopelessly poor. Not to mention the numerous individuals, friends and strangers alike, who constantly sought her counsel and her intercession. Consuelo made time for them all.

But her work in the university took precedence. She saw her teaching not as a job, but as a mission. And though she could not explain the exact nature of this mission to me, I could sense the vision behind it.

Unfortunately, not everyone could. Within the academic circles, she was regarded with much ambivalence. Many of her own colleagues thought her a figure of fun and were openly contemptuous. Consuelo was aware of this and was human enough to be pained by it. She may have derived some comfort from the fact that these same people did not hesitate to approach her for her help when they needed it, help which she never denied them. In any case, she must have known that there were many others who not only admired and loved her dearly, but believed her to be a saint.

One afternoon, when we had known each other over cups of rather indifferent coffee, I looked around me, hoping to gain some new insight into my friend's character from the appearance of the rooms in which she worked. But what struck me was only their impersonality. I have seldom been in rooms so little revealing. Consuelo had left no mark on them. It was as though she did not belong there, and was only using them as a way station.

In fact, she struck me just then as looking somewhat like a strange, slightly disheveled bird poised for flight, dressed now in bright green, sitting at the edge of her chair behind her large, cluttered desk, jumping up every so often to attend to something or other.

During one of these interruptions, my attention was caught by a painting on the wall, which I had not immediately noticed. It was a portrait of my famous ancestor.

Desiring to examine it more closely, I stepped around the desk, and nearly stumbled over a capacious bag squatting just behind it. It was half open, and I could see that it contained, besides an assortment of files and papers, what looked like some articles of clothing and a pair of shoes. This amused me, as it confirmed my impression of Consuelo as poised for flight.

The painting was unsigned, a curious fact, particularly as it was a strikingly good one. The unknown artist had captured something that most others had missed, perhaps because they had never known their subject personally, and worked from photographs or other portraits. They painted the hero—a stiff, somewhat pompous-looking visionary, in a neat little black suit, staring fixedly at this destiny. But this artist had captured the man and an ineffable quality that must have been recognized only by those who knew him well. There was the resolve, but it was a courage born of sadness. And the eyes revealed confusion as well as resignation.

I questioned Consuelo about the painting: whose was it? where had it come from? She seemed pleased at my interest. It was hers, she told me. Her grandfather had left it to her when he died. But she had no idea who had painted the portrait.

She remembered standing at the foot of the staircase in her grandfather's house as a child, and gazing raptly at it. "I thought it was so beautiful," she said. "I thought *he* was so beautiful. I don't know if I said anything to my grandfather. Perhaps I did." Later, she forgot all about the incident. But her grandfather apparently didn't. For upon his death, many years afterwards, she learned that he had left the painting to her.

Her more affluent relatives were locked in a vicious struggle over the old man's properties. But, strangely, none questioned the fact that he had desired Consuelo to have the painting.

It was too large for any of the walls in her mother's little house, so Consuelo thought of donating it to her old convent. The Sister Superior thanked her, but told her gently that it did not belong in a convent; it was of this world.

Consuelo decided to bring it to the college where she was teaching at the time, and a suitable place was found for it in the office of the Dean.

When she accepted a position in the university, she left the painting behind. But some months later, her former colleagues brought it back to her. They had grown uneasy with it, they told Consuelo. Somehow, it no longer seemed to belong in the college.

"As you can see," Consuelo said ruefully, "I couldn't get rid of it."

She hung it up in the cubicle, which was her office in the university, where it dwarfed everything, including the room itself. But it kept her company while she worked, and the students seemed comfortable with it. She fancied that it had a good effect on them. They seemed to think more clearly, to express themselves more easily in its presence.

Then Consuelo was appointed to an administrative position, and she and her painting moved to this office.

I asked whether she felt the portrait was content in its present perch, and laughing her hearty laugh, Consuelo said, "Well, he's helping me a lot with my work, so he must be."

I noticed the shift in the personal pronoun but did not comment on it.

Consuelo guessed my thoughts. "Oh, yes," she said, "I have a very intense personal relationship with him. My friends think it's all part of my craziness. They kid me about it, calling him my 'boyfriend.'"

Consuelo and I did not meet often. Her work and mine were too demanding to enable us to attend the gatherings of the *kapatiran* with any regularity. And even when we did manage to go, it was rarely to the same group at the same time. Nonetheless, our paths did cross now and then. And whenever they did, we would find ourselves slipping with ease into a close camaraderie, as though the intervening periods had never been.

However, I kept from her my own connection with the man in her painting. To this day, I am not sure why.

I was curious about the circumstance which had led *her,* a former nun, to the *kapatiran,* assuming that she was as aware as I was of the established church's opinion of these "sects." And she told me that, initially, she had indeed taken them to be esoteric cults. Later, she had discovered a wealth of material unsuspected by most scholars and had gradually become involved in the movement, not as a researcher but as initiate (this being the only way to truly understand them). Eventually, she had decided to do her doctoral dissertation on the *kapatiran.* She was fortunate in having for her advisor an elderly anthropologist, himself a great scholar, who understood the originality of her mind and the importance of her research, and encouraged her to be as unorthodox as she pleased.

But what was it that had so intrigued her in the first place? I asked Consuelo. And what was it that bound her now to the *kapatiran?*

She replied that she honestly did not know. It was simply a strong force drawing her deeper and deeper. She had resisted at first, having some doubts about the nature of this force. For she well understood that there are malevolent forces in this world, as powerful as the benevolent ones. But she had become convinced that there was no evil in the *kapatiran.* Only this mysterious drawing power. It touched something within her, the existence of which she had not been aware of. It was like listening to a melody one somehow recognized, though one had forgotten the words, she said. She thought that perhaps by listening longer, she would remember the whole song, remember perhaps the entire symphony.

For their part, the *kapatiran* had welcomed her into their midst as one of themselves. In fact, they saw in her the prophetess of whom their own traditions had spoken, the woman who would deliver their message to the world.

And that, indeed, was what her dissertation came to be: both testimony and prophecy. What in the *kapatiran* is called *patotoo*.

"Why you?" I asked Consuelo.

"Oh, Father," she cried, "don't you think I have asked myself that question again and again? Why *me* of all people? Perhaps because I am open. Perhaps simply because I am here. You know better than I the strange ways in which God works."

And, though she had not intended it, I felt justly rebuked.

Consuelo's fieldwork had taken several years. The writing took no more than a couple of months. After she had successfully defended her dissertation, it was immediately published.

"I feel *he* was behind it all," Consuelo told me, indicating the painting. "And do you know something funny? My publishers decided to launch the book on *his* birthday. And at the last minute, they decided to launch it in *his* house, yes, the national shrine in his old hometown. Can you imagine that? I had never dreamt of writing a book, much less launching it in my hero's ancestral home."

The memory appeared to have set in motion a train of recollections, for presently, Consuelo continued, "Now that I think of it, I realize that his birthday and his death anniversary have always been special to me. Somehow, I find myself always getting involved in some way with some ritual or other every time those dates come around. It's almost as if I were compelled to do so."

And then we both recalled that the following day was my ancestor's death anniversary. There was to be a big *kapatiran* celebration in the city, at the monument honoring the hero's martyrdom. Consuelo had been invited, and as I too was planning to go, we agreed to meet there.

It was one of those perfect evenings, unusual for the city even in December—cool and cloudless, the stars more brilliant than jewels, the breeze blowing in from the sea, redolent of old galleons and faraway lands.

A large crowd had gathered at the park, mostly members of the *kapatiran,* and a few curious tourists. I did not immediately find Consuelo.

There were the usual speeches, songs, trance dances. I watched without attending too closely, more engrossed (as I always am) by the participants than by the ritual itself.

After a while, I spotted Consuelo. She was standing a bit to one side, not part of any group, but apparently as enthralled as the others.

I made my way towards her, but before I could reach her, another man detached himself from the crowd and approached her. Something—I am not sure what—prevented me from walking up to them.

The man was dark-skinned and not very tall. His clothes were clean but faded. And he had the rough features and heavy build of a factory worker.

He said something to Consuelo, and she turned around abruptly, a startled expression on her face. What she saw must have reassured her, for the alarm receded, to be replaced by her customary attentiveness.

I was close enough now to overhear what the man was saying without calling their attention to my presence.

He was asking Consuelo what she thought of the celebration. I did not catch her answer. Then he said: "Why does it center on the monument? Have they forgotten everything else?"

Consuelo looked puzzled, but she allowed him to lead her away from the main crowd.

I followed at some distance, making sure that I was within earshot, but never intruding into their line of vision.

The man was showing Consuelo some slabs of unpolished marble in which were engraved passages from the hero's writings. "There was a time," he said, "when these words were lit up. Now they are left to darkness and oblivion.

"If this place is as sacred as they all claim it to be, why can't they clean it up?" he added, and I was struck by the sadness in his voice. "Do we not clean the graves of our dead at least once a year in November?"[1]

Consuelo had stooped to read the engravings, but she could barely make out the words. The man began to read them out for her:

A nation wins respect not by covering up abuses but by punishing them and condemning them. . . . All people are born equal. Naked

---

1. This refers to All Saints' Day, which is celebrated on November 1. Filipinos clean and repaint their relatives' tombs, bring fresh flowers, and spend the day at the cemetery.

and without chains. They were created not in order to be lead astray. . . . I wish to show those who deny us patriotism that we know how to die for our duty and our convictions. . . .

I noticed that he was looking at her, not at the marble slabs. Was he reciting them from memory? I wondered.

"What is the point of making fine speeches?" the stranger asked, gesturing towards the crowd around the statue of the hero. "They will change nothing, nothing." And now, I caught the anger beneath the weariness.

"Are you a member of the *kapatiran*?" Consuelo asked him.

"I am a Filipino," the man replied shortly.

They were moving now towards another part of the monument. The stranger had taken hold of Consuelo's elbow and was helping her over the low fences that separated the various sections of the monument. The steps here were littered with pieces of paper and other rubbish, and in the darkness, it would have been easy to slip.

I was puzzled by Consuelo's willingness to follow a strange man in the gloom of that park and at her allowing him to touch her at all. I knew that she did not generally permit any kind of physical intimacy, a bit of prudishness that I had attributed to her years in the convent. But even more astonishing to me was my garrulous friend's unfamiliar silence.

The odd couple had stopped now before the fountain that had been brought over from the European country where the hero had spent part of his exile. Consuelo was examining it curiously. But the mysterious stranger's gaze had wandered to a group of people nearby—a little boy with blank eyes, his bare skin showing through his rags, moving his limbs mechanically in a small grotesque dance, and beside him, three elderly men sitting idly on a stone bench.

After watching them for a while, Consuelo's companion said, "Look there. That boy has lost his mind from being half-starved all his life. And those old men are on the prowl for young street girls who will do anything to get a bite to eat and a roof over their heads for the night."

At the skeptical expression on Consuelo's face, he said, "You are wondering how I know that. Believe me: *I know.* This park is my home. I literally live here. The problems have not changed. It was all for nothing. All useless!"

Once again, taking Consuelo's arm, the man guided her towards the spot where the hero had actually fallen. The slabs on which were engraved the various translations of the hero's final poem, written from prison as he awaited death, were as mildewed and grimy as everything else around them.

Silent himself now, the stranger pointed to one verse. Consuelo read it aloud in a strangely soft voice:

> *Y cuando ya mi tumba de todos olvidada / No tenga cruz ni piedra que marquen su lugar, / Deja que la are el hombre, la esparza con la azada, / Y mis cenizas que vuelvan a la nada, / El polvo de ut alfombr que vayan a formar.*

> And when my grave is wholly unremembered / and unlocated—no cross upon it, no stone there plain— / let the site be wracked by the plow and cracked by the spade / and let my ashes, before they vanish to nothing, / as dust be formed a part of your carpet again.[2]

When she had finished reading, Consuelo turned to the stranger. And I saw that her eyes, as she looked at him, were filled with compassion and that his were bleak with pain.

I felt a shiver go through my soul. Who was this man? Who was this woman? They were standing in the shadows, very close to each other, frozen in that pose of immeasurable suffering.

As I gazed at them, the world around them seemed to fade away—marble slabs and piles of rubbish, idiot boy and lewd old men, devoted members of the *kapatiran* and idle onlookers—all vanished. They were alone together in a young land over which blew a gentle wind. He was a lean young man in a dark suit, his face bright with the promise of all his gifts. She was a beautiful young woman in a gown that swept the ground, pale with the passion he had just awakened. Shyly she gave him her hand. Humbly he clasped it in his, and raised it slowly to his lips . . . But now the wind was rising. It shook the trees, whipped her skirt about her legs, rumpled his hair. It was turning into a gale . . .

Then the vision was gone. The spinster schoolteacher stood before me, and beside her, the stocky worker in his faded work clothes.

I stared at them in consternation. Had they felt it? Did they suspect . . . ?

---

2. The lines are from "El Ultimo Adios," by José Rizal, translated into English by the Philippines' National Artist, Nick Joaquin.

But now, someone was calling to Consuelo. A member of the *ka-patiran* walked up to her. As they talked, the man beside Consuelo quietly withdrew. I watched him slip through the crowd and disappear into the shadows of the trees in the distance. When Consuelo remembered and turned around to look for him, he was gone.

I saw the perplexed look in her eyes. And then she recognized me and hailed me with her usual enthusiasm, her recent adventure slipping away from her mind.

But I could not forget so easily. Feeling immensely drained, I left the gathering early. My mind was too agitated, my heart too heavy, for prayer. After undressing, I simply went to bed.

You must understand, my conscience does not allow me to believe in reincarnation. My religion forbids it. But all my instincts told me that the mysterious man in the park had been none other than my own ancestor. And that Consuelo, poor Consuelo, was the great love of his youth, the woman he had lost, and whom he had sought both to punish and to save in his literature, since he could not do so in his life.

It seemed to me I was gazing at Consuelo's life now as at an anagram suddenly beginning to make sense. It seemed to me I understood now what drove her, understood her groping, her searching, understood why, though she thought she worshiped Christ the Redeemer, she could not be his bride, but must bind herself to the followers of another savior whom she knew only from his portrait, faithful at last to the man she had betrayed in the willful ignorance of another lifetime.

It saddened me deeply that their sufferings were not at an end. That as she had failed him, he had failed himself and, it seemed, his country. Or was it his country that had failed him?

What karmic force had yet to be worked out before his work could be considered done, his destiny accomplished? How long before he and she could finally find peace?

The following evening, there was to be a banquet given by a historical society to honor the living descendants of the hero. I assumed Consuelo would be there, and I had planned to be absent. But now, I decided to go. I felt that it was time for Consuelo to learn who I was, though I did not know what I hoped such a revelation would achieve.

After I had decided, I felt a great desire to give her something, something she could keep, something that had belonged to *him*. I think I entertained the notion that it would serve her as a kind of talisman, give her strength until the next, and perhaps the final meeting.

But my family no longer had anything that had belonged to him.

Except for a few very small articles—and I had no idea where those might be—everything that had ever been remotely connected to him had become part of the national heritage.

And then I remembered there was one thing, and it was in my possession.

As you probably know, we take the vow of poverty when we enter the priesthood. I had therefore left behind everything that had belonged to me—everything save one small object. This was a little silver medal that had been given to me by my mother. She told me it had come to her from her grandmother, who had received it, along with a few pieces of jewelry, from my famous ancestor's sister, in exchange for some money urgently needed by him in his exile. He had won the medal for an essay he had written as a schoolboy.

My mother had presented me with the medal upon my graduation from the university, the same university he graduated from.

When I received the Holy Orders, this was the one thing I had been unable to give up, perhaps from some idea that it might someday earn me my ancestor's forgiveness. (All of you must remember what he thought of priests.)

But now I felt I was being given this chance to truly earn that forgiveness.

During the banquet, I was seated at the presidential table, along with the other members of our family. Consuelo arrived late and was given a place in the opposite side of the room. It was therefore only after the banquet was over that I found the opportunity to approach her.

If I had expected her to be offended at my having kept my identity a secret for so long, the broad smile with which she greeted me was proof of how I had misjudged her.

"Oh Father, you are a sly one!" she exclaimed, her voice ringing out in the stately hall and causing several people to glance at us in amusement. "I should have known you were hiding something up your sleeve. No wonder you kept questioning me about my painting and everything. Now, confess, Father: what's your excuse for this great deception?"

I humbly acknowledged my guilt, offering no excuse save the usual one of finding people's reactions, when they learned the truth, acutely disconcerting.

And then, because I knew that we would soon be carried off by opposite currents, as always happens at large social affairs of that sort, I hastily dug into my pocket and produced my gift.

"It was his, Consuelo," I said in a low voice. "I think he would want you to have it."

Consuelo stared at the little silver medal in my hand. She did not ask who "he" was, or why I was giving her this little relic. Perhaps she thought I meant it as a reward for her years of fervent study of my ancestor's teachings.

I had nothing else to say. Somehow I could not bring myself to mention the sad man in the park, or my own strange vision.

After a long moment, Consuelo took the little medal from my hand. I waited for her to speak, expecting one of her usual voluble outbursts. Instead, she threw her arms around me and clasped me in a fierce embrace. Then, without a word, she turned around and walked swiftly out of the hall.

The young priest had finished his tale.

In the silence that followed, the stranded travelers became aware that the storm's fury had abated. There was now only a cozy patter of raindrops on the roof of the roadside noodle house.

The bald dentist rose to open the windows.

The thin man with a cane shifted in his chair. "But, Father, was it really *him* in the park?" he asked.

"I do not know, sir," the young priest replied. "I only know what I saw."

"But why did you not speak to him, Father?" cried the aging ballerina.

"Ah, I could not," said the young priest.

"And Consuelo, what has happened to her?" asked the large lady in the green dress.

"Why, nothing," the young priest said. "She is muddling along as she always has, watched over by the portrait of her hero."

"Only now she also has his silver medal," said the elegant old lady with the sleeping grandchild, wiping away the tears that had come to her eyes.

"Yes," said the young priest with a smile, "now she has his silver medal."

1992

Alfred A. Yuson
"The Music Child"

Alfred A. Yuson, born in 1945, has received a number of awards for literature, including Second Prize in the 1991 Carlos Palanca Memorial Awards literary contest for his short story, "The Music Child," and the 1992 SEAWrite Award. His second novel, Voyeurs and Savages, *won a Centennial Literary Prize in 1998. He is currently vice-chairman of UMPIL (the Writers Union of the Philippines); contributes a weekly literature and culture column to a national broadsheet,* The Philippine Star; *and teaches fiction and poetry at Ateneo de Manila University.*

"The Music Child" has the flavor of reportage embedded in autobiographical narrative. The protagonist, a journalist from Manila, sets out for the countryside to obtain an ethnographic human-interest story about indigenous music but finds himself embroiled in violence against a tribal group trying to protect their environment from illegal deforestation. The story's lyrical quality acts as a counterpoint to the themes of social injustice and environmental destruction, two important subjects for a number of Southeast Asian writers, such as Sila Khomchai in "The Family in the Street" (Thailand) and Seno Gumira Ajidarma in "The Mysterious Shooter Trilogy" (Indonesia).

When I first heard of the hair-string fiddlers from Fil, I thought it was just another of his blustery inventions.

But then the odd and curious never seem in short supply in these islands. Quickly have I learned to keep the brow down upon getting wind of possibly interesting copy.

I was in the southern Philippines for a follow-up story on *muro-ami* fishing, having already sent a report on the Manila end of the ecologically ruinous operations.

"The Music Child," by Alfred A. Yuson, first published in the 6 and 13 November 1991 anniversary double-issue of *Midweek* magazine, republished in *The Music Child and Other Stories* (Manila: Anvil Publishing, Inc., 1991) and later reprinted in *Manoa* 4 (spring 1992). Reprinted here with the author's consent.

I had interviewed the big bosses of the Frebel Fishing Corporation, as well as a few legislators involved in a committee on natural resources. Easy enough to get into these high offices when one represents Western media.

It was a dying issue as far as the local papers went. Officials had upheld the ban on boy divers pounding the reefs with iron balls to drive fish into giant nets. All that the greedy operators could do was take it on the chin and shrug.

But for the *Examiner* back home, the triumph of environmental concern would always rate a banner story in the features section. So had my editor assured me as soon as I faxed part one of the series.

Ecology couldn't die as a cause in the world's leading democracy. And where better to flush out tales of horror than in Third World enclaves run by petty politicians?

Cebu City was a smaller Manila, just as dense, dustier, hotter, more humid, except at the seafront, where I found the usual spot of calm amid the chaos, by sitting alone over cold San Miguel beer in a small restaurant.

The day I flew in I hired a jeepney, or rather, had Fil hire a jeepney to drive us down to the southernmost tip of the elongated island. There we had sought out the boy divers, who were now all out of work.

Fil provided the free translation as I explained to their fathers and the barrio chiefs that I wasn't taking any sides. It was strictly a human-interest story.

The good old Polaroid helped us along, until I brought out the Nikkormat for more professional images this side of posterity.

Indeed awash in human interest were the boys' accounts of their lives at sea—packed by the hundreds in a small ship for months on end, diving daily with only makeshift goggles for protection, tugging diligently at the scare lines underwater to ensure a profitable catch of all kinds of reef denizens, at the expense of battered corals.

Short-term gains for everyone, of course. But the perilous work earned the family some credit in the barrio store.

When occasionally a boy of thirteen or fifteen didn't surface, attacked by sharks, or worse, the bends, then so sorry. One life less at sea, one mouth less to feed in the poor southern tip of the island. The victim's kin need not mourn over the body. If recovered at all, it was buried on some anonymous, far-off isle where luckless divers were destined to spend their eternal summers under a few feet of sand and some tropical shade.

The tapes would have to be transcribed for the next night or so. A simple chore then, a few hours of holding fort in the hotel room. I'd pare down Fil's translations of the boys' stories. Adding no more than a brief intro, I'd let the barrio kids speak for themselves. The cause of ecology would best be served by the voices of the innocents.

For the present, languorous time enough to idle at a *resto* by the quay.

The San Mig isn't quite as chilled as I'd prefer. But my thirst for local color is no sooner provoked than quenched here in this apparent hotbed of cargo cults.

A tuna's jaw is paraded along the row of tables before it's plunked down upon a grill resting on red-hot coals. The instant hiss wafts the call of the sea. Surge of smoke dies back into imminent succulence.

I slide a fork under a cluster of fresh green seaweed swimming in cane vinegar. There it is again, siren song of brine, tart picture of boys diving a hundred feet to pummel the magnificent corals. It's a life. For an American enervated by the afternoon heat, the philosophy of sea breeze is the sole recourse.

Violins with strings made of human hair, Fil had said. Up north, in some obscure settlement no tourists had yet heard of, far from the gleaming white sands of the bewitching coastline.

What is it in these people, I ask myself, that makes light of the uncommon, serves it as fodder to guests of bland interest?

Fil said they saved the tresses of the tribe's departed, twined it round for weeks in a vat filled with tree sap, and pulled on the thickness to create a certain pitch. Then they strung up the instruments, not really violins, said Fil, but similar, without a waist, and no frets, just a small round hole where the bow caressed the belly.

He said he wasn't sure what the bowstring was made of, perhaps some fiber drawn from jungle vine. He hadn't seen the instrument himself, had never heard the tribesmen play. But he had gotten word of how they had performed in some barrio in the hinterland, where they had been chanced upon by a musicologist who taught in one of the city's universities. The professor had asked the musicians to give an evening concert for the coming fiesta in the big city.

That wouldn't be for a month. I could go north with Fil as soon as I faxed the follow-up piece on the aborted rape of tropical reefs, answer to another disquieting call of human interest.

This could be bigger game, worthy of Ripley's.

The tuna's jaw is flopped over. Again its juices drip on the live coals and send whiffs of smoke to ride the sea wind. Incredibly mouth-watering it is, a hint of Pacific heaven, and certainly worth more than I bargained for when I agreed to go East for the *Examiner*.

Fil arrives in a tricycle. He is all high-ho and bluster—a lean, dark man with a grin wider than the tuna's in its grilling throes. He comes lunging towards my table on the balls of his feet.

"OK, Pardner! We go tomorrow by bus. Leave at nine. Three, four hours' trip. Then we get jeepney from small town. If none, we walk. Only a few hours. Right, Pardner? Ahh, Fil needs beer. Beer and tuna to make Fil and Pardner strong for long trip tomorrow!"

As Fil had warned, the bus ride proved to be an exercise in inertia. We stopped at every barrio to pick up old women and young pigs, baskets of corn and cassava, a couple of soldiers with their M-16s swinging awkwardly to threaten everyone as we creaked and groaned along the winding dirt road.

Soon there was no sight of sea. The rain forest closed in on us, and the implacable jungle stench seemed to quiet even the trussed-up piglets.

Fil and I got off five hours later, way past noon, and headed straight for a small store to pick up some sardine cans. We opened one, dipped some stale buns into the blood-red sauce, and washed it all down with warm Coke.

Between bites and sips, Fil spoke to the pregnant woman tending the store. She sent off a scrawny kid, who came back with a fat guy in a greasy undershirt.

I could tell the kind of jeepney the fellow had just by counting the oilstains round his beer belly, and the way he looked up at the sky and scratched his head as Fil plied him with questions.

In another hour we sputtered off, taking a narrow, overgrown trail up a hill before descending into a small valley. Fording a stream, I asked for a quick stop to fill an empty Coke bottle with cool mountain water. Then we struggled up several steep inclines again, with the jeepney surprisingly coughing up enough power to make it, but barely each time.

It was an old logging road, Fil said, now unused. The loggers had moved a number of mountains away. This tribe we're visiting, he said, no one wants to tangle with them. Everyone's afraid his scalp will wind up making strange music. Ha ha ha ha ha, Fil laughed, elbowing the driver's paunch. Ha ha ha ha ha. And the clattering tailpipe laughed along with him.

We stopped at a clearing where the driver said we couldn't go any further. The road didn't end, but he had never made it past that ridge before, he said and Fil translated. We had to walk the rest of the way. The driver would come along, even spend the night with us, for Fil might not make much sense to the tribe, ha ha ha ha ha.

Nonoy the driver was right. The village was just a couple of cigarettes away, off the old logging road and down some damp path through thick jungle. Suddenly we stumbled upon a cluster of huts in a grassy clearing. A good thing it was too, for the mountain dark was fast closing in on us.

The villagers were all excited at the sight of the visitors, especially the white man with the Cokes and cameras. They offered freshly boiled yams I couldn't believe the sweetness of, and sat us by an early fire.

Much of the evening was taken up by Fil's exchanges with the elders, helped along by Nonoy, to much tittering among the women and occasional nodding from the men.

Fil said it was all right to take pictures. I didn't really feel like it but decided to try a new trick by aiming and clicking both cameras simultaneously so they could share the flash. The kids squealed and chattered about how they had gone blind, according to Fil, ha ha ha ha ha.

The squeals grew louder on the part of the women when they saw themselves taking shape and color like slow magic on the white square. Everyone jostled to take a look. One man said that he had lost a snapshot like that taken by a cousin who had worked a year in Saudi Arabia.

For dinner we had salted meat, salted fish, boiled vegetables, and crushed corn steamed with rice. Still sitting on our haunches, we shared two bottles of rum and more of Fil's jokes, this time about Japanese tourists flocking to the island's beaches in their floppy hats.

Before we knew it, the band had formed before us, nine men and women fiddling with their bows while smiling shyly to themselves. As we all quieted down, they proceeded to play a tune in unison.

The kids continued to run about and twirl the Coke bottles in the dust. The moon rose above some distant treetops, gibbous and bright orange. The music seemed to rise as well from all the nameless vines and tendrils in the forest.

The tune was rather cloying. The sounds the extraordinary instruments made were terribly scratchy at times, with some of the players frequently sliding up or down into another key. But they were a pretty picture all right, seated on low stools in an irregular row beyond the fire, smiling and laughing at false screeches as they nodded in time over their bows.

The wooden instruments were set on their laps or propped against a hip and strummed downward like a fiddle.

"*Ginse*," an old man said. "*Ginse*," Fil repeated to name the instrument. Its sound was a mite unearthly, incredibly high-pitched, and I couldn't tell if it was the tune that required short stabbing notes or it was just the *ginse*'s limitations, until the musicians fell upon a passage where their bowstrings sawed long and graceful curves to produce extended wails that finally brought the piece to a lugubrious close.

Fil and I clapped loudly and raced one another to the players. A *ginse* was quickly handed over and I plucked innocently at the strings, noting them to be as taut as any bow fiddle's. I slid a thumb upwards and elicited a sharp whine that sent a musician into a mock grimace.

"Is it really human hair?" I asked Fil, still a bit incredulous.

He pressed his own palm up and down the strings before turning to the players to relay my query.

Yes, they all nodded, their faces lighting up with a mischievous glint that seemed to say you don't have to believe it.

An old woman explained in all seriousness how they had made such instruments since as far back as her own mother could remember. The women grew their hair long and had it cut only twice in their lives. The hair was often preserved in separate packets, but sometimes mixed together, until the old men felt it was time to gather the sap of a particular tree, from which the wood for the fiddle's body also came. The hair was boiled in the sap for days, then brought out to cool as thick clumps, pulled in quick jerks, and returned to the frothing sap. The process was repeated for weeks.

Fil was getting excited translating what Nonoy said that the old woman said, at times heedlessly racing on until Nonoy would shake his head and tug at his arm and correct what he said. A long argument ensued between them over what the old woman had really meant. Then Fil would nod vigorously and so would Nonoy, and they'd agree before Fil turned to me again to alter his initial version, but only the slightest bit.

I asked if it was true that they'd be performing in the city for the fiesta. Yes, they said, it would be the first time they'd face a large crowd. Could you give me the name of the musicologist, and where I can find him in the city? One of the men ran off to his hut and came back waving a calling card.

I copied the name and address, resolving to rely more on the professor's likely notes on the oddity than on Fil's elaborations, which I had grown to suspect. I'd take more pictures in the morning, and come up with a story that should titillate the punks in Frisco.

Meanwhile we could sit back around the fire and enjoy the rest of the evening's casual performance. The group continued with their esoteric repertoire long after we ran out of rum.

"It's a pity," one of the women said in the morning, "that Luisito can't come with us to the city. If he did, they'd really hear something."

Again Fil and Nonoy had to argue endlessly over the full import of the woman's utterance. She continued to speak to them, and Fil's eyes grew extraordinarily large as he turned around to interpret, then caught himself and questioned the woman further while Nonoy attempted to help.

The story I eventually heard had to do with a boy, not of their tribe, but the son of a mestizo farm owner some hills away. They called him the music child, for he had a truly wondrous voice, the woman said—a boy who never spoke but sang his every phrase, and mimicked to perfection all the bird sounds and jungle calls, the roar of the waterfall by his father's cornfields, the monsoon wind and rustle of stalks.

They had visited the farm some months back, and played before Don Julio on their hair-stringed instruments. He had admired their talent, played along with them on his piano, then introduced his son. The boy couldn't have been more than twelve, but there was no telling for he was probably big for his age, having a large mestizo for a father. Luisito was himself dark-skinned but looked robust. His mother, a native of the place, had died in childbirth.

The father told them the infant had sung, not cried, when held aloft by the midwife upon delivery. His first song had been eerily plaintive, reeking of death, as if he knew, and indeed was describing, his mother's slippage into the afterlife at that very moment.

Don Julio recounted this in near tears before them. He hadn't been too sure if he could share the boy with them that evening, but realized that his son had to meet people who also made music.

The boy was brought out of his room, from where he had obviously been listening. He came out all in smiles, sang his greetings and deferences with the purest voice they had ever heard, then launched, with a twinkle in his eyes, into an imitation of their fiddles' sounds. He replicated passages of the music they had played as if he were one of those music boxes the professor had once brought to record their songs.

No, they hadn't told the university man about the boy. They had agreed to honor Don Julio's request to keep him a secret until he grew up.

But since I was of fair skin like the Don, he might not mind, said the woman. He is lonely, she pronounced gravely. He has to share his treasure of a son.

"This isn't just a fancy story?" I kept asking Fil. He turned to the woman again. Some of the other musicians had joined us and now repeated her claims. Never had they heard such a voice, so sweet and powerful, bereft of quaver, and of such assurance and luster that anyone who heard him could not help but gasp. It was effortless singing, they said, as if he were only talking. He had sung with them that night, making up words to fit their music, which he was hearing for the first time. But he never fell out of step, predicting correctly where the passage would course even before they strummed the next notes.

Don Julio's eyes were full of joyful tears at the music they made together. And when it was over, he kissed his son and told him to go to bed. The music child sang goodnight and farewell in the most becalming way, using phrases that were a mixture of birdcalls at twilight and certain words from the area's dialect.

They didn't dare ask Don Julio if he would allow the boy to sing with them in the fiesta, not after he had stressed that the boy should remain unknown. He had admitted, however, that it was just a matter of time before someone breathed a word about the boy to the outside world.

On our return to the city, I immediately sought out Dr. Cesar Abellana at a Catholic university.

He proved extremely helpful and articulate, expounding on what he knew of the hair-string fiddlers, as he had chosen to call them. He said he hadn't finished his research on the origin of their uncommon instrument, but had more or less codified the range of its musical capabilities.

He rattled off terms that had me scribbling like a freshman in choir school, then allowed that he feared he wasn't doing the right thing, exposing the musicians to possible exploitation by local tourism officials.

He didn't want them to turn into a sideshow, Dr. Abellana said in all earnestness. But he thought that the benefit program would at least make his own students aware of the varieties of musical expression, and of how music was such a crying human need as to defy all convention. Of course, the school would also raise funds from the unique attraction of the instruments as much as the cultural fascination with the performers themselves.

I wondered silently how he would react to reports about the music child. The boy had been in my mind for days. The possibility of finding out if what I had heard about him was true had intrigued me no end.

I resolved to finish the transcription of part two of the *muro-ami* story, wrap it up, and send it off, then go back to the hinterlands with Fil to see what we could come up with on the story of Don Julio and his son.

Fil came to the hotel the next day raring to go. He had taken a lease on an old Willys jeep, four-wheel drive. We could have it for an entire week, he said, although I had only given him enough cash for three days at the normal rate.

Fil always seemed to get everything at a bargain, that much I can say of his aim-to-please attitude. My contact in Manila hadn't fed me a live one when he gave me Fil's address in Cebu. The guy was proving so effectively gung-ho that I could forgive him his rapstyle.

He did his own research, too. We would pick up Nonoy and take a different road to Don Julio's farm. No trekking this time. We could cart in all we wanted of warm Cokes and sardine cans, just in case the music child's recluse of a father proved inhospitable.

Fil had also found out that the Don's farmhands were tribesmen who had only recently been identified by a church group running a linguistics institute.

"What's that? They deal with lingo, huh, Pardner?"

"Yeah, that's what they do all right. You're pretty sharp, Fil. So what are they called, these tribesmen of Don Julio?"

"Maligta," he answered quickly. "Aborigines. Short, dark, curly-haired. They go around with spears, bow and arrow . . . But not to worry, Pardner. Safe, peaceful people. Only problem is, you step on them at night. No see them, very small, very dark, ha ha ha ha ha . . ."

Drove like a laughing demon, too, Fil did.

We reached Nonoy's barrio well before noon, and were treated to a sumptuous lunch prepared by his wife—rice and stewed cabbage with sardines.

Fil suggested bringing along a case of beer for the Maligta ("They will like it better than rum, believe you me, Pardner!") and a bottle of local brandy for the Don, whom he said was part-Spanish.

The road was carved out of a deeply forested mountainside. Nonoy took over the wheel and kept wheezing as he struggled over the narrow turns and inclines. Fil bounced around on the back seat as he tried to keep a lid on the case of beer and assorted foodstuff.

Almost an hour into the rough, unused road, we were surprised to find it joining a wider track that appeared to have only recently been gouged out of the mountainside. Nonoy screeched to a stop, his brows furrowing.

"Loggers," he said simply.

"They're not supposed to have reached here," said Fil as he craned his neck out one side of the jeep.

Nonoy said something in the dialect as he drove forward and swung the Willys towards the right fork, following the freshly dug-up road, marked with heavy truck tires.

"He says it's the new company, Pardner,"offered Fil. "They have protection from the soldiers."

In less than another hour, in which we slogged along no more than five miles past a couple of dried-up streambeds, we reached a scenic plateau ringed by low hills. A small road branched off from the loggers' tracks, and Nonoy eased us gently into it. More rolling terrain lay ahead. After a couple of miles, we reached the edge of a vast cornfield and knew that we were on Don Julio's land.

Nonoy drove on until we spied a modest cabin that stood on a hillock. Clumps of tall bamboo sheltered it from behind. A solitary figure appeared on the porch. He was a tall man, fair-skinned, bearded. I took him to be Don Julio.

I had earlier thought of presenting myself as a writer concerned with tribal minorities. We would say nothing about the hair-string fiddlers, or of what we had heard from them of Luisito. We would pretend that we were totally unaware of the music child's existence. Our interest had to do with the Maligta.

But upon getting off the jeep and striding purposefully over to the man, who stared at us with hard eyes, something told me that we should change our cover.

I said hello and introduced myself while Fil and Nonoy remained by the jeep. Don Julio didn't say anything. I went on about how we had been traveling in pursuit of reports of illegal logging on the island, and how we had heard of the presence of his farm. I wanted to know if the tribal farmers' existence was now being threatened by the loggers, whom I had heard were in cahoots with the corrupt military.

"You're American," Don Julio said matter-of-factly, relaxing his stare somewhat.

"Yes," I replied, making a move forward to shake his hand. "I write for the *San Francisco Examiner.* I'm here for a series of reports on environmental problems. Perhaps you can help me, sir. This island is obviously experiencing uncontrolled denudation."

He met me halfway and offered his hand. "My name is Julio Cortez."

We shook hands firmly and I repeated my name. "And those guys are my guide and driver, Fil and Nonoy."

"Come in for coffee," he said without acknowledging my companions' presence in the distance.

I hesitated on the porch, wondering whether the invitation had been for myself alone. I decided he couldn't care less if it seemed so, and entered the cabin without any further word. The guys by the jeep would understand. Besides, I figured Don Julio would be more comfortable chatting one-on-one.

It turned out to be a correct assessment. We settled ourselves cozily across from one another in low, thickly upholstered armchairs with paisley prints, the kind I had last seen in Aunt Maggie's ranchhouse near San Diego. My host poured steaming coffee into a pair of large ceramic mugs that said "Yo" and "Barcelona" with a red heart between the words.

"Do you play chess?" he asked casually as he gestured at the bowl of brown sugar. I noticed that the square table between us was topped by an intricate chessboard of inlaid mother-of-pearl.

"Haven't played in years," I said truthfully. "But I understand the game, and would be most willing to take it up again with you, sir."

He nodded and took a sip of his dark coffee.

"There's a new logging consortium that's out to terrorize everyone in this part of the island," he said slowly. "We may not be able to stop them, but we will not give up without a fight."

He took a heavier sip, dipped a cigar end into the cup, and lit up to smoke. He went on to recount his life in brief, quickly leading to recent events that had clearly disturbed his idyll of seclusion. He spoke in measured tones, with a deep melodious voice that betrayed unmistakable good breeding as well as the gravity with which he regarded his current plight.

He had started his farm almost twenty years ago, after tiring of life as a wine importer in Manila. His half-Spanish father and Scottish mother had perished in a fire that struck their ancestral home, in a fashionable section of the capital.

He had no other close relations. As a bachelor at thirty-five, he had decided to close down his business, move south, find a large parcel of land, and start an orchard. He had sufficient savings for an early retirement. He wanted to be in solitude, away from commerce and civilization. He had no wish to leave the country of his birth, no desire to trace his European roots. Living in the tropics was just fine for him. There was a particular stillness at most hours, if one knew where to go, deep in some mountain where only forest sounds entered one's consciousness.

He had planted mango, banana, and papaya, among other indigenous fruit trees. His dream of a self-sustaining orchard was partly realized. But then it meant constant relations with middlemen and a large workforce, something he had increasingly grown averse to.

When the Maligta came to befriend him, he decided they were the only people he wanted to commune with. He had them cultivate fields of corn on his land and grow tubers and vegetables, enough for them all to live on. The fruit trees were maintained, their bounty gathered every season. But he stopped caring for them as extensively as he had on a commercial basis. The fruits turned sweeter, he noted. They also became less than profitable to truck down to the city markets. The people who tended his land contented themselves with whatever they could gather.

Five years ago they began to have problems with big logging companies. But they had stood their ground and the encroachment stopped. Now it appeared that the new group was determined to have its way. He himself was quite resigned to the thought that their mountains would soon be stripped naked and dry. He had hoped, however, that his land would not be touched in any way.

But the little people around him were sure to resist the newcomers, and he would have no choice but to help the Maligta. They were peaceable, but turned fierce when fighting for their lives.

It all seemed inevitable now, Don Julio said wearily. Violence had already claimed the lives of his friends who had tried to block the new road with rocks and dead trees.

Accompanied by soldiers, the loggers had exacted swift retribution, stealing onto his land a few days ago and shooting down two of the tribesmen. Worse, they had threatened to return to wipe out all resistance.

"You've come at the right time to record all of this," Don Julio said. "We're prepared to do battle. I have an old shotgun that can take a few lives. The little people are fashioning their old weapons. This afternoon they bury their dead, our dead. Your arrival is well timed. You can take a lot of interesting pictures."

He had settled back on his chair, his eyes resting on the ceiling. It was as if, resigned to the outcome, he had taken to addressing himself, recounting for his own ears what had brought him to this moment.

Once again I wondered whether I had just heard a tall tale. We were nearing the end of the twentieth century, after all. Bad guys didn't just show up and kill off recalcitrant natives. It couldn't happen. We were only several hours away from a bustling city. And yet this man before me was painting a scenario of crude confrontation, between two sets of primitives, with himself, surely a civilized man, being drawn into the fray. Did these things still happen?

And he hadn't mentioned his son at all. But before my suspicion grew that I had again been welcomed to the province of fiction, I saw a photograph resting atop the upright piano. It was some distance from where we sat, but I could make out the bright young face of a boy, eyes large and unafraid. He looked about seven or eight years old.

Don Julio seemed to have heard my thoughts, for he suddenly sat upright and took cognizance of my presence.

"My son, Luisito, is with them now, helping them prepare to bury the dead. You should come with me and meet them. Meet my son, who is ten years old. He is a special child, with a special gift that will amaze you. Perhaps it is time too, for it cannot be helped anymore, that his existence is made known to others. Like yourself."

He lifted his great bulk and waved a hand in my direction.

"Come. They wait for me. We agreed to bury the dead before twilight."

On our way out, Don Julio nodded a quiet greeting to Fil and Nonoy, who had made themselves comfortable on the porch. Our host maintained his large strides as we followed him up a path towards the jungle beyond the cornfields.

We trudged on silently for a mile, the shadows on the trail deepening with every step. We crossed a stream and hauled ourselves up a ridge. As we broke our run down into another gully, we were greeted by a faint, elegiac tune that was being sung in the distance. It was a young boy's voice, sounding clear and precise as it lured us on.

The words sung in dialect were unintelligible to me, but I noticed wonder and apprehension merge in Nonoy's face. He muttered something to Fil, who quickly apprised me that someone had died. I nodded and ran on after Don Julio, not wanting any other voice to join the marvelous sound I was hearing with increasing clarity at each step.

Soon we burst upon a small glade where close to a hundred dark-skinned men and women had gathered. Pygmies, I thought instantly, noting that the bows by their sides stood taller. They looked at us with hardly any change in their mournful expressions. Some had tears flowing down their cheeks. Beside a deep pit, a couple of bodies lay wrapped in strips of palm leaf and vine. Their faces were uncovered. Above them stood Luisito, singing to his young heart's content, face thrown up to the heavens, eyes virtually closed, phrasing long, curling lines that soared powerfully above the silent group. His features were sharply chiseled, his skin bronzed by the sun. And he was taller than some of the small men standing beside him.

Don Julio walked forward and touched the dead men's faces. When he moved back, two women fell forward and cradled the dead men's heads in their arms, rocking them gently in time to Luisito's plaintive singing. Soon they lay the heads down and made way for the men to lift the bodies carefully and pass them on until they rested on the bottom of the pit.

The special child sang on, seemingly oblivious to everything around him. His arms swept up to encompass the sky. Now there was rage in his voice. Then slowly his lament turned into a veritable whisper, still lucid in its lowest registers, as earth was piled upon the bodies and the women wailed softly as one.

I felt no urge to record the scene except with my eyes and ears. But I shall remember with ferocity how the twilight descended slowly upon us while the common grave was leveled, and how the boy fell into mellifluous sobs as he ended his song.

We trooped back in silence to the cabin. A meal was prepared for us. We ate wordlessly, even Fil, whose eyes darted constantly about. Until suddenly the boy broke into song again, phrasing lilting questions in the dialect, which Don Julio answered in Spanish.

The boy shifted to Spanish himself, then lapsed into a charming, twittering patois that included a few words in English. He turned to me and asked, in a melody I could swear approximated the first bar of the "Star-Spangled Banner," whether I was from America. I smiled and said yes. He munched briefly on a corncob, then sputtered into "Oh so proudly we hailed, / at the twilight's last gleaming . . ."

Don Julio smiled appreciatively as the boy burst into full song, ranging lyrically through half of the anthem before breaking into a different melody with unfamiliar but unmistakably English phrases. His father slapped a knee and roared in laughter.

Finally containing himself as his son wove on with his stirring rendition, Don Julio turned to me and explained. "'The Flower of Scotland.' I sang it once for him and he has never forgotten. I'm afraid he favors it over your own anthem. The Spanish one he doesn't like at all, thinks it's too sentimental. Which I find strange, since he performs with great emotion during wakes and burials."

Don Julio laughed again, mussed the boy's hair as he finished his song, and waved at him to finish his supper.

Later that night Don Julio sat before the piano to showcase his son's admirable gift to the full. Incredibly, Luisito ranged from Manuel de Falla's "Canción" and "Seguidilla murciana" to the popular aria "Una furtiva lágrima," and then from "Hey, Jude" to the lilting folk songs Fil and Nonoy knew and shamelessly hummed along to. He sang "Cu Cu Ru Cu Cu Paloma," which he obviously took delight in, embellishing it extensively with his own improvisations in the dialect, and much to his father's resounding approval, as manifested by a jazzy thumping of the keyboard. Luisito's "La vie en rose" couldn't have been more sultry or heartfelt, his "Bonnie Banks of Loch Lomond" an unforgettably emotive confluence of garrulousness and poignance. The boy was magnificent, and after a while we tired of applauding him and just sat back to listen in tremulous awe, wondering if there were any limits to his genius.

Don Julio gently ordered him to bed after he finished a sportive medley that married "God Save the Queen" with "La Marseillaise." Then our host led me to the porch while Fil and Nonoy found their bunks for the night.

"My boy hears a tune once and repeats it flawlessly," Don Julio said proudly. "Hearing a passage, he can bring it to its proper conclusion. When I taught him to read words on paper, he was only four, and he lost no time in showing me that he could read notes as well. He would rummage through all the music sheets I kept inside the piano seat, and burst out in Italian, getting the accent right, too. He'd turn a score by Wagner upside down and make sport of it, as a boy would the most terrible of toys. It was frightful. It still is."

Bats flapped noisily past the roof and swooshed around the bamboo grove. The night wind lofted across the valley, the cornfields hissing before us.

"Not only is he a great mimic, repeating exactly what he hears. He takes it further where he will, adding his own touches of whimsy, curing it here and there to suit his taste for the game, his own special game. Then too he makes up his own music, chanting epic tales of courage and gallantry, or of how two mountains coupled and gave birth to a new forest. Indeed, he was born to sing. Yet never has he sung originally of love. I remember the day his mother died. The midwife almost dropped him in fright. It was as if he was born to sing of death."

Don Julio drew a long puff from his cigar. Its end glowed like a terribly distant hearth.

"Whatever will I do with him, Señor?"

I couldn't answer. I averted my eyes, and found myself gazing at a low, bright star that was repeatedly erased by a tree branch with each gust of wind. I shivered momentarily at the cruel wonder of it all.

Luisito took me to the waterfall and mocked it with his own song, an echo that drowned its source. He hooted like an owl and clucked like a gecko, then merged these sounds into a playful nocturnal syncopation. He asked me, in his quaint way of trilling melodic refrains, how the birds were in my country. He had heard that they were different, and he had longed to hear birds other than those he had matched notes with in his valley.

I described the largest birds I knew. Even as I was sure that he failed to grasp most of my words, he sensed the shapes and sizes and imagined the sounds they made while soaring high over a great expanse of land. He became the bald eagle and the mighty condor, the buzzard and the whooping crane. He sang the mating dance and the tale of migration. He breathed the flapping of powerful wings and the constant whoosh of wind, before ending his impressions with a sustained, sibilant cry of free fall.

We joined the Maligta in a hunt for monitor lizards and came back with three large specimens of the glistening reptiles. As they were skinned and stewed in vinegar before Don Julio, the dark darling prince of the tribe sang his tribute to their past lives, how they slithered under rotting leaves and fallen branches, how they skulked after rodents and sank their teeth into fowl.

Fil and Nonoy were wordless before him. They could only shake their heads in disbelief as he silenced the treetops with flute-like bubbling trills and prolonged warbling. He would essay the meadow pipit's accelerating sequence of tinkling notes, which ended in a high-pitched and far carrying pee-pee-pee, or the blackbird's staccato dik-dik-dik, which wound up in a jarring screech.

Once when we were alone by the porch, I brought out the Polaroid and took his portrait. Luisito pressed his face close to the curious blank square. As he saw the colors come into play and his features take shape, he began to sing softly to himself, how Luisito was born one day and said good-bye to his mother, and grew up with his father and his brothers and sisters, the little people, how he swung himself down a tree and bathed in the river.

When the print was complete, he stared at his face and sang to it repeatedly, Lu-i-si-to, Lu-is-it-o, Lu-iss-ii-ttooo, chanting his name in various modes of self-celebration.

Other than that time, I had no urge to photograph him or the Maligta. Or anything else that presented itself before us. We walked around in an apparent daze in the magical valley. But we knew it would not last. It was as if the acknowledgment restrained me from making a serious effort to record any part of the implausible sojourn.

Fil and Nonoy never even asked how long we would stay, or what our next move would be. We shared our supplies with our hosts until we found ourselves relying on the tribesmen's fruits and tubers. We drank brandy with Don Julio and listened to Luisito sing with effortless passion.

On our fourth day at the farm, the loggers came back.

They had parked their truck at the edge of Don Julio's land, where the Maligta had narrowed the road and made further passage impossible.

Cries came from the distance when the interlopers were seen marching up the trail.

Don Julio brought out his shotgun and inserted the cartridges without a word. He stepped out calmly onto the porch. I followed him, my heart beginning to pound at the thought of fearful consequences.

Shots rang out from beyond the cover of trees. The Maligta were shouting to one another from different directions. Two figures stumbled out of the woods. They were Nonoy and Fil, dragging one another in panic across the field.

Luisito rushed out of the cabin and ran headlong to where more gunfire was erupting. He was bare above the waist, unarmed, bellowing his version of the rifle shots as he hurtled onwards.

His father made no effort to stop him. Don Julio's eyes had turned steely as he stood on the porch, gripping his weapon.

Nonoy grabbed the boy as they met, and both fell to the ground. Fil had crumpled down himself, and I realized that he was hurt. As I ran forward, I heard Don Julio's imperious cry behind me. "Go! It is not your fight!"

Nonoy grappled with the boy, until Luisito let out an emphatic cry that seemed to propel him out of his pleading captor's grasp. Nonoy fell to his knees again as he reached out desperately. Luisito hurdled the bushes and disappeared into the trees.

I reached Fil as he struggled to crawl away. His thigh was oozing blood. Nonoy helped me right him and drag him towards the cabin. "We must go, we must go," panted Nonoy. "To the jeep!"

We pushed Fil into the Willys, and Nonoy quickly ran around to take the driver's seat, the key shaking in his pudgy hand. I turned and saw Don Julio still motionless on the porch, his face a mask as he peered into the direction of the motley din: running feet, shouts, gunshots, screams of pain—each sound replicated by that familiar wondrous voice, which also filled the interim silences with a defiant song.

Nonoy grabbed me from behind and tried to push me into the jeep. I resisted and threw down his thick arm. Fil moaned and writhed in the front seat. Don Julio barked once more: "Go! Get away! It is not your fight!"

Automatic fire burst out in the distance. The fighting had spread, and the shrill, chattering voices of the Maligta seemed to cover another hill. Nonoy whimpered, his hands pressing feebly against my chest. I jumped into the backseat and he lost no time in starting the jeep and speeding down the trail towards where the firefight was taking place.

I peered out and saw Luisito running up a bare hillock. He threw his arms up as he reached a mound, and from his throat cascaded what seemed a hymn of fury that soon dissolved into vibrant waves of lament as we sped by.

My hands gripped the restraining bar as I arched halfway out the jeep to see him. More shots were fired and bullets whizzed by. Nonoy whined and crouched low against the wheel as we lurched on.

The boy was still out there, atop the bare mound, his arm sweeping across the valley and his head thrown back as he sang. Then I lost sight of him for the final time as we rumbled past the loggers' empty truck and onto the wider road.

But I could hear his lusty praise for all the bravery taking place around him, and his voice seemed to turn even more luminous as we sped away.

We were all crying in the Willys. Fil sobbed in agony while I tried to make sense of a kerchief and tie it above his ugly wound. Nonoy wailed in gratitude for slipping past unhurt. Tears flowed down my face as I knotted the tourniquet and patted Fil comfortingly on his shoulders.

It seemed a long time before the song of the music child trailed off.

It was hard to tell as we drove on if it was just the ineradicable memory of his voice that accompanied our flight farther and farther away from all the deaths he celebrated.

1991

Marianne Villanueva

"The Mayor of the Roses"

Marianne Villanueva, born in 1958, is the author of Ginseng and Other Tales from Manila *(Corvallis, Oregon: Calyx Books, 1991). She is a graduate of the Stanford University Creative Writing Program and, in 1993, was a California Arts Council Literature Fellow. In 1992 she was a finalist for the Manila Critics' Circle National Book Award. Currently, she is a senior project advisor with the Master of Arts in Writing Program at the University of San Francisco.*

"The Mayor of the Roses" is unprecedented in its explicit depiction of sexual violence against women. The subject of the sexual double standard and its negative impact on women is addressed by a number

"The Mayor of the Roses," by Marianne Villanueva. Permission to publish granted by the author.

of contemporary Southeast Asian writers of both genders, including Ma Sandar in "An Umbrella" (Burma), Mey Son Sotheary in "My Sister" (Cambodia), K. S. Maniam in "The Kling-Kling Woman" (Malaysia), Leila S. Chudori in "The Purification of Sita" (Indonesia), and Sri Daoruang in "Sita Puts Out the Fire" (Thailand). Issues of class privilege are also reflected in Khai Hung's "You Must Live" (Vietnam) and Outhine Bounyavong's "Death Price" (Laos).

My mother: *They used her vagina as an ashtray. Did you know that?*

My grandmother: *Afterwards, there were ten different kinds of semen in her body.*

My mother, a few months later: *There was a whole pillowcase stuffed down her throat.*

I grew up in a country of torrid heat, a country that, if I were to try and describe it, might be summed up simply by saying that the smells were not like anything we know here. The smells I remember were pungent smells of raw meat, blood, and rotting garbage, of human sweat. The sun beat down constantly.

In that country, I heard stories. It didn't matter whether they were true or untrue. The last time I was home, visiting Manila, I asked my mother, "Whatever became of your friend, the one who had all her clothes stolen during a holdup?"

My mother froze. She looked at me. "What are you talking about?" she said. "I never had a friend who had her clothes stolen."

"Yes," I told her. "You said she was picked up outside a bank, while she was using the ATM machine. A car of men. They dropped her off on Makati Avenue, without her clothes."

"No," my mother said, "no such thing ever happened."

So where did this story come from? I couldn't have pulled it out of my head. I always had this picture of a middle-aged woman, breasts dangling, being kicked out of a car, right in the heart of the commercial district. At least, I used to think, the men didn't do anything to her. They wanted to humiliate her, but she wasn't raped.

The other story, the one I am about to tell you now, is true. I know it really happened. In a small town in Laguna, Calauan. Near the University of the Philippines at Los Baños, the place where my family used to go to buy the famous Laguna cheese, and milk that tasted as close to American milk as my mother could find in the Philippines.

I never knew anyone who came from that place. We'd stop some-times at a gas station to ask for directions. Sometimes we bought pots for plants from shacks set up by the side of the dusty roads. The people were dark and thin; they were like the people of any small town we passed through on our way to the mountains or the beach. I never even knew anyone who went to the University there. So when I first heard about it—the case—I couldn't quite see the face of the woman. Even when they put her picture in the papers, I couldn't quite imagine her. And she didn't look at all the way I thought she might have looked. That is, she wasn't extraordinarily pretty.

The men were different. The men I could imagine. They looked like our drivers or like our houseboys or like our gardeners. They had secre-tive eyes, always. They threw dice and drank beer and had bellies that hung over the cinched belts of their tight khaki pants. They had loud, slurred voices.

The Mayor himself, the chief perpetrator, was a caricature. When I saw him for the first time, in the courtroom, I thought he was wearing a rug on his head.

That first day, the courtroom was close and noisy. Cigarette smoke hung in the air, obscuring the face of the woman who presided in her judge's robes. The light slanting in from the louvered windows was filled with dust motes.

I was dazzled by the play of light and dark on the people's faces. I knew no one there. I had come merely as an observer. Because of the stories.

The judge had a very strange name. It sounded Greek, I thought. But when she opened her mouth to speak, she was very Filipino. She spoke that kind of formal English with the long words that I never come across except in college books. The Mayor's family was ranged alongside; on the opposite benches was the family of the victim. The mother, I remember thinking, looked holy. She kept her head bowed, but she was not crying.

All through the trial, she sat there. Sometimes her husband came with her. He was a sad-looking man. But most of the time, the mother came by herself. Sometimes, during the testimony, she would utter a lit-tle gasp. Then someone would stand up and offer her a glass of water. She always took it gratefully.

I myself didn't know why I wanted to listen to those things. The number of times the girl was raped. They way they tied her down. The shot in the face, at close range. What horrified me was what they did with the body afterwards. The way they drove around in a van, stopped at all the beer halls, showed it off.

The priest at Sunday mass: *The body is nothing but a vessel. Not holy in and of itself, but holy when imbued with a spirit . . .*

She must have prayed, must have reminded them of their mothers, sisters, daughters. Oh holy God, she must have wept.

She was a gift, a gift to the Mayor. Since his fiftieth birthday, he'd been feeling blue, the driver said. Everyone talked about it.

How do we please the Mayor? How will we find something to give him that will make him happy?

He had plenty of money, so it couldn't be that. It had to be something else, something that would restore the bloom of youth to his pallid cheek. Fifty! That's not so old. Jaworski's still playing basketball, after all.

The chief of police suggested it first.

"*Ulol*! You are fucked up, you are crazy," they told him.

But when someone broached the matter to the Mayor, he liked the idea.

And then the Mayor's nephew. His sister's boy. Didn't he like the idea, too? Yes, he liked it. In fact, he was the one who chose the victim. A classmate of his at the University. She had a boyfriend; the two were always together. "No problem, no problem," said the chief of police. "We'll get rid of the boyfriend."

Which they did. Shooting him in the face and tossing his body down a ravine.

The girl was screaming. Her screams went up and down the scale, like a woman practicing for the opera.

Stupid. It was stupid. He'd never expected her to behave that way. They'd dragged her off screaming. Even in the car, they were already starting to rip off her denim shorts.

And then the numbers, the numbers, the numbers.

"The numbers," the Mayor said. Today had to be the day because the numerology charts said so. It was extremely propitious.

So he sang to her first. Sinatra songs. "Strangers in the Night." "It was a Very Good Year." "When Somebody Loves You."

But then he grew tired of her constant sniveling. She was crouched in a corner, no shorts now, panties half-ripped.

"Tie her up," he told his men.

And then the fun began.

It was a birthday to remember, and the fun lasted all night.

The Mayor: *It is my faith in God and Mother Mary that keeps me strong.*

He was the lord of *jueteng* in town. *Jueteng,* a poor man's lotto, a numbers game. Everyday, runners took bets from the jeepney drivers, the corner-store owners, the cigarette vendors. The people gave the runners their few crumpled pesos and then waited anxiously for the results of the daily raffles. Winners were announced in the late afternoon. There was always someone who won just enough. The rest of the money, the Mayor got to keep.

He had three children, including a girl named Ave Maria. He had a wife named Bai, who swore to all in court that her husband was with her, every night, may she rot in hell if she was not telling the truth.

When they came to arrest him, the men were understandably nervous. The Mayor was having breakfast on his patio, where he likes to listen to the sounds of birds trilling in the garden. The maid was pouring him a cup of hot chocolate. He was just bringing the cup to his lips when he saw them, the three men in khaki uniforms, crossing the living room. The chocolate scalded his tongue just then. He put the cup down and waited.

He heard one of them say, ". . . for the murder of Mary Eileen Sarmenta." He tried to remember what his numerology chart said.

He rose from the table. The maid screamed to see the teacup, all the breakfast things crashing to the ground.

"Señora! Señora!" she called.

The Mayor's wife came running from the bedroom, her slippers going slap, slap against the tiled floor. She was still in her housedress, her hair uncombed. Her eyes bulged. She stopped short when she saw the men.

"How dare you! How dare you—!" she stammered.

No one looked at her. The men's sweat trickled down the backs of their necks, staining the sleeves of their uniforms. Yet it was November, a cool month.

Their jeep was waiting on the driveway. He was snarling now; he couldn't help it.

Well, you know, it was the driver who cracked.

The driver? I asked my mother.

Yes, she said. *They offered him a chance at her, but he refused. He said he kept thinking of his two little girls at home. So he only watched while they did it.*

And who is "they"? I wanted to know.

Oh, my mother said, nonchalantly sprinkling water on the leaves of her orchids. *The nephew, the gardener, the houseboy, the five bodyguards . . .*

You see now what I mean by the stories. On my last trip home, I had to sit in the airless Pasig courtroom. I had no choice. I had to see it played out: the mayor, his bodyguards (beefy and mean-looking, just as in my dreams), his wife, the girl's mother. I had to see them all, arrayed in the courtroom, figures obscured by smoke and dim light. I had to see them, to convince myself this was real, it had really happened. It wasn't a nightmare. That this, everything I had been told, was not just some figment of my imagination, but had actually happened, in that town.

Sometimes, because I'd lived apart so long, I couldn't quite be sure of who I was. There were letters, of course, letters from back home. The letters told me nothing of who I was or who I had been. They were always filled with details of birthday parties, weddings, births, and funerals. None of these occasions affected me personally. I felt like someone looking at fish swimming around in a fishbowl.

When I went to the courtroom, I had this idea: that if I could feel hate, if I could feel that pure emotion burning up my body, then I would know where I belonged.

I didn't have any reason to be there. I was on vacation. I should have been sunning myself by the pool in my mother's backyard. Languid, I should have been languid. My arm outstretched for a cool, tall glass of *calamansi* juice. I would feel the weight in my hand—that coolness. Perhaps I'd press the glass to my hot cheek and let the drops of moisture creep down my chin.

But I couldn't be that way. There was something tearing up my insides. And every time I thought of the girl, tied down on the mayor's expensive *narra*-wood bed with her legs spread-eagled, I couldn't think. I'd have to stop whatever I was doing—yes, even stop walking, even if I was in the middle of a busy intersection—and take a few deep breaths.

The prosecutor: *And so what did she scream, while you were doing it to her?*

They were holding her arms so tight, so tight. She couldn't breathe. She had had ten of them already, and between her legs was a gaping wound where the milky semen leaked and leaked. Yet they were laughing and calling her names now. Cunt. Bitch.

Today was her mother's birthday. In the morning, before leaving for school, she had handed her mother a *gumamemela* flower from the garden. Her mother's face had broken out into a smile. *O sige na,* she had said. Go on; you'll be late.

Allan was waiting for her in his car. They always rode to school together now. Since the night of the Santacruzan, when she had been Reyna Elena, the queen of the religious procession holding a miniature cross in her arms, he'd always wanted to be by her side.

When they saw the police car at the side of the road, they didn't think anything of it, but then the policeman walked right out into the middle of the street and Allan had to stop. Then, suddenly, there were men at either side of the car, yanking open the doors. She was thrown into the back of a jeep, a firm hand covering her mouth, another holding her wrists. She twisted and kicked. She could see Allan being dragged away somewhere.

Tears sprang to her eyes. She was suddenly helpless and small. She was the little girl hiding behind the *santan* flowers, the one whom everyone was looking for because she had been throwing stones at the kittens. She was the little girl hiding in the closet because her mother was angry at her for using up the perfume that was in the cut-glass bottle on her mother's night table. She had been naughty; she shouldn't have worn shorts that day. She could feel fingers at the edges of her shorts, straining toward her crotch. Hard fingers, with nails that scratched. But she didn't want to die, so maybe she should just lie very, very still. If she lay still, the fingers might stop pushing so much, and it would hurt less. Would that help? No, it didn't help. So she continued her writhing.

Allan was nowhere now and all she wanted to do was to live.

When they took her to that house, she recognized it. That was the terrible thing. And she thought: "So it's true, all those stories about the Mayor."

He was the one who had put the crown on her head at the Santacruzan procession. He'd been there with his wife, his children. He'd smiled at her. The parish priest, Father Antonio, had clapped him on the shoulder.

After he'd done it, after he was through, she relaxed a little. She thought now he will let me go. I've survived. But she didn't realize he would hand her over to the others, the others who'd been watching at the sides of the room. His nephew, first. She recognized him from school. She screamed. He was worse than the Mayor; she couldn't bear the tearing pain between her legs.

Even after she'd had ten of them, she still wanted to live. She went on her knees. She said, "Have mercy." She put the palms of her hands together in supplication. A hand covered her eyes. She didn't feel the gun blast that spattered her brains over the floor of the jeep.

In the courtroom, I began to notice a veiled figure who appeared every day, always in the same place. She was slender; she wore a light blue dress. Over her face was the lace veil that I remembered wearing to church before Vatican Two did away with the rule about covering one's head. I never saw this woman's face, only the merest outline of her profile. The more I saw her, the more I wanted to find out who she was.

She spoke to no one. She always sat demurely, her hands folded on her lap. After many weeks, I began to get the feeling that she was Mary Eileen. I thought her hands, with their faint tracery of blue veins, looked very familiar.

When I asked people who she was, they would shrug, because no one had noticed her particularly. There were so many spectators in that courtroom, it was actually difficult to breathe. There were days when the smell of human sweat, and all the tension collected in people's bodies, was so overpowering that I literally kept a handkerchief to my nose the whole time I sat there.

I didn't want to be there and yet I was there.

When it was all, all over, when the Mayor was being taken away in handcuffs, when his wife was wailing and gnashing her teeth, when the flashbulbs were popping and there was general pandemonium, desks toppling over and people scuffling to be the first to get the story out, I couldn't move. People shoved me from behind, cursing. They were trying to get to Mary Eileen's mother.

"What do you think about the verdict?" they asked her. "Are you happy?"

That was the first time I saw the woman's eyes fill with tears. She didn't answer, only pushed her way wordlessly out of the room.

Much, much later, when I was myself again, I opened a newspaper and there was his picture. I couldn't mistake that shock of hair that looked like a rug, those pig eyes. He was sitting in a bathtub, and, from what I could see of him, was apparently naked. The caption said that the picture had been taken in jail. But the Mayor was smiling. The article said the Mayor's bathwater was sprinkled with rose petals provided by his loving wife, Bai, the new Mayor of Calauan.

1999

Paulino Lim Jr.

"Mother Lily and the Mail-Order Groom"

Born in the Philippines in 1935, Paulino Lim Jr. earned a bachelor's degree in education and a master's in English at the University of Santo Tomas and a doctorate at the University of California, Los Angeles. He is the author of a scholarly monograph, The Style of Lord Byron's Plays; *a short-fiction anthology,* Passion Summer and Other Stories; *and a quartet of political novels. Currently, he is Professor Emeritus in the English Department at California State University, Long Beach.*

Many modern Filipino writers, including Bienvenido Santos and N. V. M. Gonzales, have written from different perspectives about Filipinos in the United States. Paulino Lim Jr.'s story has a contemporary transnational edge as it explores the human consequences of globalization on the Philippine economy through the protagonist's desire to pur-

"Mother Lily and the Mail-Order Groom," by Paulino Lim Jr. Permission to publish granted by the author.

sue imagined opportunity in America. The Southeast Asian exile's experience has been explored by a number of writers throughout the region. The experience of exile resonates with another familiar subject: that of the economic migrant within the ASEAN nations, as illustrated by Daw Ohn Khin's short story "An Unanswerable Question" (Burma).

If you get tired of reading the same sad news about the country's debt of twenty billion dollars, circa 1985, and its attempts to secure new loans to pay the interest on the principal, you can always turn to the personal columns. There the items are decidedly human interest—some will even make you smile. Take this ad, for example: "Selected rich Americans seek Filipino wives." Selected by whom? Rich by whose standards? A gas station attendant earning twenty thousand dollars a year is phenomenally rich, if you consider the eighteen pesos, roughly a dollar, that his counterpart in the Philippines makes a day. One may point out, of course, that the country's foreign debt and personal want ads both relate to one thing: a bowl of rice on the table.

Another ad promises much more: "Australian European businessmen now in town to meet attractive single educated ladies view friendship-marriage come to Video Match Ambassador Hotel." One wonders how many college graduates, unable to find work, will appear at the Ambassador for the interview and videotaping. Is it naive to expect that the prospective friend or husband be single? How does the shy Filipina overcome the embarrassment of answering questions that test her intelligence as a college graduate and then mimicking Madonna or Jane Fonda in front of the video camera? Is it the same steaming bowl of rice?

This next ad supplies an answer: "Slim, pretty, genuine sisters want *balikbayan*, foreigners for marriage." Forthright, not bashful at all, either a Filipino from abroad or a foreigner will do. The idea of sisters being "genuine" might intrigue the foreign reader, but not the Filipino who may grow up knowing that in another household he has half brothers and sisters, not considered genuine by the town with its double-standard morality. "Genuine" also tells the native readers that the sisters are virgins.

In contrast to the Australian and European items, this seems straight from the horse's mouth told in one breathless neighing: "Single American traveler just arrived looking for a beautiful Filipina slender intelligent at least 5'3" age 18–26 single no children for friendship or

possible relationship." To an American blessed with a bounty of over-
weight Caucasian girlfriends, a slender and intelligent Filipina must be
special, but she must not be married nor be a single parent. He must
have been warned about the *queridas,* or concubines, raising the inau-
thentic offspring of errant husbands.

Only recently have I begun to read the personal columns, as well as
job listings, in the classified sections of magazines and newspapers. It's
all because of Cecilio, who answered a personal ad by an American
woman. If a visitor from Iowa wants a beautiful, slender and intelligent
Filipina, why shouldn't a liberated woman from Philadelphia advertise
for a handsome, slim and intelligent Filipino? This came out when we
heard that Cecilio's family was selling a rice field in a barrio six kilometers south of our town.

At first we thought they had become fearful of the communists who
came down from the mountains at harvest time and took two sacks of
rice for every ten gathered, leaving the remaining eight to be divided
between the farmer and the landowner. Call it tithing, securing protection, or paying tax. The truth or versions of it were gossiped about with
wonder and envy—Cecilio was going to America and needed the
money for fare.

The young men of my age who gathered in late afternoons at the
plaza to shoot baskets, many of them college graduates unable to find
jobs, including myself, talked about Cecilio's good fortune. He was neither a doctor nor a nurse, the most common émigré, who staff hospitals
across the United States—from Long Beach, California, to Long Island,
New York. Nor was he a recruit in the United States Navy, putting in
twenty years as a steward before retiring with relatives in America or
repatriating to the Philippines.

"Cecilio, how did you do it?" we asked him one afternoon on the
basketball court. Cecilio stood tall among us; next to him we seemed
darker, swarthy. He was tall—five eleven—and wore white shirts and
Converse shoes. If anything, the shoes, costing as much as two sacks of
rice, set him apart from the rest of us who played basketball wearing
rubber slippers. He shot baskets but didn't play games. He did not
want to injure his piano-playing hands and infuriate his mother, a
woman who boasts of a Spanish priest in her family tree.

"Well, about a year ago, I wrote to this woman who wanted a pen
pal."

We all laughed. A pen pal! It had to be something more involved.

"Her name is Amanda, a psychologist. She owns a house in Philadelphia. She has sent me a fiancé visa."

No one laughed. The man who was dribbling rested the ball against his hip. From the way we looked at one another, we all wondered about the situation of a woman sending a fiancé visa to one who is gay, as the Americans would put it.

If anyone felt like condemning Cecilio for passing himself off as straight and deluding his pen fiancée, he kept it to himself. Instead, we asked him about the processing of his own visa at the American embassy, which looks more like a fort than an office building on the edge of Manila Bay.

"It's slow. Visa applicants average 350 a day. There's a little racket going on at the gate. To be among the one hundred whose visas will be processed on any given day, you have to pay. The first fifty pay one hundred pesos, the next fifty pay fifty pesos. I read a letter to the *Bulletin* editor denouncing this extortion."

Cecilio got his visa, his ticket from the rice-field sale, and we all wished him a safe trip as he joined the thousands that made the Philippines second only to Mexico in sending immigrants to the United States.

About this time two sensational news items involving Filipinos in America appeared in the papers. One was a letter to "Dear Abby" by a woman who discovered that the man she married already had a wife in the Philippines to whom he sent money regularly. Another recounted the killing of a wife and her mother by the Filipino husband. She also found out about the man's other family and left, moved back to her mother's house, and filed for annulment. The man begged her to return, she threatened to tell the immigration authorities, and he killed her and her mother. The man was apprehended in Tijuana attempting to book a flight to Mexico City with his two children, a boy and a girl.

Cecilio didn't quite make the news as these two Filipinos did, but stories about him began to circulate on the basketball court. We heard talks about Cecilio's escape, his going underground in Los Angeles, and a fake marriage in Las Vegas. We did not get all the facts until Lilia, a nurse at a hospital in Los Angeles, came home for her mother's funeral. The town calls her Mother Lily because of what she does for Filipinos needing a temporary home in Los Angeles. Cecilio hid at her place after the scorned woman had told the immigration authorities that she wanted the visa canceled and the fiancé sent back to the Philippines.

I am running ahead of my story, or rather Cecilio's story. I'm prompted by much more than curiosity or interest in gossip. God knows we have enough gossip in this town. If anything, the woman psychologist interests me as I am a psychology major myself who hopes to find a counseling job at a local school or college. I heard she even bought a piano for Cecilio.

"I never saw Amanda," Lily told us. "She's in her thirties, older than Cecil, late twenties. Cecil said she's fat."

"Cecil? Is that how he calls himself now?"

"Yes."

"Nice name."

"Cecil said it shocked him that she was big, not like the picture she sent him."

"Is that the reason he gave for running away from her and not because he is, you know . . ."

"He lived with her for almost a year in a house with a swimming pool. Amanda supported him all this time while he waited for his green card."

"What's a green card?"

"A green card gives an alien permanent resident status—the first step to becoming a full citizen. With a green card you can have a social security number and find yourself a decent job."

"Did Cecil tell you what he did during the time he lived with Amanda?"

Lilia smiled, dropped her lovely face and raised a hand to cover her mouth as she laughed, palm towards us. I said to myself, Lily may seem plumper than her sister and have a scrubbed look about her but she is still a Filipina, demure and shy. She must be well liked at the hospital where she works.

"You could say that he repaid Amanda every cent she spent on him."

"How so?"

"Well, he was Amanda's houseboy, pool-maintenance man, musician, gardener and her personal cook."

"And sexual partner?" I said.

Lilia shook a finger at me and said, "You have a dirty mind."

Laughter.

"Cecil is such a good cook, I found this out when he lived at my place. Can you imagine having your own Asian cook in America, and I mean Asian. Cecil can cook Chinese, Filipino, Thai and Indonesian.

You see, ethnic restaurants are very popular in Los Angeles. They are the poor man's excuse for dining out, as cheap as some of them are. Cecil does Japanese also, but he says that Amanda hated anything Japanese."

"Any reason?"

"Cecil said something about Amanda's father being laid off by the Ford Motor Company."

"I wonder what Amanda misses the most—the houseboy or the Asian cook?"

"You are being foolish again," she told me.

"Go on with your story."

"Cecil said that the most difficult thing was pretending that he was enjoying himself. Oh, he liked doing the yard and had started a flower garden. He told us about a plant with long red tassel flowers, called 'Love Lies Bleeding.' And he loved cooking. He was amazed at the spices and the quality of the meats he found at the supermarkets. But he said he could not stand it when she touched him, especially when they swam."

I had other things in mind that I was afraid Lily would call dirt.

"So he decided to run away. Before he left the Philippines he had compiled addresses and phone numbers of Filipinos he knew living in the States. He studied bus and train schedules and kept part of the grocery money Amanda gave him. And one day he boarded a Greyhound bus and took off."

A Greyhound odyssey.

"Cecil said that the families he stayed with gave him money to get him out of their houses."

"And that's where you came in, Mother Lily?"

"I got Cecil's phone call as soon as he arrived in Los Angeles. L.A., you see, is a sanctuary for all kinds of illegal aliens. You hear mostly of Mexicans and Salvadorans coming from south of the border. But I once read of Chinese aliens being flown across the border aboard a Beechcraft airplane. It's crazy out there."

"Are the immigration people still looking for Cecil?"

"Oh, yes, and they'll deport him if they catch him. He's working in a Japanese restaurant and, get this, he has a Japanese boyfriend."

Lily meant this for me. She knew I'd find it amusing.

"What's going to happen next?"

"Well, right now, he's living with his Japanese boyfriend. He's trying to save up and get his green card. He could get married. The going rate right now for a fake Las Vegas marriage with a citizen is three thousand dollars. It's as good as marrying a U.S. serviceman at Clark Air Base or Subic Bay. But if they catch Cecil, they'll deport him, put the woman in jail for five years and fine her ten thousand dollars."

"Lily, why don't you marry me and take me with you to L.A.?"

Lily lifted a finger, poised to admonish me again, but instead gave me the kindest and warmest look.

1997

Vietnam

Vietnam has a long history of resistance and accommodation to outside domination: first, Chinese cultural and political influence from 111 B.C.; then European incursions from the fifteenth century. The French successfully colonized Vietnam from 1862 to 1954 and were succeeded by American involvement from 1954 to 1975. Traditional Vietnamese literature reveals the direct influence of Chinese genres and language; nevertheless, it reflects a uniquely Vietnamese aesthetic in its lyricism and its authors' propensity to examine the emotional depths of human relationships, an aesthetic also found in modern Vietnamese literature.

The modern short story in Vietnam arises from a preexistent template, the rather didactic Chinese short-story genre called *xiaoshuo* that was adopted over the centuries by the Vietnamese literati. This style of short story was published in the early newspapers of the late nineteenth century to instruct the public in *quoc ngu* (romanized Vietnamese) script. Western literary influence melded to this tradition. Modern French romanticism, naturalism, and realism were introduced during the French colonial period, along with French-language education for a restricted number of Vietnamese. New Chinese translations of modern Western literature also influenced Vietnamese writers during the early twentieth century.

Popularization of the modern short story grew with the spread of *quoc ngu,* modern printing techniques, and the appearance of newspapers and periodicals during the first decades of the twentieth century. The first generation of Vietnamese journalists appeared during the 1910s. They became the initial group of modern short-story writers in the North to experiment with a Vietnamese style of realism and a new form of literary language. By World War I, *quoc ngu* had become the vehicle for a new body of Vietnamese nationalist literature emphasizing social critique.

During the late 1920s, the progressive and French-trained monarch

Bao Dai promoted a more liberal intellectual climate that led to an explosion of literary creativity. The 1930s saw change and turmoil. This period also saw intense literary activity as new journals and newspapers flourished, providing a venue for short-story publication. Different literary trends developed into Vietnamese styles of realism, romanticism, naturalism, and social critique. Popular literature came into being with romances and spy, detective, and adventure fiction. An important debate influencing the entire modern period emerged between proponents of realism (art for society's sake) and romanticism (art for art's sake).

Japan seized French military bases in Vietnam in 1940, and a pro-Vichy French administration remained in place until 1945. Meanwhile Ho Chi Minh organized an independence movement known as the Viet Minh. At the end of World War II, his followers seized Hanoi and declared Vietnam to be an independent republic. The French quashed this hard-won independence in 1946.

Resistance against the French continued until their bitter defeat at Dien Bien Phu on 5 May 1954. The 1954 Geneva Conference left Vietnam a divided nation, with Ho Chi Minh's communist government ruling the North and Ngo Dinh Diem's regime, supported by the United States, ruling the South. Government policies in both areas impacted post–World War II writers.

Under the Democratic Republic in the North, a clear party policy advocating socialist realism and writers' participation in the daily lives of peasants, workers, and soldiers had developed by the 1960s. The first American bombings mobilized a resistance literature.

Although writers had more freedom in the South (the Republic of Vietnam), they still suffered censorship if their writing became too political. Several literary schools flourished, including existentialist, romantic, realist, socialist, and progovernment; each school was associated with a specific newspaper or literary magazine. Since many South Vietnamese writers had been involved in the war of resistance, they wrote about the psychological impact of war on families and love relationships or about the French destruction of the environment. Other writers focused on changing gender roles and individual alienation. Women writers became more prevalent throughout Vietnam in the 1960s.

Years of bitter conflict passed before Vietnam was again reunified as an independent nation in 1975. Skirmishes between the communist Viet Minh North and the American-backed South had developed into full-scale civil war as the United States became embroiled in the area and completely altered its economy. Saigon finally surrendered on 30 April 1975 while the remaining U.S. military and diplomatic personnel were evacuated from the city. Nearly thirty years had passed in civil war. An entire generation of Vietnamese had endured a divided Vietnam, knowing only continuous warfare. After 1975, writers in the South found their literature suppressed; many fled into exile or ended up in reeducation camps. A reemergence of the tension between "art for society's sake" and "art for art's sake" ended in a victory for socialist realism.

A ruined economy and infrastructure made the next two decades difficult. In 1986 Doi Moi, a new policy for economic renewal, allowed for some privatization and outside investment. In October 1987 writers were encouraged to "never curb your pen," and a number of "dissident" writers quickly emerged. This Renovation literature evidences several trends that are not necessarily "anticommunist." Among them are a Vietnamese postmodernist revision of conventional history and a critical realism rooted in the work of Vietnamese writers of the 1930s. Some dissident writers' work is still banned for being too outspoken, and writers are frequently harassed or jailed. The stories in this section have been selected to represent writers of the modern period from North, Central, and South Vietnam.

Nguyen Cong Hoan

"Tu Ben the Actor"

Nguyen Cong Hoan (1903–77), from North Vietnam, is considered one of Vietnam's great writers of satire and realist fiction before 1945 and subsequently a writer of socialist realism. A prolific author, he produced eight collections of short stories, twenty-five novels, and three memoirs. Before his retirement, he served as president of the Vietnamese Writers' Association.

In 1935 his collection of short stories Kep Tu Ben *(Tu Ben the Actor), from which this story is selected, created a literary controversy between adherents of "art for art's sake" and "art for society's sake." With subtle irony, in a style later known in Vietnam as critical realism, Nguyen depicts the struggle between poverty and humanity in his portrayal of the protagonist, Tu Ben. Also found here is the poignant sensibility of pathos that distinguishes some Vietnamese fiction. Other Southeast Asian writers, such as U Win Pe in "Clean, Clear Water" (Burma), are also masters of satire and realism. A more humorous satirical approach to humanity is expressed in Sila Khomchai's "The Family in the Street" (Thailand).*

Among true opera fans, everybody knows Tu Ben the Actor. He is famous, above all, for his extraordinary comic skills. When on the stage, he need not utter a word, for just his facial expressions and over-the-top satirical gestures are more than capable of provoking hysterical belly laughs and thunderous applause from any audience.

Although originally from Saigon, he has performed in Hanoi for the past three years. Due to his independent nature and unique talent, he has never joined a stable company. Any theater fortunate enough to

"Tu Ben the Actor," by Nguyen Cong Hoan, first published in 1935. This translation is based upon the manuscript in *Nguyen Cong Hoan—Truyen Ngan Tuyen Chon: Tap I* (Nguyen Cong Hoan—Selected Short Stories: Volume 1) (Hanoi: Nha Xuat Ban Van Hoc, 1996). Permission to publish granted by the translators, Peter Zinoman and Nguyen Nguyet Cam, with the consent of the author's estate.

cast him can be sure to sell out the house. When leaflets or newspaper notices announce one of his upcoming performances, Hanoi audiences stampede to the theater. Latecomers, who invariably must return home, money in hand, can be heard complaining about the small size of today's theaters! It is no surprise that Hanoi's playhouses always offer him top billing.

However, for over a month now, he has not performed. For over a month now, his father has been sick. For over a month now, in a dark loft in the small house at the end of Sam Cong Lane, Tu Ben has listened to his father's moans mingling with the sad whistle of the medicine kettle. The sound depresses Tu Ben and he cannot think about work. As his father's condition worsens, Tu Ben exhausts his savings to buy medicine. Finally, with no other options, he begins to borrow money from several wealthy theater owners.

One day, the owner of the Stage Drama Theater stopped by for a visit. Following a perfunctory greeting, he inquired abruptly after his loan.

"So, where's the money you owe me?"

"Please, I need more time. I'll pay you when I return to work."

The owner pursed his lips. "Enough. I've heard it all before. Pay now or I take you to court."

Tu Ben forced a grim smile and turned away. Fearing the conversation slipping away, the owner sweetened his tone.

"It's been so long since you performed. My audiences always ask about you. Why not come back to work?"

"I'm planning to, but . . ."

"I've recently commissioned an old-style operatic comedy by a talented young writer. You'd be perfect for the main role. No one but you can really do it."

"For a new role, I'd have to rehearse . . ."

"Of course, but it shouldn't take half a month to learn the lines and get down the blocking."

"Half a month!"

Tu Ben repeated the words over in his head. Half a month. Fifteen long days. Each day, he would have to leave his father for rehearsals. His father was sick and there was no one else to look after him.

"Forget it. I'm too busy." He pointed to the mosquito net. "My father's weak. I must stay with him."

Tu Ben's father coughed fitfully. Reaching out from his sickbed, he grabbed a spittoon sitting on a nearby stool. But his frail trembling hand lost its grip. The spittoon crashed to the floor, splattering saliva around the room. Startled, Tu Ben hurried to help his father.

"Father! Why didn't you call me?"

With a small broom, he cleaned up the saliva. He glared at the owner.

"See. How can I leave him alone?"

"If you work for me, I'll send someone to take care of the old man."

"Thanks, but I just couldn't."

At that moment, the faint sound of a chopstick tapping a ceramic bowl rose from under the mosquito net—a signal from his father. Tu Ben hurried to his side. In a low voice, his father asked for water. Seizing the opportunity to ingratiate himself, the theater owner approached the bed. He lifted the net and spoke to the old man.

"Hello, Uncle. Do you recognize me?"

The old man strained to open his eyes. Feigning recognition, he flashed a grim, toothy smile, nodded and extended an unsteady hand. Don't imagine, Dear Reader, that the old man was familiar with this style of Western greeting. His grim, toothy smile was no more than a feeble attempt to conceal a profound discomfort. Rather, his effort to offer a polite Western greeting reflected a pathetic desire to help his son receive a favor from this man.

"You're not so weak, Uncle. Why won't Tu Ben work for me?"

The old man nodded nonsensically.

"I'm producing a new opera, Uncle. I want your son for the lead."

The old man forced a grin and readied an answer, but Tu Ben cut him off.

"You're tired, father. I must stay with you."

The old man frowned in a way only Tu Ben understood. His father didn't want to cause trouble between his son and his son's creditor. The owner tried a more soothing tone.

"Try to help me out. If you accept, you can repay me whenever you get the money. And you can use all the money you make by starring in my play 'The Obsequious Mandarin' to buy medicine for your father."

The persuasive power of the last sentence made Tu Ben pause, and filled his father with hope. The old man took a deep breath to calm himself. The owner tried again.

"What do you say?"

"You will look after my father?"

"Don't worry. You can rehearse at home. Given your talent and intelligence, you'll only need to come to the theater for final rehearsals. Why waste your talent?"

This last sentence struck Tu Ben as if he had just taken holy communion. A thoughtful expression came over him, and he stared at his father.

Tired of his son's hesitations, the old man wrinkled his brow and snapped: "Take the job!"

The utterance faded in a stream of wheezing.

Tu Ben's resolve disappeared. He turned to the owner of the Stage Drama Theater: "Okay. I'll do it."

After waiting so long and working so hard for Tu Ben's tenuous agreement, the owner feared a future change of heart. What if the old man took a turn for the worse on opening night? What if Tu Ben pulled a sudden no-show? He pulled out a contract and politely requested that Tu Ben sign on the dotted line.

When the day came, publicity-mobiles circled Hanoi's streets announcing the performance and distributing leaflets. Banners displayed at prominent intersections apprised theater lovers of the special event: "A New Play—Starring Tu Ben."

That evening, the exterior of the Stage Drama Theater was lit as brightly as day. The brightness revealed a vast throng of people unevenly lining the street. It looked like a huge field of colorful flowers surrounded by swarms of butterflies and bees. Under awnings, atop balconies, in the middle of the street, a thousand teenage girls and boys flocked together, impatiently chirping and flirting with one another. The melodious symphony music, broadcast from the theater, was rich and seductive. It urged people forward, told them to forget their troubles, and impelled them to hypnotically exchange the contents of their pockets for tickets.

Gradually this human wave disappeared into the theater. After taking their seats, members of the crowd happily recited Tu Ben's past routines and mimicked his signature gestures. The audience waited anxiously for the stage curtain to open. They wanted so much to laugh, clap their hands and memorize Tu Ben's inevitable zingers, which they would then repeat incessantly. These, no doubt, would bring smiles to their lovers' lips. Glory to Tu Ben the Actor! But pity him as well! For unbeknownst to the crowd, back at home, his father had taken an abrupt turn for the worse. As the old man's final breath drew near, Tu Ben sat in his dressing room, a knot boring through the pit of his stomach.

Indeed, Tu Ben's misery was apparent to everyone who peeked into the dressing room. Grim-faced before the mirror, his stomach churning, his brow furrowed, he still had to dip his hands into the tin of rose-colored powder and apply it to his face. He dabbed his fingers into the ink plate and rubbed them over his lips. He then had to slip backwards into a scholar's gown, put on silly-looking green boots, and place a mandarin's bonnet upside-down on his head. In costume, he looked absurd—both rich and merry. Now came the time when he must satisfy his boss, impress his peers, make the audience double over in laughter and clap until their palms ached. But how close to death his father was! Before leaving home, he had realized the danger. Oh God! He had to put it out of his mind. He had to forget in order to joke, to jest, to wise-crack on stage, so that we might laugh, so that we might roar with laughter, so that we might laugh until we roll in the aisles.

The first act ended and the curtain closed. A rousing round of applause, hailing the King of Comedy, exploded like fireworks. Tu Ben walked out to take a bow. Bewildered, he stopped before the ferocious applause. The sight of his queer costume and painted mouth drove the audience to fits of sheer delight. The longer he stood there in silence, the more they gaped, reveled in his comic genius, and cackled hysterically.

Such cruelty! In this play, Tu Ben's character was always on stage and constantly hamming it up. In each scene, his character was required to break out in gut-wrenching laughter.

Act I had dragged on interminably. During the short intermission, he sent a stagehand to check on his father. But before his return, Tu Ben took the stage for Act II. Once again, he had to shout, to sing folk ditties, to enunciate his words, to control his delivery, to perform the requisite gestures, and to laugh just as heartily as in Act I. But by this point, the sight of his face alone was enough to send the audience into fits of convulsive laughter. They remained oblivious to the hints of anxiety that were beginning to appear on his face. Suddenly, while preening in response to the rhythmic clapping of the crowd, he overheard low whispers coming from the wings.

"It's worse than before. The old man seems to have slipped into a coma."

A coma! It can't be true! But just at that moment, his character was scripted to embark on an elaborate comedic bit. Thousands of eyes fixed silently on his every move. Eager for another chance to clap wildly and roll in the aisles, the crowd hung on his every word.

Act II seemed even longer than Act I. Alone in his dressing room, he received the news: his father had lost consciousness. The old man's hands and feet had grown stone cold.

What news could be more painful?! Tu Ben burst into tears. He cried aloud.

"Father!"

Overhearing this cry, the theater owner worried that his play might be aborted. He tried to console Tu Ben and forbade the stagehands to report further news.

The stage was set for the final act. The theater owner ordered Tu Ben to touch up the powder on his face, and to rearrange his gown and hat to their former humorous positions. Upon seeing Tu Ben sobbing and weeping as he adjusted his belt, the theater owner commanded him to quiet down and wipe away his tears. Then he directed him toward the stage. Again, Tu Ben shouted and sang, chanted and laughed, jumped and danced—the requisite quest for applause.

Picture the sad scene of Tu Ben. The more his sadness grew, the more he had to make merry and perform gaily. And the absence of news from home gnawed deeper at his intestines, rubbed salt deeper into his wounds.

While the final act seemed never-ending to him, it was much too short for the audience. As the curtain fell and he took a bow, steady rhythmic clapping filled the theater. It echoed for what seemed an eternity. Just as his obligation seemed at its end, just as he was about to rush to his father's bedside to see his father's face one final time, a thunderous chant rose up from the front rows:

"Bis! Bis!"

The theater owner raised the curtain. Tu Ben quickly hid his melancholy face—the face that reflected his true feelings. He began a final humorous sketch for the crowd.

The trumpet blared and applause shook the theater to its very foundation. The curtain slowly descended and he took his final bow. But, without a moment's notice, audience members rushed to the stage and surrounded Tu Ben. They offered him flowers, grabbed his nose, and sang his praises. He felt his insides grow cold and brittle.

Finally, too tired to accept the compliments of another audience member, Tu Ben retreated to his dressing room, changed his clothes, and scrubbed his face clean.

As he stood confusedly, wondering about his father's condition, a fellow actor approached and hurriedly pressed into his hand a stack of money given him by the theater owner.

"Hurry home, Tu Ben! It's too late! I'm sorry! I'm really sorry!"

1935

Translated by Peter Zinoman and Nguyen Nguyet Cam

Khai Hung
"You Must Live"

Khai Hung (1896–1947) is the pen name of Tran Khanh Giu, a cofounder (along with Nhat Linh) of the powerful Self-Reliance Literary Group and also its most prolific writer and most popular member. He was born in Hai Duong Province, North Vietnam. His best-known short story is "You Must Live" (Anh Phai Song) (1934), and one of his better-known novels is Nua Chung Xuan *(Halfway through Spring) (1934). In 1941 he was arrested for anti-French activities. Following World War II, he supported the anticommunist Vietnamese Nationalist Party with his own newspaper,* Viet Nam. *In 1947, while fleeing for safety to his wife's village, he was captured by the Viet Minh and died at Gua Ga in Nam Dinh province.*

"You Must Live" reflects a consistent theme in Khai Hung's fiction: the strength of human character. Like many of his stories, it challenges the roots of traditional Vietnamese society and advocates the need to recognize individual rights and freedoms. In this story a peasant couple, at the bottom of the socioeconomic ladder, finds society to be devoid of compassion for their poverty, like an indifferent river. The vicissitudes of peasant life and marriage relationships are important themes for other Southeast Asian writers, including P. H. Muhammad Abdul Aziz in "The Plankway" (Negara Brunei Darussalam).

"You Must Live" (Anh Phai Song), by Khai Hung, published in *Van Xuoi Lang Man Viet Nam (1930–1945)*, vol. 3 (Hanoi: Nha Xuat Ban Khoa Hoc Xa Hoi, 1994). Permission to publish granted by the translators, Bac Hoai Tran and Courtney Norris, with the consent of the author's estate.

A summer afternoon on the Yen Phu dike.

The water of the Nhi Ha River had just begun to rise, flowing power-fully, as if it wanted to yank loose the small island in the middle of the river. The dull red water was littered with tree trunks and dead branches from the forests, bobbing like a line of small boats racing swiftly toward the open sea.

Standing on the dike, the bricklayer's assistant Thuc followed the driftwood intently, then turned to his wife and fixed his gaze upon her, asking silently for her opinion. Observing the river and the sky, his wife shook her head and sighed.

"The wind's so strong. And those black clouds on the horizon are rolling in fast. It'll rain soon, honey!"

He also sighed, walking away slowly. Then he paused and asked her, "Have you made dinner yet, dear?"

"Yes, but there's only enough rice for the two children to eat tonight," she told him sadly.

The couple looked at each other without a word . . . They seemed fixated by the same idea, one that compelled them to return to the river. The tree trunks continued to rush by in the red water.

Thuc smiled a rather vague smile. "Let's risk it!" he ventured. She shook her head, without saying anything.

"Did you go to Mrs. Ky's house yet?" he asked.

"I did."

"How did it go?"

"No good. She said she'll only hand over the money if we bring her the driftwood first. She won't give us a loan beforehand."

"So that's the way it is, huh?"

His words sounded as final as the last swipes of a trowel putting a brick into place on a still-unfinished wall. Thuc was resolved to carry out something extraordinary, so he turned again to face his wife.

"Listen! You go home now and take care of the boy Bo."

"He already has the girls Nhon and Be to play with."

"But it would still be better if you go home. Nhon has only just turned five; how could she possibly take care of her little brother and sister?"

"I'll go home then . . . But you'll also come home, right? What are you doing standing there?"

"Sure, sure, you go ahead. I'll be right along."

Obeying him, Thuc's wife went back to the village of Yen Phu.

When she got home to the rundown house, musty and dark, Thuc's wife lingered in the doorway, painfully observing their poverty.

Crowded together on the matless wooden *kang* were her three children, weeping and sobbing, calling out for their mother. The boy Bo was crying to be breast-fed. He hadn't had anything in his stomach since noon.

The girl Nhon patted her brother but he didn't stop crying, and this made her lips start to quiver. She urged her sister Be, "You go look for Mom and tell her to come home and feed him."

But Be refused to go and flung herself onto the *kang,* cursing and yelling.

Thuc's wife rushed over to them and picked up the baby, comforting him. "Oh dear! I'm never home, and here I've let my child go hungry. And now he's crying."

She sat down on the *kang* to breast-feed him. But no matter how much he sucked, no milk came. His mouth opened to release his mother's breast and he howled even louder than before.

Thuc's wife sighed, and tears glinted in her sunken eyes. She stood up, moving about the room while singing a lullaby. She tried to comfort him again. "Oh dear! I haven't had anything to eat, so there's no milk for you, my child."

After a little while, the boy fell asleep from exhaustion. Meanwhile, the house had become quiet. The two sisters had been chased into the street to play so their brother could sleep undisturbed.

Thuc's wife sat there silently and reflected on her life. In her unsophisticated, unimaginative mind, the plain country woman had never known how to put her memories in order. The things she could recall appeared to her as a jumble of shapes of people and objects, jostling for their place in a picture. Of only one thing was she sure, remembering very distinctly that she had never enjoyed any happiness or leisure like wealthy people.

When she was twelve or thirteen, still using her maiden name Lac, she worked as a mortar mixer. Her life was nothing unusual. Day after day, month after month, year after year . . .

At seventeen, there came a time when she and the bricklayer's assistant Thuc worked in the same place, she as a mortar mixer, and he as an apprentice. They teased each other, fell in love, and then got married.

For five long years, in the rundown, musty house at the foot of the

Yen Phu dike, there had been nothing tranquil to speak of in the empty lives of these two miserable human beings. Their misery only grew when they had three children in three successive years.

On top of that, it was a time of hardship, with scarce work and low wages, forcing them to try a little of this, a little of that. They labored endlessly day after day, not able to support themselves or their children.

During last year's flood season, the assistant Thuc unexpectedly stumbled on a new way of making a living. He borrowed some money to buy a small bamboo boat. The two of them took it out daily to catch driftwood in the middle of the river. After two months, he was not only able to pay his debt, but earned more than enough to spend unconcernedly.

So in this year of poverty, the couple had anxiously awaited the day when the floodwaters would come again.

Then only the day before, Heaven began to deliver a livelihood to his family.

Thinking of that, Lac smiled to herself, very softly putting her son down on his cloth diaper. She tiptoed outside and went up to the dike, seemingly resolved to carry out her plan.

When she reached the dike, Lac didn't see her husband anywhere.

The wind was as strong as ever, howling fiercely, and the current hurtled like a thundering waterfall. Lac looked up at the sky—it was so dark.

She stood there thinking, the tails of her blouse flapping noisily like waves crashing against the shore. Suddenly an idea struck her, sending her sprinting in a panic down the dike toward the river.

Reaching the place where the small boat was moored, Lac spotted her husband wrestling with the knot of bamboo strips that secured it. She watched her husband quietly, waiting for him to finish the task, then stepped into the boat. "Where are you planning to go, honey?" asked Lac.

Thuc scowled at his wife.

"Why didn't you stay home with the boy?" he scolded her.

Lac was frightened and stammered, "He's . . . he's asleep."

"What did you come here for?"

"Where are you taking the boat?"

"What are you asking me for? Go home!"

Lac covered her face with her hands and sobbed. Thuc was moved.

"Why are you crying?"

"Because you're going out to catch the driftwood by yourself and won't let me go with you."

Thuc thought it over, glancing up at the sky and then down at the water.

He then told his wife, "You can't go . . . it's too dangerous."

Lac laughed. "If it's so dangerous, then let's brave it together . . . But there's nothing to be afraid of. I can swim."

"Okay!"

His response sounded so cold that Lac shivered. The wind continued to roar and the water raged. The sky was growing darker by the minute.

"Are you frightened?" Thuc asked.

"No."

The couple began to guide the boat towards the middle of the river, with Thuc steering and his wife paddling. They struggled against the force of the current, fighting to turn the bow upstream. But the boat was swept downriver, bobbing up and down in the silty water like a dead bamboo leaf sinking in a puddle of blood, like a mosquito drowning in an inkwell.

It wasn't until a half-hour had passed that the boat reached the middle of the river. Thuc kept a tight hold on the helm while his wife hauled up the wood.

After a short while, the boat was almost full. The couple was about to make their way back to the riverbank when it started to pour. Suddenly thunder and lightning tore through the black clouds, as if the whole world was coming apart.

The small boat grew heavy with water.

They tried to paddle, but were swept away by the force of the water . . .

"Good heavens!" they yelled out.

The boat was sinking. The logs that had been hauled up onto the boat now joined their former companions in the river, and floated away indifferently, carrying with them the capsized boat . . .

"Do you think you can swim to the shore?" Thuc asked his wife.

"Sure!" she answered with certainty.

"Swim with the current . . . Ride the waves!"

"Sure! Don't worry about me!"

The rain was still coming down hard, and the thunder and lightning continued unabated. They felt as if they had fallen into an abyss. Soon Thuc saw that his wife was close to the point of exhaustion, so he swam over to her.

"How do you feel?" he asked.

"Okay! Don't worry!"

She had just uttered those words when her head went under. It took all her strength just to come to the surface again. Thuc hurried to her rescue. With one arm grasping his wife, he used his other arm to paddle. Lac smiled, looking at him with tenderness. He smiled back.

A moment later, Thuc said, "I'm too tired. Hold on to my shoulder and let me swim! I can't hold your weight anymore."

After a few minutes, Thuc was even more drained, and his arms felt limp.

"Can you keep swimming?" his wife asked gently.

"I don't know. By myself, maybe I could."

"I'll let go of you so you can get to shore, okay?"

He laughed. "No! Let's die together."

It was only a moment, but to Lac it felt like an eternity.

"Lac my dear! Do you think you can swim anymore?" her husband asked again.

"No! . . . Why?"

"Nothing. We'll die together then."

Suddenly Lac spoke in a trembling voice.

"Baby Bo! Daughter Nhon! Daughter Be! . . . No! You must live!"

All at once Thuc felt much lighter. His heavy burden no longer weighed him down. Thinking only of the children, Lac had silently released her hold on him and sunk to the bottom of the river, allowing her husband to swim to the bank.

Electric lights shone brightly on the riverbank. The wind had died down, and the waves were calm. A man holding a baby boy sat crying, with two small girls at his side. It was Thuc the bricklayer's assistant and his children. They had come down to the riverbank to say their last good-byes to the soul of the woman who had sacrificed her life out of love for her children.

In all its immensity, the water of the river continued to flow, indifferently.

1934

Translated by Bac Hoai Tran and Courtney Norris

Vo Phien

"Unsettled"

Vo Phien is the pen name of Doan The Nhon. He was born on 20 October 1925 in Binh Dinh Province, Central Vietnam. A prolific writer, he was well known in South Vietnam from 1954 to 1975 for several novels and many short stories. Since his resettlement in the United States in 1975, he has continued to be quite productive. His Lit-erature in South Vietnam: 1954–1975 *(translated into English by Vo Dinh Mai) was published in 1992 by Vietnamese Language and Culture Publications of Australia.*

"Unsettled" reflects Vo Phien's literary style, which is noted for its complexity, possibly due in part to European and American literary influences. He is also known for stark character portrayals and a penchant for detail. In this short story he unfolds a psychological landscape covering the war years in Vietnam through the 1950s, including war's toll on human relationships and the will to love. The sadness of life and the poignancy of love relationships are also depicted in Khai Hung's "You Must Live" (Vietnam) and Pramoedya Ananta Toer's "The Silent Center of Life's Day" (Indonesia). The enduring effects of war on human relationships are also reflected in Bunthanaung Som-saiphon's "A Bar at the Edge of a Cemetery" (Laos).

It was drizzling. Hieu covered his head with a leaf fan, and walked home without hurrying. The scattered raindrops grew smaller, and finally almost disappeared, leaving a cool vapor in the air. When he reached the front gate of the house, he looked up. Like so many times before, he paused unintentionally to take in the view of the small house, then suddenly felt depressed, realizing his life had been wasted. He looked at the thin fence made from rotting, thorny bamboo sticks, at the *han the* herb growing at the foot of the fence, and then at the low

"Unsettled" (Ban Khoan), by Vo Phien, published in *Truyen Ngan 1: Tap Truyen* (Westminster, CA: Van Nghe, 1987). Permission to publish granted by the translators, Bac Hoai Tran and Courtney Norris, with the author's consent.

and narrow house belonging to teacher's aid Thi. It was five meters in length and four meters in width, including a kitchen, a place to sleep, and a place to receive guests. He looked at the boards plastered with cow dung that had been used as walls, now deteriorating. He viewed all these things as evidence of a failure in life, even though they weren't his, nor were they his responsibility. To make matters worse, it had been like this for decades.

Strangely enough, usually after he stepped into the house and saw teacher's aid Thi lying there smoking his pipe, that feeling of depression and despair seemed to dissipate. Thi's familiar pose, which projected an air of unconcern, made him feel warm and reassured, even though that pose belonged to a person smoking opium. Hieu would look at Thi and smile: the old man attentively heating the powder or scraping its residue, appearing important, full of confidence. So full of presence, in fact, that when he looked up and reminded Hieu to go eat, the very act of having a meal took on greater importance.

Thi had lived for three-quarters of a century; for nearly half a century, he'd been lying there smoking opium. When told that opium was harmful to his health, Thi would silently look down at the wooden *kang* and busily scrape the opium residue as if he hadn't heard. And when told that opium would shorten his life, he would open his mouth wide and emit a terrible laugh, a soundless laugh that wrinkled up his whole face and shook his entire body. It was a horrible sight. In fact, he was no longer in good health; it was undeniable. Hieu could lift him up and hold him with one arm like a child, or he could use one hand to push him down onto the surface of the *kang*, preventing him from moving at all. Thi's health was nothing more than a bad joke.

But how does one determine the relationship between health and longevity? Living in a time of war, when life is full of hardship and witness to fierce combat, even young and healthy people find it hard to stay alive. Being strong as a water buffalo and fast as lightning might not save your life amidst bombardments and raids. Working one's hardest: wife working, husband working, children working, exhausting the best fields and having to move into higher terrain, still not being able to find enough to eat, still going hungry, still wearing rags. Teacher's aid Thi, despite being so weak, so untalented, so slow, not only managed to eat and clothe himself, but also found a way to supply his opium habit. How had he been able to avoid the destruction of war, much less find rice and opium? How could he still be alive at the age of seventy-six? It was inconceivable.

During the war years, everyone was so busy looking after themselves, no one paid attention to this amazing feat. Not until all the guns and bombs had stopped and all the smoke and fire had vanished from the landscape did things begin to become clear again. Then people took another look and saw that the tiny house five meters in length and four in width was still there. They saw the rotting bamboo hedge with *han the* herbs growing at its base, and in that same house, teacher's aid Thi still lay and smoked. Everyone in the neighborhood was at first startled, and then praised him with awe.

This in itself was touching and comforting for Hieu but at the same time very sad. He felt like a commando who, after days of jumping into enemy bunkers, attacking bases and trenches with bullets tearing his fatigues and making holes in his helmet, finally wins and lies down to rest in sheer exhaustion. After looking down at his torn fatigues and reflecting on how close he'd come to being killed, he unexpectedly notices a small, perfectly intact ink stain on his sleeve, made by his kid brother the previous year—a memory that is soothing, but also a painful reminder of separation.

That afternoon, while Hieu stood at the gate with the leaf fan in his listless hand, he found himself bewildered about his past. He realized that his life hadn't progressed a single step; it hadn't gone anywhere, lost like an abandoned wagon car standing lonely on the tracks in a vast and deserted field.

He stepped into the dark house. Teacher's aid Thi stopped what he was doing, and spoke in a gravelly voice: "The sky this afternoon was so unusual. One moment it was golden, the next it was drizzling. There are only a few more days until fall is here. I wonder about more unusual weather ahead."

Why was it important to him? Teacher's aid Thi sat in his house year-round, so what connection could he possibly have to the colors in the sky? How could he even see such things to be able to talk about them? Why should he eavesdrop on other people's incidental conversations just to speak in that self-important tone? Hieu didn't answer his question, raising no objection nor discussing it any further. He enjoyed leaving Thi's query unanswered as a way of retribution. He had such an aversion to that kind of pompous attitude.

Hieu banged against the low bed that came up only to his shin. He lay down, and hid himself in the darkness, looking at teacher's aid Thi sitting there busying himself with something on the *kang* in the middle of the house. His face had become more sunken, the nose sharp and thin, the lips puckered and sharp. His cheekbones rose up, also sharp, and his chin was even sharper. He looked attentive, unperturbed by Hieu's cruel intentions.

Was he aware of Hieu's intentions? Hieu had the impression that Thi knew everything. It was just like that late night ten years ago when Thi had been lying on his back dozing on the *kang*. At that moment Loan was sitting on the *kang*'s edge right next to Thi while Hieu, lying on this very bed, stretched out his right hand to cover hers. Hieu had gently caressed and stroked Loan's plump hand. On those nights, they both kept an eye on teacher's aid Thi's sharp face to see if he knew. Hieu had detected the same pompous and inscrutable attitude even then. The two of them had wondered whether Thi discerned the secret activity of their hands in the dark. Hieu felt that if they were not prudent, he would certainly find out. But actually, teacher's aid Thi knew everything, as if he possessed omniscient vision, apprehending every detail without needing to perceive it.

Night after night Thi lay smoking, while Loan either stayed by his side feeding his opium pipe or sat brewing water for tea. Hieu would be on the other bed. Even though Thi's pose never changed, both felt like they'd been tiptoeing around a light sleeper since that night when Hieu had stealthily put his hand over Loan's. It was so useless! Thi could hear everything without needing to open his eyes.

The first time it happened was around eleven o'clock at night and teacher's aid Thi had just made a comment about the story of Pham Cong and Cuc Hoa. Hieu was gazing on Loan's face and neck, his chest heaving with excitement. Hieu knew with certainty that he had to make a move. He found himself passionately in love with Loan, desiring her. His throat was dry and full, and he swallowed hard. Loan sat like a silhouette in the silent room while raindrops sprinkled down outside. The moment was ripe with anticipation, making Hieu's heart pound with nervousness. Loan stared fixedly at the flame of the oil lamp, sitting so still: people are only capable of sitting motionless like that during moments of extreme anticipation. So did Loan also feel that it was time for Hieu to act?

Softly, very softly, Hieu put his hand over the back of Loan's. Her nostrils and eyelids moved slightly, so imperceptibly that for years after that moment, Hieu was never sure whether that movement was real, or whether he had just imagined it. He doubted himself, half feeling as if Loan's hand had moved, but half suspecting that it had been the trembling of his own. Hieu's hand had pressed hers for a long time while she calmly looked at the flame of the oil lamp, keeping still as if nothing had occurred. Her demeanor really puzzled Hieu; he hadn't known what to do next.

Loan lowered her head, biting her lower lip while shifting her thumb upwards. Hieu hurriedly withdrew his hand, but she kept hers where it was. Although Hieu didn't believe that Loan would withdraw her hand, he still didn't try to cover it with his again. He looked into her eyes, and she glanced in the direction of teacher's aid Thi who was lying on his back staring at the ceiling.

The next morning, Hieu was washing his face by the water jar when Loan, carrying a kettle, came out from the kitchen and stood behind him waiting for the gourd. Hieu turned around, and seeing her, said quietly: "Loan! Loan are you mad at me?"

Loan whispered: "Yes."

Loan took the gourd from Hieu, filled it with water and then turned on her heels. In desperation, Hieu softly called after her: "Loan!"

She hung her head, smiling, and kept walking. Upon reaching the kitchen, she turned around and grinned. Hieu found the whole situation quite amusing and couldn't help thinking about his behavior.

A few nights later, when the three of them had taken a break in their conversation—in fact, only teacher's aid Thi and Hieu had been talking to each other—Hieu started to worry. He looked around the house, at Thi's head on the folded pillow and at the geckos waylaying roaches on a house post in the shadows. Thi's quiet, wakeful state was impossible to decipher, and seemed to bolster Hieu's suspicion that teacher's aid Thi had known about the two of them all along.

In the same unspoken way, Hieu had come to know a few details about Thi's life without ever having heard about it from anyone. Thi suspected that much. His life had never been any good since his youth. Thi had given himself to his vices too early. When he stopped his revolutionary work and turned into an opium addict, he abandoned his first wife and took a second. This woman grew larger and larger, while Thi himself became thinner and thinner. His appearance was so comical that whenever he ventured into the street, children ran after him pointing their fingers. He had tried to maintain the dignity of a proud man, making an effort to look proper and well dressed, with all the creases pressed until they looked very sharp. Whenever he went out he carried a cane and kept a serious expression on his face. But his second wife had found no attraction in that, so without asking for his consent, she had gone ahead and built a new life. She rented an apartment, moved

out and went into business for herself. From then on, people never saw
any sign of a relationship between Thi and his wife. However, in order
to keep up appearances, she'd had to accept a few conditions
demanded by Thi—otherwise, he threatened to force her to resume
their previous legal relationship by noisily meddling in her affairs. The
terms were that she had to contribute some money towards his addic-
tion and make arrangements so that he wouldn't be completely abandoned, that is to say, find someone to care for him and cook his meals.
That year, Thi's wife asked her niece Loan to come and help her uncle.

Such a complicated family situation, with all those conditions. The
people in the neighborhood didn't bother to pay attention because
teacher's aid Thi lay and smoked in an obscure alley. Loan hadn't said
anything, nor had Thi said anything, but gradually, with one detail one
day, another the next, without remembering who whispered it, a young
clerk named Hieu came to understand it all.

Thi liked talking. It was the reason that drew Hieu close to him and
Loan. He enjoyed talking about people and about the past, but without
ever injecting any humor or lightheartedness into the conversation.
Thus for months, the relationship between Hieu and Loan progressed
with silent gestures, in a sober environment. They concealed their relationship, even though both were under the impression it was impossible to conceal. The two had never had a date nor held a long conversation, because the house was too small, with no garden, and Thi rarely
went out.

On the one occasion when Thi left the house and the two of them
had an opportunity to talk, Hieu told Loan that he'd joined the libera-
tors and would have to go South. After the revolution began, he'd given
up his clerkship in order to become head of the district youth league.
But now, he had joined the army.

The two of them sat side by side on the low bamboo bed. Hieu
talked in a low voice for a long time, while Loan sat silently, hanging
her head. He'd noticed many times that Loan possessed the ability to
remain silent for long durations whether sitting or lying, without moving a leg or an arm, or making any gesture at all. Because of this, each
of Loan's movements had value, as if it had been contemplated carefully, and was absolutely necessary. Hieu wondered whether Loan's
tranquility made her beauty that much more mysterious and attractive.

Hieu paused, and Loan waited for a moment to make sure that he
had finished. Then she asked: "When did you make plans to become a
soldier?"

Hieu hurriedly explained: "I know that I'm to blame. But current circumstances and events leave me no choice. Once I'm gone, you won't be able to live forever like this, with your uncle. You'll be drawn into the events of these times. I don't know where or how you'll be when I come back!"

Loan remained silent. Hieu worried about using words that may have sounded boastful and impractical, words that confused her. But being able to talk at length, he had become bolder. Seeing that she was miserable, he smiled and said: "I'm afraid that from now until the day I return, you'll go through changes in life, maybe encountering unexpected things . . . they could be exciting, and you'll forget me, abandon me . . . Loan, would you abandon me?"

"I would!"

She still had that playful tone like the other day. But this time Hieu also found it filled with affection and intimacy. He put a hand on Loan's shoulder, the shoulder he'd admired and desired from the moment they'd sat down together. Hieu smiled and asked: "If you abandon me, who will love me?"

Loan stole a glance at him, smiled, and looked down again. Hieu's hand caressed her shoulder, as if to see how she would react. Loan reached up and pulled Hieu's hand down, and then squeezed it between her own hands. It was a promise. They sat looking at a fly buzzing around the oil lamp set in the middle of the *kang*. It was so quiet and deserted. Hieu heard a mosquito bump into his ear, and then buzz away in panic . . .

The sound of teacher's aid Thi's footsteps resounded from the direction of the alley. Loan lifted his hand and brushed it against her face, then dropped it, stood up, and went into the kitchen. Hieu felt warm tears on the back of his hand. Teacher's aid Thi stepped into the house. Hieu felt nervous and embarrassed.

Only after teacher's aid Thi had removed his robe and settled down on the *kang* did Hieu recover and steal a glance at the flickering flame that shone through the door of the kitchen. He suddenly remembered and touched the back of his hand, but the tears had dried.

Why had Hieu returned to Thi's house after the war? Since then, he had often examined his behavior and concluded that his willpower had weakened considerably. Too often he showed no determination, acting listlessly and desiring stability at any cost.

Before coming back, he had heard rumors about Loan's life over the previous nine years. He learned that Loan had officially had a husband, but then had an affair with another man, which had resulted in numerous brawls. He learned that Loan was involved in the execution of her own paternal grandfather, and also took part in the decision to kill Hieu's aunt. Since he had been orphaned when small, that aunt had raised Hieu and sent him to school. That aunt was his entire family. Now he had no other relatives in the old village.

The day he came back from the front, he wasn't particularly enthusiastic. He had no intention of rushing to find Loan, or of making inquiries about her. He had heard bits and pieces about Loan's life, but still he came back. He was like a person who casually sits on the rim of a well and, glancing down at the water, sadly sees a clear reflection of moss and leaf fragments mingled with the reflection of his own disheveled hair and beard. Now, back in this town, Hieu gradually came to see those ten years of Loan's life more clearly, like replaying a depressing scene in its entirety again and again until there is no longer any strong emotion, just a lingering malaise.

Teacher's aid Thi also felt there was no need for any admission on his part for Hieu to understand either his past or Loan's. As the three grew closer, they could understand each other in silence without having to ask any questions. Even so, there was still a certain awkwardness between them, just like when Loan and Hieu had engaged in a secret love affair by the side of teacher's aid Thi.

At dusk, Thi usually lay down and smoked in the middle of the *kang*, while Hieu lay quietly on the low and narrow bamboo bed. Occasionally, Hieu would brush off a swarm of buzzing mosquitoes, eyes focused in the direction of the flickering flame in the kitchen where Loan was crouched next to the stove.

At times like these, Loan thought about the night when she went through Hieu's village with another comrade. The two had waded across a stream, in water so cold it had made their flesh tingle. With her feet still wet, Loan had held her pant legs up to her knees while she walked. The comrade followed her, looking at those ivory calves under the moon.

Loan had asked: "Hac, do you really think vengeance is necessary for a revolution?"

Loan had been thinking about the upcoming public denunciation intended for Hieu's aunt. Knowing that expressing such concerns to a comrade could be very dangerous, Loan nonetheless had understood the state of mind of the comrade walking behind her then. Loan trusted her woman's intuition.

Hac answered: "Landowners have to repay what they've taken from their victims. It's the right thing to do."

"We have to take back land, property, and power for poor people . . . That's right. That way we've established a new society. But as for revenge, beating them or killing them to relieve our anger is an emotional reaction. I can't see how revolutionary reasoning can lead to an act that carries that sort of emotional baggage. I don't see it as being necessary for the establishment of a new order."

"There's no need to kill them off in order to redistribute property justly. But it's necessary to sacrifice them in order to train the proletariat in hatred, and thus help them to fulfill their revolutionary mission."

"So these are only training sessions, then. Surely you can see there are unjust cases, people being framed, exaggerations of their crimes just to incite hate?"

Hac had thought about it, and then said slowly: "If it happens like that, it's still logical. The revolution aims at organizing a new society, not exacting justice for all the crimes committed under the old system. If you find a landowner who in fact isn't quite guilty, but his sacrifice is needed for the revolution to move forward, then what do you think of that? The success of the revolution doesn't rely only on doing what's fair. The future of humanity gives us the right to treat some landowners without complete fairness!"

Loan hadn't pursued it. After a moment Hac asked, in a different tone of voice: "Do you have any relationship with this Mrs. Le?"

Loan had shaken her head. In fact, Le was Hieu's aunt. She steered the conversation in another direction.

As the night wore on, it grew colder. Loan, feeling distraught, looked toward the bamboo hedge, which appeared vague in the white mist. Behind it was Hieu's village.

Coming upon a bridge built only of two unsteady bamboo trunks that spanned a large stream, Hac had gone ahead of Loan. He then took her hand and led her across. Hac's move had been so natural that Loan had felt too shy to withdraw her hand. But with her hand pressed against his, by the time they got to the middle of the bridge, she had begun to feel an unusual warmth. When Loan jumped onto the road, she felt a bit unsteady. Hac put a hand across her back, then quickly dropped it. The two of them continued to walk along the deserted road in the mist.

After that night, Loan felt uneasy when she thought about her husband and Hieu. But gradually Loan grew accustomed to it and became bolder. With an active life that took her from place to place, Loan constantly found herself in situations like this one, making it difficult for her to maintain her self-control for very long.

Loan sat next to the stove, reminiscing about her past—a bustling and chaotic life, filled with lofty passions along with sorrowful and awful sins. Now, sitting by the stove in teacher's aid Thi's house, listening to the water in the rice pot bubbling, Loan felt as if she could sigh with relief, having returned to a normal life after a violent storm. Still, this kind of peace was so dreary. And so wretched.

Meanwhile, in order to arrive at some insight that could explain her behavior, Hieu lay and thought about Loan, putting pieces of information together, all the rumors surrounding the life of cadre Loan. Hieu had no hatred for her cruel treatment of his aunt. It wasn't a special case, nor a personal one. A whole class of people like Loan had behaved like that. Upon leaving her cooking and opium duties in Thi's household and entering society, the young woman—completely perplexed by all those political lines of reasoning and social issues—was immediately guided, educated, and trained to carry out those acts. All her knowledge convinced her that this was the right thing to do. When she did it, she was certain that if Hieu found out, if Hieu had been there, if Hieu were in her position, he would have approved and done exactly the same thing. Indeed, throughout the years, hadn't Hieu himself been guided by the same kind of reasoning, rigid and one-dimensional, that led to acts that even he no longer understood?

The incomprehensible thing that needed some explanation was not why Loan had been cruel, but why Loan had defected and given up her husband, her lover, all in order to stay in the South. Hieu found that his feelings for her had become less harsh; not only did he have no animosity towards her, he also felt a tolerant compassion. He sensed his singular closeness to her, the only one who understood her.

Hieu believed that perhaps even up till now, Loan had never thought that her husband or Hac had done anything wrong, anything blameworthy. Everything that she had done alongside her comrades had been logical and necessary, even the way she had mistreated Hieu's family and her own. That line of reasoning could have carried Loan further, had it not been for the execution of her paternal grandfather. Indeed, Hieu thought this must have been the event that made Loan decide to defect. It didn't mean that Loan thought her side had been wrong, only that when Loan witnessed the comrade picking up a pole and hitting her grandfather on his silver-haired head, then the rational part of her was deeply shocked. When this happened, a different person emerged, screaming in rebellion.

For the young woman, the old man with the silver-haired head was sacred. Her education had imprinted that concept in her subconscious mind. That way of life, how people treated one another, had been molded and maintained in Asian society throughout the ages. Occasionally, that way seemed to have been conquered by the new line of reasoning, but in reality, it still had extraordinary strength. Especially in a woman. Thus, when that comrade and Loan interrogated and finished off Hieu's relative, Loan was greatly upset but could still control her emotions. Yet when Loan's comrade hit her grandfather's silver-haired head with a pole, the conventions of twenty centuries rose up in protest within her.

Loan no longer knew how to rationalize these acts, but one thing was certain: she couldn't bear it anymore. Loan was stunned, then defected and ran back home to find a little peace. Now both Loan and Hieu felt terrified whenever they thought about the lines of reasoning from those years.

Hieu lay down and looked at the dancing shadows cast by the flame on the dirty narrow walls, sporadically hearing Loan's noises in the kitchen when she dragged the bamboo kettle pad, lifted the wok and stirred it with chopsticks. Unexpectedly, Hieu sympathized with the humble life she would lead from now on. He felt that in fact there was no significant barrier between them. Hieu contemplated how right now, if he could spontaneously go to the kitchen and sit down by her side without startling her, he would calmly say: "Don't be shy. I understand you more than anyone else. I was also confused, having lost my faith like you. You have hurt my family, and also hurt your family and your own life. I was just like that—I have also harmed many people. So now both of us are bewildered, unable to understand our behavior during the past years, and now we are at a loss, not knowing what to do. Perhaps we are even closer now than ten years ago. Both of us have been murderers, killing each other. Because both of us have been in the same situation, now we can sympathize with each other! Am I right, Loan? What are you pondering by the stove? Do you agree we shouldn't avoid each other forever? Loan! . . ."

Gradually, there were no longer any rationalizations in his mind; in their place were enchanting words filled with emotion. Hieu found his heart overflowing with love for Loan. These thoughts became sweet endearments in his mind. Hieu kept repeating them until suddenly he jumped a little and stopped, not knowing whether he'd spoken them out loud.

Hieu brushed off the mosquitoes, and looked up to gauge Thi's reaction, and then once again turned his face towards Loan. She was in the kitchen and Hieu in his dark corner, each of them in a separate place, greatly unsettled. Teacher's aid Thi lay dreamily by the side of a steadily burning oil lamp, separating them. Keeping them apart was the obliviousness of an unaffected old age that had withstood the ups and downs of life.

Since the day they'd reconciled and started living together, Hieu had realized that their new life wasn't taking them anywhere, and he felt even more tortured.

As for Loan, perhaps she had already accepted it. Finding the protection of a faithful man, the young woman felt reassured. It was an exaggeration to say that Loan had fulfilled her purpose in life, but now she found a warm joy in taking care of Hieu's clothing, food and drink. She no longer felt unsettled or yearned for anything else.

But Hieu still found life meaningless and without direction. He was already over thirty, not knowing what to believe in, housebound with an addicted old man. Where would his soundless steps back and forth through Thi's gate take him?

Family, fatherland, compatriots, lofty ideals . . . all those things had already lost their sacred meaning. After all the brutal destruction during the past ten years, all that was left in his soul now was a desolate landscape where it wouldn't be easy to rebuild anything significant in the foreseeable future. Right now a big question mark had suddenly appeared in that void. What was the meaning of his life? What meaning did life have? Since he could no longer understand it, he became deeply depressed and tormented.

For the past few years, taking part in the hustle and bustle of a movement, amidst the roar of drums and bugles, he had acted with passion, going forward as if pushed from behind, thinking that the purpose of his life naturally was to lunge headlong in a predetermined direction. Now the party had disintegrated, organizations had dispersed, and the guiding lines of reasoning had collapsed. Life had become wretched, just like after a night spent dancing with bewitching sirens only to discover the next morning they were just paper and straw. He became worried when he examined his life and found only emptiness.

Hieu thought about the myth of Orpheus going to the underworld to ask for his wife's return to earth. His request was granted, but he was only allowed to bring Eurydice back on the condition that he not gaze upon her before their return. Orpheus was elated. But on the way back, his curiosity got the better of him. He took one look at his wife, causing her to vanish. Hieu suspected that if he were still caught up in events, still being pushed forward, perhaps he could be blind and have faith in what lay at the end of the road. But he had given up halfway, paused and looked directly at life. His scrutinizing gaze made life lose all its color, becoming pale and distorted, like Eurydice! What could he do now?

Every evening when he went home and paused before the rotten bamboo hedge in front of Thi's small house, he was filled with dread and a terrible emptiness in his soul. Even though he tried to allay his anxiety and could even forget it for a little while, sometimes the reality of a meaningless life would hit him again unexpectedly, still fresh, still as shocking as his initial realization. It was not unlike the story of Lord Guan's severed head, placed in a sealed box.[1] When Cao Cao opened it, the head suddenly opened its eyes and mouth wide, as if Lord Guan was still alive, causing Cao Cao to faint from shock.

After moments like these, Hieu would once again enter the dark house and sink onto the low bed by the *kang* of teacher's aid Thi. He'd hear the buzz of some mosquitoes, the sound of Thi smoking, the noises that Loan made in the kitchen. It would be like that until Loan finished setting the table and invited the two men into the kitchen to eat. Usually, when teacher's aid Thi busied himself tidying his opium set, Hieu would pull his wife down to sit next to him, and in silence caress her hand. If Thi took a long time to finish, Loan would allow Hieu to wrap his arm around her hip, then sit quietly waiting.

That gesture brought back a memory. It had rained heavily the day they had reanimated their love affair. Teacher's aid Thi had been out and couldn't come back because of the rain. Throughout the afternoon, they were forced to stay close to one another in the wet and narrow space of the house. Despite any reticence, their mutual feelings had

---

1. Lord Guan and Cao Cao are major characters in the Chinese war epic *Three King-doms*, attributed to Luo Guanzhong.

been revealed for some time through every move in this life of close confinement. Loan had stood leaning against the window, gazing out into the yard. Hieu had lain in his bed looking at her. They had stayed that way for so long that both of them felt it wouldn't make sense to continue on like this. Hieu got up and walked over to Loan. She'd appeared nervous, but stood still.

Softly, Hieu had said: "Loan!"

She hadn't turned her head but suddenly burst into tears. Hieu had felt strangely relieved: there would be no need for any words revealing all the dark secrets, nothing to be recounted, to be explained, to be answered. He had stood watching Loan cry, listening to her weep. They were standing together and feeling as if everything had been explained and all had been forgiven. Hieu placed his arm around Loan's back, and with an intimate gesture, she pulled his arm up and pressed it against her. A warm feeling passed through Hieu, dazing him.

He looked down upon her. Tiny droplets of rainwater covered her face, her hair, and her eyelashes. Hieu noticed, now so near, that Loan's complexion was no longer fresh; the skin had become dry, the facial muscles slack. At that moment, from his loving and firm gaze encompassing Loan's face and the gesture with which she held his arm, he sadly felt that both their faces and love seemed tired, a bit indifferent, timeworn, but still very sincere.

After that day, they continued their love affair by the side of teacher's aid Thi. And even though no one talked about it, Thi knew all about this surreptitious relationship, and they knew that he knew everything. At this point Loan was already five months pregnant.

One day, when she appeared to invite them to eat their evening meal, she sat down next to Hieu while waiting for teacher's aid Thi to clear his opium set. Loan tugged at Hieu's wrist resting on her hip, and drew his hand to her belly. Loan wanted him to feel the movements of the fetus. At first Hieu was indifferent, but gradually he discovered some vague hope, a little joy, that gave his life some meaning. Quietly, he smiled in the dark. From then on, every evening when Loan came up from the kitchen, Hieu lovingly caressed her belly without waiting for her to tug at his hand. Perhaps he was touching it for reassurance, to remind himself that there was hope and encouragement, albeit experienced with a passivity he would possess for the rest of his life.

At the same time, Loan was joyful, feeling that she was living in the kind of happiness that would only become even more secure. Quietly

Loan reminisced about the touch of their hands throughout the phases of their love, from their initial hesitant uncertainty, to the moment their hands had squeezed each other tightly, sometimes being raised lightly and caressing intimately . . . The strange expressions of a love that endured amidst floating opium smoke, in a house so confining that the whispers between two people would certainly be overheard by a third person more alert than them. A type of love that had always relied more on a sense of touch than upon the sound of words, two people involved in conjecture and sensitivity more than verbal expression.

While Hieu was smiling, Loan also smiled in the dark. They didn't see each other, and each followed a different train of thought.

1957

Translated by Bac Hoai Tran and Courtney Norris

Duong Thu Huong

"The Story of an Actress"

Duong Thu Huong was born in 1947 in Thai Binh Province (the Red River Delta). She is recognized as one of Vietnam's most talented writers. Her fiction is typically composed of self-reflective excursions into memories of wartime reality and human relationships. By the time her novel Paradise of the Blind *(1988) was published, she had been labeled a dissident writer. She was subsequently expelled from the communist party for her insistence on open speech, which was advocated by the Doi Moi policies of that same party. She was arrested and imprisoned in 1991 but released due to international pressure. Most of her material is now published outside of Vietnam because of censorship.*

Some critics describe Duong's writing as a "literature of disenchantment," but "The Story of an Actress" reflects much more. It contains a Proustian sensibility, consistent with Duong's attraction to

"The Story of an Actress" (Chuyen Mot Nu Dien Vien), by Duong Thu Huong, published in *Chan Dung Nguoi Hang Xom* (Hanoi: Nha Xuat Ban Van Hoc, 1985). Permission to publish granted by the translators, Bac Hoai Tran and Courtney Norris, with the author's consent.

memories and self-reflective fiction but imbricated with an existential poignancy about life and self-obfuscation. We are led into a childhood epiphany in the rain-streaked, fecund rice paddies of Vietnam—ruptured with the self-consciousness that adulthood brings. An existential sensibility is also reflected in writing by other Southeast Asian authors, such as Cristina Pantoja Hidalgo's "The Painting" (the Philippines) and Pramoedya Ananta Toer's "The Silent Center of Life's Day" (Indonesia).

"In those days, we lived so happily and joyfully."

"Those childhood days. Why bother talking about them?"

"No. In those days we really lived."

She had choked as she said this during her last visit with me. Then the tears welled over her eyelashes, streaming down her cheeks. Cheeks that only two years ago had been so youthful and full of vitality, now had become washed out and faded.

There was a sound of shoes thudding up the stairs—slowly, weakly. Each thud was a dry, muffled sound, hitting the wooden boards at regular intervals.

She listened and said, "He's home."

"I should go home too," I answered, standing up.

She kept quiet. Her infant son was trying to lift his big head off the mattress, teaching himself how to roll over. His head was so big, his forehead so full of wrinkles. His thin neck couldn't lift the watermelon resting on top of it.

I went to the door. Before going down the stairs, I turned back one last time and saw her following me with tear-filled eyes.

"In those days, how happily we lived."

That's what her eyes said. But they weren't looking at me. They were looking at those months and years that had receded into the past . . .

Truly we had experienced happy days. Now I understand why people often reminisce about their childhood . . . That year, I was still a girl by the name of Bê, and she was a girl called Thom. We were both twelve. Even then, Thom was already beautiful, and I was a bit more ugly than

I am now. I was as black as a crow, and my hair, exposed to the sun, had turned as red as corn silk, as unkempt as a bird's nest. My head was full of lice. Every time the newly hatched lice started to bite, I went crazy from the itch and scratched my scalp until it bled. I didn't inherit anything from my father, except his sooty complexion, hooked nose and big eyes that were protruding and insolent. I had two buck teeth that stuck out like the short wings of a mole cricket. Fortunately, though, I was never unhappy about my appearance. After school, I roamed the fields catching crabs, picking up fish left behind in drained ponds, stripping sticky rice off its stalk on the sly, using my fingers to dig for watermelon seeds . . . sometimes I hunted for duck eggs laid in ditches.

On the other hand, Thom already looked like a young woman, even though she was only twelve. A lot of young men had an eye on her, and one even dared to declare his love for her publicly, for fear that he would lose her to someone else when she became a woman.

It made me want to bean those guys on the head with dry *xa cu* cones. I don't know why I was so jealous . . . We had been playmates since the days when we still ran around naked. Our families shared one wall under the same tile roof. Our parents had bought the neighboring apartments, set in a row of houses built with foreign aid in 1952. The apartments were identical, like drops of water. A large sidewalk paved with stone running along the national route had been our playground ever since we were able to toddle. A *kim phuong* hedge dropped yellow flowers onto the sidewalk, mixing with tiny green leaves. On the other side of the national route were fields, ditches, paddies and hillocks . . . It was the mysterious and beautiful world of childhood. Thom was only average when she was small, but overnight, at age ten, she became unusually beautiful.

The neighbors were surprised by the sudden change in Thom, exclaiming, "Good heavens, look at that little girl, Thom. All of a sudden, Heaven has changed her looks!"

As for me, the older I grew, the more ugly I became—so much that my mother complained to my father: "We only have one daughter, who is naughty as a devil and ugly as Chung Vo Diem.[1] When she grows up, who will do us the favor of taking her away? . . . And look at Thom . . .

My father exploded and shot back: "I am ugly, and that child who resembles me is also ugly. If you want to have beautiful children, then

---

1. Chung Vo Diem: a plain-visaged Chinese concubine known for her intelligence.

go marry someone else. In this life, there's no shortage of people with superficial beauty . . ."

My mother held her tongue. Father continued his tirade: "A mother who says her daughter is a devil? . . . I don't know what sort of person you are . . . Would you rather be a second mother to Thom? Why don't you just go over and ask her parents' permission?"

At that moment, I happened to be in the bathroom cleaning a gaping wound on my knee with salt water, having fallen off a *phuong* tree after being bitten by a tick. I giggled quietly at their argument. After that incident, my poor father grew cold towards Thom. Every time she came over, he pretended to be busy reorganizing my commendation letters and pictures of me receiving awards at school.

Clicking his tongue, he would complain: "It's time to find another drawer to hold all of Bê's stuff. The drawer in this tea table is already full . . ."

Thom never understood his intent. My friend was an average student. I pitied my father and found it funny since I wasn't jealous of Thom's beauty at all. I loved her. Her fair, rosy, oval face looked so gentle. Her black eyes always appeared distant and dreamy, and the straight bridge of her nose was so elegant. Her full, rosy lips were like ripe fruit on a branch. I loved Thom so much that I was jealous of all the boys who came near her—they were very dangerous. As for the girls, I didn't stop them from approaching her. Girls always had fewer tricks up their sleeves than boys . . . Oh, how strange those adolescent years were.

Yes, but in those years, Thom and I lived beautiful days. In the morning, we went to school. From one to three in the afternoon, we would finish all of our homework assignments and quizzes. After that, it was our magical time. I would go ahead into the fields, with Thom following. If it was May, there would be sudden showers, splashing our heads and shoulders with large drops of water, sweet and fresh, and sowing our minds with the happy, warm sound of falling rain. Those sudden showers displayed a vast silver sheet, shining bright, woven from crystal clear water and bright sunrays. The air was filled with sounds and light shining through pouring rain, giving us a feeling of utter happiness. We walked in that magical rain, with the golden rice flowers, wet and sharp, scraping over our skin. The water flowing over the walls of the bunds tugged at our legs. Slippery frogs darted between our feet, leaving a strange sensation, both terrifying and delightful. Sometimes, after a flash of lightning had torn apart the water-filled heavens, a gunshot would explode in the sky. At that moment, Thom would scream, and throw her arms around me.

I would laugh, trying to keep calm in the middle of the vast open field. "Don't be afraid," I would say as my heart filled with a sense of pride and happiness that I could protect that little, gentle friend of mine.

Summer rains were like a noisy dream, violent but fleeting. When the rain let up, we would try to catch fish in the canals. Occasionally, we would come to puddles filled with *thau dau* fish—a kind of fish only two fingers wide with a long body, white scales and a fat belly that women would bring home to cook with pickled mustard greens and tomatoes. We might be able to catch a whole basketful of these. And you, have you ever caught any fish? If not, you should try it once. Not so that you can hold in your hand a scaly animal in the same taxonomic class as the frog, having cold blood and gills—as pointed out in biology lessons of the sixth grade—not any of that. Rather, to experience an indescribable joy.

Moreover, have you ever eaten fish baked in a field?

Good heavens, Thom and I ate fish that way so many times. We would go into a small guard station on a dike, a temporary refuge for farm laborers, or to a familiar mound in the shade of a tree. Before we settled in, we would have to find a few banana leaves, a spoonful of salt, some firewood, and a matchbox. And then we would bring out our fresh fish with their gaping mouths. We would wrap them up very tightly in three layers of banana leaves and cover them with mud. If it happened to be a sticky kind of clay, then it was even better. We would build a fire and lay the wrapped fish on top, baking it until the mud became completely dry and cracked. After removing the cracked mud and unwrapping all three layers of banana leaves, we would have the most delicious delicacy in the world. Only the steaming white meat remained with all its sweet juice intact after the fish had been cleaned. The fat from the fish's belly would have melted into the juice and mixed with the singed young banana leaves, smelling so fragrant. Then sprinkled with salt, it would be ready for us to savor.

The field was vast and soulless. The only sounds were a frog chorus and water gurgling over the bunds. And the rice was golden, but it didn't look like rice—more like a sheet of silk the color of ripe apricots draped over the fields. We had baked fish and eaten them like that so many times, and each time our happiness was boundless, as if we had encountered a rare kind of joy sent here from a distant star. Sometimes we imagined being Robinson Crusoe on a deserted island, or two detectives in an African desert. Other times, we felt like two explorers in America searching for gold, taking a lunch break on a wild high plateau. Yes, it was just like that . . . Please don't laugh at the happiness of adolescence. When we're twelve, we have so many illusions that bring true and genuine moments of joy. This sort of happiness remains with us throughout our lives . . .

"In those days, we lived so happily and joyfully."

That's what she had said, her eyes filling with tears as she looked up at me. The girl Thom of younger days had become a woman. Her face was pale, dazed, with an ugly child resting feebly on her arm and gloomy thoughts inhabiting her mind. At which moment had my beautiful friend been transformed forever? Yes, I still remember those days perfectly, as if they had happened only last week. In those days, we had just graduated from high school. Thom had barely slid by, and I was worried about her performance on the upcoming university entrance exam. Because we were so close during all those years in high school, Thom had studied hard with me and never had to repeat a grade. Still, she was never more than average, and passing the university entrance exam was, of course, much more difficult. But that year, we were seventeen and Thom had many new girlfriends.

When I encouraged her to study, she seemed annoyed. Before, everyone had teased us about being inseparable like husband and wife: "Hey, Bê and Thom, Bê and Thom . . . husband and wife, where are you going!" "Hey, you husband and wife, come here."

Every time it happened, Thom would giggle, and I would reveal my two cricket wings of teeth, feeling elated. Even by the tenth grade, people teased us like that sometimes; but while it still made me happy, Thom would feel ashamed and turn away angrily, blushing. Gradually, I began to understand that Thom no longer wanted to be near me. Yes, when a person is seventeen, who would want a friend like me, regardless of how good, loyal, and devoted I was?

Thom had become a beautiful girl, mature and magnificent—so gorgeous that the young teachers at school would go into a frenzy like electrons surrounding a nucleus, and students, upon getting up each day, would bite their pens dreamily, trying to squeeze out clumsy and burning verses to her . . . Yes, surely Thom could no longer be close to me. I was a girl born of crude games from the countryside. I still waded in the fields, catching crab and fish. Of course, I now went not with Thom but with some younger children; I looked like a tailless rooster among young chickens.

In the tenth grade, I was still fond of playing soccer and basketball with the boys. Sometimes we elbowed each other hard in the ribs when competing for a good ball. I didn't know how to dress properly, usually looking more like a scarecrow than a girl. Yes, it was just like that. And I should have understood that Thom's distance from me was to be expected. But I couldn't understand, so I was sad. Human beings can never get used to losses, whether it's reasonable or not. So I roamed the fields, abandoned, while the children amused themselves playing other games. I conjured up the precious rains of childhood, the delicious baked fish with the fragrance of burnt hay, and the expansive autumn horizon, so crystal clear and inviting.

After graduation, I asked Thom to study every day, knowing that she had just slid by. But she refused every time. First, Thom had to go have a dress made with her friend Lan Anh; the next time she went to see a Vietnamese opera with her two cousins from Hanoi; the third time, Thom had to see a young man off at the train station, someone I had never met. This was the last straw, making me lose my temper and stop going there to ask her to study. Several times after that, she came to my house and waited just outside the door, but I stayed in my room. Thom soon ran out of patience and gave up on trying to salvage our friendship. She was probably just fed up with me. Her new girlfriends came constantly, entreating her to get new clothes and permanents, to act in plays, to sing, and to study with them . . .

Thom had more than enough distractions to forget me. So we no longer saw each other, even though just a wall separated us. Sitting on my side, I listened to Thom's familiar voice, her soft giggles or sometimes a few phrases from mixed-up songs . . . it made me so sad. At times like these my poor father consoled me. Every night, we would read books together, or solve algebra or geometry problems. Sometimes he took me on his bike to see a movie or have some ice cream. It was like that until the day of the exam. And then my poor father received a just reward: I passed the exam with the highest score in the school, more points than I needed to study abroad. Although I'd inherited his sooty skin, as tough as termite-resistant wood, and his hooked nose, protruding eyes, and aggressive disposition, I didn't love father any less for it. I especially loved him on the day the test results were announced.

I was only mildly excited, but I watched as father's tears streamed down his face, all the way to his chin.

My girlfriend had less than half the score needed to enter the teacher's training college. How could Thom be expected to pass the exam when she studied only with her group of new friends? They all loved to have fun, decked out in stylish clothes. They would flock together and go to the park or a deserted classroom, huddling close to one another. They would crack watermelon seeds, gossip, make *nom* salad or cook sweet soup. When they had finished eating, their eyes would start to droop. Each sat in a corner, hands clutching a book, eyes closed tight, fast asleep. Group study for the lazy—exchanging views on the latest fashions, ways to flirt with young men, stories about this girl dumping that boy, that's all it was . . .

The red *phuong* flowers had wilted on the road, and the yellow *kim phuong* bloomed one last time in the canopy. Sometimes, in the middle of a sunny day, the weather would change; the sunlight would be as white as hoarfrost, spreading over the streets and the fields, a kind of gentle, soft and bewildering light. And the wind would suddenly shift direction, hesitating for a moment in space. I prepared to enter the foreign-language university. According to the program, I would study there for a year, and then transfer to the school of advanced math in Germany. My father eagerly prepared clothes, suitcases, and shoes for his daughter. In those days, I felt pity for Thom and vaguely wondered if I had been at fault. Granted, Thom was the one who had decided to keep her distance, but if I hadn't taken it so seriously, if I had loved Thom more selflessly, perhaps she wouldn't have failed the exam. I decided to cross over the wall that for three long months hadn't been breached by even half a centimeter.

Thom was home, but she wasn't alone. Two young men were sitting there, one of them holding a guitar, the other jotting something down on a notepad. On the *kang* sat an old man. He must have been the most important person there, because every move by the two young men was under his control. Thom wasn't expecting me, so she awkwardly stood up to make introductions. I knew that they were the director and two actors from the national theatrical troupe, here doing an audition. For so long, Thom had hopes of becoming a movie star. She was so beautiful, but it seemed to me that to become an actor, beauty alone wasn't enough. Despite my misgivings, I followed the special audition for my girlfriend with suspense. The two young men took turns asking questions. While beating time and trying a rhythm, they pressed Thom to sing a song and act out a small piece. It was so intimidating. Because of her beauty, she had been assigned supporting roles—hugging a bouquet of flowers or walking across the stage—but Thom had never acted. Even when it came to singing, Thom had been given a spot on one of the higher rows only to display her beauty, since her singing was poor and usually out of tune with the rest of the choir. The two young men shook their heads in disappointment, but the old man sitting on the *kang* did not. Instead, his eyes shone unusually bright in their two deep sockets. His gaze was sentimental and attentive, flickering with an opaque and faint red flame. In my entire life, I had never seen such a gaze in any of the old men I had met.

"Be your natural self. You guys stop and let her calm herself," he said.

The two young men kept quiet. One put the notepad and the pen down on the table, and the other let his hand fall down across the body of the guitar to rest on his knee.

"Don't be afraid, dear." He turned to Thom, speaking sweetly.

"Uncle, I don't . . ."

"Take a drink dear, and let's sit back and talk naturally. Just forget this audition . . ."

Thom looked up at the old man like a drowning person spotting a rescue boat. She sighed with relief and sat down.

"Excuse me, but allow me to ask, how old are you dear?"

"Uncle, I'm seventeen."

"Seventeen, the most beautiful age in the world . . ." He spoke softly, accompanied by a smile and a sigh.

Once again, deep in his eyes, I saw the flicker of a shadowy and faint red flame. Fleetingly, his gaze revealed a furtive passion, of the kind usually seen in the eyes of young couples deeply in love. I don't know why, but at that moment my face grew hot and my insides boiled, both from indignation and shame. I stood up and went home. I realized that I had become totally alienated from, and unneeded by my girlhood friend.

Two days later, I left home.

The train departed at four A.M. Before I got on my dad's rickety motorbike, I glanced at Thom's door. It was firmly shut, and so that's all there was to our farewell.

At the train station, my dad reminded me: "Focus on your studies. Once a month, your mom and I will come visit. Don't worry about us at home."

"Yes dad, I'll remember what you've said."

The train entering the station blew its whistle insistently, as if rushed and impatient. I lifted my suitcase onto the train and sat looking at the teary eyes of my poor father. It pulled away, and still I heard his voice through the window: "Try to study. Don't think about anything else, my daughter."

Yes, I had studied. But how could I avoid thinking! . . .When my hometown faded in the mist, when the familiar fields receded beyond the tracks, I felt they were abandoning me. They said good-bye to me and the lingering images of my childhood—the banks of the ditches, the sparkling water and the waving grasses and plants, the gigantic flash of lightning in a spacious sky, the sound of rain falling passionately, the cacophony of insects and plants . . . And above all these images and sounds, floated a gentle and beautiful face with mysterious dark eyes and an elegant nose, a face with sweet, cute lips like ripe fruit in the fall. Yes, only in childhood can people love each other so passionately and so innocently like that . . .

Once a month, my father took my mother on his old iron horse of a motorbike to visit me in Hanoi. They brought me everything from chicken eggs to packages of peanuts. They wouldn't let me leave the dorm, and especially wouldn't let me think about returning to visit our hometown. They never mentioned Thom in any of their stories. One day, I couldn't resist, so I asked: "Thom is still home; is that right, dad?"

My father kept quiet, but my mother replied: "So you don't know anything? She's married."

"Married? To whom?"

"I'm not sure. I only know that she married an old man even older than your dad or her father, Mr. Thao. He arranged for his own car to come pick her up and take her to Hanoi, where the wedding was held. It was rumored that the wedding was very big. The neighbors didn't know about it, but later each house got a bag of Dai dong tea and a package of Hai chau candies."

She paused for a few seconds, and dropping her voice, said: "There's a rumor that he already had grandchildren."

I was stunned. I pictured the old man whom I had met. A wrinkled mummy. His neck was thin and withered, with an Adam's apple bobbing up and down between his shirt collar of gaudy print. His eye sockets were sunk deep into his face, and in his passionate gaze, there flashed that shadowy and faint red flame.

"Do you know where her house is?" I asked.

They looked at each other, worried. "How would we know? And why are you asking? Your job is to study." That was my poor father's reply.

"I was only wondering. Don't worry," I said to calm him down.

As soon as they got on their motorbike and left for home, I boarded the Ha Dong trolley to go into town. That very morning, the troupe was rehearsing inside the theater. Because of the power outage the stage was pitch dark. In place of the lights, there was the sound of merry laughter from the novice actresses, which brightened up the place and gave it a youthful and fresh atmosphere.

I didn't see Thom among them. I asked a girl in white with big, bold eyes: "Do you know anyone in the troupe by the name of Thom?"

"There are two girls by that name. One is that girl over there with a rather dark complexion wearing a shirt printed with red dots. The other is Lady Thom, wife of Mr. Trang Tuy, president and general director of the company. Which one do you want?"

"I wanted to ask about an old schoolmate. Her name is Vu Thi Thom."

"It must be the wife of the general director of the company. She doesn't live in this row of cheap houses with us. She lives in a private house. In just a moment she'll arrive in the car with Mr. Tuy."

I was taken aback, and looked up at the billboard advertising the show. So that old man was Trang Tuy, the most famous person in the theater world; at least, his name had made us feel dizzy ever since we were small children. In the press, on the radio . . . his name had been repeated over and over like the chorus of a song. He probably had been born several generations before us. Now, Thom had become the wife of that glorious old man.

Seeing me standing dazed, the girl with big, bold eyes laughed: "How's that? You're friends? But you didn't know about the most important event that could happen in anyone's life? It was the most famous wedding in the city!"

In shame, I asked, "What does Thom study? Acting or singing?"

"Both . . . and perhaps in the near future, dancing and opera as well . . ."

She let out a peal of laughter, without trying to hide her arrogance and sarcasm. I turned away. Just then, a flashy car pulled up to the steps of the theater. The car stopped, the door opened, and the old man that I had met jumped out. He opened the car door wide, and my girl-friend stepped out. Yes, it was Thom. In a fresh, gorgeous and sleek outfit, she looked like an empress.

She saw me. "Bê, when did you come?"

She rushed toward me, stumbling. Her excessive joy told me that surely she hadn't had a happy life among the novice actresses. She must have been isolated and lonely. I held Thom's hand, thinking nostalgi-cally about what had existed and been lost between us. Director Trang Tuy approached. He was precisely that glorious, renowned celebrity. He wore a shirt with oversized checks, and fastened to his left lapel was a platinum pin shaped like an arrow, with a pearl on the tip. A pair of well-tailored jeans couldn't hide the pathetic sight of his withered but-tocks. The very famous person shook my hand, but I wasn't as excited as I should have been to meet such an idol.

"Hello . . . sir . . ."

I pondered for some time which title I should use to address him. Of course, I couldn't call him by the common ones, such as Mister, Senior Uncle, Junior Uncle . . . Thom surely had to call her husband by the usual title of *Anh*. But for me to address him that way would have left a bitter taste in my mouth.

"Please come visit us. Thom has told me a lot about you. I also crave grilled fish out in the fields, just like you used to make."

He was smart. He completely understood my thoughts and why I was annoyed with him, so he changed forms of address perfectly, talk-ing in a friendly and charming manner. He did this so smoothly that I didn't have time to react, having no choice but to follow him into the car. The driver was a young man with a face careworn from hardship. He sat indifferently, without turning his head once. Thom sat in the backseat with me. Trang Tuy got in front, but then had to go inside to tell the assistant director of the theater that he would be going home to entertain a guest. Once that was done, he came back out.

"Let's go. Drop us off at Dong Xuan market for a little while."

"I understand clearly boss," the driver replied civilly but coldly.

Trang Tuy was unperturbed, as if he hadn't paid any attention to him. He turned his head and said: "Dear, you take Bê into the market, okay? I'll wait. Today, we should show off your talent a little. We can make noodles and grilled fish or eel soup."

He winked at me: "Do you know! Thom cooks excellent food. One could never wish for a better housewife."

His eyes glittered in happiness. His smile showed his complete satisfaction, even though he had lied. Thom was extremely clumsy—whenever she had to clean a fish, she had to come ask for my help, afraid of mistakenly puncturing the gallbladder full of bile. Whenever she prepared an eel, it was never completely clean of its slimy mucus. And when she cooked *rieu cua,* she had to ask her mother to filter and boil the broth from the crushed crabs. My friend blushed at her husband's compliment, truly happy. Suddenly, I was sick of both of them.

I said, "I can't stay for lunch. I have a class at ten o'clock."

Thom protested. "No. Bê, you must stay. How can there be a class at ten o'clock?"

"At ten I have German conversation," I firmly replied.

Mr. Trang Tuy looked at me. "But you'll come visit us in the near future? Don't put it off, because we're really looking forward to it. Now, let's have a cup of coffee. The driver will take you back to school."

We stopped at a coffee shop famous for its delicious brewed coffee and chocolate egg custard. Afterwards, Trang Tuy told the driver to take me back to school. I thought that he was very sophisticated and guessed that I would have respected and admired him a great deal, if only he were still that distant, glorious man and not the husband of my friend—a person forty years his junior.

On a Sunday two weeks later, Thom came to school to pick me up for a visit at her house. The driver spoke very little, with a face shut tight like a coffin. I hesitated, and wanted to refuse, but felt that I couldn't. Thom clearly didn't understand my hesitation.

"You must come visit us. Tuy keeps talking about it. Yesterday someone gave him a pair of fat, castrated roosters as a present, so we can make vermicelli and chicken soup. The janitor at the theater has just taught me how to prepare broth with shrimp paste, the way her family traditionally makes it."

My friend talked, innocent and satisfied. I steered the conversation to another topic: "How's your job, Thom? Have they assigned you a role yet?"

"Not yet. Tuy says that there's no need to hurry. In art, we cannot hurry. Perhaps for the time being I can keep participating in the training group. But when the opportunity arises, Tuy will send me to an official training school. It could be the theater school in Moscow or Berlin."

The driver sat in front like a statue, his hands grasping the steering wheel and eyes focused directly on the road. But I had the feeling our conversation was being taken in by those ears, yellow as wax. I felt he was silently smirking.

I changed the subject a second time: "Hey, Thom. Have you heard any news from Lan or Thuan?"

"Lan pulled some strings to get into the elementary teachers' training school. All the way up there in Thai Nguyen. After graduating, she'll teach at an elementary school in the middle of nowhere, so that will be it for her. What's more, she married a forest ranger, which ends any chance of her going back home. Thuan has been luckier; she got an accountant's position in a shipping company. It seems she's just been transferred to a freighter, so at this moment, she's probably floating on the water somewhere."

I challenged her. "That's good, isn't it?"

"Well, sure . . ." Thom replied weakly.

The car stopped in front of a small villa.

"We're home. Bê, go on ahead," Thom said.

I went through the gate while Thom stayed behind to negotiate something with the driver. I couldn't catch his response; I only saw the flashy car take off like an arrow through the intersection.

My friend hurried to catch up with me, saying awkwardly: "This driver is so insolent. I'll have to tell Tuy to have him replaced."

We went inside. The villa had two floors, with four large rooms, built under the French occupation. The State rented it to two families: a certain department chief lived downstairs and Trang Tuy upstairs. Thom's room was in the back. In light of the housing situation as it was then, it was an ideal place. Her living space was twenty-eight meters square, with a tile floor, an extra room, and a bathroom. The main door that opened into the front room had been boarded up with wooden planks nailed together with big nails. It looked crude and ugly. Thom didn't talk about it, but I guessed that the front room belonged to Tuy's own children. Perhaps they were around forty years old, married. Trang Tuy wore a pair of red and brown striped pajamas. In his sleepwear, he looked even worse since his knotted joints protruded everywhere under the thin fabric. We cooked our meal, and afterwards, Thom showed me the poems Tuy had written for her.

They were poems in a 1930s style: days like jade, golden nights, a fairy from paradise, you are the reflection of my life, you are a dream with wings . . . A host of noisy, picturesque words, sparkling and glittering like the stuff in a jewelry store display case. In front of that pile of treasures, my friend was giddy. "This one, Tuy wrote for my birthday. This one, he wrote before our wedding day:

> Had I not met you, my life would have withered away
> Like the *phu dung* flowers fading in the garden
> Oh, my gentle, dainty fairy . . ."

Thom folded the serrated pink sheets, exuding the scent of cheap perfume, and placed them in her jewelry box. Seeing her holding them with such care and love, I understood that those weary verses had been her sole source of comfort in these surroundings, outside of her husband. Because clearly, in this house, she had no relationship with the others living around her, other than one based on hatred and contempt. I also recalled the cold attitude of the novice actresses toward Thom. Then I realized that my friend was climbing a fraying rope and this rope she clung to for dear life was the president and general director—Trang Tuy—and her fantasy of the glory his power could bring her.

Her savior was sleeping. A thin curtain separated him from us, but that gauzy piece of cloth couldn't hide the signs of old age as he slept. When he wasn't trying to be charming, wisecracking, or telling jokes, or wasn't raising his hand to dismiss a class . . . he revealed his true self, an old man approaching sixty. Lines—cruel lines—had appeared all over his cheeks, his temples, and below the bags under his eyes, enveloping his neck. His legs were crossed, the cuffs of his pajamas raised just enough to reveal thin and bony legs.

Suddenly I felt overwhelmed with pity for my friend. "I'm very glad that you're happy. But you should pay more attention to your work," I said.

Thom smiled, "Sure, I'll urge Tuy. Maybe when spring comes, I'll go study in Moscow or Berlin. The contract for sending students over there has been signed. Tuy said so."

I stood up. "I have to go home, okay?"

My friend panicked and grasped my hand. "Going home already? Why so soon?"

I looked at my watch. "It's three forty-five."

Thom stood dazed, sighing. I picked up my handbag. My friend pulled me back, and said in a voice that had lost all its composure: "Bê, come see me often, okay . . . don't abandon me . . ."

In her eyes, the contented glimmer had disappeared. Her happiness must have died, along with the perfume-filled verses in her jewelry box. Other than these, she had nothing left to shield herself or to cover the emptiness in her life. I was trying to find some words of consolation, but the driver, right on time, had pulled up in front of the villa and honked his horn. I was scared of his cold face and I rushed down to the car.

The following week, I took the early-morning trolley from Ha Dong to visit Thom. Seeing me, she was close to joyful tears, like a child waiting for its mother to come back from the market, or like our teenage years, whenever I kept her waiting too long—whether in a corner of a hut, or on the bank of the paddy while I looked for firewood, or down in a ditch while I searched for duck eggs. In my heart, I felt a longing that people get when they love, cherish, and want to protect someone. My friend was paler than usual.

"Are you sick? Why are you so pale?" I asked.

Thom shook her head without replying. She brought out a basket of black *tram* and we cut each of them in half to make steamed *tram* with meat filling. Suddenly there was a knock on the door, and Trang Tuy stood up to answer it. A man appeared: small and bad-tempered, with a mustache that looked like an army of ants crawling above lips stained purple from nicotine.

"Hi, dad," he said and went straight to a chair and sat down. He didn't bother to look around or greet anyone else.

Trang Tuy went pale and shouted: "When you come into a house you must acknowledge your host. You lack even the most basic social graces."

"I already greeted you."

"Not just me, what about . . ." He looked at us, making me feel awkward.

But his son cut him off with a defiant, adamant gesture. "That's enough, dad. Don't make me look like a clown. I don't want to."

The father bellowed: "But I want you to. I want you to do it."

His son didn't back down. He jerked his head up, and thrust his black mustache forward. "Then what do you want me to call her? Keep in mind that I'm already thirty-six. And your first grandson is already thirteen."

"Age is one thing, rank is another."

"Yes," the son replied angrily. "Greetings, my father's wife."

Thom didn't say anything, but her fingers trembled so violently that the fruit she was cutting slipped, falling to the floor. Her face turned paper white. Trang Tuy, brooding and impotent, glanced at his wife.

His son, after having obeyed his father's order to greet his step-mother, turned back: "I've explained everything to you carefully. Please give me your opinion."

"I don't have an opinion. I don't owe you anything."

"No. You fathered us children, so you have to be fair to us. I'm not an adopted son; I'm not someone you picked up in the street, so you can't treat me like this. If things were like they were before, this entire house would be mine . . ."

"So you plan to kick your two younger siblings out into the street?"

"No, but they have to know how to behave. They have to pay their fair share to me based on whatever the commissions are for housing these days. I can't live in my wife's house forever. A son-in-law living in his wife's mother's house is like a dog cowering under the pantry."

"Then you can go right over and tell them. Tell them face to face; you don't need my help." The father was shouting and pointing at the wooden door leading into the front room that had been boarded up with some big nails, looking crude and ugly.

The man's face was as cold as ice, and his jaw muscles jutted out: "Dad, you have to do it. You have to settle it. Otherwise, I'll . . ."

Trang Tuy was so angry that his face went purple. His hands trembled uncontrollably. All at once, he began to stammer: "I . . . I . . . won't do it. Then . . . what?"

"Then . . . ," the son continued, looking not at his father, but at my friend. "Then you have to split this room in two. This is my room, not that woman's . . ."

Thom rushed to me and clutched me tightly, bursting into tears. The general director grabbed a glass jar filled with sugar for coffee and heaved it at his son's face, but he ducked. The sugar jar hit the wall and shattered, pieces of glass flying everywhere, and sugar scattering onto the floor like white sand. The son stood up and left the room, slamming the door angrily behind him.

The director threw his hands in the air and shook his head: "How monstrous—a monstrous generation. These young people nowadays are no longer human beings. They've lost their virtue . . ."

I didn't answer him. At that moment, there was another knock on the door. By then, Trang Tuy had lost his composure and usual poise. He asked curtly, "Who is it?"

The door opened and a fresh-looking young man stuck his head in the door. "Boss, a cadre from the Ministry of Culture paid an unexpected visit at the theater. They want you to come at once."

The director didn't reply, but changed his clothes in angry silence. The young actor glanced at us with apprehension, then whispered to Thom: "Are you coming?"

"No, I'm sick," my friend responded. She hung her head so that the young actor couldn't see her swollen eyes.

When Trang Tuy and the actor had left, I asked her: "The other day, you said that Tuy could send you to study at the school of drama in Russia or Germany, right? I think you should apply to study abroad right away . . ."

"How could I go now?" And with that, she started to sob loudly, like a child. "I'm pregnant . . . three months now . . ." Tears streamed down her face. A vein was throbbing on her slender, ivory neck.

Blood rushed to my face: "How could you be so stupid? You haven't been through training yet . . ."

"But Tuy told me that . . ."

"Told you what?"

"That we had to have a child, as a memento."

"He already has a bunch of children. A bunch of children and a bunch of grandchildren."

"But Tuy said . . . ," she mumbled, then collapsed on her bed, pushing her face into the pillow embroidered with the white *phu dung* flowers.

I loved Thom, but I couldn't suppress the anger that was rising in me like a roaring fire. "Now you're in training. After you give birth to the child, you'll have to raise it for two or three years before you can go back. What will happen then?"

"Tuy said that . . ."

"Never mind Tuy, it's you. You have to be responsible for your own life." My friend looked up at me, her beautiful eyes full of tears, her face bewildered and pitiful.

"But tell me, what can I do?"

It was my turn to be bewildered. She was right, what could she do now? She couldn't become an actress, or a singer, and worse yet, she had no ability to study dance or the other arts. The only thing Heaven had bestowed on Thom was a spellbinding beauty. But her dream was to become a movie star, a star of the stage. She aspired to glory and fame. Thom could never be content with the life of an elementary school teacher like Lan, living in the middle of nowhere. Nor did she want to spend her days on a freighter like Thuan. She needed glory; yes, it was the foremost thing in her mind. And my friend had looked for glory up a dark staircase.

The city whistle screamed. Twelve noon. I told Thom I had work to do that afternoon, so I had to go home right away.

My friend pleaded with me: "Bê, come visit me, don't abandon me."

I nodded, but thought to myself: "You abandoned me first. I'm always the first one to be abandoned." My nose filled with bitterness, and I felt on the verge of tears.

A few days later, my head teacher had the day off due to illness, so I took the trolley to visit Thom. She had given up work completely and no longer went to the theater each day. She looked wooden, and it was clear that she was pregnant. Her eyebrows stood out above an unfocused gaze, and her two pale cheeks had become sunken. Thom's beauty seemed to be diminished. The director, however, had regained his good humor. He apologized to me, sorry that "my ill-bred son ruined our fun last Sunday"—and then gossiped about what had been happening backstage at the theater, and about his plans for the future, to produce a series of love tragedies by Shakespeare and Schiller . . .

Once a week, I visited Thom. With each visit, I witnessed her gradual emotional breakdown. Thom no longer mentioned going to study theater in Moscow or Berlin. She no longer opened the jewelry box to take out the love poems to read to me.

Once, I said to her, "Well, the truth is, life is very long. After giving birth, you should try to arrange some care for your child and go study. Who knows, you might become a stage actress. In life, who doesn't run into hardship along the way . . ."

She looked at me and shook her head miserably. Her eyes were empty, like a house whose walls had been removed, leaving only a tattered, thatched roof still standing. They no longer had any spark of hope, or to be more exact, illusion. The moment when a person with illusions recognizes her true worth is horrible—when she discovers that illusions are just that, and they can never come true. Their effect is like a dose of a hallucinogenic drug, or a cloud at twilight.

One day Thom saw me to the gate. Just then, the car bringing Trang Tuy home from the theater pulled up.

Thom said to the driver, "Could you take Bê back to school?"

He looked at her coldly. "The company assigned me to serve Comrade Director during business hours, not to serve you."

Having said that, his eyes lost some of their coldness. He turned to me and said, "Get into the car, Bê, and I'll drive you to the school. But not because someone told me to."

Thom choked and her face turned deadly pale, but Trang Tuy only shrugged and went inside. Even he, as intelligent and experienced as he was, couldn't find a way to defend his wife at that moment.

I told the driver, "Thanks, but I'll take the trolley." And I left, not waiting for a good-bye.

After that day, I had to start preparing for semester final exams, so I couldn't visit my old friend. Two weeks later, my finals were over. On the Monday of the third week, the office secretary handed me a piece of paper, on which was written: "I'm sick. Come visit me, Bê."

I changed my clothes, but the minute I arrived at the school gate, I heard the sputtering of that old motorbike. My poor father pulled up, with my mother riding on the back carrying a heavy rattan basket. I feigned being in a big hurry, and said to my parents: "Today I have something important to do. You can give everything to Phuong Hoa to keep for me, then you can visit Uncle Hong and go on home. Don't wait for me."

They were taken aback. My mother wondered aloud, "What is it?"

Without looking at her, I determinedly stepped out of the school gate and replied, "Something very important, mom."

Having said that, I felt guilty, so I ran up and hugged her from behind. "Dad, mom— please go home. I have to go now." Then I quickly released my mother and left without looking back.

My poor father tried to call after me: "Something to do with your studies, right?"

"Yes, my studies . . . ," I answered loudly.

Reassured, my parents entered the school grounds. He went ahead, and she followed, the rickety motorbike between them, laden with the heavy rattan basket. I hid behind the wall surrounding the school building, and before going on my way, watched them secretly until they disappeared from sight.

It seemed that Thom had been waiting for me for a long time, because the moment I pushed open the door to enter, she burst into loud sobs. Her beautiful face was swollen and a little wrinkle could be seen along the corner of her eye. One hand covered her face, while the other rested on her prominent belly that moved up and down under her robe with each breath. I sat down next to her; and suddenly, tears streamed from my eyes, hot on my cheeks. We wept silently for a long time—one of us because of shattered dreams; the other because her heart had been broken from helplessness. What could I do to save Thom now?

After a long while, I asked, "Have you eaten since morning? I'll go buy some *pho* for you, okay?"

My friend shook her head.

"Should I go buy *che* with ice?"

She shook her head again. Her blurry eyes were fixed on the gray door.

Looking into her lifeless eyes, I asked, "What do you want, Thom?"

My girlfriend remained silent for some time, then said slowly, "Either I die . . . or he must die."

Her small hand fumbled under the pillow. My intuition told me that something was wrong, so I grabbed her arm and flipped over the pillow. Underneath was a shiny knife lying on the sheet. The knife was made of steel as black as an animal's horn, with a glistening, thin blade. One look at it was enough to give me goose bumps. I held the knife, shouting, "Don't be crazy, aren't you afraid that people will laugh at you?"

Thom kept silent, like a statue.

I went on, "I'll tell your parents."

"Don't. My mother would die, she would die . . . ," Thom whispered.

Pain echoed in those disjointed, trembling and feeble utterances. I knew that in this game, Thom's mother had illusions as strong as her daughter's. Mrs. Thao had supported this ill-fated marriage. Perhaps she had believed with all her heart that it would help her daughter climb to heights of fame.

I sat for a while unable to express any words of much comfort. Finally, I couldn't help but repeat some phrases from a third-rate novel: "Life is long, don't be foolish . . . You must live . . ."

But upon hearing my words, Thom looked up and asked coldly, "But am I living?"

A bitter feeling ran down my spine, spreading fear throughout my body. It was true, Thom had not been allowed to live. Why hadn't I understood that until now? . . . A person had to be allowed to live, true to herself. She couldn't live as if she were something totally unnecessary.

Thom suddenly bellowed like a crazy person: "Have I been allowed to live? . . . It would have been better for me to be like Lan, like Thuan . . ."

Sure, now Thom wanted to be like our two girlfriends with their sad fates: an elementary school teacher living in the middle of nowhere, married to an obscure forest ranger, and an accountant spending her days on a freighter, who in all probability would marry a sailor or a mechanic, a nobody . . . But that was life, exactly. A healthy life, a real life.

"Either I die . . . or he must die." Thom repeated it, but she was no longer yelling; instead she was whimpering like on old woman. Then she put her face down on the pillow. The mattress shook under her agonized tossing and turning.

There was a knock on the door, and Trang Tuy came in, asking in bewilderment, "What's the matter?"

"Nothing. You should go and leave Thom alone," I answered. My face at that moment must have made me look like a killer, because Trang Tuy stepped backward in panic. That person of such celebrity opened the door without protest, glancing at me while moving towards the stairs, not uttering a word.

After that episode, Thom calmed down. Perhaps she had already tried to reconcile herself to a meaningless life. She put away her pointed knife in the jewelry box where the perfume-filled love poems now lay unread and neglected. She sat cutting cloth diapers, making baby shirts, and knitting tiny booties; and when her term ended, she gave birth to a wrinkled and ugly son, like I recounted to you at the beginning of the story. That son was indeed a memento, but a depressing one.

I studied hard for my exams, especially because German was not an easy language to learn. When Thom's son was three months old, we received our instructions for departure, so I paid her one last visit. I had planned to tell her many things before I went so far away—things like, each person has to find his or her own place in life, that people need glory but shouldn't look for it up a dark staircase, that life by nature is fair so don't expect to enjoy its fruit if you're not ready to sweat for it . . . But when I sat in front of Thom, the words choked in my throat. She looked at me through her gloomy eyes, in which the distant dreams had died.

"In those days, we lived so happily and joyfully."

"In those days, we really lived."

In her eyes, I found a shadow of the childhood rains. The rains that weren't rains, but an overflowing, endless celebration. In our hearts they created melodious sounds and sparkling magical colors, remaining like a fresh breeze for our souls. And thanks to those memories, we'll again find the blue smoke, the taste of delicious baked fish, and the clear autumn horizon, so inviting . . . Those fish we catch ourselves in a pond, that is real happiness . . .

1985
Translated by Bac Hoai Tran and Courtney Norris

Glossary

Ama: elder sister; form of address in Burmese for an older woman

ambuyat: a type of food made from flour mixed with boiled water

amin: amen

Amma: "mother" in Tamil; also used to address any older woman with affection or respect

angpow: a monetary gift of thanks

Anh: a Vietnamese title used for one's husband or with a sense of friendship to a man

baht: Thai currency

baju: usually a plain, long-sleeved, collarless top worn over loose long pants or trousers. For formal occasions, the material is usually silk. The entire outfit includes a sarong, which is worn over the *baju*, and pants. The sarong, usually of silk and gold or silver thread for royalty, is tucked in at the waist and reaches the knees or below, depending on Straits Chinese fashion.

bakau: a type of Mangrove tree growing along the seashore

calamansi: a type of fruit similar to a lemon in taste

char kuay teow: a type of noodle fried with cockles and black sauce

che: a dessert or sweet snack with the consistency of soupy custard

cheongsam: Chinese dress with a high mandarin collar

chi: a Cambodian unit of money. Ten *chi* are worth one *domlong*.

Cikgu: a form of respectful address used for a teacher

Dang: a form of address used for a lady, girl, or woman

domlong: a Cambodian unit of money; a measure of gold equivalent to about 450 U.S. dollars

ginse: stringed instrument

gumamemela: a showy Philippine flower, usually red or orange

Haji: a term of respectful address for someone who has made the pilgrimage to Mecca

haji: someone who has made the pilgrimage to Mecca

Hanuman: the magical white monkey in the *Ramayana* who assists Rama in finding Sita. In "Sita Puts Out the Fire" he appears as the son of Ravana and Sita

HDB: the Housing and Development Board, a government agency. Most Singaporeans live in apartment blocks built and managed by the Housing and Development Board.

Hsunthein Pwe: Burmese term for an important merit-making Buddhist ceremony and festival that occurs in Southeast Asian nations with a strong Theravada Buddhist influence

IC: identity card

imam: the man with Islamic religious training who leads prayers either at home or mosques

Indra: king of the Hindu pantheon of gods and a character in Buddhist mythology who sometimes materializes to assist people in trouble

kampung: Malay village

kapatiran: term whose closest English equivalent is "brotherhood" or "sisterhood." The translation, however, is not quite accurate since *kapatiran* has no gender bias.

kashatriya: warrior, the second of four major castes in India

kazun: rabbit greens

Kempeti: the Japanese secret police

keroncong: popular Indonesian music, originating from Portuguese songs

kip: Lao currency. In the early 1990s, when this story was written, the exchange rate was approximately seven hundred *kip* to the U.S. dollar.

Kitha Gawdami: personal name

kulimpapa: a kind of tree in Negara Brunei Darussalam *(Vitex pubescene)*

kum: gold

kyat: Burmese currency worth four and a half *lakh* or about fifteen U.S. cents in 1999

kya-zan hinga: a noodle and sauce dish believed to preserve one's good fortune when offered to monks

lahpet thouq: pickled tea-leaf salad

lakh: a unit of Burmese currency

lao: the name of a species of grass commonly found in Laos

lapu: a type of sea fish *(Pteropterus antennata / Centrogens vaigiensis)*

LEKRA: Lembaga Kebudajaan Rakjat; an Indonesian writer's organization devoted to literature for society's sake

Liao: a term of address used for old or respected people

maghrib: the fourth of five daily prayers in Islam

Mahabharata: one of the two great Hindu epics, along with the *Ramayana*. In this epic, two branches of the Bharata family fight over the kingdom. The god Vishnu, in the form of Krishna, acts as an advisor to the Pandavas, who eventually win the war.

Mau Lam: a type of musical theatrical performance popular among the Lao

muro-ami fishing: a type of seasonal fishing in the Philippines, in which small boys are recruited to drive fish into nets

narra: a very rare and expensive Philippine wood

New Paper: the afternoon tabloid in Singapore

Nga Kyweh: a variety of rice prized for its good flavor

nom: sweet and sour grated salad

pakomah: a length of cloth used variously as a wrap-around garment, belt, headgear, carrying bag, etc.

Pancasila: the embodiment of basic principles of an independent Indonesian state, as set forth in the 1945 constitution of Indonesia. The five principles are belief in one supreme God, humanitarianism, nationalism expressed in the unity of Indonesia, consultative democracy, and social justice.

patotoo: testimonial; bearing witness to something

peranakan: the Straits Chinese, who adopted some Malay customs and produced a distinctive culture that included richly patterned fabrics and intricate jewelry

Pham Cong-Cuc Hoa: an epic love poem by an anonymous author that is an important part of Vietnamese folklore

pho: beef noodle soup

phuong: *Royal poinciana;* a showy tropical tree with flamboyant scarlet and orange flowers

pottu: a red or black dot Hindu women wear between their eyebrows

pya: smallest unit of Burmese currency

rakshasa: demons with magical powers popularized by the Hindu epics

Ramayana: one of the two great Hindu epics, along with the *Mahabharata.* The plot revolves around the abduction of Sita, Rama's wife, during their period of exile in the forest. Ravana, a ten-headed (or ten-faced) demon has transported her to his island kingdom. When Rama finally finds her with the help of the magical white monkey, Hanuman, and defeats Ravana, Sita must enter fire in order to prove her fidelity.

Reyna Elena: queen of the Santacruzan procession, selected from among a town's beautiful girls

rieu cua: short for *bun rieu cua;* crab noodle soup

rotan: a cane used for corporal punishment attached to certain criminal offences

rupiah: Indonesian currency

samsu: a cheap, illegal brew

Santacruzan: a religious procession held in the month of May

sato: the rice liquor made by farmers everywhere in Thailand

Semar: the grotesquely fat clown servant in Javanese *wayang* shadow theater

Shan: an ethnic group in Burma

Shiva: the destroyer deity of the Hindu trinity, which also includes Brahma (creator) and Vishnu (preserver)

shwe-yin-aye: a kind of cold drink made from sago, sugar, and ice believed to cool one down in hot weather

Si (Sri): a prefix of respect used with names of people

"Singha Gry Pope" ("Singhaa Krai Pop"): the televised version of a heroic poetic tale by Sunthon Phuu (1786–1856)

sinseh: a professional herbalist

The Straits Times: the morning newspaper in Singapore

Suprema: a female leader of the Katipunan

thanakha: a yellowish paste ground from the bark of Murraya Paniculata. Burmese women wear it to protect their skin from the sun.

tong tin: lending groups in Cambodia in which people pool their money then draw lots to see who receives an interest-free loan in a given month

Tosakan (Totsakan): the Thai name for Ravana, from the epic the *Ramayana.* This demon is depicted as having ten heads or ten faces—thus the name Tosakan. In the epic he abducts Sita. After Rama defeats him in battle, Rama refuses to take Sita back, since the public may no longer believe in her chastity. Sita enters fire to prove her purity, and they are reconciled.

tram: fruit of the Canarium album tree

Tuan: "sir"; an honorific form used to refer to a white colonizer

tuka-tuka: a type of stingray

ulol: crazy

University of Phnom Penh: now known as the Royal University of Phnom Penh

Wunnapahta: a personal name

Yathawdaya: the name of Siddhartha's mother in Burmese. Here it refers to a song that narrates the episode of the four signs in Siddhartha's life.

Suggested Readings

Burma

Allott, Anna J. *Inked Over, Ripped Out: Burmese Storytellers and the Censors.* New York: P.E.N. American Center, 1993.

Beikman, Sarpay. *One Thousand Hearts and Other Modern Burmese Short Stories.* Rangoon: Sarpay Beikman Management Board, 1973.

Thein Pe Myint. *Selected Short Stories of Thein Pe Myint.* Trans. Patricia M. Milne. Cornell University, Southeast Asia Program Data Papers, No. 91. Ithaca: Cornell University, Southeast Asia Program, 1973.

———. *Sweet and Sour: Burmese Short Stories.* Trans. Usha Narayanan. New Delhi: Sterling Publishers, 1999.

Indonesia

Aveling, Harry, ed. and trans. *From Surabaya to Armageddon: Indonesian Short Stories.* Singapore: Heinemann Educational Books, 1976.

———, ed. and trans. *Gestapu: Indonesian Short Stories on the Abortive Communist Coup of Thirtieth September 1965.* University of Hawaii, Southeast Asian Studies Working Paper, No. 6. Honolulu: University of Hawaii, Southeast Asian Studies, 1975.

Frederick, William H., ed. *Reflections on Rebellion: Stories from the Indonesian Upheavals of 1948 and 1965.* Trans. John H. McGlynn and William H. Frederick. Papers in International Studies, Southeast Asia, No. 60. Athens: Ohio University, Center for International Studies, 1983.

Kartodikromo, Mas Marco. *Three Early Indonesian Short Stories.* Trans. Paul Tickell. Working Paper, Centre of Southeast Asian Studies, Monash University, no. 23. Melbourne, Australia: Dept. of Indonesian and Malay, Monash University, 1981.

Lingard, Jeanette, trans. *Diverse Lives: Contemporary Stories from Indonesia.* Oxford: Oxford University Press, 1995.

McGlynn, John H., ed. *Menagerie, 1: Indonesian Fiction, Poetry, Photographs, Essays.* Jakarta: The Lontar Foundation, 1992.

Laos

Outhine Bounyavong. *Mother's Beloved: Stories from Laos.* Ed. Bounheng Inversin and Daniel Duffy. Seattle: University of Washington Press, 1999.

Rains in the Jungle: Lao Short Stories. N.p.: Neo Lao Haksat Publications, 1967.

The Wood Grouse. N.p.: Neo Lao Haksat Publications, 1968.

Malaysia

Ahmad, Shahnon. *The Third Notch and Other Stories*. Trans. Harry Aveling. Singapore: Heinemann Educational Books, 1980.

Aveling, Harry, trans. *Fables of Eve*. Kuala Lumpur: Dewan Bahasa dan Pustaka, 1991.

———, trans. *Sayembara Esso-Gapena: Malaysian Short Stories*. Kuala Lumpur: Dewan Bahasa dan Pustaka, Kementerian Pendidikan Malaysia, 1987.

Fernando, Lloyd. *Twenty-Two Malaysian Stories: An Anthology of Writing in English*. Singapore: Heinemann Educational Books, 1968.

Lee, Kok Liang. *The Mutes in the Sun, and Other Stories*. Kuala Lumpur: Rayirath (Raybooks) Publications, 1963.

Keris Mas. *Blood and Tears*. Trans. Harry Aveling. Petaling Jaya, Selangor, Malaysia: Penerbit Fajar Bakti/Oxford University Press, 1984.

Wignesan, T. ed. *Bunga Emas: An Anthology of Contemporary Malaysian Literature, 1930–1963*. London: A. Blond, 1964.

Singapore

Baratham, Gopal. *Love Letter and Other Stories*. Singapore: Times Books International, 1988.

Chia, Corinne, K. K. Seet, and Pat M. Wong. *Made in Singapore*. Singapore: Times Books International, 1985.

Choo, Sylvia Toh Paik. *Lagi Goondu!* Singapore: Times Books International, 1986.

Chua, Rebecca. *The Newspaper Editor and Other Stories*. Singapore: Heinemann Educational Books (Asia), 1981.

Chua, Terence. *The Nightmare Factory*. Singapore: Landmark Books, 1991.

Fernandez, George, ed. *Stories from Singapore: Twenty-four Short Stories by Eighteen Authors*. Singapore: Society of Singapore Writers, 1983.

Goh, Sin Tub. *Goh's Twelve Best Singapore Stories*. Singapore: Heinemann Educational Books (Asia), 1993.

Heng, Geraldine, ed. *The Sun in Her Eyes: Stories by Singapore Women*. Singapore: Woodrose Publications, 1976.

Jeyaretnam, Philip. *First Loves*. Singapore: Times Books International, 1988.

Lee, Russell. *The Almost Complete Collection of True Singapore Ghost Stories*. Singapore: Flame of the Forest, 1989.

Lim, Catherine. *Little Ironies: Stories of Singapore*. Singapore: Heinemann Educational Books (Asia), 1998.

Lim, Thean Soo. *Blues and Carnation*. Singapore: Federal Publications, 1985.

Moey, Nicky. *Army Ghost Stories: and other Tales*. Singapore: Promethean Integrated, 1994.

Nair, Chandran, ed. *Singapore Writing*. Singapore: Woodrose Publication for the Society of Singapore Writers, 1977.

Tham, Claire. *Saving the Rainforest and Other Stories*. Singapore: Times International, 1993.

Wong, Swee Hoon. *A Dying Breed*. Singapore: Heinemann Educational Books (Asia), 1991.

Yeo, Robert, ed. *Singapore Short Stories.* Vols. 1 and 2. Singapore: Heinemann Educational Books (Asia), 1978.
——, ed. *Singular Stories: Tales from Singapore.* Washington, D.C.: Three Continents Press, 1993.

Thailand

Anderson, Benedict R. O'G., and Ruchira Mendiones, eds. and trans. *In the Mirror: Literature and Politics in Siam in the American Era.* Bangkok: Editions Duang Kamol, 1985.

Atsiri Thammachoti. *Kun Thong* (You Will Return at Dawn). Trans. Chamnongsri Rutnin. Bangkok: Lo Kai Publishers, 1987.

Bowie, Katherine, ed. and trans. *Voices from the Thai Countryside: The Short Stories of Samruam Singh.* University of Wisconsin, Center for Southeast Asian Studies, Monograph 6. Madison: University of Wisconsin, Center for Southeast Asian Studies, 1991.

Draskau, Jennifer, ed. and trans. *Taw and Other Thai Stories.* Hong Kong: Heinemann Educational Books (Asia), 1975.

Kepner, Susan Fulop, ed. and trans. *The Lioness in Bloom: Modern Thai Fiction about Women.* Berkeley: University of California Press, 1996.

Khammaan Khonkhai. *The Teachers of Mad Dog Swamp.* Trans. Gehan Wijeyewardene. St. Lucia: University of Queensland Press, 1978.

Lao Khamhøom (Khamsing Srinawk). *The Politician and Other Stories.* Ed. Michael Smithies. Trans. Domnern Garden. Singapore: Oxford University Press, 1991.

Masavisut, Nitaya, and Matthew Grose, eds. *The S.E.A. Write Anthology of Thai Short Stories and Poems.* Chiang Mai, Thailand: Silkworm Books, 1996.

Phillips, Herbert P. *Modern Thai Literature: With An Ethnographic Interpretation.* Honolulu: University of Hawaii Press, 1987.

Siburapha. *Behind the Painting and Other Stories.* Trans. David Smyth. Singapore: Oxford University Press, 1990.

Sidaoru'ang. *A Drop of Glass.* Ed. and trans., with introduction Rachel Harrison. Bangkok: Editions Duang Kamol, 1994.

Smyth, David, and Manas Chitakasem, trans. *The Sergeant's Garland and Other Stories.* Kuala Lumpur: Oxford University Press, 1998.

Thai P.E.N. Anthology: Short Stories and Poems of Social Consciousness. Bangkok: P.E.N. International Thailand Centre, 1984.

Treasury of Thai Literature: The Modern Period. Bangkok: The Thai National Identity Board, Office of the Prime Minister, 1988.

The Philippines

Arcellana, Francisco. *Selected Stories.* Manila: A. S. Florentino, 1962.

Arguilla, Manuel Estabillo. *How My Brother Leon Brought Home a Wife, and Other Stories.* Manila, Philippines: De La Salle University Press, 1998.

Brillantes, Gregorio C. *The Distance to Andromeda and Other Stories.* Manila: Benipayo Press, 1960.

Bulosan, Carlos. *The Laughter of My Father.* New York: Harcourt, Brace, 1944.

Casper, Leonard, ed. *Modern Philippine Short Stories.* Albuquerque: University of New Mexico Press, 1962.

Dalisay, Jose Y., Jr. *Sarcophagus and Other Stories.* Quezon City: University of the Philippine Press, 1992.

Francia, Luis H., ed. *Brown River, White Ocean: An Anthology of Twentieth-Century Philippine Literature in English.* New Brunswick: Rutgers University Press, 1993.

Garcia, Neil C., and Danton Remoto, eds. *Ladlad: An Anthology of Philippine Gay Writing.* Pasig, Metro Manila, Philippines: Anvil Publishing, 1994.

González, N. V. M. *The Bamboo Dancers.* Manila: Benipayo Press, 1960.

Jubaira, Ibrahim A, ed. *A Canto of Summer: A Collection of Fifteen Moslem Short Stories from the Heart of Southern Philippines.* Colombo: Times of Ceylon, 1974.

Lumbera, Bienvenido, and Cynthia N. Lumbera, eds. *Philippine Literature: A History and Anthology.* Metro Manila, Philippines: National Book Store, 1982.

Mojares, Resil B., ed. *The Writers of Cebu: An Anthology of Prize-Winning Stories.* Manila: Filipinas Foundation, 1978.

Santos, Bienvenido N. *You Lovely People.* Manila: Benipayo Press, 1955.

Yuson, Alfred A. *The Music Child and Other Stories.* Manila: Anvil Publishing, 1991.

Vietnam

Banerian, James, ed. and trans. *Vietnamese Short Stories: An Introduction.* Phoenix: Sphinx Publishing, 1986.

Duffy, Dan, ed. *Focus on Contemporary Fiction, the 1920's and Visits Home.* Viet Nam Forum 14. New Haven: Yale University Council on Southeast Asia Studies/Yale Center for International and Area Studies, 1994.

———. *North Viet Nam Now: Fiction and Essays from Ha Noi.* Viet Nam Forum 15. New Haven: Yale University Council on Southeast Asia Studies/Yale Center for International and Area Studies, 1996.

———. *Literature News: Nine Stories from the Viet Nam Writers Union Newspaper, Bao Van Nghe.* Trans. Rosemary Nguyen. Lac Viet 16. New Haven: Yale University Council on Southeast Asia Studies/Yale Center for International and Area Studies, 1997.

Ho Anh Thai. *Behind the Red Mist: Fiction.* Ed. Wayne Karlin. Willimantic, Conn.: Curbstone Press, 1998.

Karlin, Wayne, Le Minh Khue, and Truong Vu, eds. *The Other Side of Heaven: Post-war Fiction by Vietnamese and American Writers.* Willimantic, Conn.: Curbstone Press, 1995.

Le Minh Khue. *The Stars, The Earth, The River: Short Fiction by Le Minh Khue.* Trans. Bac Hoai Tran and Dana Sachs, ed. Wayne Karlin. Willimantic, Conn.: Curbstone Press, 1997.

Linh Dinh, ed. *Night Again: Contemporary Fiction from Vietnam.* New York: Seven Stories Press, 1996.

Nguyen Huy Thiep. *The General Retires and Other Stories.* Trans. Greg Lockhart. Singapore: Oxford University Press, 1992.

Tran Vu. *The Dragon Hunt: Five Stories.* Trans. Nina McPherson and Phan Huy Duong. New York: Hyperion, 1999.

References

Herbert, Patricia, and Anthony Milner, eds. *South-East Asia Languages and Literatures: A Select Guide.* Arran, Scotland: Kiscadale Publications, 1989.

Kratz, E. Ulrich, ed. *Southeast Asian Languages and Literatures: A Bibliographical Guide to Burmese, Cambodian, Indonesian, Javanese, Malay, Minangkabau, Thai and Vietnamese.* London: I. B. Tauris, 1996.

Olson, Grant, ed. *Modern Southeast Asian Literature in Translation: A Resource for Teaching.* Tempe: Arizona State University, 1997.

Translators

Anna J. Allott is currently a Senior Research Fellow in Burmese studies at the School of Oriental and African Studies, University of London. From 1980 to 1996 she was honorary secretary of the Britain-Burma Society. She has written extensively on Burmese literature, including *Inked Over, Ripped Out: Burmese Storytellers and the Censors* (New York: P.E.N. American Center, 1993).

Harry Aveling is Senior Lecturer in Indonesian/Malay in the Department of Asian Studies at La Trobe University, Australia. An eminent translator of modern Indonesian and Malaysian writers, he has translated and compiled numerous short-story collections and anthologies over several decades.

Patricia B. Henry is an Associate Professor in the Department of Foreign Languages and Literatures, Northern Illinois University. Her areas of specialization are Austronesian linguistics and Javanese and Indonesian language and literature. In 1991 she authored the article, "The Writer's Responsibility: A Preliminary Look at the Depiction and Construction of Indonesia in the Works of Pramoedya Ananta Toer," which appeared in *Crossroads: An Interdisciplinary Journal of Southeast Asian Studies*.

Susan F. Kepner teaches mainland Southeast Asian cultures and literatures and Thai language at the University of California, Berkeley. She has published many translations of Thai literature and is the author of *The Lioness in Bloom: Women in Modern Thai Literature* (Berkeley: University of California Press, 1996).

Peter Koret graduated from the School of Oriental and African Studies, writing his doctoral dissertation on traditional Lao literature. He has contributed chapters on Lao literature to *Laos: Culture and Society,* edited by Grant Evans; *The Canon in Southeast Asian Literature,* edited by David Smyth; and other works. He is currently working on a study of the traditional Lao poem *Leup Pha Sun* and its twentieth-century interpretation.

John Marston has a Ph.D. in anthropology from the University of Washington in Seattle. He was twice coordinator of Cambodian-language instruction at the Southeast Asian Studies Summer Institute. He is now teaching Southeast Asian studies at Colégio de Mexico in Mexico City.

Patrick A. McCormick received his master's degree from Northern Illinois University, where he studied Burmese language and literature. He is currently working toward a Ph.D. at the University of Washington, Seattle, where his research interests include ethnicity; ethnic identity; minority languages of Burma, including Mon and Manipuri; and contact linguistic issues between Tibeto-Burman and Mon-Khmer languages.

Nguyen Nguyet Cam graduated from the University of Hanoi in 1992 and is currently a graduate student in Asian studies at the University of California, Berkeley. In 1995, she served as guest editor of a special issue of Vietnamese literature for the journal *Manoa*.

Courtney Norris is a consultant in the field of agricultural development, specializing in Vietnam and other parts of Southeast Asia. She recently coauthored a textbook with Bac Hoai Tran entitled *Sinh Hoat Bang Anh Ngu* (Living With English) (Tokyo: Tan Van Publisher, 2001) for Vietnamese learners of English. She lives in San Francisco and is currently researching a book on Vietnamese silk weaving.

Tomoko Okada is a Senior Lecturer in Cambodian studies at Tokyo University of Foreign Studies. She has published numerous articles on Cambodian literature. Her latest book is a Japanese translation of modern Cambodian short stories, *Gendai Kanbojia Tampenshu* (Tokyo: The Daido Life Foundation, 2001).

Vuth Reth received a master's degree in linguistics from California State University, Long Beach. He is currently associated with the Royal University of Phnom Penh.

Claire Siverson is associated with Smith College in Northampton, Massachusetts.

Bac Hoai Tran received his master's degree in English with a concentration in linguistics from San Francisco State University in 1999. He has been teaching Vietnamese at the University of California at Berkeley since 1992. He is the author of the textbooks *Anh Ngu Bao Chi* (San Francisco: Mo Long Publisher, 1993) and *Conversational Vietnamese* (Tokyo: Tan Van Publisher, 1999) and has published numerous translations.

Kheang Un completed a bachelor's degree in political science and economics at the University of Hawai'i at Manoa and a master's degree at Northern Illinois University, where he is currently a doctoral student.

Robert Vore completed his Ph.D. in English at Northern Illinois University in 1997. His publications include an afterword to the 1991 translation by Margaret Aung-Thwin of Ma Ma Lay's *Not Out of Hate* (Athens: Ohio University Press, 1991).

Than Than Win received her Ph.D. in English from Northern Illinois University in 1998. She is currently a Burmese-language instructor at the Southeast Asian Studies Summer Institute and has taught Burmese at the University of Hawai'i. She has published an article, "Going to America: I Always Wear My *Longyi*," in *Asiaweek* (1993).

Teri Shaffer Yamada received a master's degree in Southeast Asian languages and literatures in 1975 and a Ph.D. in Buddhist studies from the University of California, Berkeley, in 1985. Currently she is an Associate Professor in the Department of Comparative World Literature and Classics at California State University, Long Beach. She has written numerous articles on modern Cambodian literature and the diaspora.

Peter Zinoman received his Ph.D. in Southeast Asian history from Cornell University in 1995. He is currently an Associate Professor of Southeast Asian history at the University of California, Berkeley. His translations of recent Vietnamese fiction have appeared in numerous journals. His most recent publication is *The Colonial Bastille: A History of Imprisonment in Vietnam, 1862–1940* (Berkeley: University of California Press, 2001).